SCREAMS

SCREAMS

THE WILL TO KILL
FIREBUG
THE STAR STALKER

THREE NOVELS OF SUSPENSE

BY **ROBERT BLOCH**

UNDERWOOD-MILLER
San Rafael, California
Lancaster, Pennsylvania
1989

SCREAMS

ISBN 0-88733-079-7
Signed Edition 080-0

CONTENTS

For Elly --
Who has dedicated so much of herself to me.

SCREAMS

The Will to Kill

ONE

I RAN DOWN THE STREET.

It was a beautiful, sunny day, and no one was chasing me—that is, no one I knew about. But I ran down the street as though all hell was at my heels. And maybe it was.

When you're running, and everybody else is walking, people look funny to you. They look as if they're all moving in slow motion. Some of them seem almost frozen—particularly the ones who actually stop and stare after you.

You'd think that they'd never seen a man running before. You'd think that they were shocked at the very idea of anyone who dared to move fast, who hurried to get somewhere or to get away from somewhere else.

Well—which was it? Was I running *to* or *from*? I didn't know. I honestly didn't know. But was that any reason for them all to stare at me, as though I was a thief, or a murderer?

My heart began to pound as I turned the corner and ran up the block.

Thief or murderer. Was I either, or both? I didn't know. I just knew that I was running, had to keep running. And now my heart and my feet were pounding in rhythm: *rich man, poor man, beggar man, thief* . . .

I concentrated on the rhythm. Another part of me took over, guided me across the street, down the other side, to the store front. Another part of me brought the rhythm to an end before a small door. Then I stopped and I knew where I was, who I was.

This was my store. This was my name on the door.

TOM KENDALL
STAMPS—COINS—SECOND HAND BOOKS—MAGAZINES

Yes, I was Tom Kendall, all right. I was the tall, crewcut character with the puzzled brown eyes staring at my own reflection in the window pane.

I was Tom Kendall, I was alive and breathing in the city of Empire on this fine day of August 25th.

But where had I been last night?

I took another look at the mug in the mirrored window surface. Yes, it was good old Tom to the life; good old Tom, badly in need of a shave. Badly in need of food, rest, and a few answers. I could see it in those big brown eyes of his. *My* eyes. They'd been open for a long time and they'd seen things.

What had they seen last night?

I couldn't remember.

Oh, I could remember plenty of nights before the last one. I could remember the night I left college. I could remember the night before I joined up, the night before I married Marie, the night before I shipped out, the night before I cracked up, the night before Marie died.

I could even remember the night before last. But that was the kicker. It was always the night *before* something big happened. The big things themselves were lost and forgotten.

I nodded at myself in the mirror. "Come on, you sad-looking bum. I'll buy you a shave and a cup of coffee."

The coffee came first, over at Nick's.

"Hello, Tom," he said. "The usual?"

"Sure." He poured it black and edged the sugar nearer to me.

"Boy, I didn't expect to see you around this early," Nick told me. "Not after last night."

"Was I—pretty high?"

"Not high at all, far's I could tell. Whattsa matter, don't you remember? You was in here and you musta had four-five cups, just like that. You and this frienda yours, you know, whatsis-name."

I nodded, but I didn't know whatsisname. That's what I wanted to find out.

"Big fellow?" I asked.

"Naw. Whattsa matter'th you today? The skinny guy, one you allus argue with. Boy, you sure was fannin' the breeze."

Art. It must have been Art. I breathed a little easier as the coffee went down. I could call him later and find out—not ask any direct questions, of course, but find out what had happened. If anything. Art didn't know about the forgetting; that is, I'd never told him and I didn't think he suspected. If he had notions he kept them to himself. *Even your best friends won't tell you—*

"Fill 'er up!" I said.

Nick poured for me again, and I glanced down below the counter while he wasn't looking. My coat was all right. A bit rumpled, but nothing torn. And no bloodstains. That was a relief, too. I'd found several times in the past—I could remember that only too clearly. Maybe I'd gotten into some fights. Maybe I'd gotten into—

But that I couldn't remember, didn't even want to think about.

I stood up, laid a quarter on the counter, and went out. Nick was busy with the early morning stenographer crowd, so I didn't say good-by.

That stenographer crowd. "Gimme a cuppa coffee 'n a cruller." Then out with the cigarettes. Day after day, week after week, month after month, year after year. Never a change.

Up until recently, I never drank coffee in the morning. I preferred cocoa, or hot chocolate. And I wouldn't be caught dead with a cruller in my hand. "Cruller." There was a word for you. Whatever became of the good old American breakfast of ham and eggs?

Went up to ninety cents, I told myself. And I suppose that was the answer, or part of the answer. The rest of the answer was the course of least resistance. You go into a one-arm joint or a counter place, and the first thing they do in the morning is slap a cup of coffee in front of you. If you tell them you don't want it, didn't order it, they look at you as though you were a freak. And it's the same with the cruller and the cigarettes.

Up until about a year and a half ago, up until the crackup and getting out of the hospital, I'd been willing to let them think I was a freak—anything, just as long as I didn't have to sear my sensitive stomach lining with rancid coffee, greasy doughnuts and acrid cigarettes.

But I didn't want to be a freak any more. I didn't want to be different. So I conformed all down the line, and I was all right—except that I couldn't remember what happened last night.

Last night.

I lay back in the barber chair, and George put on the hot towels. I tried opening my eyes, and everything was dark and hot . . . dark and hot . . . and the chair was way back so I was off-balance. It felt a little bit like the restraint, like the hydro-therapy, and I wanted to get up and run out of the place.

But I had to conform. Conform and conform. Doctor Greene had told me I was all right. Hell, I had my discharge certificate. Everything was down there in the black and white.

Only there was no white now, only black. Dark and hot. Like restraint, like hydro-therapy, like something else. Something else I couldn't remember. I wanted to remember, but I was afraid.

What was it?

George took the towels off and cranked me up, and then he went at me with the razor. Razor and tongue. Neither of them were too sharp, either.

"How's business?" As if he cared.

"Oh, so-so."

"See you got the front painted."

"Yeah, last week. Getting pretty shabby."

"Soak you much for it?"

"Hundred and fifty."

"Boy, that's the racket! I should of been a painter, that's the line I should of went in for."

Maybe he was right; he certainly wasn't much of a barber.

As for his conversation, I could answer it in my sleep. Talking was almost like that, with me, because I kept trying to remember.

Then the hot towels went on again, and then he was working me over with the razor once more, and then—

"Oops! Sorry!"

The edge of the razor cut my chin. The edge of the razor, and it was bright and gleaming, and so was the blood, only the razor was silver and the blood was red. Red blood, Jimmy's and Sam's and Marie's—

"No!"

I threw off the towels and the cloth and stood up.

"But it's nothing, Mr. Kendall, only a little cut. Here let me put something on it—what's the matter?"

I turned away from the mirror so that I couldn't see the razor or the blood on my face, and then it was all right again.

"Sorry," I said. "Guess I've got the shakes. Bad hangover—you know."

"Brother, do I ever? Take like last Sattiday night, me'n my uncle Steve, we—" He halted. "Boy, you had me scared for a minute, though. The look on your face!"

I grinned. "Not much of a face, is it? But I hate to have anyone spoil my manly beauty. No, it's all right, George, I don't need any tonic. The bleeding's stopped."

I tossed him half a buck and left.

Does the bleeding ever stop?

Fine questions to ask myself, and the day hardly begun. Such a nice day, too. My watch registered five to nine. The mail must have been delivered already.

Sure enough, after I opened the door I scooped it up from the floor. Eleven pieces. I walked over, switched on the overhead light and then the light above my desk. I sat down and looked over the morning's loot.

Light bill. A memo from a jobber in New Jersey—special offer on Coronations. Old stuff, and I was overstocked. Coronation sets hadn't gone as well as had been expected.

Nine other letters. Five were returning approvals, with payments. I counted up the money-orders and the checks. Eighteen dollars. Not too bad. And here were four new requests. I checked the files to make sure they were new, then put the letters on the other desk.

Then the door opened and Kit came in.

Kit came in, and for the first time I truly realized that it was a beautiful day. Oh, it wasn't the sunshine and the sudden singing of birds; it wasn't the blue sky and the balmy breeze.

It was hair the color of fresh honey, and eyes that slanted upward with the oriental inclination of the true Norwegian. It was the swaggering stride of long, slim legs, the rounding upthrust of a sweater that was just tight enough, the tantalizing tan of neck and throat and bare arms. Kit made my days for me—and some of my nights, too.

Coming in this way, the least I could do was tell her about it.

"I love you," I said.

The oriental eyes gave me a long-lashed look. She smiled that smile of hers—the one da Vinci almost captured in his Mona Lisa. Then she spoke.

"Go to hell," said Kit.

Two

IT MIGHT HAVE BEEN the start of a very interesting conversation, but it wasn't. Because Ferguson came in just then, and he wanted me to stock up on a new album line.

I'd just gotten rid of him and was going over to Kit's desk, where she was sorting approvals for the mail, and in walked two amateur numismaticians, aged ten and twelve, with their inevitable, "Hey, Mister, what'll ya give me for an Indian head penny?"

Kit took them over immediately, but by this time I was trying to find a copy of the April, 1943, *Astounding*. The science-fiction fans were out in force today, because right on the heels of this request came Doctor Kleiner, to paw over that new stock of British prozines I'd gotten in. Then somebody wanted to see what I had in 19th Century Newfoundland—it turned out to be a twenty-dollar sale before I got through—and Kit sold a bunch of pocket books, and a copy of *The Golden Bough*, of all things.

It went on like that all morning, with the cash register ringing merrily, and then it was time for lunch.

Nora came in with her little tray. "What'll it be, folks? I got ham, egg salad, peanut butter, cheese—"

"Two hams," I said. "What about you, Kit?"

"I'm not hungry."

"Egg salad for the lady," I told Nora. "And a coke. Make mine a root beer."

Nora set the stuff down on the desk, and I paid her. "Ain't it a grand day?" she asked.

"It was." She wasn't really listening for my answer, so she said nothing as she waddled out.

Kit observed the silence and contributed to it, heavily. I unwrapped the sandwiches and brought over two paper cups for the drinks.

"There's salt in the drawer, if you want some," I said.

"I know." Kit ate daintily, like the cat she was—the soft, sleek, supple feline with the slanted eyes.

"Pretty hot," I said.

"I don't notice it."

"Hot in here, I mean. *Down* here."

"Down where?"

"In hell. Where you told me to go this morning. I've been here ever since."

"Well, fry there."

"Now, Kit. Come on, what's it all about?"

"You know what it's all about."

Typical woman's answer. And it was typical, too, that she carefully finished her sandwich before she started to sniffle.

I suppose my reaction was also standard. I went over and put my arms around her shoulders, standing behind her chair. She shrugged a little, but not too much.

"Come on," I said. "Tell me."

"As if you didn't know. After last night . . ."

There it was again. *Last night.* Had I seen Kit last night? And if so, when and where? To say nothing of *what.* Nights with Kit could be so interesting: nothing I'd want to forget.

"What about last night?" Not a very brilliant approach, but I didn't feel brilliant. I just felt confused and lonely, and as though I wanted to hold Kit very tight for a very long time.

"Oh, what's the sense of talking about it any more? I meant what I said, Tom. We've had a lot together, we've had so much—but it isn't enough. It can't be enough, not for any woman. It isn't that I'm a prude or anything like that. But dammit, I love you, and I want to get married."

So that was it. A little, a very little, was beginning to come back to me. Not enough really to add up, but I could guess at a bit more. Last night wouldn't be the first time we'd gotten onto that subject.

"You know how I feel about you," I said. "And you know how I feel about the business. Everything I could beg, borrow or steal—the G.I. loan, every penny I had—went into this thing. I'm almost clear, now, after a year and a half. In a little while we'll be in the black, and then we can really get rolling.

"After all, Kit, I know something about marriage." I wished I hadn't said that, but it popped out. I went on hastily. "Takes a lot of moola to set up housekeeping. All that furniture and appliances, and a car, and a decent place to live. Isn't it worth waiting for a while longer? Why, we can get a down payment on one of those homes they're putting up out in Longwood, we can do it in another year at the most, and—"

But she was crying again, really crying this time. When Kit cried, her eyes never seemed to get red and swollen. She cried like a little kid, with her fists clenched and her mouth screwed up as though she was more angry than hurt.

"Please, honey," I said.

She turned around and pushed my hands away. She had stopped crying quite suddenly.

"What's the matter with you?" she said, quietly. "Can't you stick to the truth once you come out with it? Or was that just another lie, too?"

I didn't know what to say, so I waited.

Kit stood up. "Everything you say you've said a dozen times before. And I always believed you. Even last night I did, until you went on and told me the rest. So why do you come back with the same old line today, when I know the real reason?"

So I'd told her. Told her the real reason. That was bad.

"Do you think I'd forget, overnight? Loving you the way I do, worrying about you the way I do? And do you think I'd care? I'd marry you today, if you'd have me. But no. You've got to be noble, you've got to be self-sacrificing, you've got to be the martyr, the hero! Except that you expect me to go on this way, without marriage. It's just as apt to happen whether I'm wearing a wedding ring or not, if what you told me is true.

"So don't give me any more of that 'I love you' line, Tom. If you really loved me, you wouldn't be afraid. Because that's the real reason, isn't it? You're afraid, Tom. Not of what you told me—you're just afraid to get married, to start over again and lead a normal life. Don't you see, I want to help you. But I can't unless I can be with you and—"

This time, when she broke down, she wasn't angry. It was grief that made her quiver against me, grief that sent her shoulders snug against mine, pressed her close to cling for comfort.

But it was something else that made her break away once more, break away and stare up at me for a long moment.

"I can't take any more," she said, quietly. "I've tried, and I want to—believe me, I want to—but I can't. I know you really think that what you told me is true, even though you were cleared. But that only makes it worse. Because it means that nothing I can say or do will ever make you change your mind.

"No, Tom. A year won't help, two years won't help. Not as long as you believe what you do. If doctors couldn't change your mind for you, I wouldn't have a chance. So I'd better go."

"You're leaving?"

"Right now." And she walked over and picked up her purse. I stared at her because I couldn't believe it was happening this way. Kit, who loved me, just walking out.

I thought of a million things to say, but none of them were any good. Nothing was any good. She was walking out on me, leaving me alone in the dark.

She was moving toward the door, and the sunlight was captured in her hair, and every golden inch of her I knew, and loved, and—

Kit stopped and turned around. She looked at me, sighed. "I know," she said. "I know I'm a heel. Walking out on you when you need me. When you need someone to take care of you during your blackouts, so it won't happen again—if it ever did happen."

I *had* told her, then. *Everything.*

"But it's your fault, too, Tom. If you loved me as much as you say you do, you'd go to another doctor. To ten doctors. You'd get rid of your trouble, somehow, and be a whole man again—for me."

I could only nod. She was right, of course. She was so right. And I knew, of course, that she was giving me another chance. Another chance, now, to tell her that I'd do just that. I'd go to a psychiatrist, and I'd find out the truth, and then Kit and I would get married. It was all so simple, so easy. Except that the blackouts weren't as bad as really knowing, really being sure. If I was sure, then nothing and no one, not even Kit, could help me.

So she waited for my answer, and there was only one answer I could give her.

"Good-by, Kit," I said.

"Good-by." She turned away. She said the rest very softly as she went out the door, so softly I almost didn't hear her.

"I still don't think you really killed your wife," said Kit. "And what's more, I don't care."

I cared. I cared a lot. It's a habit you get into—caring. Some people seem to cultivate it and others don't.

There's the old story about the man attending his wife's funeral. He breaks down at the church, he breaks down at the cemetery, he sobs and sobs uncontrollably all the way home.

His best friend, who accompanies him, tries to cheer him up. "Look," he says, "it isn't that bad. Why, in six months or so, you'll get over all this sorrow, forget all about it. I'll bet before a year is out you're likely to meet a new girl, get interested in her, take her out, even marry her. Then you'll be sleeping with her just as if—"

"Sure, I know," wails the guy. "But what about *tonight?*"

Every time I hear that story, it reminds me of some people I know. The lucky, lucky people; the ones who don't seem to care. But I'm not that way. And I wasn't that way when Kit walked out of the door, out of my life. I wasn't that way when Marie died.

Sitting in the store, that afternoon, I'd think about it, when the customers weren't bothering me for Zanzibar #156, unused (watermarked multiple Crown and Script CA) or *Galaxy*, June, 1952.

It was no use fooling myself. I'd loved Marie just as much as I now loved Kit. Kit was tall and blonde, Marie was—had been—short and dark. Kit was forthright, Marie shy and reticent. But she'd loved me, and we were both scarcely past the fumbling-discovery age, and I was going in for a hitch and people had just begun to find out there was a place called Korea.

And so we were married and lived happily ever after—for about two weeks. Then she followed me to boot camp, and she followed me to embarkation, and then her letters followed me.

After I went to the hospital, after the long time when I wasn't reading anything, I had the stack of her letters to catch up on. Thirty-seven of them, one hundred and ninety-two pages. I know, because I counted them. I even counted the words, the number of times she wrote, "I love you."

Then I counted the weeks, and the days, and the hours, and the minutes until I was discharged and we were together again. We had our first dinner at the Top of the Mark. And we spent our first night in a cabin outside of Redwood City. Those things I could remember, now.

But I couldn't remember my first blackout with her, nor any of the others, including the last. I could remember what went on between, though.

She didn't know what was the matter with me, of course, any more than I did. She tried to understand. She tried not to question me—ask where I'd been, or why—and it helped. Because I asked myself those questions, often enough. She never complained, no matter how bad I got, and that helped, too.

The trouble is, it didn't help enough. It didn't help to prevent her from having those crying spells, and from sitting up nights worrying, wondering where I was and how I was.

That was when we were still on the Coast, and I had this job over in Oakland. Just a working stiff, and on the intermediate shift, but the job was enough to keep us going. Or it would have been, if anything could have kept us going.

But instead of complaining she cried, and perhaps that had something to do with it. There were times when I wondered if she was ready to crack up, if she was even closer to it than I was. All that seemed to happen to me were these blackouts—temporary amnesia. But her melancholia was chronic, acute.

I managed to check up on myself, from time to time. Actually, what I did during those periods of blankness wasn't startling or unusual in the least. I'd go off for a few drinks, take a bus ride thirty or forty miles up the line, or just wander around by myself. I never, to my knowledge, got into any trouble or created a disturbance. Others who were with me didn't even realize that I'd gone under. Apparently it was just a secondary reaction to a severe concussion—service disability.

I didn't wonder then, but I wondered now: what had happened to Marie during those times? I'd go out and get lost in a city. Marie would stay home and get lost in her own mind. That's melancholia.

If it hadn't been for Art Hughes, I don't know what either of us would have done. Art Hughes: plant supervisor, Gershwin enthusiast, best friend of the family. I knew him in all three roles, but it was the latter one I admired the most, and came to lean on.

It was Art who went out, many's the night, and located me somewhere in town, or beyond town. It was Art who sat there and cheered Marie up, talked her out of her depression, slipped on the Iturbi duo-piano version of the *Rhapsody*, or the Levant variations on *I Got Rhythm*, or old George himself doing the *Preludes*.

Art was trying to help. I know Marie tried, and I tried too. But it didn't work out in the end. Nothing worked out to prevent the final blackout.

This one started like all the others. I was walking down the street, after the shift was over, heading for the two o'clock bus and hoping I wouldn't miss it. The next one wouldn't be around for another hour. I wanted to get home (yes I did, I wanted to very badly) because Marie had been crying when I left. She had been crying yesterday, too, and when I'd asked her what was wrong she wouldn't tell me. Or couldn't.

I remember I was thinking again for the tenth time that perhaps I should persuade her to see a doctor. She'd been to a g.p. just two weeks ago, but I wanted her to see a specialist. If she could only get hold of a good psychiatrist, a top man like Greene—although he was a neurologist, really—perhaps he'd find the answer. As it was, she was all tightened up inside, tightened up and ready to explode.

Explode. That was the last thing I remember thinking about. Then, without any warning, the roof fell in, the curtain came down, and I was lost. "I" was lost. Not the person that walked, talked, ate, drank, functioned on the surface level. I'm talking about the real "I"—the observed Observer.

But "I" was lost, and the blackout came. The fugue. Fugue and variations.

Usually, coming out of it was simple. There'd be a moment of panic—always the panic, upon realization of who I was and where I was, together with wondering where I'd *been*, where I was *now*. Then I'd gradually reorient myself and get ready to pick up the pieces and go home. So far there had never been any pieces. So far, I'd never snapped out of it and found myself at home.

Only *this* time—

This time I came out of it standing in our bedroom in the apartment. Standing there in the moonlight with the scissors glinting in my hand.

Standing over the body of Marie and looking at the place where those same scissors had cut her throat . . .

THREE

IT WAS ALMOST five o'clock. Kit had been gone now for about four hours, and it seemed like only a minute. Only a minute, but long enough for me to live it through all over again with Marie. Long enough for me to deal with Mr. Simpson and his copy of the *Decameron*, with Buzzy Foster who wanted some of those new airmails in blocks, with the fat woman who collected *Planet Stories* but ripped off all the covers from her purchases.

It seemed like only a minute, and I wondered if it would always seem that way, if a part of me would always be standing near the counter telling Kit good-by.

That's when I decided I was going out to get drunk. I watched the minute hand edge up to eleven, then go past it to twelve. Two more minutes and I'd close. I picked up the outgoing mail—some more approval requests had come in during the afternoon and I had a respectable pile—and then the door opened and he came in.

Sherlock Holmes would have loved my business. Dealing as I did in stamps, coins, magazines and second-hand books, I got an odd assortment of customers. After a time, I was able to size them up and make a pretty reasonable snap judgement. One look usually told me what the newcomer was seeking. I could even refine it down to categories within categories. That is, if my customer was a stamp collector, I could peg him as U.S.—general, strictly airmail, a completist, or a professional philatelist specializing in British Guiana only. In books, I could separate the "just looking, thank you" browser from the obscurantist; the Proust addict from the furtive individual in quest of "them there Jack Woodford books, hey."

So when my late client arrived, I gave him the benefit of all my experienced appraisal—and drew a blank.

Oh, not because he wasn't a type. He was as typical as they come; except that his type didn't make a practice of coming into my shop. There was nothing for them here.

The man was porcine: hog-fat, hog-jowled, with pork-bristles on his neck and chin, little pig-eyes set in folds of fat on either side of his blunt muzzle. He wore a bright blue suit that was designed to drape; on him, it merely bulged. A long-collared maroon shirt bunched up around his thick neck, and it is almost unnecessary to add that a nude was portrayed on his hand-painted tie. He was almost a self-caricature; the fake "hood," the Central Casting mobster. Actually, he was probably a petty gambler—the real dealers don't dare to dress that way any more.

"Say," he said. "Got a minute?"

"Certainly."

He lumbered over and tested one of my chairs to the uttermost. It creaked when he sat down, but did not collapse.

"You sell stamps?"

Good Lord, don't tell me I'd slipped up after all! Maybe I was looking at my golden opportunity to unload one of those Coronation sets! I ventured a bright smile.

"That's right. Something you're particularly interested in?" I turned around, thankful I hadn't yet locked the safe.

"No, not me. I was just wondering. You ever buy stamps, too?"

"You mean collections?"

"Uh-yeah. I guess so. I mean, books full of 'em."

"You have an album you wish to dispose of?"

"Right. A album."

"Might I take a look?"

"Here."

He hefted the album up onto the table. It was a green Gibbons—British album for British colonies, the kind only a specialist would own. I riffled through the pages, fast.

What I saw interested me greatly. There was almost a complete Barbados here, mint. Ditto for most of the West Indies. Strong early Canadian. Most of the Cape triangles in excellent condition—used, no forgeries. Early Labuan, excellent showing of high-value Rhodesia without revenue cancellations, nice St. Helena.

"Would you mind telling me how much you want for this collection, Mr.—?"

"Calgary. Joe Calgary." He shrugged. "I figure it's worth mebbe a fast two hunnert."

A fast two hunnert wouldn't have touched his Canadians. I closed the book. "I suppose it's fairly complete," I said. "You have the 1839 Mauritius?"

"Oh—sure."

"And the 1940 Tanganyika?"

"All them there. Diden' you see?"

I nodded again. There is, of course, no 1839 Mauritius and no 1940 Tanganyika, either. Any more than there was the faintest possibility that this man owned the collection.

"Well, whaddya say? Is it a deal?"

I hesitated. "Could you tell me just how many countries are represented in your collection?"

"Countries? Uh—I dunno. I mean, it ain't really my album, see? It's—it's my brother's. He saves 'em. Onny he needs some dough kind of fast like. You know how it is, and I figured—"

I stood up. "I understand. But unfortunately, I'm rather heavily over-stocked right now. I'd suggest you try elsewhere, or return the album to your brother and let him try. He could probably answer more of the questions that will be asked. On second thought, I recommend that—give it back to your brother."

He got it, all right. He stood up, slammed the book against his side, and moved off without another word. His heels crunched against the floor, then clicked against the sidewalk outside as he slammed the door.

I stood there, watching a good thousand dollars' profit disappear. It was a wonderful collection; I could have used it a dozen times over, and it was hot. I wondered where he'd stolen it.

Then I sighed, shrugged, and locked the safe—almost before the sound of his heels and the echo of his door slam died in the distance.

The sound of his heels . . .

I glanced down at my own shoes. Better get a pair of cleats put on, I thought. Then maybe I could hear myself walk. Next time I went off the deep end, I'd at least have a familiar sound to keep me company.

The deep end. I was going to get drunk, I reminded myself. All right. But first the cleats, and then something to eat.

Fratney was still open, and his boy put the cleats on for me. Then I went over to Rourke's and had a steak. Big, manly deal. Cleats on the shoes, big blood-rare steak for dinner, and then a night on the town.

A night on the town? Why not? Anything was better than the memories I had, the memories I'd lost, the sound of voices I wanted to remember, the sight of faces I wanted to forget.

Walking down the street, after the steak, I ran into Blind Bill. He was standing on the corner at Oak, the way he always is at that hour of the evening. I dropped a dime in his hat and took a pencil.

"Thanks, Mr. Kendall," he said.

"Thought the cleats would fool you," I said.

"It isn't the sound," Bill told me. "It's the rhythm. Everybody's got his own rhythm."

"Guess you're right," I said, and moved on. He probably was right at that. Everybody's got rhythm. I got rhythm. Wonder what Art Hughes' friend Gershwin would say to that? And what about Art Hughes? He might be up at Swanee's now. He'd come to town last month, transferred to the branch plant, and I'd seen him just twice—both times in Swanee's. Art had explained he had a room just around the corner. I'd promised to look him up but hadn't because I'd been spending my time with Kit.

That is, I had until last night. If Nick at the cafeteria was right, I'd seen Art some time during the evening—probably after my visit with Kit. And now I could see him again—tonight and every night, just like old times . . . old times before Kit, and the sight of Kit.

I wondered whether Blind Bill ever had to worry about the sight of faces he wanted to forget. Then I came to Swanee's and stopped wondering.

Let's put it this way. Swanee's came to me. It was that kind of a place: big and brassy and forthright, a gaudy whore of a place, hanging over the window sill and shouting down into the street. The big neon lights blazed before your eyes while you were still a block away. Half a block and you could hear the booming of the juke box; a few feet more and you caught the overtones of conversation, punctuated by the clink and tinkle of glasses. Then the air from the joint came swooping right out to hit you, hit you and scoop you up and carry you in.

Up until a year and a half ago, I'd have run a mile to get away from such a hangout. It was the kind of a bar where the early-morning coffee drinkers go when their work is done.

But I'd learned to conform, and when you conform you go to places like Swanee's where the lights are bright and the music is loud—so loud you can't hear yourself think.

There must be fifty thousand places like Swanee's scattered all over the country, and they all have the same atmosphere. When you go in, you can't hear yourself think, and that's the big secret of their success: nobody wants to hear himself think any more. If you drink enough coffee in the morning, if you drink enough of the beer or the hard stuff at night, you never hear yourself think. In time you even get so you stop thinking, and you don't hear that, either.

I walked in, moving right up to the bar. The place was already half-filled, and so were its occupants. Only eight o'clock, but some people like to stop thinking early. I chose the far end of the bar—away from the television set—because although I wanted to stop thinking I still wished to maintain the illusion that I was alive.

The oldest of the three bartenders came right over.

"What'll it be?"

"Old Overholt. Water on the side." I didn't ask for the brand name because I was a snob; it's just that in the Middle West nobody seems to drink rye and the bartenders always do a double-take if you ask for it. Funny thing, they drink a lot of rye in the East, but once you get as far as Illinois, it's bourbon all the way.

I glanced to my right, down the side of the bar, but I couldn't see Art Hughes. My drink came, I disposed of it, ordered another. A foursome came in and sat down on the vacant stools to my left. They craned their necks to see the television set. Some drama was on, but nobody could hope to hear it above the juke-box jangle, which was probably just as well.

I picked up my drink and moved all the way to the right, way down to the corner. And there I sat, for all of thirty seconds, before I felt the hand on my shoulder.

"Art!" I said.

"So you remembered." He grinned at me, shyly. "I wasn't sure you would."

Apparently I had seen him last night, then, and made a date. But I wanted to know more.

"Sit down," I invited. "What'll it be?"

"Ale will do." Art, in addition to being a Gershwin fan, was an ale drinker and a pipe smoker. Which was all right with me, as long as he didn't take up ice fishing and expect me to go along.

The ale came, and I ordered another shot for myself to keep him company. We sat back and relaxed a bit. At least I did; I'd always found it simple to relax with Art around. He was the easy-going type. Tonight, though, I sensed a difference, or thought I did. He kept making rings on the bar with the wet bottom of his glass.

"Hard day?" I asked, just for something to say.

"The usual. And you?" He put a lot into the question, or was I just imagining things?

"Nothing special."

"Nothing?"

He really was after something. I downed my shot. "No. Why should there be?"

"No reason." He finished his ale, glanced at his watch as I signaled to the bartender. "Hey, wait," he said. "I've got to be running along."

"Time for a quick one, though," I assured him, and wondered what gave here. "Got a date lined up or something?"

"Well, no. But I've got to clean the place up, and—"

I didn't bother to listen to the rest of it. Art was always a poor liar; not that he lied very much that I could recall. But why was he in such a hurry to leave? I didn't think it was a girl; Art never ran around with anyone but the ghost of Gershwin. Those pipe-smoking ale drinkers are all alike. Marie had always tried to fix up a date for Art, and he'd always backed down. I could remember that easily enough.

So it wasn't a girl, and yet he wanted to leave. Why? And whatever the reason, if he wanted to leave, why had he bothered to show up in the first place?

I decided on the direct approach. "Look," I said. "Was I very bad last night?"

That made him blink for a moment. "Bad? No, Tom, you weren't bad. Of course, you got pretty excited, you said some pretty wild things for a guy who hadn't been drinking—but then, you must have had a rugged session with her."

I was right. I'd seen Kit, then come over here and found Art.

"You can say that again," I told him. "Matter of fact, I guess I was so excited I don't even remember half of what I was talking about."

"Is that the real reason?" His lips asked the question, but he kept his eyes on his glass.

"Sure. What else would there be?"

"Well, you know what you told me. Or don't you remember?" Suddenly he looked up at me without blinking. "Say, you didn't have one of them last night, too, while you were telling me about it?"

"One of what?"

"The blackouts. The amnesia, the spells."

I hesitated, then nodded. "That's right," I admitted. "As long as you know that much, you might as well know the rest."

Art drank, paused, drank again. He set his glass down. "I'm sorry, Tom," he said. "But as long as you're leveling with me, I'll level with you. I've known about those blackouts for a long, long time."

"How long? Since it happened? I mean, was it in the papers?" Funny I'd never thought of it being in the papers; then again, it must have been. There must have been a lot of stuff about me and Marie. Only I'd cracked and they hadn't let me look at the papers—and when I finally got out, I didn't want to. Sure, that was it: he'd read it in the papers. He and a million others.

"No, Tom," he told me. "Even before that. Marie talked to me about it."

"I see." I grinned at him and put my hand on his shoulder. "And you never let on. That was nice of you, boy—didn't want to embarrass me."

He drew back, almost but not quite imperceptibly. "That's all right. Here, let me buy you one—and then I'll really have to cut and run."

Cut and run. I didn't like that phrase. Marie had been cut and the blood had run.

When the drinks came, I said, "Tell me something, Art. Last night, did I do a lot of talking about—Marie?"

Again he turned away. He was pouring his drink and his hand slipped a little. I watched the puddle form at the side of his glass. I had plenty of time to watch it before he replied, and then his voice was so low I could scarcely hear it over the juke box.

"No, it wasn't Marie," he said. "It was this girl of yours. This Kit."

"I talked about Kit, eh? And I was pretty upset?"

"Yes, Tom. You don't remember, do you?"

"Not a moment. Not a moment until this morning, around eight-thirty. Then I snapped right out of it, just like that." I snapped my fingers.

"Tom." He was almost mumbling now. "Tom, you're all right now, aren't you? I mean you can remember what we're talking about."

"Of course I'm all right. Good Lord, I'm not crazy or anything like that. You know I've been given a clean bill of health. It's just these spells—"

"Sure, Tom. But I wanted to be certain you could remember. Because I've got a piece of advice for you. Go see a doctor, Tom. See one soon. Tomorrow."

"Now look here," I said. "It can't be that bad. So I had a little blackout last night, and I talked a little wild because Kit quarreled with me. Is that anything to make a production number out of?"

"No. But I wish you'd see a doctor. Just for a checkup." He stood up. "Now I've got to shove."

I stood up, too. "Oh, just like that, is it?" I said. "You've got to shove. Three, almost four years I've known you, and you're shoving. No 'see you tomorrow,' or 'see you next week,' or even 'see you around.' Just that you've got to shove. What's the matter, am I poison or something?"

"You know better than that, Tom."

"It's getting so that I'm not sure what I know any more," I murmured. "I thought I was sure of myself, but that was years ago. Now I get blackouts. Then I thought I was sure of Kit, and she walks out on me. All through everything, though, I've always been sure of you. The way you stuck by me when Marie had those spells, the way we used to get together night after night. . . Why, even when I was in the hospital they told me you'd come around and asked if I needed any money or anything. Art, you've been my best friend. Don't I deserve a better deal than this 'got to shove' routine?"

A novelty card salesman once pinned a sign on my store wall, next to the safe. It read THE MORE YOU EXPLAIN, THE MORE I DON'T UNDERSTAND IT. I thought of that sign now, watching Art Hughes' face as I talked.

The more I said, the more he edged away. Was I just imagining things, or was he really scared? Was Art afraid of me?

"All right," I sighed. "I give up. Go shove."

He started to walk away, then stopped. Kit's routine. "How about it, Tom?" he asked. "You'll see a doctor?"

"Maybe," I countered. "If you'll answer me just one question."

"Go ahead."

"You don't like being around me very much after last night. That's obvious, and you needn't try to deny it. But even so, you came in here hoping to see me. Why?"

He shrugged. "I just had to find out."

"Find out what?"

"Find out how everything went today."

"But why?"

"Because of what you said last night. After you talked about Marie, and the way she died, you began talking about this Kit, and your quarrel."

"Go on," I said in a flat voice, "I want to hear what I said."

"Well, it was only talk. I know that now. And if you'd just go and see a doctor—"

"What did I say? What did I say about Kit?"

Art Hughes took a deep breath. "You said that if Kit ever tried to walk out on you now, you'd kill her."

FOUR

I SUPPOSE I SAT THERE at the bar for a long, long time after Art Hughes
went away. I sat there thinking about a lot of things—first about him,
then about Kit, then about Marie. But mostly about Marie. About Marie,
and what had happened after she died.

I'd come to standing there, standing over her with the scissors in my
hand. She was dead. I didn't need to feel her pulse or anything like
that—not after taking one look at her throat. So I called the cops, and
they asked me a lot of questions, and then the photographers shot off a
lot of flash-bulbs in my eyes, and they took me down to headquarters and
booked me.

I don't blame them. Even today, I don't blame them at all for what they
did. They find a woman with her throat cut, and her husband calls up and
tells them about it. Then when they ask him where he was and what he
was doing, he says he can't remember. His prints are on the scissors and
the neighbors say his wife was always crying. He talks about amnesia and
blackouts, and when they get him down in front of the D.A. he can't even
answer simple questions.

So he's probably trying to fake it for an insanity plea. So they talk
tougher, and they say they'll throw the book at him. So he cries and goes
all to pieces and doesn't even ask for a lawyer. And the next morning, he's
in a daze: can't even remember his own name, or so he says.

Cops don't care for that kind of reaction. I can understand that now. I couldn't then; I couldn't understand anything. For a while there I guess I didn't even remember Marie was dead. The first thing I do recall was that I was crying her name when I really snapped out of it.

By this time I was already in Veteran's Hospital and Doc Greene was taking care of me.

Doc Greene was the boy I had to thank for everything. He'd spotted my picture and name in the paper the morning after it all happened. He'd hopped over to headquarters, backed up my story, got the coroner to look for Marie's prints on the scissors, too. He practically took over the case: he pointed out the suicide angle, the melancholia. He figured out just how you'd have to hold the scissors to make such incisions; it added up, pretty much, to the fact that I or anyone else would have to be a contortionist to do the job. It wasn't impossible, but it was very difficult.

And then, to clinch it all, he managed to trace back part of my route. I'd been in a tavern way over on the other side of town, from two-thirty until three-thirty. I must have walked home, because there was no bus running where I could have made a connection and been home before five. And as close as the coroner could figure out, Marie had died any time between midnight and four in the morning.

Besides, he knew my record; he'd taken care of me over there, in Korea. He made quite a witness at the inquest. I just sat there, still in a daze.

The important thing was, Doc Greene had cleared me. He stampeded them into a suicide verdict. And it would have been very hard for me to have made it home by four in the morning, very difficult for me to do the job.

But not *impossible*. And suicide—

That's what I kept telling him, even after a lot of sessions, even after there was no relapse, no need for restraint. "Suicide," I'd say, over and over again. "It just doesn't add up, Doc. Marie loved me. She wouldn't kill herself when she loved me."

Then was the time he told me about melancholia. Involutional melancholia. It sounded possible, and yet . . .

So when I was almost ready to be discharged, he told me the rest. They'd found out something during the autopsy.

"She was going to have a baby," he said. And pregnant women, in her mental condition, frequently are impelled to self-destruction. "I'm sorry, Tom, but it all adds up."

It all added up. But what did it add up to? Maybe it made me a *double* murderer. I didn't know.

I do know that Doc Greene helped me a lot after I got out. He helped me when I decided to leave town and needed a loan from the VA to open my store. He even wrote to me, for a while, until he was transferred back to the West Coast. I know he helped me as much as one man can ever help another.

But I didn't know for sure how Marie had died and even now, a year and a half after I got out of the hospital, I still couldn't be sure.

I wasn't sure about that, or about Kit, or about Art. I wasn't sure about anything, except that I couldn't stand this being alone much longer. Sitting alone here in the corner of the bar, nursing my fourth—fifth?—drink.

It's never good to sit alone at the end of the bar. I had a theory about this, too; a very simple theory which I'd never dared put to the test.

I believe that if a man walked into a strange tavern, some ordinary neighborhood place, every night at eight p.m. and ordered one drink—sat down at the end of the bar—drank it, then walked out—and if he came back the next night and the next and did the same thing, without saying a word to anyone except to give his order—I believe if a man did this for two weeks straight, he'd be killed.

It wouldn't be four nights before some of the regular customers would be asking the bartender who the creep was, after he walked out. It wouldn't be six nights before they'd be openly murmuring while he was still sitting there, minding his own business. By the tenth night they'd have him figured out as a queer, a Communist, a lunatic. By the twelfth, somebody would go up to him and try to get him into a conversation. If he didn't respond, by the fourteenth night the neighborhood bully and loudmouth would gather his cronies, wait for the man to come in, and then walk over and ask him what the hell he was doing in here anyway, coming sneaking around like that. If the man answered, the bully would hit him. If the man didn't answer, the bully would hit him. And the sight of blood would be enough to bring on the second blow. They'd all wade in, and they'd kill him.

No, it's not good to sit alone. Not good at all, and not safe. If you sit alone, you might be killed. Or perhaps you might be the one who'd be contemplating killing.

Marie had died. And I'd threatened to murder Kit. So I moved away from the end of the bar, into the crowd.

I slid onto a stool in the center of the mob, in the center of the bibulous, babbling Babel. And it was a Babel they were building, getting higher and higher with every drink.

It was hard to distinguish voices in this crowd. It was harder still, once a voice was isolated, to comprehend words and phrases. But the noise itself was comforting, it was human and familiar.

Then one voice became familiar, and its words were familiar too.

". . . awright, so gimme twenty bucks for the album. Twenny bucks for Chrissake, this here dealer said it was worth maybe two hunnert . . ."

Mr. Calgary. Sure enough, there he was, as big as life. Bigger than life, seen this close up. Because he was only two stools away from me, down the bar. Separating us was the little redhead. I looked at her as she looked at Calgary.

She was tugging him by the sleeve now, saying, "Come on, Joe. Come on, now, cut it out. He doesn't want to buy anything. Joe, come *on*, you're em*bar*rassing me!"

I suppose, on occasion, the rhino birds tug at their rhinoceros—and with just about the same results.

Joe Calgary clutched the album in one hand. The other hand was locked on the oldest bartender's tie. "Twenny bucks is all," he said. "You gotcha self a real deal, buddy. If it wasn't I had a bad day with the nags and all, I would'n even of let you smell of it. But I wanna show Trixie here a little action, so how's about it? Twenny bucks . . ."

"Shut up, Joe, will you shut up and let the guy alone?"

" . . . worth easy two hunnert. Come on, fork over, be wise for a change . . ."

"Take your hands off me. I told you I don't want to buy any album."

"Then how's for lendin' me the twenny? Until tomorrow night, see? Take the goddamn album for secur'ty. That's it, you lend me twenny now, huh?"

"Let go of me!"

"Joe, lay off the guy—"

"Oh, want to get smart, huh? Awright, you got it comin', buddy."

Then everything went into *presto vivace*. The bartender yanked himself free, signaling desperately to his companions behind the bar. The little redhead banged at Joe Calgary's thick neck with her handbag. Joe Calgary reached out and hit the bartender in the side of the face with the Gibbons album. It represented over a thousand dollars in profit, it weighed more than six pounds, and it drew blood.

The other two bartenders came up on the run, but I was closer. Close enough to swing Joe Calgary around and clout my fist into his face. I didn't aim for anything in particular. With a face that big to hit, you didn't have to aim.

I landed solidly, solidly enough to hurt my knuckles. Joe Calgary just grunted, spat, and looked at me. I saw the light of dawning recognition, followed by another light. It kindled like a sudden glare, and then Joe Calgary struck back.

He didn't strike with his fist. Instead, his hand went away for a moment, disappeared under his coat. When it came out, I saw the fist. It was curled around the handle of a knife.

The knife ripped down. I ducked and my stool clattered to the floor. Coming up, I hit him in the stomach. He wheezed, and then I heard the song of the knife. I tried to get out of the way, but it wasn't necessary. Something cracked above my head, the knife clattered to the floor beside me, and then I stood up.

One of the other bartenders had hit Joe Calgary over the wrist with a sap. Nothing had broken, apparently, but a sap can hurt even a Joe Calgary when properly applied.

He stood there, turning white, then red. The oldest bartender said, "You all right, Mister? Want I should call copper on this guy?"

I shook my head. "No. I'm okay. Just tell him to pick up his toys and beat it."

Calgary winced as he stooped over. He had the knife in his hand again, but the bartender was waiting with the sap. "You heard what he said," the bartender told him. "Now beat it before somebody changes their mind."

"Come on, Joe," said the little redhead.

That did it. He couldn't touch me or the bartender. But she was available, and he noticed her for the first time. "You lousy little tramp!" he muttered. "You hadda have a big night, huh? I'll give you a big night, you dirty little two-bit—"

The sap whistled. "Out," said the bartender. "On your way. Now!"

Joe Calgary backed away, twisting the knife in his big hand. "I'll get you," he said. "I'll fix you good for this. You hear me? I'll get you."

He wasn't talking to the bartender, or to me. He was talking to the redhead. That is, he thought he was. Actually he was talking to the whole world— to his fat old sloppy Ma and drunken Pa, and the dopey teacher and the crummy truant officer, and all the kids on the playground who were cleaner and smarter and nicer than he was.

But the redhead thought he meant her, too, and she shivered.

Even after Calgary trailed out, after the excited murmur of voices subsided and broke up into individual units of gabble, even after I'd sat down again, the little redhead still sat shivering.

"Thanks, Mister." The oldest bartender leaned toward me. "I mean about taking him off me. And about not yelling copper. Gives the place a bad name, you know."

"I know."

"How about a drink, now? On the house?"

"Good idea." I meant it, too. I was shivering, but inside. Not because of Calgary—because of the knife. It was very sharp, that knife. Sharp as a razor, sharp as a scissors.

I pushed away the thought, grabbed the one next to it and hung on: little shivering redhead.

"What about a drink for Trixie, here, too?" I asked. "No reason why she should be cheated out of her evening."

"Sure, whatever you say. Overholt was yours? And Trixie—bourbon and white for a wash?"

Trixie nodded. Her trembling subsided measurably as she turned her head and smiled. "Much obliged," she said. Then, "Hey, how'd you know my name?"

"Isn't that what he called you?"

"Sure. You were listening."

"If I hadn't listened, I couldn't have done anything."

"That's right. I mean, thanks. Say, you weren't afraid of that big slob at all, not even when he pulled a shiv on you."

"Not much." Not much was right. I'd almost passed out, but then she didn't have to know all my secrets. Or did she?

"You all alone?"

"Up until now."

This made her give out with a real smile. The drinks came, and she raised her glass in fingers that shook only slightly.

"Here's to you, Mister."

"Tom Kendall's the name. And here's to you, Trixie." We drank. And the bartender popped up like a slightly decrepit, benevolent Jack-in-the-box.

"You folks ready for another? It's all on the house tonight."

I looked at Trixie. She looked at me. Then she made the one feminine gesture I've learned to recognize—the gesture that means you're in like Flynn. She put her right hand up to her neck and smoothed her hair. And this time her hand didn't shake at all.

"There's a booth vacant over there in the back," she said.

I nodded. The nod took in the booth, the suggestion, and Trixie herself. Although, upon close inspection, Trixie deserved considerably more than a mere nod.

Oh, she wore one of those green dresses that her type of redhead inevitably wears; her shoes were a clashing crimson, and her bag was much too large and pseudoalligatorish.

But there was nothing pseudo about her red hair, or her pale, un-freckled face, or her smoke-gray eyes with the little green lights around the pupils. Her mouth was full and generous beneath the lipstick, and she walked with a complete awareness of what she so demurely displayed. She was much too good for a Joe Calgary. For that matter, she was probably much too good for me. I'm not talking about taste in clothes, or formal education, or even current moral standards. I'm talking about the woman.

And in the booth it was the woman I responded to. The woman, and the drinks on the house, and the mood of the moment which—surprisingly enough—wasn't despair any more. Sure, I'd lost a lot today. A thousand bucks' profit, a girl, a friend. I'd even lost my memory a while back. But old W. C. Handy had it right when he wrote those lines about a red-headed woman . . .

We talked a bit. Turned out she was a part-time model at a downtown style shop. Turned out I was a stamp and book dealer. Turned out I mustn't judge her by that Joe Calgary, why she scarcely knew him, and why she *ever* said she'd go out with him in the first place she didn't know. Turned out I was explaining why guys like Calgary liked to carry knives.

That must have come several drinks later, because I was using words like "psychology."

"Got to understand his psychology," I told her. "He's the bluffer type. Always making a threat or a fist and hoping that's enough—hoping the other guy will back down on account of his size."

"But he threatened me, you heard him." She was really frightened, and no mistake. So I went on, improvising my reassurance.

"Take my word for it. I've read up a little bit about the psychopathic killer, and I'd swear he's not the type at all. Your real knife artist, your actual murderer, would never display his weapon. And he'd never threaten anyone openly. He's just smile, and go away, and lurk somewhere waiting in the dark. Waiting in the dark, in the fog, in the night. Waiting silently and then striking silently. Like Jack the Ripper."

"I know about him," Trixie said, pathetically proud because she'd recognized a phrase, a name she could understand. "I saw this movie once; it was all about him and how he used to cut up these women. I was so scared I almost didn't stay to see the end."

"But it was only a movie, Trixie."

"I know. Wasn't there a real Jack the Ripper, though?"

"Yes. There was. But that was in London, almost seventy years ago. In 1888, to be exact."

"Gosh, you know all about those things, don't you?"

"Not much, really. But as I say, I've read a bit. About the Ripper and Haarman, and the other butchers."

"Were there a lot of them? I mean, are there still people like that running around loose?"

"Once in a great while. You don't hear too much about them, and as I say, they're usually very cautious and secretive. That's why they carry knives, I suppose—because a knife is silent."

All at once I didn't want to talk about the Ripper any more, or knives, or silence. I didn't want silence. I wanted voices not sharp but soft, and the slow, growing intimate warmth of possession.

What did Trixie want? I don't know. Perhaps she wanted to show her gratitude. Maybe she wanted someone to hold her and make her forget about the threats. It might be that she wanted the warmth of possession herself, or even that she wanted me.

I don't know. But I do know that she smiled, and made that gesture of hand to hair, and then she said, "Look, honey, it's awful noisy in here, don't you think? I mean, my place is only about four blocks away, and if you don't mind drinking bourbon instead of that rye—"

Well, I didn't mind in the least. I followed her out of the booth. After I said goodnight to the oldest bartender, I took her arm and we walked to the door together. Her arm was soft and yielding beneath my fingers. Her hip brushed mine, and it felt soft and yielding, too. Softness always yields in the end.

Going down the street her high heels clattered in counterpoint to the clatter of my cleats. It was almost eleven, but Blind Bill still stood on the corner. Still stood, stood still, Blind Bill . . . I was getting tight.

Tight as a tick, and tick-tick went my watch as I held it up to my ear. Then I wound it, to make sure it was tight too. Both of us tight together. Me and my watch. Me and Trixie, tight together. That's the way it should be, that's the way it would be.

I felt sorry as we passed Blind Bill on that corner. I was going to call out to him, but Trixie tugged at my arm and whispered, "Come on, let's go. He gives me the creeps just to look at him," So I went on. What could I say, anyway? What can you say to a poor blind moocher late at night as you pass him with a pretty redhead?

There were no pretty little redheads with apartments for Blind Bill. And I couldn't help it or do anything about it. So we walked along, in rhythm with her feet and heart and pulse-beat, and my hand squeezed her arm. After a moment her arm went around me because we were coming to a dark place. Or because she liked having her arm around me. Or both.

Then we got to her place. It was on the street floor, front, in one of those little six-family units over behind the park.

Inside she turned on the light, humming a little, because she was glad to be home. She pulled down the shades, still humming, because after all a girl's got her reputation to think of. She went out to the kitchen and I could hear her hum for a moment more. Then silence. No sounds of bottle or glasses, either.

I got up from the sofa and walked out there, down the hall. To get to the kitchen I had to pass the entrance to her bedroom. And—surprise— she wasn't in the kitchen, hadn't gone there at all! She was just standing in the doorway to the bedroom, and I guess she'd stopped humming because she never hummed while she took off her clothes.

She smiled at me in the semi-darkness.

"You still want that drink?" she asked . . .

We had the drink, later. Much later, we had another. Perhaps even another, but everything was so confused. The light was on, the light was off, she was laughing, she was crying, I was laughing, I was crying. Why was I crying? Because I couldn't remember, and it was hard to remember now if her hair was black like Marie's, or blonde like Kit's, or red like Trixie's. That was her name, Trixie, and she was afraid. Afraid of whom— me? She didn't have to be afraid of me. She had to be afraid of Joe Calgary and somebody named Jack. Jack the Ripper, who knew a lot of girls like Trixie; Jack the Ripper, who never got caught.

I must have told her about Jack again, or maybe I just thought I did and I was really telling it to myself, inside my head. It was dark inside my head now, and dark outside. Better to stay inside, to sleep there and hide there and lurk there in the night and the fog where all is silent including the knife. If I really went inside, really went to sleep, I'd forget about the knife. Trixie was warm, and the knife was cold. Take her warmth, cut out the cold. Cut it out. Cut—it—out!

Then I was screaming "Cut it out!" over and over again, and I was wide awake this time, wide awake at last and able to see in the early morning light.

I was able to sit up in bed and see Trixie lying there on the floor, red hair haloing her head and red blood for a necklace about her throat . . .

FIVE

THE FIRST THING I wanted to do was run. Yesterday had started that way for me—running. Then I shook my head, because there was nowhere to run to. Nowhere in the world.

Marie gone, Kit gone, Art gone, and now Trixie was gone, too. I'd be going next myself, and I needn't bother to run.

I sat up and put my feet down on the other side of the bed. For a long moment I poised there, halfway to getting up, blinking and shaking my head, trying to clear it, trying to think, to remember.

We'd had a lot to drink. And then I passed out, or thought I passed out, and I had these nightmares. They were bad, but they were nothing compared to the one I had now. And this one was real.

Once again I forced myself to look. The nightmare lay sprawled, almost spread-eagled, on the floor. The hair was red, but more of an orange now that there was something with which to compare it.

And there was something for comparison, plenty for that and to spare.

I don't like to think about it, much less describe it, even now. But I saw. Saw that it wasn't only her throat. It was her shoulders, and her chest, and her stomach—and whoever had done it hadn't just meant to kill her.

Whoever had done it—

I got up and almost bumped into the mirror. I almost bumped into the sight of my own face, staring there.

"You," I whispered. "You, Tom Kendall. You know who you are this morning. And you know, today, that you didn't do it. Not this. Not to her."

As soon as I said it, I felt that it was true. Sure, I'd spent the night here and I was drunk. I'd passed out and I had fantasies.

But I remember everything—everything except for the time when I slept. The time when I slept and she died. Could it be that I did it in my sleep?

"No," I told myself. "No, you didn't."

And I believed it. Yes, I believed it. But would anyone else?

I forced myself to walk around the bed, kneel beside her. I didn't touch her. I didn't want to touch her. But I had to look for something. I had to look for the knife: the knife, the razor, the weapon—the *silent* weapon— the weapon that came in the night, came through the door or the window . . .

There was no knife on the floor. There was no knife in the hall, or the front room. There was no knife in the bathroom, and when I opened the kitchen drawer I found only a ten-cent paring knife with a small blade.

I went back to the front room. The door was locked—and from the inside. I went over to the window. The shade flapped. I pulled it up, and there was the opening—halfway to the top!

I tried to remember now; had she opened that window? Or closed it? Or merely pulled down the blinds?

No answer. I couldn't find an answer.

I went back into the bedroom, and the old running urge came up again, strong. I looked at my watch. Six-thirty. It was still early. The front hall and the streets would still be deserted.

Now was my chance. Now was my chance to dress and get out of here, fast. That was my only chance.

I put on my clothes. The urge was getting stronger and stronger. I could hardly wait to lace up my shoes, hardly manage to tie the bows. Then I was on my feet and once again I nearly bumped into the mirror. I looked at myself and I shook my head.

I walked down the hall to the bathroom and turned on the cold-water faucet in the bowl. I let it run for a moment and then I stuck my right wrist under it. I took away my right hand and stuck my left wrist under it. Then I stooped and ducked my head, until the water was icing along the back of my neck.

I found a towel, dried off. Then I turned and walked back down the hall. It took me a thousand years, but I made it. I sat there staring for another century or so, and at last I picked up the phone.

"Hello," I said, and it took a year for every word to form. "Hello, get me the police. Yeah, that's right, the police. I want to report a murder."

Modern science is wonderful. The phone got me the police, all right; it got me the police in about two minutes flat. More police than I could handle.

But I wasn't handling the police. They were handling me. The four men from the squad car just hung around downstairs, trying to keep off the crowd which their presence attracted. The man from the coroner's office and the photographer came later, and they checked and measured and dusted and tested and shot off flash-bulbs. Two detectives cased the place thoroughly. And I sat in the kitchen with Lieutenant Cohen.

Yes, Cohen—not Murphy or Reilly or Kelly or O'Brien. And he didn't keep his hat on in the house. He didn't even wear a gray suit; it was blue, and not blue serge but brighter. He was short and stocky, and red-headed—dark red, not bright like Trixie's hair. He wore a small mustache and he wasn't much older than I was. He might have been a very good Homicide man, but he'd never get a job on a TV crime show.

He sat me down at the table and flipped open a notebook. His fountain pen leaked a little, and he shook it carefully onto the first page, then tore the page out.

"Want to talk about it?" he asked. "Or would you rather wait for a formal statement? You know, of course—"

"—that anything you say may be held against you." I nodded. "All right, I'll tell you what happened."

So I gave him my name and age and address and then I told him. He sat there writing notes, telegram-fashion, but he didn't interrupt or say anything. Once in a while he chewed at his mustache to see whether it would come off. It didn't.

I don't know what I'd expected, but it was something different. I thought he'd break in, ask for details, follow up points in my story and try to break them down. I thought he'd nod, or chain smoke, or stare at me.

But he just wrote everything down: starting with me going into Swanee's and ending with the time I got dressed and then changed my mind and called the police.

When I finished he sat back, shook his head, and chewed at his mustache once more. Then, "Henley!" he called. "Come in here for a minute."

Henley was another one of the Homicide men. He came in from the bedroom.

"What's the story?" asked Lieutenant Cohen.

Henley looked at me, shrugged, looked away. "Nothing definite yet. She's mugged and we got prints. Lots of prints. Corr is on his way back to the lab. We should get the dope tonight sometime."

Cohen nodded. "All right. Make sure you got prints from the front room window—the open one, on the right."

"Already dusted."

"Tell Flint to take this name and address and check on it." He gave Henley my name and address.

"Got it."

"And one more thing." Cohen turned to me. "Mr. Kendall, will you please give this man a description of Joe Calgary? The more complete the better, of course. And see if you can describe his knife."

I told Henley about Joe Calgary and his knife.

When I finished, Lieutenant Cohen stood up and gave Henley a push. "Get on it, now," he said. "Send out a pickup right away. No charge. If you find him, and he hasn't got the knife on him, Bronson'll make out a search warrant for you. Go up to his place and get it. One other thing—I want you to go down to Swanee's bar. Talk to the night bartenders, the customers. Get the story, and anything you can on this Trixie. Her habits, her friends, who she's come in with. The works."

Henley nodded and went out with the other man from Homicide.

"Guess that's all," Lieutenant Cohen told me. "Now let's go downtown."

We went downtown. It was anticlimax. Everything had been anticlimactic since I'd called the police.

They booked me on suspicion, and I met Bronson who turned out to be an assistant D.A. I told the whole story all over again in the presence of a stenographer. I was calm, quiet, cooperative.

They brought me a cup of coffee while I talked, and when it was all over they took me out down the hall to a cell.

That's when the photographers from the paper tried to rush me. And that's when I stopped being calm, quiet and cooperative.

At first I only shielded my eyes when the flashes went off. Then a little guy stuck his camera right through the bars in the corridor and tried to pop a bulb in front of my face.

"Cut it out!" I yelled. "Cut—it—out!" That's what I'd been yelling when I woke up, when all the knives were flashing just like the light flashed now. "Cut it out. It's just like the other time. Cut it out!"

Then I calmed down, but somehow I felt everything was different. It wasn't that anybody had pressured me. But I got this feeling that I'd been through all this before. And why did it have to happen all over again? How many times would it happen over again? And why, why, why . . .

I lay on my bunk in the cell and closed my eyes. When I did that I could still see little yellow rings from the flash-bulbs. And I still kept asking myself: why, why, why . . .

Then I slept, really slept. That was the only good part, the sleeping. When I woke up it was late afternoon and Lieutenant Cohen was tapping on the bars.

"Sorry to disturb you," he said. "But someone would like to see you. If you don't mind. This is Mr. Howard, the District Attorney."

"Hello, Mr. Kendall." Mr. Howard stepped out of the shadows and nodded at me. "Can I come in for a minute?"

"Make yourself at home," I told him.

"Will you need me?" Cohen asked.

"I don't think so." Cohen went away, and the District Attorney unlocked the cell door and came in. He sat down on the chair and I got a good look at him. He was black-browed, bald, and he wore rimless glasses. When he smiled I got a look at some expensive bridgework. At least I thought it was bridgework and I was right.

"Sorry I wasn't around this morning," he began. "But I had an appointment with the dentist."

"Hurt you?" I asked.

"It was mur—" He stopped suddenly, then chuckled. "Better watch my language around here," he said.

"I don't mind." And I didn't. He seemed nice. But then, they all seemed nice. Cohen and Henley and Bronson and all the rest of them. I was willing to bet that the guy in charge of the electric chair was ever so charming, too—but I didn't want to meet him.

I snapped my attention back to what Howard was saying.

"I read the statement you gave to Mr. Bronson," he told me. "It seems quite complete."

"Told him everything I know," I said.

"Mr. Bronson didn't try to ask a lot of questions, did he? I mean, he wasn't—"

"Nobody pushed me around. This Lieutenant Cohen seems to be a pretty good guy, too."

"Thanks. I'm glad to hear that, Mr. Kendall."

"The name's Tom." I stood up. "Seeing that you're asking, there's only one thing really bothering me. Everyone is a little too polite. It makes me nervous."

"Sorry. It's just our policy." Howard took off his glasses and polished them. "Anything else make you nervous, Tom?"

"Why—no. I guess not."

"What about the photographers?"

"Oh, you mean this morning, in the hall. Well, you know how it is. The way they come at you, and the idea of getting your picture in the papers. That's enough to make anybody nervous."

"Is that all?"

"What do you mean?"

Howard put his glasses on again. "When the photographers tried to take your picture, you yelled something. Something about it being just like the other time. What other time, Tom?"

The cell was cool, but I began to get wet under the arms.

"Why—"

"Look, Tom. You're in here on a serious charge. If it's upheld, I'm the man who's going to have to prosecute that charge in court. How I do it will depend a lot on just what you're willing to tell me now." He smiled, and the new bridgework glistened in the single shaft of sunlight from the window. The teeth were false. And the smile? And the words?

He sighed. "Don't get the idea that this is some movie you're seeing," he said. "I'm not a fighting D.A., and I'm not up for re-election for three years yet. I can play it the hard way if I have to, but I don't like it. So let's not hold anything back."

My hands were sweating, too. I rubbed the palms against the side of the cot as I sat down again. He watched me all the time he talked.

"You gave a pretty good statement, Tom," he said. "I know, because I've read a lot of them. I think I can tell when a man is telling the truth. And you told the truth so far—but not the whole truth."

"What more do you want?"

"Everything, Tom. Everything. What do you suppose we were doing while you slept? We had your name, address, previous background. Naturally, we checked. And the first thing we ran into was that—other time."

"Newspaper files?"

"Teletype from the Coast. Photostats of all the documents will reach us by tomorrow afternoon. But meanwhile it would help if you told about it yourself. All of it."

He had me. He had me cold. I was sweating but I wanted to shiver. But I talked, then. I told him everything. About Marie, the blackouts, the inquest, and the hospital.

"Good," he said, when I finished. "It checks, so far. By the way, Tom, you'll notice I didn't write anything down. And there are no witnesses."

"It wouldn't matter," I told him. "Come to think of it, I don't see why I was so panicked. After all, it was on the record, and I've been cleared. I'll be cleared this time, too. Just as soon as you find Calgary and that knife of his."

Howard stood up. "Just got a report on that, too," he said. "We haven't picked up Calgary yet, but we did go through his room. Nothing there. So we checked on his movements. After he left Swanee's we traced him to another place down the street. Dick's. He sold his knife to a bartender there, for three dollars."

Now it was my turn to stand up. "You got it? You really got it?"

"Here it is."

The District Attorney reached into his inner coat pocket and brought out a tissue-wrapped parcel. He undid it slowly, carefully.

"We checked it for prints already," he observed. "And they're all the same. They may or may not be Calgary's, but they're certainly not yours—so that's a matter of record."

I breathed a little easier, then. "What about blood?" I asked. "Did you find any bloodstains?"

Howard nodded. "Yes. Some of them may be recent."

"And there's some way, isn't there, of telling whether it would be the same type of blood as Trixie's?"

"That's difficult to say, but I believe there is a method."

"You have the coroner working on it, haven't you, or the boys in your lab?"

"No."

"Well for heaven's sake, man—I don't want to tell you your business, but it's important to me. Get on it!"

"It won't be necessary."

I stared at him. He stared right back as he spoke.

"You see, the first thing we did was to take the knife to the coroner and show it to him. He checked the wounds on Trixie's body. Look at this blade, Tom. It's big and broad. This isn't the knife that cut Trixie Fisher's throat."

"You're—sure?"

"Positive." He stood close enough so that I could see the saliva form on his bridgework. "The weapon that killed Trixie, the weapon that ripped her up, was longer and thinner and pointed. Do you know what a poniard is, Tom?"

"Yes, I do. It's a French dagger, something like an Italian stiletto. Matter of fact, I've got a wall case down at the shop and I think there's one up there. I sell them for curios from time to—"

I stopped. I was saying too much, or not enough. "But wait a minute, I've had some of those pieces up ever since the place opened and all I've ever sold was a dirk and a Malay kris."

"You know a lot about knives, don't you, Tom? Quite an expert."

"Just because I told you a poniard is like a stiletto? Look, Mr. Howard—go down to my store, take my key, go in and see for yourself. That poniard and the other pieces, I never bothered to dust them off. You can see for yourself that nothing has been disturbed for a year and a half—"

The District Attorney sighed. "The boys have already been there, Tom. They found your wall case. It holds a German hunting knife, a Bowie, two Filipino stabbing knives and an Arab dagger. But no poniard."

"Maybe I was mistaken," I said. "Maybe I sold it. I might have forgotten. A man can't keep track of knives and everything he—"

"You'll find it's very important to keep track of knives," Mr. Howard answered. "Very important. The boys do. They checked your wall case thoroughly, because they thought it was so important. Some of the weapons were dusty, as you say, but the case itself was clean. The lock, for example, was quite immaculate even though it had been recently broken. Whoever took that poniard out wanted it in an awful hurry, I might say."

"Somebody stole it?" I asked.

Mr. Howard unlocked the cell door and stepped outside. He closed the door again and smiled as it clanged.

"That's one theory," he said. "Personally, I have another. Would you like to help me out, Tom? Would you like to tell me what you did with the knife after you ripped her?"

SIX

IT MUST HAVE BEEN ABOUT AN HOUR later when the guard came by. I was lying on my bunk watching the shaft of sunlight as it turned from white to gold, from gold to red, from red to dusty rose. I watched it fade, wondering why everything had faded for me today.

"Visitor," said the guard. He unlocked the door, and the sun started to shine again.

"Kit!"

"Darling—the minute I read the papers—"

Her arms were around me tight. She was ready to kiss me, but I broke away.

"The papers. Are they pretty bad?"

"I could get you one. If you want to read it."

"No." I shook my head. "I don't want to read it."

"But you'll tell me about it. About what happened."

"Sit down," I said. I sat down in the shadows, so she couldn't see my face. "Yes, I'll tell you about it."

And once again I told my story. I'd told it so many times I thought it would be easy by now. But it wasn't easy. Not the part about Trixie, about sitting in the booth and going home with her. That wasn't easy at all. By the time I got to the end, I was barely whispering. Anyhow, I told her.

She stood up and put her arms around me. That's a natural gesture when you want to comfort somebody, or when you love somebody. Which was it this time?

She kissed me, and I found out in a hurry. Not too much of a hurry, really. She took her time.

"Then you're not angry? I mean, you understand about—what I did? I thought you'd walk out on me forever, and I had a lot to drink, and—Kit, I'm sorry. She was a nice girl, really she was."

"Don't talk any more," Kit said. "Don't talk any more."

We didn't talk for quite a while then.

"Lady, your time's up." The guard tapped the bars with his key chain.

"All right." She dabbed at her mouth. "Tom, I'll see you tomorrow. And your lawyer will be here after supper."

"My lawyer?"

"Of course. The papers said you didn't name an attorney. So I went right around to Anthony Mingo, and he promised to come up after office hours."

"Anthony Mingo? He's pretty big, isn't he? How come you thought of—"

"Don't worry. He's a friend of mine. As a matter of fact, we were almost engaged, once. But that was a long, long time ago." Kit smiled at me and I smiled back.

"Lady," said the guard.

"Coming." She turned to me. "One thing more, Tom. I'll need the combination."

"What combination?"

"To your wall safe, silly. I never gave you back my key. But if I'm going to run the place while you're here, I have to get at the stamps."

I could have kissed her. In fact, I did, until the guard came right into the cell and took Kit away.

Then they turned on the lights and brought me my supper and I found out I could eat. I was still eating when Lieutenant Cohen showed up.

"Hello, Kendall," he said.

It wasn't anything in his face, it wasn't anything in his tone of voice. But the way he switched from "Mr. Kendall" to just "Kendall" told me where I stood.

"Hi," I called. "Just eating. Want to join me?"

"No, thanks. You got company coming. I thought I'd just stop by beforehand and see if you'd thought of anything more you could tell us. The District Attorney said he had a talk with you."

"That's right. And I told him everything I know. I was hoping you might have news for me. Did you find Joe Calgary yet?"

Cohen shook his head. "Don't worry, he'll turn up. Right now we're more interested in a certain poniard."

"That's probably turn up, too," I answered.

"Feel pretty good, eh, Kendall?"

"Lots better, thank you."

"Nice-looking girl you've got there. Saw her in the office down the hall."

"Well, don't go getting any ideas."

"A wife and four kids, and I need ideas?" He chuckled, then stepped closer to the bars. "Look, Kendall. This is off the record and I shouldn't be telling you this, but I'm going to anyway. Howard's out to nail you. He was pretty sore about the way that interview went this afternoon. Don't let him fool you. He talks soft but he carries quite a big stick. If this case ever goes to court with him feeling that way, he'll get them to throw the book at you."

"Thanks," I said. "I'll remember that."

"It would help you a lot more right now if you could remember a few other things," Lieutenant Cohen told me. He took an after-dinner nibble at his mustache. "The more cooperation you show, the better it'll look in the records. You did fine this morning, you did fine right up until you talked to Howard. So why spoil it? If you could just tell me where that poniard is—"

"Sorry," I said.

"You will be," he answered, and walked away.

Then the guard brought in Anthony Mingo.

We shook hands. We sat down. He opened his briefcase and took out some note paper and asked me to tell him my story.

This time I found it quite easy, easy enough so that I could study and observe Anthony Mingo during all the time that I told it.

Anthony Mingo was dainty. Not delicate, not effeminate, but dainty. He was slight of stature rather than short; he was well-proportioned but small-boned. He had curly graying hair and a complexion like old china. His porcelain-blue eyes and thin pink lips seemed painted on, and his skin itself had this patina of daintily-preserved elegance. He looked like a doll; he looked like an elderly little boy in a fawn-colored, form-fitting summer suit.

His gestures, when he made them, were quick but controlled. Every so often, during the course of my story, his head moved forward to catch, or punctuate, or emphasize a point. Always it moved quickly; always it halted quite suddenly, without a jerk. The control was perfect every time. And I noticed that, although he sat with his right leg crossed over the left, it didn't swing back and forth, or move enough to disturb the sharp crease in the trousers. No waste motion here. And no waste emotion, either, in those painted eyes.

I kept watching them, after a time, waiting for some reaction. None came, until I finished what I had to say.

"That's all," I concluded. "You know my background. You know what happened with Trixie, and what I told the police and the D.A. this afternoon. What do you think?"

"What do I think?" And the emotion came into the eyes now, the emotion I hadn't suspected. "Why, my dear boy, I think it's perfectly fascinating! Have you seen the papers?"

I shook my head.

"They're having a field day, I assure you, a positive field day! Forgive me. I know it's not something to be treated lightly. But it's absolutely delicious the way the press has handled this affair. The knife and sex angle, of course—it's only to be expected. But I wish the reporters would get together and agree which form to use. One of them compares you to Giles de Retz and the other insists on using Gilles de Rais. Not that it matters."

I stood up. "Look, Mr. Mingo. I've had a long, hard day. Tomorrow won't be easier. So if you don't mind, please go away and be fascinated somewhere else."

He raised a delicate hand. Not too far, just far enough. "A thousand apologies, Mr. Kendall! I've been singularly lacking in good taste, as well as in tact. And I apologize, abjectly."

He registered abjectness. Precise, correct abjectness. "Do not misunderstand. If I forbear to show sympathy, it is because sympathy is not my province in this matter. I find it best for my clients that I remain objective. And at times my somewhat inane evidence of humor helps me to maintain that objectivity."

They were all good two-dollar words, but I hadn't yet heard one I could buy.

"I asked you what you thought," I said.

"Please, Mr. Kendall. Katherine warned me that I might find you a trifle overwrought—"

"Katherine?"

"Miss Munson."

Funny, I never called her Katherine or Miss Munson. And he'd almost been engaged to her, once. I wondered about that. But right now, it could wait.

"Well, I'm not overwrought," I told him. "I'm just overtired. It's only that I hoped you might have a few ideas."

"I do, my dear boy. Indeed I do. But before I say anything, I was wondering if you had any theory?"

I paced the floor for a moment, if you can call four steps forward and back a pacing job. "Of course I have a theory. It was Calgary all right. Who else? So he didn't use the same knife. He used the poniard."

"Your poniard?"

"The one from my store, yes. Look, I told you about how frightened Trixie was. She knew Calgary, that's why. Oh, I gave her a snow job that Calgary wasn't dangerous, but I only did it to cheer her up, get her mind off it. I didn't believe my own line about him not being the Ripper type—"

"Jack the Ripper?" A new emotion came into those baby-blue eyes. "What do you know about him?"

"Not too much. I've got some books down at the store."

"I should very much like to see them some time in the future. I happen—but no matter. Go on with your theory. You say you felt this man Calgary might be dangerous?"

"Felt?" I snorted. "He came at me with a knife, didn't he? And he wasn't faking. He hated my guts. Trixie was his girl, and I went home with her. So the way I figure it is this. He hung around some tavern down the street, maybe took on a load, waiting for us to come out. Then he followed, just to make sure where we were going. After that he went around to my store—he knew where it was, been there in the afternoon and probably noticed the knives on the wall. He broke in, got the poniard, listened outside the window of Trixie's place until he knew it was safe, and then—" I gestured and let my hands fall.

"Very good as far as it goes," Mingo commented. "But it doesn't go quite far enough. For example, why didn't he kill you at the same time? And if not, if he wanted to be certain of establishing your guilt, why didn't he leave the poniard in the body?"

"Ask Calgary," I said. "That's your job. Find the man and ask him."

"That's a job for the police, and as I understand it they are looking for Mr. Calgary at the moment."

Anthony Mingo leaned forward. "Rest assured that I shall investigate fully," he said. "There may be half a dozen other suspects, once the details of Trixie Fisher's circumstances are established. Women of her class have a propensity for acquiring numerous jealous friends. In a crime of this nature, a crime of passion, the old adage must properly be reversed. *Cherchez le homme*, my boy. *Cherchez le homme.*"

We were getting bilingual already, and there still wasn't a word I could hang onto for comfort.

"Tomorrow should bring us some of those answers," Mingo continued. "I'll do all I can to find out about your Mr. Calgary and any other acquaintances of the deceased. But there's one other aspect of this case which frankly worries me."

"And that is?"

"Your past record. That and the blackouts. You told me a good deal, I know, and Katherine volunteered some information this afternoon. But in this particular circumstance I'd feel better if we had some expert psychiatric opinion to go by."

"In other words you think I might be crazy."

"Far from it, my dear boy. You impress me as being remarkably sane, quite well-balanced considering the situation as it stands. But there's always the element of doubt, and the way the press has chosen to exploit this case—the Ripper angle—may cause us a bit of difficulty."

"Wait a minute," I said. "Wait a minute. Why didn't I think of it before? Give me a sheet of that paper and your pen."

I scribbled out a name and address and handed it to him.

"Doc Greene," I said. "There's your man. Nathaniel Greene. I told you about him. He's the guy who had my case in the service and at the hospital after Marie died. He helped then and he can help now. He's out on the Coast. Call him up—long-distance—tonight, now. It's still early enough out there."

Anthony Mingo tapped his chin with the slip of paper. "Excellent, my boy!" he declared. "Excellent! I'll do that. And you'll have my report in the morning."

Then he went away and I went back to my cot, feeling neither better nor worse, except that I wanted some sleep.

But I didn't get any sleep. Not yet. Because they came for me again.

This time it was Lieutenant Cohen *an* the D.A., and neither of them said a word as they marched me along the corridor.

We went into a room I guessed must be the line-up room, because there were big charts on the wall and many lights.

"Stand up there on the platform, please," Cohen said. So I stood up there on the platform.

I stood waiting for the bright lights to hit me, stood there sweating and ready to squint. But there were no bright lights, only the single overhead bulb. And in a moment, a patrolman walked over to the wall and snapped off the switch. I was standing in the dark. I couldn't see anything, but I could hear.

I could hear the D.A. bring this man in, and I could hear a sort of tapping or clicking sound for a moment. Then only voices.

"You say you knew her?" The District Attorney's whisper.

"Sure. I could recognize her anyplace. Went by once or twice every night with some guy or other. Always picking them up. But what could you expect from such a floozie?"

"And it was about eleven, you say, that she passed?"

"More or less. Clocks don't mean much to me."

"She was alone?"

"I think so."

"Think?"

"Well, it was her heels I heard. I'd swear to that. Way she clattered along, it would take an army to march with her before I'd notice."

The voice was familiar, and when it came to that part about hearing the heels, I remembered. Blind Bill was out there. They'd picked up Blind Bill!

"And then you went into the park, you say?"

"Sure. Around midnight they start going home from the bars. I get lots of handouts that time, so I stay up late. Doesn't matter to me what time of day I sleep, you know."

"I know. And you came out of the park near her apartment?"

"Must have, about one, I'd say. That's when I heard him come along."

"And you'd recognize the sound again?"

"Pretty certain to. He walked right by me, and then he stopped. Stopped and waited for me to pass. I went around the corner, but I couldn't hear anything so I got kind of nosey and sort of cocked an ear. Sure enough, about a minute later, he started walking—only back along the way he'd come. I guess he stopped right in front of her front window, then. I heard it ease up, a little, and figured he was climbing in. Well, it wasn't any of my business, you might say, so I just kept on going."

I wanted to call out, then. I wanted to call out to Bill and tell him he was mistaken, there had been two sets of footsteps when Trixie and I passed him at eleven.

But Lieutenant Cohen was suddenly beside me in the dark, and he nudged me in the ribs and he said, "Get ready, now."

And down below, the D.A. said, "You really think you can identify him, eh?" And Bill said, "I'll try," and then the D.A. called "Ready up there?" and Lieutenant Cohen nudged me again and whispered, "Walk across the platform."

I walked across the platform in the dark.

The room was silent, and the cleats on my heels sounded like nails being driven into a coffin—my coffin.

"That's it!" Blind Bill yelled. "That's the man! I'd recognize that sound anywhere. Same rhythm. You got your killer now—I'd swear to it!"

They nailed the lid down on my coffin and took me away.

SEVEN

THEY WOULDN'T GIVE ME PILLS, or drugs, or drinks, or anything that might have helped me to sleep. They just left me to sit there in the dark, sit there and listen to the noises outside my cell and inside my head.

Perhaps I could have slept if it weren't for those noises. I heard somebody laughing down the hall. I heard myself asking why Blind Bill had lied. I heard somebody cough in the corridor. I heard Blind Bill say the cleats had come by all alone, late at night. I heard the jangle of a guard's keys. I heard Blind Bill identify me.

Why did he say that? What possible reason could he have for lying?

The voices asked the questions inside my head, and there were noises, noises everywhere and not a spot of silence. Except for the red spot. The spot of blood on the knife. Because a knife is silent . . .

After a long while the noises and the questions went away, and I just thought about the knife, dreamt about the knife.

Then in the morning the noises came back again, as the dawn came up like thunder. The noises clattered down the hall with my breakfast.

There was a mirror in my cell, but they wouldn't give me a razor to shave myself with. I didn't even ask why, because I knew. A knife is silent.

I sat there after breakfast, waiting. Who would it be this time? The D.A., Cohen, Mingo, Kit? Nobody came.

Finally I made some noise myself, rattled the bars until the guard came along. I gave him a quarter and asked for the morning paper.

When he brought it I didn't want it. Not after I read the story, read the headlines and the second-page "features." They had me strapped into the chair already. Tom Kendall, the Sex Slayer.

I couldn't finish reading. Actually, I didn't have to. Because a little before noon, somebody arrived.

It was Anthony Mingo. The guard let him in and he nodded at me. "My dear boy, you look tired! Sleep poorly?"

"Insomnia," I said. "Or something I ate."

"Don't be bitter. Did anything—happen—last night after I left?"

"Sit down and I'll tell you about it," I said. He did, and I did.

Mr. Mingo pursed his lips ever so delicately. "That doesn't sound too good," he observed. "But it explains a number of things. I saw this blind man down in Howard's office as I came in. And the bartenders from this place you mention, Swanee's. Bronson tells me that they're going to bring in the deceased's former roommate, a Miss Joan Schuyler. Would you know her, by any chance?"

"Never heard of her."

"Oh, they're thorough, and no mistake. Which is all to the good, from our standpoint. Who knows what they may find out or turn up? Often a very slim lead may be the determining—"

I didn't want a lecture on criminology. "Skip it," I said. "What about Doc Greene? Did you get hold of him? What'd he say?"

The lips unpursed, parted. "I meant to tell you. I tried to reach Doctor Greene at the hospital last night. They told me there that he'd been transferred to active duty once again. He's in Korea."

And I was back in my coffin. The nails were in tight, the cleats were in tight—

"Wait a minute!" I stood up. "The cleats! I had them put on yesterday, after Joe Calgary left my store. Because he was wearing them, too!"

"So?"

"Don't you understand? I couldn't figure out why Blind Bill was lying last night. Only this means he wasn't lying. He did hear somebody walking with cleats in front of Trixie's apartment. It was Calgary coming in." I was shaking. "Get hold of Blind Bill and tell him, will you? Or tell the D.A., tell Cohen. They've got to find Calgary now, unless they're already brought him in—"

Mr. Mingo smiled. "He's not booked. I checked. And today I shall proceed upon a little private investigation of my own. I'll report back tomorrow morning, when you're formally charged."

"Formally charged?"

"Er—you must realize, under the circumstances, that unless something unexpected turns up within the next twenty-four hours, you'll have to stand trial."

"But the cleats, and Calgary—"

"Mr. Calgary is a suspect, yes. But you are the man they're holding.

Now, Mr. Kendall, if you'll excuse me, our time is limited and every moment counts."

"Sure," I said. "Every moment counts."

He went out then, and I started counting moments. The moments until lunch came. And after lunch, the moments until Cohen came.

"Just stopped by to bring you a message," he said.

"Singing telegram?"

"No. Just good luck. From a pal of yours. Art Hughes."

"Art Hughes—what's he got to do with this?"

"Just checking. He was with you in Swanee's, remember? Said he saw you the night before, too—when you blacked out. Guess you talked pretty wild and he told you to see a doctor. That right?"

"Right," I said.

"Anyway, he wanted to see you, of course. But that's out. So he said to give you his regards and to wish you all the luck in the world."

Which I needed, and which wasn't enough. They had Art Hughes now, and he could tell them all about me and Marie and my threats against Kit. Good Lord, I'd forgotten that part! And if Kit heard, why then—

"What's the matter, Kendall? You look a bit pale."

"I need fresh air," I said. "Either let me out or go away."

He went away.

The afternoon was long, long enough for me to wonder whether or not they'd found Joe Calgary, or the poniard. I sat and wondered about all sorts of people and things.

I wondered what Mr. Mingo was doing, and where he expected to collect his fee. I wondered about Kit, and the store. Did she notice the lock had been forced on the door, and on the knife cabinet too? Yes, and I wondered about Doc Greene, over there in Korea.

It got dark, and I had supper. Still nobody came, and I wondered some more. Where was Lieutenant Cohen? Had they found any more friends of Trixie's, like this Joan Schuyler they were going to bring in for questioning? Was Art Hughes over at Swanee's talking about my sad case with the oldest bartender? What were the hot-shot reporters dreaming up to write about me tonight? And where was District Attorney Howard, the man who didn't have to fight for re-election?

I got one answer, anyway. The guard came along, unlocked my door, and let Howard in.

"Good evening," he said.

"Matter of opinion."

"Sorry to have neglected you. We've been quite busy."

"I can well imagine."

"I doubt if you can, actually." He glanced at his watch. "Getting late, I see. Has Lieutenant Cohen been here?"

"Not recently. You expect him tonight or something?"

"Hardly. He's out on a case."

"Another? I thought your boys only handle one assignment at a time."

"Usually. This is a bit—irregular."

"Look," I said. "Just because we're on opposite sides of the fence, that doesn't mean I don't want to help. I came across something today that might interest you. It's about Blind Bill identifying me last night. I wish you'd listen because I think it's important."

"Go ahead," he said.

I went ahead. When I finished, I watched his face. He smiled and I got a glimpse of how his bridgework looked under artificial light. "That sounds reasonable. And we'll check into that, you may be sure, when we get a chance to talk to Calgary."

"Still haven't found him? You've had them out looking—"

"All day. And tonight there's a general alarm out. We want him worse than you do, now."

"Now?" I was beginning to hope, a little, as a thought occurred to me. "This girl friend of Trixie's, the one who used to room with her. You were going to question her. Did she say anything that might help to pin the murder on Joe Calgary?"

"Not a word. We didn't even talk to her, but she gave us a pretty good lead."

"How come?"

"You can hear all about it downstairs, Mr. Kendall," said the District Attorney. "After you're released."

"Released? You mean, you're letting me go?"

"Well, we could hold you as a material witness. And of course, we'll want you for one when the case comes up. But I don't think you'll run."

"I won't," I assured him. "You'll probably have a tail on me anyway."

That made him smile, and we were both smiling as we walked down the corridor.

"Please," I said. "I can't wait. What's all this about? What kind of a lead did Joan Schuyler furnish if you didn't even talk to her? Didn't you try?"

"We tried," said Howard, and he wasn't smiling now. "We tried, but we were too late. When we finally located her around eight tonight, she couldn't talk. She was dead."

"Dead?"

"Murdered. The same way Trixie was murdered. And apparently by the same weapon. Maybe it was your poniard, maybe not. But you didn't do it, and we did find that stamp album Calgary carried. It was on the floor in her room. That's enough for us."

"So you're letting me go," I murmured. "Even though I couldn't possibly be mixed up in this second killing, aren't you taking a pretty big chance?"

"Perhaps. But I'm inclined to trust you, Mr. Kendall. Besides, you're taking a bigger chance than we are. There's a Ripper loose in the city, somewhere—and who knows? Next time he might come looking for you."

EIGHT

KIT WAS WAITING for me in the office, and so was Anthony Mingo. "Tom, I'm so glad," she said, and kissed me.

Mingo didn't kiss me, but he said, "Wonderful news, my dear boy."

Then they gave me back my wallet and identification; I signed a receipt, and shook hands with Howard.

"I'd appreciate it if you didn't say anything to the reporters," he suggested. "They'll probably be around tomorrow. Under the circumstances, the less anyone says the better."

"There's nothing to tell them, anyway."

"I know." Howard showed me what those black eyebrows looked like when they formed a frown. "That's just the trouble with this whole case. Nothing to tell them, and they keep blowing up the Ripper angle. I don't like to think about the general reaction when Miss Schuyler's death hits the headlines tomorrow morning."

"Three years until election," I reminded him. It wasn't kind, and I regretted it.

"That's not what I mean, and you know it. I'm talking about the fear psychology—women staying off the streets, locking their kids in the basement. That sort of thing. A panic is easy to start and hard to stop or control."

"You're so right," Mr. Mingo observed. "When Jack the Ripper was—you might say—carving himself a career in London, the carpenters and cabinetmakers went from house to house, selling locks and window reinforcements. Things reached such a state of tension that the women of the East End sent a petition to the Queen. There was some talk of sending the army into Whitechapel."

"I doubt if we've reached that stage here," the District Attorney informed him. "And while I admire your encyclopedic knowledge, I suggest that the less you display in this particular instance, the better. You know what happens whenever we get this sort of a case, Mingo. The news seems to stir up every psychopath in town. Which reminds me." Howard glanced at his watch. "I'm due for the show-up. I've issued orders to bring in everyone with a previous record in affairs like this, and the boys have been busy. So if you'll excuse me—" He hesitated and turned to me. "Mr. Kendall, would you care to join me? It might be that you'll recognize someone or something that would help give us a lead."

I shook my head. "No, thank you. I may not have a lot of friends, but I've chosen them pretty carefully. And none of them are pathological degenerates."

"Thank you, darling," said Kit, sweetly.

"Right now I want out of here," I went on.

"Can't say that I blame you," Howard observed. "But will you keep your eyes open during the next few days and report anything unusual? People who try to contact you, people who say things that might have a bearing on the case?"

I nodded.

"And keep in touch with us, will you? Call me, or Lieutenant Cohen."

"Of course I will."

"And remember one thing more. No heroics. None of this boy-detective stuff, going out on your own and hunting down the killer while I just sit in my office here and twiddle my thumbs. That's all right for the comic books, but we have a solid law-enforcement agency in this town. Understand?"

"You needn't worry. The farther away I stay from the whole business, the happier I'll be. And my happiness will be complete when you pick up Joe Calgary. Take my word for it, he's your Ripper."

I left him with this nugget, this brilliant example of my deductive powers, and went out into the night with Kit and Anthony Mingo.

Mr. Mingo had a car. It was a Lancia with delicate lines, but big enough so that the three of us could occupy the front seat.

"I'd like a word with you, my dear boy," he said, as we drove away. "But I appreciate how you must feel. Perhaps tomorrow, after a good night's sleep, you might favor me with a visit at the office?"

"Anything you say."

"I'll drop you off at your place, now."

"Fine."

Kit held my arm tight. "I still can't quite believe it," she told me. "Wasn't it lucky that—" She paused, and her fingers dug deeper into my elbow. "No, I don't mean it, not about that poor girl. Tom, what's happening? Two murders in a row like that—it's frightening."

"Not when you consider precedent, Katherine." Anthony Mingo talked as he drove. "For example, I recall the Black Dahlia murders, out on the Coast. In that series—"

"I don't want to hear about any more murders tonight. Please, Tony, you promised."

I looked at Kit. Then I remembered she had almost been engaged to him once, whatever that meant. Even so, I couldn't quite swallow the "Tony." Anthony Mingo, whatever place he occupied in my life now or in the future, would never be "Tony" to me.

Kit was upset. I didn't want to disturb her any further, but there was one thing I had to know. I tried to make it sound casual.

"How did things go at the store today?" I asked. "Any trouble?"

"No. We did thirty-seven in the stamps on walk-ins and about thirty on approvals. Nine on books, nothing in coins. Reeber brought in those magazines you ordered—a complete file of *Fantasy and Science Fiction*, in good condition."

"Fine," I said. "Anything else."

She drew in her breath suddenly, and cat claws raked my arm. "I—I forgot! The most important thing of all, and I forgot. Somebody broke into the store the other night. The glass was splintered all around the lock, but—"

"Nothing was stolen," I finished for her. "Nothing that you could see. Yes, I know about that, Kit. Somebody broke in and took that poniard, that French dagger. Cohen's already checked on it, so don't worry."

"I do worry, darling. I can't help it. I'll worry all night until I see you in the morning."

I had an answer for that, but not in front of Mr. Mingo. After all, he had been almost engaged to her, once.

But when we pulled up in front of my apartment, I opened the door and said, "Come on up for a while, Kit. It's still early and I want to talk to you about those approvals." I leaned over and nodded at Mingo. "It's all right. It'll see that she gets home safely."

Kit sat there in the car.

I reached for her arm. She moved away. She didn't pull away, just moved. But the withdrawal was unmistakable.

"Please, Tom. Not tonight. I'm a little upset, and—"

"Sure. I understand. It'll keep until morning. You'll drop her off, Mr. Mingo?"

He nodded, quickly—too quickly to suit me.

In fact, nothing suited me right now. Nothing would ever suit me as long as I knew that Kit was afraid of me.

I clenched my fists and bent down to kiss her. She didn't draw back.

She was willing enough to kiss me as long as Mingo was there. I didn't even doubt that she still loved me and would go on loving me. But she wouldn't come up to my apartment. Because Marie had died, and Trixie had died.

All of a sudden I realized that my promises to Howard weren't meant to be kept.

I couldn't stay out of this, because I was still in it, up to my neck. I'd be in it until the killer was found, until I was really cleared, and Kit knew it and wasn't afraid any more.

"Goodnight, Tom." She pulled her head away.

"Tomorrow in my office, then? You'll call first?"

I nodded at Mingo, nodded at her, and the car pulled away.

Then I went inside, went upstairs to my apartment. There was no mail, but I wouldn't have opened it if there was. Instead, I wanted to open the windows, open my shaving kit, open my pores under a shower. And I wanted to open a bottle.

I did what I wanted, all of it. The cork came out of the Old Overholt at precisely eleven. I know, because I was looking at the clock when the phone rang.

"Hello," I said.

"Tom! I just heard you got out. Is it too late, or can I come up?"

"Are you nearby?"

"Just down the street. Ten minutes, huh?"

"Sure," I said. "Sure, Art. See you."

Art Hughes was paying me a visit.

I made the necessary preparations. That is, I got out the ice cubes, a second glass and a bottle of white soda. Art never took his straight. I rummaged around looking for my bottle opener, but I couldn't find it. I ended up by prying the cap off with a butcher knife.

Then Art knocked on the door. When I opened it, I realized my preparations might be superfluous. Because Art was drunk. Not "high" and not "loaded"—just drunk. He hadn't sounded that way on the phone, but there always seems to be an extra effort to disguise the condition when a drunk telephones. Besides, he'd been out in the air after his call.

He stood swaying there in the hallway until I motioned him to come inside.

"Tom!" he said. "Good to see you. Good old Tom." No slurring. No "Good *ol'* Tom." He could talk straight enough. But he weaved when he walked, and his eyes didn't track properly.

"Where were you?" I asked. "Swanee's?"

"How'd you guess?"

"Psychic. Here, have a drink." I poured and indicated a chair for him alongside the kitchen table. He sprawled, reached, gulped.

"I'll bet Swanee's is doing a roaring business tonight," I said. "Everybody in there, asking questions. You ask any questions, Art?"

"Who—me?"

"Don't try to fool me." I grinned at him. "I'll bet you could hardly wait to rush down there and look for clues."

"Well, I was only trying to help. You know. Only trying to help." He wasn't grinning. He meant it.

"What about the cops, Art? Did you help there, too?"

"Sure. All I could. You know about that, huh?"

"Of course. And I appreciate it. Told them about Marie, eh?"

He looked puzzled, then worried. "Not me, Tom. It wasn't me. They knew all about her before they asked me. And I couldn't deny it. Could I, now, could I, Tom?"

"No. I guess you had to tell them."

"After all, it was for your own good. I mean, this other one—this Joan somebody—she hadn't been killed yet, and I thought that if—if—"

"You thought that if I had killed Trixie, it would be better if the police figured I was crazy. Is that it?"

"Right, Tom. Right. You can understand that, can't you? I'm your friend."

"You're my friend, but you believed I killed Trixie."

"No, Tom. Look, you're getting me all mixed up. I come—came around here now because I'm your friend. Because I'm glad you got out. Now you're free, Tom. You can go away. You can go away to some other town and see a doctor like I told you. Those blackouts, Tom—did you ever think maybe it was some kind of brain tumor? Gershwin had a brain tumor, Tom. He used to get those—"

"Never mind Gershwin tonight." I poured him another drink. "And I'm not angry because you talked to the police. I know you did what you thought was right, and you want to help."

"That's the truth, Tom. I want to help." He reached for the glass. "All day long, that's all I've been thinking about—how I could help." He took a mouthful, swallowed, shuddered. "I did my best."

He did his best. The thought hit me, then: why Kit was afraid.

"One thing I don't like, though," I said. "And you might as well know it."

"What's that?"

"You didn't have to call Kit and tell her. Tell her that I'd threatened her, that she wasn't safe with me.":

His mouth worked, struggling to get the words out. "But Tom, I didn't—!"

"Don't lie to me." I stood up, stood over him, and for the second time that night my hands formed fists. "You called her when you left the District Attorney's office. You called her and warned her to keep away from me."

He cringed. Once, in the shop, when we worked together, I saw Art Hughes in action. A crane mooring snapped, and three tons of steel started to slide down to the floor. There was a little sweeper working right underneath, and Art Hughes was twenty feet away. He ran forward and tackled the sweeper, rolled over twice and out of the way just as the steel fell.

And now, when I stood over him, he cringed.

All of a sudden I had to sit down. "Sorry, Art," I said. "This whole thing's too rough for me, I guess."

He nodded, and it was the nod of a man who was sobering up, fast. But he didn't look at me. He stared down at the table as he talked.

"You got to remember one thing," he said. "I'm your friend, Tom. That's why I did it. That's why I want you to see a doctor and get straightened out again. It's for your own good. Don't forget, I saw it happen to Marie."

"Good God, man, you can't believe that! You were there, you know I didn't kill Marie."

He sighed, but he still wouldn't look at me. "That's right. Not with a knife, you didn't. But why do you think she died, Tom? You wouldn't know, would you? But I know. I know because I used to sit with her, times when you were away, out wandering around with those spells of yours. I listened to her cry, I know what she was thinking, worrying and wondering and waiting, night after night, until—"

"All right, Art," I said. "According to you, then, I really did kill her in a manner of speaking. Only Oscar Wilde said it better. Each man kills the thing he loves, isn't that it? The coward does it with a kiss, the brave man with a sword. And maybe it's better that I don't do any more kissing until this thing is over with."

He wouldn't look at me. He just stared down at the kitchen table, and kept mumbling.

"See a doctor, Tom. See a doctor before it's too late. That Kit, she's a fine girl. See a doctor and don't talk about killing any more. Or swords. I come up to help you, and you're sitting here at the table with—"

Then I knew why he didn't look at me. I knew what he was looking at instead.

It was resting next to the white soda bottle. The butcher knife.

"Go home, Art," I said. "Go home. It's all right. There's a plainclothes man downstairs, watching the place. I'm sure of it. So I wouldn't harm you. Go home, Art."

He went home.

After he left I sat there for a long time. It was my turn to stare at the butcher knife. And as I stared, I wondered. I hadn't killed Joan Schuyler. That was certain. But I'd threatened Kit—

I couldn't remember what happened just before Trixie died . . . I'd come out of a blackout to look down at Marie's body . . .

No, this case wasn't over for me. Staring down at the butcher knife, I knew it was just beginning.

NINE

WHEN I CAME TO THE STORE the next morning I took out my key, then realized I didn't need it. In the first place, Kit was already inside, at her desk. In the second place, the smashed lock hadn't been repaired yet. I stared at the jagged glass around the frame, near the doorknob. It was a messy job. Somebody had been in an awful hurry, or somebody had been very clumsy. Or both.

I walked in. "Good morning, Kit," I said. "Sleep well?"

She just looked at me and flushed. She didn't blush. Instead she had the kind of blonde complexion that flushes.

I wondered what embarrassed her, then realized the reason as she hastily shoved the morning paper under the desk and out of sight.

"That's all right," I said. "Here, let me take a look."

Kit watched me as I read. I wasn't bothered by the headlines—I'd expected them. SECOND RIPPER KILLING would naturally provoke such stories. I read a little about Joan Schuyler; later I wanted to read it all, but right now I was interested in the lesser details. I wanted to read if they'd found Calgary yet.

They hadn't. At least, there was no report. And I was pretty certain they'd call me downtown if and when they had him.

"Here's the mail." Kit handed me the correspondence.

I looked it over. All routine stuff, and I wasn't in the mood.

"Want me to take care of it, Tom?"

I shook my head. "Later, maybe. Right now I'd like you to go over to Harry's—you know where it is, down a couple of blocks—and see if he'll come and fix that door. Need a new pane, I suppose, and a new lock."

"All right." Kit stood up. "Mind if I stop for a cup of coffee on the way?"

"Go ahead." I tossed her a dollar. "Maybe you can bring back a cup for me. And some pie."

"Didn't you eat breakfast yet?"

I shook my head. "I started to go into Nick's, but he saw me coming. And maybe I'm just a sensitive soul, but I didn't like the way he looked at me."

Kit flushed again. She picked up her purse and walked out, and I was alone.

Well, I might as well get used to it. Looked as though I'd be alone quite a bit of the time from now on. Art Hughes wouldn't be coming around, and Kit would keep a desk between us. Even people like Nick didn't want to see me.

Nobody wanted to see me any more, except possibly the man who was just coming into the store now. And he *couldn't* see me.

"Hello, Bill," I said.

"Mr. Kendall! When I heard they'd let you out, I came right over."

"Here." I walked over to him. "Let me get this chair for you." He tap-tap-tapped his way over to it, and I steered him by the shoulders. He sat down heavily, and the sun from the window glared pitilessly into his face, into his eyes. But it didn't matter.

Bill's face was big and battered, and something about his closed eyes made the rest of his features stand out in unnatural prominence. His nose and forehead were ridged and welted, and I wondered if he drank a lot or if he had some skin disturbance. I could ask him, of course, but there were other things I wanted to find out first.

There was, it turned out, no need to ask. He told me.

"Came right over," he said, again. "Wasn't far. We're sort of neighbors, Mr. Kendall. You know where I live, right over Peck's Grocery?"

I nodded, then remembered he had no use for nods. The blind face searched for mine in the sunlight. "I had to apologize to you, Mr. Kendall. I made a bad mistake. If they wouldn't have let you out, I was coming down to tell them about it anyway."

"Thanks, Bill," I said. "I'd already figured it out, though." And I told him about Calgary and the cleats, and why it was that he'd confused the two of us. "One other thing, though," I said. "I walked past you at eleven with Trixie Fisher. But you told them downtown you only heard her footsteps. How could that be?"

Blind Bill shrugged. His knotted knuckles moved over the shaft of his long black cane. "It's the rhythm, Mr. Kendall. That's what I recognize— the rhythm. Chances are, you were walking the way she walked. Feet coming down at the same time, and her heels making more noise than yours." I caught myself starting to nod.

"Yes," I said. "I see—I mean, I can understand that."

"Get up and walk now, Mr. Kendall," Bill urged. "I want to check on something."

I stood up and walked the length of the store, then returned.

"Sure," said Bill. "There's a difference. The man I told the police about is slower. Heavier, I'd say."

"He's big and fat." I leaned over Bill. "You tell the police all you know?"

The cane hit the floor with a thump. "Of course I did! Why shouldn't I? Those cops, if they wanted to, they could run me off the street. I got nothing to hide, Mr. Kendall."

"I believe you. But you see, it's important to me, Bill. I'm still under suspicion, in a way. I want to see this man Calgary caught and convicted. And you're apparently the last person who saw—I mean, heard him. On the night of the murder."

Bill shook his head slowly. The blind eyes blinked, the mouth smiled. "That wasn't the last time, Mr. Kendall."

"You mean you've heard him since then?"

"Sure. I was just going to tell you. I came from the District Attorney's office right over here. Like I say, I play ball with the cops, and I told them first."

"All right, let's have it," I said. "When was the last time you heard those footsteps?"

"Last night," Bill said. "Last night, right after supper. I was standing on the corner just outside the park, near Wentworth. The cleats came past. The same rhythm."

"You're certain?"

"Positive. Of course, it took me a little while to figure it out. Don't forget, I'd identified you and I knew you were locked up, and so at first when I heard the noise I just thought here's another fellow who wears cleats. Then, when the extra came out about the second murder, I got to thinking. And I remembered the way you walked without any cleats. Faster. Then I recollected that the cleats I heard under Trixie's window were slow—and so were the ones I heard last night."

I sighed. "Too bad," I said. "When you heard him he was probably just on his way to Joan Schuyler. You might have saved her."

"Maybe she wasn't worth saving," Blind Bill said.

"What do you mean by that?"

The cane thumped down. "Nothing." He sighed. "Oh, hell, I guess I didn't have any call to say that, did I? It's just that—well, you don't know what it is when a fellow's blind. The way the little things get big, more important." The cane thumped again, the knuckles moved. "Now take yourself, Mr. Kendall. You slip me a dime now and then, and that's nice of you—but it's not the most important thing. Most important thing is the way you always say hello. Every time you pass, you say hello."

"I wish to God I'd remembered to say hello when I went by with Trixie," I told him.

"Bet she was the one who wouldn't let you."

"Why do you say that?"

"I was right, wasn't I? I know. Because those kind never say hello. Not the hustlers. They're too snooty to say hello to a beat-up blind bum."

"You're pretty bitter, aren't you, Bill?"

He sighed. "Guess so. Only it's been a long time since I got a hello from a woman—"

"Hello, Bill!"

He jumped when he heard that. But it was only Kit, returning. "The man will be down to fix the door right after lunch," she said. "Here's your coffee. I got apple pie."

"Thanks," I said. "My favorite."

Blind Bill stood up. "Better move along," he said.

"Here, let me help you," I told him. "Watch out for that broken glass."

"Somebody busted in on you, eh?"

I told him about the poniard. He nodded. "French weapon, isn't it? Too short to swallow."

"What's that about swallowing?"

Bill grinned. "Didn't you know? Before I got these cataracts, that's what I used to do. Sword swallower in a carny outfit, sideshow."

"Well, whoever stole my dagger didn't intend to swallow it," I said. I guided Bill over the threshold. "You'll be sure and let the police know if you hear those footsteps again?"

"Right away," Bill promised. He started to tap along the street, then turned his head. "I'm sorry about my mistake, Mr. Kendall. I'm glad you're out, now."

"Thanks. I'll be seeing you."

It came out before I could stop it, but he didn't mind. He was used to it. He must have gotten used to a lot of things, hidden away in that eternally dark world in which he tapped along, groping his way to the grave.

Well, we were all blind, in a way—all groping our way to the grave. Trixie and Joan Schuyler had already made it. Who'd be the next one?

I went back into the store, trying to shake off the sudden depression. Perhaps the coffee would help. And I wanted to talk to Kit. —But there wasn't time for coffee, or Kit. The phone rang. I recognized the well-modulated voice.

"This is Anthony Mingo speaking."

"Yes. Oh, about our appointment—I was going to call you. How about this afternoon some time?"

"I'd appreciate it if you could make it sooner. That's why I called. I find

I shall be out of the city for a day or so, and plan to leave after dinner. Could you possibly come down now?"

I hesitated. "Of course. Be right over."

"Excellent. You'll be able to close up without any difficulty?"

"Why should I close up? Kit's here."

A brief, hesitant silence. Then, "Yes, of course. I'd forgotten. I'll expect you, then."

"Right."

I hung up. Kit opened the paper container and passed me the coffee. I shook my head. "No time. Got to go."

"Don't tell me that was the police again?"

"No. Just your ex-boy friend. Mr. Mingo." I put on my hat. "By the way, he seemed a little surprised to find out you were here. Did you tell him you were quitting?"

"No." Mingo had been too slow and Kit was too fast. "Whatever gave you that idea?"

"Hard to say where my ideas are coming from these days." I grinned. "See you at twelve, for lunch. We've got a lot to talk about."

"Yes," she said, and tried to look pleased about it. I went out and started walking down the street, and the shadow moved after me.

TEN

THE SHADOW WALKED QUIETLY, slowly, pretending to be interested in the windows. Of course, going through the park, there were no windows. There were only curving paths.

I took advantage of that to loop back after rounding one curve, and stepped out of the bushes right in front of him. He was a small, sandy-haired shadow and he startled easily.

"Anything new from headquarters?" I asked.

"Now look, Mister——"

"Kendall's the name. As if you didn't know." I smiled at him. "I'll bet this isn't any more fun for you than it is for me. So why don't we cut out all the funny business and walk along together?"

"I've got my orders," he said.

"That's right. Lieutenant Cohen wants you to keep an eye on me, doesn't he? He wants to know where I'm going. Well, right now I'm on my way to a lawyer. Anthony Mingo. And if you'll just cooperate, you can park yourself in a big easy chair outside his private office instead of hanging around the lobby downstairs. Good deal?"

We walked along together, out of the park and down the street.

"How's it coming?" I asked.

"Nothing new."

"The Lieutenant still looking for Calgary?"

"I wouldn't know."

"Not even after that new tip Blind Bill brought in?"

His eyes flickered for a moment. "I—wouldn't know."

"What's your name?" I asked. "Or wouldn't you know that, either?"

"Flint."

"I remember, now. Lieutenant Cohen mentioned your name at my apartment."

"I wouldn't know."

The needle was stuck again, so I left it there. We entered a lobby, took an elevator to the eighth floor. Flint eased into a chair, as I gave my name to the receptionist in the anteroom.

She smiled. "Go right in. Mr. Mingo expects you."

I nodded and glanced over my shoulder. Flint was sitting there, his face half-hidden in a book. I hoped for his sake it was a memory course.

Then I walked down a long hall, opened a panelled door, and said hello to Anthony Mingo.

"Come in, my dear boy." Today, sitting behind the desk, he was wearing a dove-gray suit, but in a room this size he looked more like a little boy than ever.

Everything in the room seemed enormous by way of contrast. The big desk, the huge bookcases, the voluminous drapes—all outsize. Even the weapons on the farther wall. *Weapons.*

Everywhere I went, the knives were following me. The poniard, the butcher knife; and Blind Bill had to be a former sword swallower. It was a conspiracy. It was also slightly ridiculous.

Or maybe I was just suddenly sensitive to the theme. I remember my old boss at the factory telling me what happened when he bought a house.

"Funny thing," he said. "We decided to landscape the grounds, and the first thing you know, wherever I looked I saw fertilizer ads. I was reading the same papers and magazines I always read, and I'd never noticed one before. But now it seemed like they were all over. And everybody I knew seemed to be talking about fertilizer and lawns. It was all fertilizer."

Sure. It was all fertilizer. And so was this notion about being pursued by knives.

But the swords hung from the wall. There was a yataghan, a cutlass, a scimitar. All of them big weapons, of course. I stared at the cruel curves.

"Interesting, are they not?" Mr. Mingo stood up and minced over to my side. "Care to look around a bit?"

"Why not?" I replied. And why not? Silly to let my imagination run away with me—nobody'd pay the ransom. No sense in thinking as I did, that perhaps Blind Bill had swallowed my poniard, or Mr. Mingo had concealed it in the scabbard of a sabre, or Art Hughes might be afraid of knives because he'd just used one.

When the mind is troubled, it can take refuge in a book. So I looked at the bookshelves. The usual assortment of legal window dressing, plus. The plus interested me.

This was carrying coincidence—or fertilizer—too far. The shelf, right behind his desk, with its titles neatly arrayed: Barnard's anthology, *The Harlot Killer*, plus *The Lodger*, plus *The Mystery of Jack the Ripper*, plus the books of Pearson and Roughead, and Dr. Wertham's *The Show of Violence*. Yes, and here was another name I knew—*Justine*, by the Marquis de Sade. I knew I wouldn't have to go much farther before coming across Krafft-Ebing. It might be this book here. No, this was the 1954 Scott catalogue. I was glad to see a friend at last.

"You a philatelist?" I asked.

"Formerly. That book is misplaced on the shelf."

"You can say that again! Where did you amass such a library of crimes of violence?"

"Here and there, through the years. But sit down."

I sat and waited for him to continue.

"After all, it's quite natural that I should be interested in the more—bizarre, shall we say?—elements of my calling. I trust you're not sensitive about such things." The delicate mouth made a delicate *moue*.

"It doesn't bother me. Only for a man who makes his living defending people you seem to spend a lot of time studying those who were convicted."

"Accused? Convicted? You miss the point, Mr. Kendall. I am interested solely in the phenomenon of murder itself."

I had heard that word many times during the past three days, and it had issued from a lot of mouths, including my own. But when those delicate little lips formed the syllables, something special happened.

Suddenly, the room grew dimmer as though the echo of the word had summoned shadows. Murder often lurks in just such shadows.

For the first time I really got the feeling—the feeling of murder. Murder in the air, murder around me. And it wasn't my imagination. Somewhere, some place in this city, there was a murderer. A silent man with a silent knife. He'd struck twice in two days, struck close to home. And that's why the word bothered me now. Because it wasn't just a word, something for me to read in books or newspapers. It was a personal threat.

I glanced around, half-expecting to see a shape emerge from the shadows. Nothing there, of course. But then, murder can hide anywhere. Sometimes it can even hide inside a person.

Little Mr. Mingo was watching me. Maybe he guessed my thoughts. Maybe he shared them. Whatever it was, he looked amused, as though he were chuckling over some private joke. From the looks of his library, I could imagine what kind of private jokes a man like Anthony Mingo might find amusing.

But I really didn't have to guess, because he was telling me, now.

". . . since you're not unduly sensitive, I might mention that this affair has certain piquant aspects which intrigue me: the hired assassin, the barroom brawler, the enraged or outraged lover. Through the years I've seen so many that I must confess to a certain boredom. This instance is much more to my taste, I assure you."

He didn't have to assure me. I could see it in his face.

"I've often regretted that I was not born a generation earlier. Those were high times for the true *aficionado* of the crime of violence."

"You'd have liked to be alive when the Ripper was around, I suppose?" My sarcasm was obvious.

"No, not precisely. Say five or ten years later. It's a delicate point you raise and one worth considering, but on the whole I'd choose the nineties." My sarcasm, apparently, hadn't been obvious enough. Either that or his enthusiasm surpassed it. Because he went on with obvious relish. "Yes, the nineties. The Ripper would still be fresh in memory, with the delicious possibility of his imminent return. And meanwhile, one would be reading about Mr. Holmes. Not Sherlock, the fictional detective, but H. H. Holmes—the Chicago mass-murderer. You recall his story? The castle, the dungeon, the bodies of the women found in the torture chambers? And then there was Neil Cream and Dr. Crippen, of course, and—"

"Oh, for the good old days," I said. "You sentimentalists are all alike."

This time he couldn't ignore my implications.

"Sorry," he said. "I perceive that I'm boring you."

"Not at all. It's just that, as my lawyer, I'd expect you to be a little more interested in the present case. For example, what did you find out about Joan Schuyler that might help us?"

Mingo shrugged. It was a complete gesture, yet so delicately executed that it wouldn't have dislodged a butterfly from his shoulder.

"The papers told the story," he said. "Joan Schuyler ate supper at a cafeteria, alone. She came home and the janitor's wife was out. Otherwise she would have received the message telling her to report at headquarters for questioning. She went to her room and apparently lay down for a nap. She locked her door but not her bedroom window. That was a bad mistake, Kendall. Her last."

There won't be many open windows in town today, I thought.

"The killer must have entered from the alleyway. He found her lying face downwards on the bed; they know that because the wounds indicate the striking angle. Perhaps she died after the first thrust—I understand they were very deep. But the killer didn't stop then, Kendall. He went on. He turned her over, and he thrust again. And again. One can only surmise how long he might have continued or what he would have chosen to do next. But he was interrupted. The janitor's wife came in and the door slam outside disturbed him. By the time she came down the hall and knocked, he was gone, leaving the album behind him."

"That's the part bothering me," I said. "It's such a stupid plant—so obvious."

"Ah, but is it? Your deduction is logical, normal, to be expected. Undoubtedly the police feel the same way. But this killer is cunning. He may assume such a reaction, may even intend it." Mingo turned and gestured toward the bookshelf. "Read the cases," he said. "Your true artist in murder is skilled in subtlety."

I tried to think about fat Joe Calgary being skilled in subtlety. I couldn't make it. But a man like Anthony Mingo, now . . .

"That album," I said, trying to read his painted-on eyes. "It seems like a pivotal factor to me. If only someone would show up and claim ownership—"

"My dear boy," laughed Mr. Mingo. "Would you, if it were yours?"

I shook my head.

"Well," he said. "Of course not." Suddenly he sat up and his face sobered. "But there's no point in discussing this matter any further. I had another and entirely different reason for calling you in."

"If it's your fee," I said, "I guess I can take care of it. There's some cash in the bank, and you'd be willing to take the rest in installments—"

A hand made a gossamer gesture and the fee disappeared. "Consider it paid," Mingo told me. "As a courtesy to an old and very dear friend."

"Kit?"

"Miss Munson has always meant a great deal to me," he said. "And that, actually, is what I meant to discuss with you."

I stood up. "You told her to quit, didn't you?"

"Yes, of course I did." He caught the look on my face, but he didn't flinch. "Please, spare me the melodramatic rage. I advised her to resign and for a very good reason."

"It had better be," I said.

"She's in danger. Serious danger."

"From me? So you think I'm crazy too, do you—"

"My dear boy, no need to raise your voice. That isn't my implication at all."

"If not me, then who?"

"I wish I knew," Mingo murmured. "And so do the police. Who killed Trixie Fisher and tried to implicate you? Who broke into your store, for the same purpose of implication? Someone, whoever he is, bears no good will toward you. And it's quite likely he may try to strike again."

"I've got a tail on me night and day. He's sitting in your anteroom right now."

Anthony Mingo smiled. "I'm sure he'd come bounding in here—within thirty seconds *after* I struck you down with one of those swords on the wall." The smile faded. "No, Kendall, you've been emotionalizing, not cerebrating, or you'd realize the facts. Somebody dislikes you. Somebody who has already managed to kill two women. Until he is found and captured, you aren't good company for any young lady. Nor is it wise for a young lady to sit alone and unprotected in your store, which has already been entered. I haven't distorted the circumstances in the least, you must admit. And if you consider the matter sensibly, you'll agree. Katherine would be better off out of your life until this affair is over."

I nodded. "You have a point. I'm sorry I blew up. And I'll tell her to go."

"She's always assured of a temporary position with me, you know."

I knew that, too. Mingo didn't fool me. But the devil of it was, he had talked sense. It wasn't safe for Kit to be around me. And the only way to change matters was to find the killer, fast.

"I'll see her at lunch in a few minutes," I said. "She'll leave after I talk to her."

"Excellent. You might ask her to call me. I am leaving town this afternoon and won't return until the day after tomorrow. I'd feel better if she'd inform me as to her decision before my departure."

I walked over to the door.

"Meanwhile, if you need anything, my office here will be instructed to cooperate fully."

"Thanks," I said. "Thanks for everything."

"Quite all right, my dear boy." Mr. Mingo offered me a smile of dismissal. He turned it on with his usual precision.

He turned it off with precision, too. As I closed the door I caught a final glimpse of his face. He was staring at the swords on the wall, and his thin lips moved soundlessly. Some might have said he was praying. But I had a hunch I knew better.

Mr. Mingo, the *aficionado* of Bluebeard and Jack the Ripper, was scared.

Eleven

AS I LEFT MINGO'S OFFICE and entered the long hall once more, I caught sight of the door at the farther end. I walked up to it, pushed, found it would open. Mingo's private exit, no doubt.

It would serve for me, I decided; it would serve very well. I emerged in a hall corridor on the other side of the building and took the elevator down. I didn't know what Mr. Flint would do about lunch, but one thing was definite—he wasn't eating with Kit and me.

I called Kit from the drugstore down the street.

"Anything?"

"Just customers. Did you see Tony?"

"Tell you all about in ten minutes. Meet me at the Copper Kettle. I'll be inside, at a table."

I was, and she did.

"Tom, did Tony say anything? About me, I mean?"

"Yes. He said he told you to quit."

Kit bit her lower lip. "He had no right to tell you! He had no right to interfere—"

"Maybe. But what he said makes sense. Kit, I want you to go. If anything happened to you because of me, I'd never forgive myself."

She gave me the first real smile of the day, then. Also her hand to play with.

"Look, Kit, I've had a lot of time to think things over. Mingo's right. And you're right, too."

"About what?"

"About us. About me. I'm going to see a doctor and get things straightened out once and for all. So that we can get married, be together."

"Tom!"

"You will marry me, won't you, when this thing is over? If it's all right?"

"Of course I will."

"Then start acting engaged."

"Right out here in front of everybody?"

"That's not what I mean. Start taking orders, young lady."

"Such as?"

"Such as not going back to the store this afternoon. Such as taking that temporary job in Mingo's office."

The sun went behind a cloud then. "No, Tom. I draw the line at that. I won't work for Tony again, ever."

"Again?"

"I—I never told you this, did I? Two years ago I was Tony's secretary." My eyes narrowed. "And he made a hard pass at you."

"No. That's not it at all. I told you, we were almost engaged."

"I've been meaning to ask about that. I don't like that word 'almost.'"

"Oh, it's not what you're thinking. It might have been, but I wouldn't let him. Not after I found out—"

"What did you find out, Kit?"

"Please." Her shudder was genuine. "I don't like to talk about it."

"I want to know," I said, slowly. "And it's not just out of curiosity, or personal reasons alone. I'm beginning to get some peculiar ideas about our friend Anthony Mingo."

"Was it something he said or did this morning?"

"Partly. And it was also what he didn't say or do. Let me tell you, and then you tell me."

So I described our interview. I told her about the swords, and the books, and Mingo's charming little theories about murder. "Any of it sound familiar?" I asked.

"All of it." She shuddered again, and I could feel the tremor running clear down into the hand I held. "But you only know part of it. He's got more books out at his house. And more swords. And he's got a recreation room; only it isn't just that. It's a place where he keeps a collection of—oh, Tom, don't make me talk about it any more! He took me down there once, just to show me, he said. And he watched me when I saw, and then he tried to make love to me—" The angry sobbing came.

"It's all right, Kit," I said. "I know. So you quit. And he's still after you to come back."

"I'd never go back, never," she declared. "The only reason I went to him was because you were in trouble, and he's a good lawyer, Tom, really he is. That's just the trouble. Tony isn't bad. He's just twisted up inside. He's sick, Tom. You understand."

I understood, all right. I understood about being sick and twisted up inside. But I also understood something else, something I had to tell her.

"Kit, something happened when I saw Mingo this morning. I got a feeling. Call it a hunch, call it anything you like. But I'm beginning to sense that he knows a lot more about all this than he's saying."

"But, Tom, how could he? You don't really believe he killed those girls? I—I think he'd be the kind who might hurt them, but he wouldn't murder."

I shook my head. "I keep remembering what the District Attorney said. How this kind of crime seems to bring out the latent lunacy in every aberrated individual: starts them to imagining, thinking, planning, gloating—and maybe, acting. And when I heard Mingo talk this morning—"

"Remember your promise," Kit said.

"Promise?"

"You're going to keep out of this case."

"Sure," I told her.

"I mean it, Tom. If you want me to quit until the police find the killer, I'll quit. But you've got to keep your part of the bargain, too."

"All right."

"When are you going to see a doctor?"

I grinned. "This afternoon. I've already made the appointment."

She smiled back at me as we rose. "That's wonderful, darling. Who is he?"

"Doctor Crippen," I said. "I hear he's a good man."

We went out and parted on the corner. She was going to her place, and I was going off on my appointment.

I hadn't liked lying to Kit that way. Actually, I hadn't even liked ducking out on poor little Mr. Flint. But neither of them would have approved of my present plans. What had the District Attorney said? Something about not playing boy detective.

Well, I wasn't wearing a tin badge and I wasn't carrying a water pistol. But I had a job to do. If the police couldn't find Joe Calgary, it was up to me. After all, I had a right to look for my knife, didn't I?

The papers had given me one bit of help after all—their stories listed Calgary's address as the Court Hotel. I knew where that was, all right. Every town has its Skid Row, and ours is one of the biggest and best.

So I went slumming.

The crum-bums were out in force today. Some of them wear khaki, and some of them wear blue shirts, and some of them wear the same beat-up old overcoat winter and summer both, rain or shine. Rain or shine, you find them on the sidewalks and on the concrete steps—the bugs that swarm out from underneath the stones of a big city. The red-rimmed eyes look at you, but seldom see. They're really gazing out of present time—at yesterday's dreams or tonight's bottle. The cracked lips move, because the winos like to talk. Sometimes they talk to each other, sometimes they talk to themselves, but most of the time they talk to people who aren't there: people who haven't been there for years because they're dead, or divorced, or run away.

Oh, it's easy to be smug and smart and superior about the crum-bums—until you look in the mirror and wonder what a week without shaving would do to your face, and what would happen if your clothes got worn and you couldn't afford the price of a haircut. Almost anybody can look like a crum-bum after just a month. And all you need to make a start is just one little push. Lose the job, lose the house, lose the wife or the kids, or just plain lose your nerve—and then start looking for what you've lost in the bottom of a bottle. A month? You can turn into a crum-bum yourself in one minute, if the minute is bad enough. Sometimes, though, you don't go all the way. I know, because I'd come mighty close after Marie died. And I pulled out of it. Blind Bill—he wasn't a crum-bum, but he'd gone halfway. On the other hand, there are those who are all gone.

Like the character who tugged at my arm in front of the Court Hotel.

"Hey, buddy."

That's what they all say. "Buddy." Everyone's their buddy, everyone with an ear to lend and a dime to give.

"Hey, buddy, you gimme somethin' forra bite ta eat? Honest, I ain't had nuthin' all day."

"Sure." I fished out a quarter. "Say, you wouldn't happen to have seen Joe Calgary around, would you?"

"Joe who? Who's he?"

Of course not. Even boy detectives aren't that lucky. I handed him the quarter and he headed across the street for the tavern and I went into the Court Hotel.

There was no lobby, of course; only a stairway and a small desk with an elderly man sitting on a stool behind it. That would be Pop. You find lots of guys like Pop around. And he'd shoot the breeze with me, sure. And he'd tell me that Joe Calgary had a room, but let me see now, he hasn't been around for two-three days, and are you another one of them detectives, Mister?

And then I'd slip him a couple of bucks and he'd let me go up to Joe Calgary's room and I'd search the place and find an important piece of evidence the stupid police had overlooked. And just as I found it, I'd get sapped over the head, and when I woke up there I'd be in a dark cellar someplace with Joe Calgary looking down at me. And he'd beat me up pretty bad—but not so bad that I couldn't escape and then knock him out two chapters later in time for the usual happy ending.

I uttered a single four-letter word to myself that summed everything up. This was no good. The District Attorney was right—it was a waste of time playing boy detective. I turned around to head out.

Then I noticed the side door. It led to the bar. I walked in.

This place was no Swanee's. They had a juke box, but none of the customers would ever waste a nickel that way. There was only one bartender on duty, and he wasn't working at the moment. After all, it was scarcely three o'clock, and the crum-bums are noctambulists. Among other things.

There were only two people sitting at the bar when I came in. One of them was a sailor and the other was a—well, sometimes they're called "hostesses" and sometimes they're called "B-girls." Whatever the designation, they're usually dark and sullen-looking. This specimen was no exception. The sailor didn't seem to mind, because he was half out.

I didn't mind, either. I walked up to the bartender.

"What'll it be?"

"Make it a shot and water." No sense starting off on the wrong foot by asking for rye here.

He poured.

"I know the heat's on," I said. "But I've got a message for Joe."

"Joe." He didn't even make a question out of it, merely an echo.

"Yeah. Some money I owe him. Figured now was the time he could use it. If I leave it here, will you see that he gets it?"

"That'll be fifty cents." The bartender took the money and leaned over until I got a good look at the place where he'd cut himself shaving yesterday or the day before. "All right, now I heard everything," he said. "First off it was a hot tip at Belmont a fella wanted to give him. Then it was I better come out with it or they'd take the license. Then it was would I like to make a fast buck for myself. Hell, they even sent a broad in—one of them lady cops! And now you come along. That makes four today already. Do me a favor, will you—go back downtown and tell 'em I ain't seen Joe since the night before it happened."

Tom Kendall, boy detective, was baffled. He stood at the bar sipping his shot of rotgut and wondered which way to turn.

He didn't wonder long.

Somebody turned him. I gaped around and stared into the familiar mustache of Lieutenant Cohen.

"Thought we'd lost you," he said. "I might have known."

"Give Mr. Flint my best regards and tell him I'm sorry, but I had a previous luncheon engagement."

Lieutenant Cohen managed a smile. "He's already been given a message. Next time you go anywhere, he comes inside."

"Some of those pay-toilets are awfully small," I said.

"All right, Kendall, you've had your fun. You've come looking and you've gotten your answers. Are you willing to run along now?"

"Is that an order?"

"Call it a suggestion."

"Then I'm staying here." I faced him. "Look, I'm not having fun, as you call it. I'm looking for Joe Calgary. Your department has been looking for him for three days and from what the bartender here tells me you've done a pretty shabby job."

Cohen took a big bite out of his mustache. From the face he made, he didn't like the taste today.

"I don't want to make trouble for anyone," I said. "But finding Calgary is important to me. And if your boys can't do it, I will. I'm not very smart and I'm no detective. So all I can figure out is this: if Calgary's still in the city, he'll come back here sooner or later for his clothes, for money, for information. I don't say he'll come in the front door, and I don't say he'll come in during the next half hour, either. But sooner or later, he'll show. And unless you drag me out of here by the ears, I'm going to stick here until he does show."

Lieutenant Cohen nodded. "Sometimes the dumb idea pays off in the end," he said. "That's why we've had a man planted outside every hour during the last three days."

I looked at the floor. "Sorry," I said. "I guess I sounded off a little too much. But I still mean what I said. After all, you had a man planted on me this morning—but I left by the back door. And you can come in that way, too. Or somebody can come in who knows Calgary. So I'm sticking here."

"All right," said Cohen. "All right. So you stick here. And finally, who knows, through the back door or down the chimney comes Joe Calgary. Then what happens?"

"I don't know," I told him. "I just want to see him and talk to him. I've got a hunch he's scared, Lieutenant. He's off some place hiding and scared, and he doesn't know what to do. I'd just like to talk to him."

"I see." The Lieutenant would run out of mustache some fine day if he kept on like this. "Now you're a psychologist, is that it?"

"Psycolgist!" The sailor came to life suddenly. He raised his head from the bar and stared around, heavy red jowls hanging. He looked like a bull looking for a place to charge.

"Who said anythin' about psycolgist?"

"Nobody's talking to you," Cohen snapped.

"You psycolgist?"

"You'd better get some fresh air, chum," Cohen told him.

It seemed like a sensible suggestion, but the sailor wasn't having any. "My name's Sweeney," he yelled. "You wanna make somethin' out' it?"

"Pipe down, honey," whined the B-girl.

"You shut up!" The sailor rose and stumbled toward us. One hand gripped the empty beer bottle from the bar. "No goddamn phoney psycolgist gonna crap me! Why you—"

He swung. I ducked. Cohen sidestepped and grabbed the sailor by the arm. The sailor dropped the bottle and butted Cohen with his head. Cohen hit him once, and then the two of them were stumbling and punching across the floor. Cohen managed to get close enough to the door to shout outside.

"Flint!" he yelled. "Get in here!" He got a good grip on the sailor's collar, now, and dragged him out into the street.

I played impartial observer. The sulky-looking hostess drifted over and I wondered if she had me sized up as a prospect. She opened her mouth and I waited for the familiar "Hello, honey," routine.

What came out instead was just a whisper. "Beat it out of here while he's still busy," she said. "I'll meet you three doors down at the Blue Jay in five minutes. Go in the back way, nobody'll notice, and when Eddie asks you, tell him you're waiting for Helen."

"Helen," I said.

"That's right," said the hostess. "Helen Calgary."

TWELVE

THINGS WERE MUCH QUIETER in the Blue Jay down the street. I ducked into the rear booth, although I didn't think there was much chance I'd be spotted. Cohen would figure that I'd run fast and far.

The bartender turned down his radio and came over. "What's yours?"

"Hold it a while. I'm waiting for Helen."

He favored me with a gold-toothed smirk and returned to the endless escapism of the ball game.

I sat there wondering how Lieutenant Cohen had made out with the sailor. I wondered what he would say to Flint when he realized I'd given him the slip again. Then I started wondering about Helen Calgary, but not for long.

She drifted in through the back entrance and sat down across from me. The table between us was narrow, and I could smell the cheap perfume and all the other odors it was meant to conceal. I could see the cheap powder and the lipstick, and what they were meant to conceal, too.

The bartender was back. "Hi, Helen," he said. "You folks ready for a—"

"Never mind," she said. "This is personal."

He walked away. When he got back to the bar he turned up the radio, loud. We were left with our twentieth-century version of privacy.

"Got a cigarette?"

I extended my pack, held out my lighter as she reached over, sucking in the flame with a nervous hunger. She took four long drags in rapid succession.

"You wanted to talk to me," I said.

"You said you had some money for Joe."

I opened my wallet, took out a ten-dollar bill.

"Is that all?"

"There could be more. If you want to talk about it."

"How much more?"

"That depends."

She took another deep drag. "What's your name?"

"Tom Kendall."

She let the smoke out right in my face. "Why you're the guy who—" I nodded.

"Hell, and when you talked to that dick, I thought maybe you really was a friend of Joe's—" She started to get up, but I guessed where her hand would go before she left and clamped down on her wrist as she reached for the money.

"Sit down," I said.

"Not me, Mister! You better get the hell out of here before I call—"

This was the third time I hadn't let her finish a sentence. I got out my wallet with my free hand. "Another ten if you sit down," I said. "I can't hurt you just sitting across from you."

"You bet your sweet life you can't," she said. But she sat down again. She picked up both ten-dollar bills and put them away. She didn't carry a purse, so they disappeared under the table.

"If you won't talk, I will," I told her. "I take it you know my name and why I'm interested. But that doesn't make me your enemy or Joe's enemy either. I don't expect you to tell me where Joe is—matter of fact, I don't even think you know."

"That's the God's truth," said Helen Calgary. "I don't know. And I'm worried sick."

"You're not the only one. That's why I'm down here, trying to get information."

"Well, you won't get it out of me. I don't know anything about it." She ground out her cigarette and I passed her another, quickly, before she decided to get up again. My lighter came out, her lips sucked in.

"I take it you don't believe Joe is guilty," I said.

"I know he's not." She leaned forward again so quickly that four things bobbed—two of them earrings. "I ain't talked to no cops, because what would be the use? They don't know who I am so they haven't bothered me. I live over here, see, and Joe stayed down at the hotel. That's how it was. And I wouldn't tell them nothing anyway. Fat chance I'd have getting them to believe me." She took a puff and a breath simultaneously. "But he didn't do it. I know he didn't do it."

"What makes you so sure?" I asked. "He could have used the knife he stole from me, and then they found that stamp album he stole—"

"He didn't have your knife. He didn't have any knife, not even his own, because he sold that in Dick's for two bucks. And he sold the damned album for twenty."

It was my turn to lean forward. "Who'd he sell the album to?" I asked.

"He didn't say."

"But he told you about it and about the knife. That means you saw him after the murder."

Her mouth opened, but no smoke came out. She stared at me as I reached for my wallet again. I was running out of tens so I gave her two fives.

"All right," she said. "All right. I don't know nothing to harm him, anyhow. And you're not a cop."

"Believe me, I'm in this thing just as deep as he is. Deeper. Maybe I can help us both get out of it."

"Somebody better." The mascara was thick, the eyelashes were false, but the look in the eyes were genuine. "I'm scared, Mister. I ain't never been scared like this before." She scowled. "I ain't never seen him scared like this before either."

"When did you see him?" I asked.

"Three o'clock Wednesday morning."

Three o'clock Wednesday morning. That's when I was sleeping with my nightmare. That's when Trixie was sleeping with her nightmare—the one that never ends.

"He came here?"

"He came upstairs to my room. Back entrance. He said he spent the knife money for drinks at Dick's but he still had the twenty. And he needed more, because he had to get out of town, fast. I gave him fifteen. All I had."

"Did he tell you why he was leaving?"

"No. He was scared, though. I never saw him shake like that before. He said he couldn't tell me; it would only get me messed up in it."

"Did he say any more about where he'd been earlier that evening?"

"A little. He picked up this Trixie Fisher right after supper. He figured on maybe making fifty bucks, he said, even if it cost him a fin or so to get her plastered."

"He told you that?"

"Sure, why not? I knew how he got his dough."

I didn't yet, but I was beginning to get ideas. "Go on," I urged. "Anything more?"

"Well, he'd started drinking early, I guess, before he met her. And he told me about Swanee's and the fight with you. That really burned him, so he went over to Dick's and sold his knife and drank some more. Then he sold the album. I guess he was really sloughed or he'd of never done a fool thing like that. But he gets that way when he has too much, you know."

I nodded.

"And then what happened?"

"I don't know. I don't know any more except what I already told you—how he come in and acted so jumpy and beat it."

"Maybe he was still drunk when he talked to you."

She shook her head. "No, he was sober. Scared sober." She dumped the second cigarette. "I tried to get him to tell me, but he took the money and beat it. And that's all . . . until I read in the papers that morning, and the cops came around, and then that night I read about the other killing."

I was beginning to sense a pattern, and just then something else clicked into place.

"Joe knew Joan Schuyler, too, didn't he?"

"Joan? Of course he knew her. Just like Trixie. And that's why I'm so scared. Whoever did it might know about me, too."

I gave Helen her third cigarette. "Helen," I said. "How did Joe figure on getting fifty bucks out of Trixie?"

She shook her head.

I took out my wallet, but she shook her head again.

"Did he ever get fifty bucks out of you that way?" I murmured. "Did he, Helen?"

She stood up, and this time I didn't grab her wrist.

"Is that why you're frightened?" I asked. "Helen, have you guessed who the ripper is?"

Helen Calgary sat down again, sat down and started to sob. Long, hard, dry sobbing. "Oh, let me alone, for God's sake, let me alone!"

I put my hand on her shoulder. "All right. I'm sorry. It's only that the more you tell me, the easier it will be to catch him. Then we'll all be safe."

She nodded, still sobbing. I took the last five out of my wallet and laid it on the table. "Thanks for helping," I said. "And one thing I'll promise you—your name won't be mentioned."

Helen Calgary looked up. Her shoulders shook, then the shaking subsided.

"That stamp album," she said. "Joe told me where it come from. He said he stole it off his lawyer—Anthony Mingo."

THIRTEEN

I DIDN'T GO BACK DOWNTOWN. I took the alley exit and circled around, looking for more alleys. I walked way over to the near north side before I stopped into a neighborhood restaurant for supper.

It was dark when I got out, and the taxis were going by. But I didn't want a taxi. Lieutenant Cohen had probably sent out an order covering taxis, if he wanted to see me. And I had a hunch he did.

Drexel Boulevard was a long way out, but I took the trolley bus. I transferred, rode some more, and then I walked. There's never any public transportation running near the real Gold Coast, because the wealthy like their privacy.

Right now, Anthony Mingo's privacy was about to be invaded. I came along the street and stopped before the thick hedge which extended back for over a hundred feet. Then the trees began, another thirty feet of them. And behind the trees was the big house: the big dark house.

It would be dark tonight, because Mingo had left town. Possibly he had servants. Maybe there was a big dog loose on the grounds.

This I'd find out about, the hard way. And it was going to be the hard way. Tom Kendall, boy detective. What was that business about going up to the killer's room and searching for evidence and then getting slugged? All very amusing, and yet here I was. Here I was, without a gun, or a knife, or a file, or a jimmy, or even a flashlight. Nothing but a small hunch and a big hole in the head.

That was why I couldn't turn to Cohen for help. He'd call Mingo in, certainly he would. He might even issue a search warrant after talking to him. But I doubted that latter possibility very much. Mingo was no fool—he'd cover his tracks thoroughly. And once he knew that the heat was on, the tracks would stay covered. My chances of finding anything out would be over.

So I'd do it the hard way.

I walked up the stone path, then paused. *What are you doing here?* I asked myself. *You're crazy. Better to cut it out. Run away.*

The night was dark, and the wind bent the trees, and their shadows nodded at me. The shadows knew, the shadows agreed. I'd better run away.

But I was sick of shadows and running. I was sick of blackouts and being afraid to remember. I wanted to be free, I wanted to have Kit. I'd lied to her when I said I'd see a doctor—and then again, maybe I hadn't lied.

This was the therapy I needed. To focus on the problem, face it, and follow through to a solution.

I started walking again, reached the door.

No dogs barked. I peered through the mullioned panel, saw a dim light burning in the hall. There were windows off to my right. I could try them in just a moment. But first I had to make sure about the servants.

I hesitated. Suppose there were servants, what then? What if somebody answered the door, and I said—

The answer was ridiculously obvious. Anthony Mingo was my attorney, wasn't he? So I'd come to talk to him about the case. Simple. No gun, no knife, no file, no flashlight. Just common sense.

Common sense pressed the buzzer. Common sense stood there while the echo died away. Common sense waited, then subsided. I began to think about the windows again after all. About no gun, no knife, no file, no flashlight.

I turned, started away.

And then the door opened, and Anthony Mingo said, "Come right in! Good to see you, Tom."

It was as easy as that. He led me down the long hall, past a library, past a parlor entrance. In these lofty corridors he seemed more than ever like a little boy to me—a little boy who had lost his way.

But Anthony Mingo knew where he was going.

"Let's step down to the recreation room, if you don't mind," he said. "I was just preparing to run off a film."

So I was even going to see the recreation room!

"We can talk while it's on," he told me, as we descended the stair. "It's a silent. Quite a stroke of luck, my being able to locate it—and it's on rental to me for tonight only." We walked through the basement. "So you called and found out I'd changed my plans about leaving town," he said. "Fortunate that I heard your ring way down here."

So he'd notified his office he wouldn't be leaving town. I breathed a bit more easily after I heard that. Then I tightened up again as we entered the recreation room.

I don't know what I expected to see, after Kit's hints and what I'd surmised since. I was prepared for almost anything: a bastadino, a rack, even an Iron Maiden. But that's what comes of reading too much fantasy or science fiction. Anthony Mingo was no mad scientist, and he wasn't operating a torture chamber or a private morgue.

What he had, instead, was a private museum. At least, that's what it looked like to me. There were more bookcases, of course, and big leatherbound files of old newspapers. I saw just one weapon—a Yezidee knife, hanging on the wall behind the bar. The rest of the room was lined with glass cases on wooden mounts.

Mingo hadn't been lying. On the wall opposite the bar was a beaded screen for home movies, and in the center of the floor stood a projector, film already wound.

But at the moment I wasn't interested in that. I had to see what was in those cabinets.

"Look around," Mingo invited. "I'll mix us a drink. Let me see—you would take rye, wouldn't you?"

"How'd you guess?"

"Katherine told me."

I shrugged. I wondered just how much Kit had told him, and why.

That could wait. I wanted to look into the cases. I did. What I saw was disappointing. A piece of rope. A torn fragment of a skirt. An old shoe. And—so help me—a pair of false teeth!

"Landru's," Mingo murmured, from behind me. "Here's your drink."

"Thanks," I said. "Landru?"

"The Frenchman. The Bluebeard. Fifty, sixty women—perhaps more. An interesting memento, is it not?"

Yes, it was not. But I began to sense the pattern here. The shoe, now.

"Annie Chapman wore it the night the Ripper found her. At least such is the claim of the unsavory gentleman who sold it to me in London some years ago. Of course, it might be that I'm the victim of an imposture, since there's no way of authenticating it. The skirt, now, I'm reasonably sure of. Edinburgh. Helen McDougall. She was the paramour, you know, of one William Burke. You've heard of Burke and Hare."

I'd heard of Burke and Hare. Then the rope.

"Thug strangling cord. Thuggee hasn't been entirely stamped out, contrary to common belief."

I'd heard of Thuggee, too.

Within the next few minutes I heard new names, saw new souvenirs:

Palmer, Jesse Pomeroy, Strangler Nelson. A glove, a weskit button, and a belt buckle with the initial "N."

And all the while my courteous guide was talking, talking, and it was quite commonplace, really. The objects he displayed were utterly prosaic; everything was normal, and nothing was frightening. Except, perhaps, the realization of the thoughts that crawled through Mingo's head.

"I've quite a newspaper file, too," he was saying. "Recently, I've taken to collecting a new category. I call it my ex-soldier file." We were back at the bar now, and he was pouring another drink. "During the past several years, I've been struck by the number of cases in which ex-soldiers have literally run *amok*, you might say. They all seem to follow the same pattern. Breakdown, confinement, discharge—followed by a period of seemingly normal adjustment to civilian life. Then, suddenly, something snaps. And they kill, in blind and berserk fury. Wives, mothers, sweethearts, children, strangers. During one year alone the clipping bureaus have supplied me with over a hundred items." I caught sight of a grimy hand as he waved.

He paused. "Wasn't that your trouble, Tom? Crackup while in service?"

"Sorry," I said. "I've never gone berserk. Not yet."

He glanced up over the bar. "That's interesting." He indicated the dagger. "Ever hear of the Yezidees? In Crusader times, they furnished the Assassins: the hasheesh-drugged killers who terrorized the Moslems and the Christians alike. The dagger is one of a pair; pity I couldn't obtain the other." He broke off. "Do you find my tastes interesting or am I guilty of boring you?"

"Not in the least. But weren't you going to show a movie?"

"Ah, yes. Indeed I was. And if you do share my interests, to a certain extent, you may be pleased."

That's what makes your deviate truly unbalanced. He comes to believe that his tastes are normal, that everyone shares them.

But in this instance, I nodded, I wanted to see the movie.

"Sit down, make yourself comfortable," Mingo invited. "I'll snap off the lights and we'll start running. I got it from a foreign exchange this morning and the print isn't too good, I fear. But then, it's thirty years old. *Das Wachsfigurenkabinett*."

"What?"

"*Waxworks*. The Paul Leni film. I'm not running the first episode, with Jannings. It's the second and third, the Veidt and the Krauss, I want to see. You remember way back, Tom? No, of course you wouldn't. Conrad Veidt—there was an actor for you! And Werner Krauss. Both of them were together in *Caligari*, too."

So here was another facet of Mingo's personality; he was a movie fan. Or was it another facet? As the screen flickered, I began to wonder.

Mingo sat down next to the projector and stared at the screen in rapt silence. I stared, too. I stared at Veidt and realized Anthony Mingo wasn't

interested in the acting. He was interested in the story—the story of Ivan
the Terrible and the lovers in his torture chamber. On one level it was
merely an excellent weird fantasy—but in terms of Mingo's reaction, the
film was a pathological study.

I gathered that, despite the fact that Mingo never stirred or uttered a
word. But I heard him breathe, heard the changing rhythm. Midway in
the film, when I judged him to be utterly absorbed, I moved. I slipped out
of my seat and slipped back in again, all within the space of forty-five
seconds. His head never turned in the darkness.

Then I sat and waited. I waited as the Krauss sequence came on. I might
have known what it would be. The Ripper, of course. The Ripper following
me everywhere. The Ripper and the knives, following the two lovers now,
through the deserted carnival. Peering around the merry-go-round, leer-
ing through the spokes of the ferris wheel. And the scene was distorted,
and doors opened of their own accord, and the lovers fled slowly while
the Ripper pursued them to inevitable doom.

Halfway through the sequence Mingo spoke for the first time. His voice
was quite soft.

"You know, of course, that I never informed my office I wasn't leaving
town. Or did you bother to call at all?"

"No," I said. "I didn't even try."

"You came out here expecting to break into my home?"

"That was the idea, yes," I admitted.

"Might I ask why?"

"You might. But perhaps you'd rather answer my question first."

"Proceed."

"Why didn't you claim your stamp album? You must have known it was
your collection."

"Is that all you wanted to know?" Mingo's head turned in the darkness,
but I doubted if he could see my face, any more than I could see his. And
Jack the Ripper prowled across the screen, across both our brains.

"Not entirely. Because I think I can guess the answer. You were afraid
the album would tie you to Joe Calgary. Was he a client of yours, Mingo?"

No answer.

"Was he a client? Or were you *his* client?"

"What do you mean by that? Who told you? Nobody knows, nobody
could know—".

"It's pretty obvious, Mingo. You're a practicing sadist. You like the
whistle of whips, you like the sight of the marks they leave. Oh, I'm not
condemning you, I'm not even shocked. I've heard of such things before.
But you had to be careful. It didn't work out, trying such tricks with girls
like Kit. So you got them elsewhere. Joe Calgary furnished them, I believe.
I think he'd pick them out, pick them up, get them drunk, and then bring
them here to you. And you'd pay them—and him—off."

"Go on."

"What more is there to say? Perhaps the last time he was here you had a quarrel. Maybe he wanted more money. In any case, he stole your album and tried to sell it. Then, when the murder broke, you were afraid to claim it. Because the album would establish a connection between you and Calgary, and the police would find out."

The drama on the screen was coming to a close. Here in the room it was still going on. The Ripper and his victim—but which was which?

I didn't know. Even when he cracked, I didn't know.

"All right, Tom. All right. It's true, all of it's true. You don't understand what it is to be like this—to want to hurt and to know that you can't really. I never really hurt any of them, Tom. It was all more of a make-believe, like the movies, like collecting the relics and reading the books. You know that, don't you, Tom? I never tortured, I couldn't bear the sight of blood. But if anyone found out, I'd be ruined. Can't you see that, Tom? Can't you—"

"Yes." I sighed. "I can see that. And I wish that was all I could see."

The nightmare was almost over on the screen. But only on the screen. I had to go on.

"But there's more, Mingo. More."

"What are you trying to say?"

"Nothing that you don't already know. I'm telling you that when Calgary got mixed up in these killings, he came to you. After all, he only had about thirty-five dollars and he wanted to get out of town because he was frightened. Do you know why he was frightened, Mingo?"

"No. He wouldn't tell me." The little man gasped. He'd said too much, but it was too late now.

I kept on. "So he asked for money. And you gave it to him, to get out of town."

"All right." Mingo stood up. "Now you know, Tom. You know everything. And what are you going to do?"

"I don't know," I said. "But I still want to locate Joe Calgary."

The film flickered off. Mingo moved toward the light switch on the wall. "He wouldn't tell me where he was going," he said.

It was my turn to take a deep breath. I could leave it like this and promise Mingo I'd never say a word. He'd believe that was all I knew and take my promise, and things would go on.

But things mustn't go on any more. I let the air out of my lungs as I spoke.

"Wouldn't tell you where he was going?" I asked. "Or *couldn't*?"

Mingo's hand hesitated on the switch.

I kept on, because there was no other way. "You didn't give him the money after all, did you? You knew that if you paid him off, sooner or later he'd be back for more. That's the way blackmail works. Sooner or later something would slip, and you'd be implicated. And meanwhile you'd always have it hanging over your head, as long as he was alive."

"You don't know what you're saying," Mingo told me.

I stood up, quietly. "You killed him," I said. "That's why you gave out that you were leaving town tonight. You wanted time to dispose of the body. Where is it, Mingo?"

"No," he said. "No."

"The movie was just a cover-up, in case somebody happened to come in. You had other business in the basement tonight. I saw the dirt on your hands, and you aren't the kind of a man to soil your fingers unless you have to. But there's dirt on them now. Where's the body, Mingo?"

He snapped on the switch. He was all ready for me; the pretty little automatic was cocked and aimed. "I'll take you there," he said.

I took one step forward, then raised the knife—the knife I'd sneaked down from the wall behind the bar while he watched the film.

The light glittered on the blade. I could see the reflection in his eyes, as he stared at it. He forgot about the gun. All he could see was the knife.

"You!" he whispered. "I knew it. You're the one, after all. You're the Ripper!"

I moved forward. His hands began to shake. "Don't come near me," he whimpered. "Don't! Don't rip me. I can't stand the sight of blood. I can't stand it—"

I took another step, pulled the knife back, and let it go.

It didn't hit him. I didn't intend for it to hit him. I only wanted him to flinch and duck—just long enough for me to reach his side and grab the gun out of his hand. Then I twisted his arm behind his back.

"I'm not the Ripper," I said. "But you'd better show me the body, now."

I kept hold of him as we went out the door, down the length of the basement, past the oil-heating unit, into the little storage room. Originally it had been intended as a fruit cellar, but Mingo had changed all that. He'd made it into a wine cellar.

A wine cellar, and now, a tomb. He'd just started digging, apparently, when I came, and he hadn't gotten very far. He was frail and delicate, and the job of smashing through concrete with a pickax wouldn't have been easy. Cementing everything over again might have presented another problem. In fact the whole setup was slipshod and hastily contrived—like something out of one of those early Victorian case histories Mingo gloated over.

I stared at the preparations for interment while Mingo whimpered beside me. He wasn't looking at the hole in the floor. He was looking at the hole in Joe Calgary's forehead.

He'd shot him with the little automatic and dragged him down here. Now Calgary lay face up on the floor and his face was dead white—but no whiter than Anthony Mingo's face as he watched and whimpered.

"I didn't hurt him," he whined. "Believe me, I didn't hurt him. Just the one shot, and it was all over. And there wasn't any blood. I couldn't have gone through with it if there was blood."

I had Mingo's automatic in my hand now, and I used the muzzle to prod him over to one corner.

"Stay there," I said.

"What are you going to do?"

I moved back to the door.

"I'm calling the police, of course."

"No—you can't—don't leave me in here with him—for the love of God—"

How did Poe phrase it in *The Cask of Amontillado*? *"For the love of God, Montresor!"*

I locked him in the wine cellar with Calgary's body and went upstairs to call Lieutenant Cohen.

FOURTEEN

"I GUESS THAT washes everything up," Lieutenant Cohen told me. We were riding downtown now, to headquarters. Ming wasn't in the car; he was in a police ambulance, behind us.

I still don't like to think about that part—the way he really went to pieces when the police came and we opened the wine-cellar door. We found him sitting there mumbling, and at first we thought he was talking to himself. But he was talking to Calgary's body, explaining that he wasn't really a killer, he just liked to pretend, and he'd never hurt anyone to draw blood.

Cohen hadn't wasted much time trying to talk to him. He called for an ambulance, we went upstairs, and I told him what I knew, and how I'd come to know it.

Then we got rolling. Cohen was still shaking his head, now, in the car.

"Hard to figure a smart guy like him planning to bury a body in the cellar," the Lieutenant said. "He's been around enough to know it never works."

"He wasn't thinking like Anthony Mingo the attorney," I answered. "In his own mind he was acting out the role of one of those perverted monsters he was so fond of reading about."

"He pulled a pretty childish stunt," Cohen sighed.

"Murder is always childish," I told him. "Real murder. Think about it a while, Lieutenant, and you'll see it's true. The smart boys—the ones who write the movies and the TV shows are always ready to supply their fictional murderers with clever gimmicks. But your real killer seldom is rational or mature enough to reason things out—particularly when he kills suddenly, unexpectedly, on impulse. Oh, there are exceptions. Only by and large, you cops will go on finding bodies under coal piles and culverts, corpses tossed hastily into the river, or just left lying where they fell as the murderer fled."

"I just can't figure it out," Cohen sighed. "A guy like Mingo pulling a stunt like this." Another sigh. "I suppose if he doesn't calm down, we won't even get a conviction. They'll stick him in the fun-house for keeps."

"That's the key to the whole thing," I said. "Anthony Mingo hasn't been really sane for years. He's been dramatizing himself in the role of a murderer for a long, long time. And then, when he actually faced the act, he bungled it. He killed like an amateur, covered up like one. Because he told the truth when he said that none of it was real to him. All the stories of violence and bloodshed were just extensions of his own fantasies. He didn't learn anything from the celebrated criminals he admired. He just bungled."

We pulled up in front of headquarters.

"Lucky for you he did, Kendall," Cohen remarked. "You weren't too smart, either, going down there that way. Seeing how it turned out, I'm not going to make an issue of it. But you disobeyed orders twice today, running out on us, and you're going to give the whole Department a black eye when the story breaks." He started to chew his mustache, then stopped. "That's on the record, Kendall," he muttered. "Off the record, I admire your guts. And I'm glad it's all over."

"Is it?" I said, and followed him inside.

Bronson and Howard were both waiting. They spent only a minute or so with Mingo. Some doctor went in with them and they came out shaking their heads.

I caught the phrase "catatonic reaction" and heard the doctor issuing orders to the attendants. They took Mingo away, then, and turned to me.

"Well, Kendall, congratulations." The District Attorney's smile was wry, but genuine. "I understand you took matters into your own hands. We won't say anything about that now, because it's all turned out for the best. But I'd appreciate as full a statement as you can give us, before we admit any reporters."

"You're going to be quite a celebrity tomorrow," said Mr. Bronson. He didn't seem too happy about it.

"All right," I said. "Here's your statement. But before I give it, you'd better send somebody down to Otis Street. Either the Court Hotel Bar or the Blue Jay. Pick up Mrs. Helen Calgary. She's the one who gave me the tip."

I described Helen Calgary to Cohen. He went out and relayed the description, sent the order on down.

Then I sat back and told my story from the beginning. They listened quietly, and every word was taken down.

There were only two interruptions. The first came when Henley stepped in for a moment. "What'll I tell those guys?" he asked. "They're getting antsy for a chance to interview Kendall, here."

"Ten more minutes and we throw him to the lions," Howard said. Henley went out.

I finished what I had to say.

"So you see," I concluded, "it isn't really over. All we can do is guess. Calgary could have killed Trixie Fisher with my knife. But I doubt if he killed the Schuyler girl, and you seem to think both murders were the work of the same man."

"Or woman," Cohen muttered.

"True. It might have been a woman."

"It might have been Mingo," suggested Bronson.

"Impossible. The man who fumbled with Calgary couldn't conceivably have executed such crimes." I was suddenly quite an authority—look who was going around telling assistant D.A.'s about murder! I shook my head. "No, this doesn't really solve anything. It's my belief that the Ripper is still at large."

Howard stood up. "Belief," he said. "Have you anything tangible to back it up with?"

"No," I said. "Nothing."

"You aren't holding back any further evidence?"

"I'm through with that. I've had it tonight."

"Then all you're offering now is your opinion. Is that correct?"

"Right."

"Under the circumstances, then, I am going to ask you to refrain from airing that opinion. Because some of us here are inclined to think otherwise. Despite what you say, it is by no means impossible that Anthony Mingo is the Ripper. We shall, of course, check back on his movements during the times when the crimes were committed. And we shall question him as soon as he is in a condition to talk. Meanwhile, our Department is still following up other leads—"

"Let me get this straight," I said. "You want me to go out there and tell those reporters I think the Ripper murders are solved?"

"You don't have to tell them that. Just tell them the truth—tell them you don't know."

"Now, wait a minute." I was on my feet.

District Attorney Howard waved his hand. "I know what you're thinking. You're thinking I want you to cover up for us. Well, that's not true. There's more to this case than that." He walked over to the window. "Kendall, take a look out there."

I joined him and gazed down at the city by night, flaunting its neon necklace.

"Three hundred thousand people," he said. "Three hundred thousand human beings. Old folks, young folks, women and kids—and tonight they're all afraid of one man. The Ripper. They all read the papers. They've all got theories. We've had over fifty phone calls and another fifty anonymous letters. They're seeing Rippers everywhere. And we're checking everything that comes in, no matter how screwy it sounds.

"Yes, Kendall, they're all afraid and they've all got theories. But because of what you did tonight, they'll listen to you. Tomorrow they'll be reading your theory. What are you going to tell them? Are you going to keep them frightened, keep those kids crying whenever they see a shadow? And if you do, what possible good can you accomplish?"

"Suppose I don't," I murmured. "What good will that do?"

"It might do a lot." Howard faced me. "It might give us just what we're looking for—a chance to catch the real killer with his guard down. Once he thinks we've accepted Calgary or Mingo as the Ripper, he may grow careless.

"You understand, I can't coerce you. This is still a free country, and there's still a free press—and I like it that way. I can't even hold out a promise that my theory will pay off. It's only a chance, but I'd like to have it. Not for my sake, but for everybody's.

"Well, Kendall, it's up to you. What do you say?"

I stood there, ready to give him my answer, when the second interruption came. Henley again.

"Yes?"

"We got Mrs. Calgary."

"Bring her in."

Henley shook his head. "Can't move her yet. Got to check for prints and take the pictures."

The room started to spin. I could see the open mouths, hear the sudden, sharp inspiration of the gasps.

Somebody, I don't know who, asked the inevitable question.

Henley nodded. "That's right," he said. "It's the Ripper, again."

FIFTEEN

REPORTERS ARE A FICKLE TRIBE. It turned out that none of them were really waiting to see me, after all. They were all anxious to get down to the Blue Jay, to the little upstairs room off the back hall where Helen Calgary had learned the secret of the Ripper.

A secret she'd never share, now.

Lieutenant Cohen left for Otis Street right away. Henley stayed around and told us what he knew. It wasn't much.

Helen Calgary, after my departure, went back to the Court Hotel. Her sailor was gone (Cohen put him in a cell until he sobered up, then turned him loose without charges), and she decided it was time for supper. She ate alone across the street at some greasy spoon. And she came back alone, to the Court Bar.

Around seven, according to the bartender—not the man I'd seen, but a night man—she struck up a conversation with a young Mexican gentleman named Jesus Ramirez. Mr. Ramirez, who was available for testimony, was anxious to improve his acquaintance, and to this end accompanied Helen Calgary up the stairs leading to the second floor of the Court Hotel. According to Pop, they were occupied in Room Four for the better part of an hour. Whereupon Mr. Ramirez returned to the Court Bar below and Mrs. Calgary, pleading slight fatigue—"I'm getting out of here, I'm sick of this crummy joint": these were her last recorded words— left by the rear exit and presumably went directly to her own room upstairs over the Blue Jay. Her entrance through the back way was unobserved. That was not unusual, for the Blue Jay was crowded and the bartender busy. He habitually paid no attention to the comings and goings in back.

"Hell, if I had a nickel for every bum who crawls up and down them stairs in a night," he phrased it.

Nor could he help to identify any suspicious-looking characters from amongst his clientele.

"They're all a bunch of crooks," he reported. "Ain't a one of 'em wouldn't slip a shiv to his own mother for a fast fifty. Or less."

The time was nine o'clock, give or take a few minutes. And the bar was crowded, and the juke box blared, and upstairs Helen Calgary sprawled across her unmade bed, reading a comic book. She was smoking a cigarette, and there was nothing to disturb her. Apparently she was used to sounds on the stairway, too. Sometimes those sounds meant profit, and she never locked her door. You meet all kinds that way: Mexicans, and Puerto Ricans, and Greeks bearing gifts.

But it wasn't a Greek bearing a gift this time. Someone came in very softly and very slowly. Something came up very softly and swiftly. And then something came down.

Again the wounds were narrow and quite deep, and again there were many of them. This time the Ripper took his time, working in the dark, perhaps, after turning off the switch. And then he went away again. Possibly there might be prints on the doorknob or door frame; possibly not. There weren't in Joan Schuyler's room; and in Trixie's apartment the only prints found were hers and mine. The Ripper went away as quietly as he had come, and by the same route.

He missed meeting Henley and the squad car by just seven minutes.

"That's it," Henley told us.

That's it, and all of a sudden it was too much for me.

Howard noticed my face. "What's the matter?" he asked.

"Look, would you excuse me," I said. "I don't feel so good. I want to go home."

He nodded. "Henley, tell one of the boys to take Mr. Kendall home in a car, will you please?" He glanced down the corridor. "All clear. No reporters—they probably won't bother you now, until morning. You'll check with us then?"

"Sure," I said. "Thanks."

We went downstairs and out a side door and one of the squad cars drove me home. I didn't talk. I didn't feel like talking any more. We passed the park, and I wondered if Blind Bill was peddling his pencils. We passed Swanee's and I wondered if Art Hughes was trying to locate a Gershwin selection on the juke box. We swung around and—just to complete it—drove by Kit's place. I wondered if—but no, I'd had it. I was through.

Then I was home, and I said goodnight, and the shape rose up out of the shadows.

"Come on up," I said. "Talk all you like. But don't expect any answers."

She helped me up the stairs. She opened the door for me. She took off my coat and my shoes. She even brought me the Overholt.

"Maybe this marriage business won't be so bad after all," I said. The drink was beginning to help a little.

Kit draped herself over the arm of my chair and investigated the rim of her glass with her tongue.

"You didn't see a doctor after all," she said. "Where were you?"

I closed my eyes. "Not now," I said. "Tomorrow."

"But it's important. I have to know."

I stood up. "Give me fifteen minutes first," I said. "Here, mix yourself another drink."

She did. I went into the bathroom and took three showers. A cold one, then a hot one, then a cold one again. I slapped myself with the towel. I swallowed two aspirins. Then I put on my robe and came out and had a drink.

And I told Kit about Anthony Mingo and Helen Calgary.

No need to go into her reactions. They were vivid and appropriate. I ended up by kissing her and stroking her hair. But I didn't think of it as an ending—right now it was more of a prelude. I let my hands slip.

She pulled away.

"What's the matter? Still afraid of me?"

"No. No, Tom, it isn't that." She frowned. "I just can't make up my mind. You've gone through so much today, maybe I'd better not tell you. It can wait until morning. Yes. It can wait."

She reached out and put my hands back where they'd been resting, although not exactly resting.

They rested now.

"What did you have to tell me, Kit?"

"Never mind, darling. It doesn't matter. Not now, it doesn't. Just relax."

This time I pulled away. "All right, Kit," I said.

She looked at me without any expression at all, and she said, "I saw your friend Art Hughes again tonight. He came around to my place right after supper."

"Did he tell you to go away again?"

"No." The voice was expressionless, too. "He told me he had killed Marie."

I managed to stand up. "Kit, you're sure of this?"

"He didn't say he murdered her with the scissors, no. But he said he'd lied about you, lied to you. That he was responsible for her death. And that he was going to kill himself."

"Kit—you listened to him, and you let him get away?"

"I was afraid. Because he acted so—crazy. And all the while he was talking, I had the funniest hunch."

"What was that?"

"Did you ever stop to think that maybe he was the Ripper?"

I was already halfway across the room.

"Where are your going?"

"To put my clothes on. How long ago did he leave your place?"

"Eight o'clock, a little after."

I glanced at my watch. It was about ten-thirty. So much had happened, in so little time. So much could happen—

I dressed quickly. Kit picked up her purse.

"Are you sure you feel all right, darling?"

I nodded. But I wasn't sure. I wasn't sure of anything, and I had to find out.

We went downstairs. It was a fine summer night with lots of stars and a generous helping of moon. A fine night for a stroll in the park. But we didn't stroll—we almost ran.

Blind Bill wasn't working the park tonight, and neither was anyone else. Despite the moon and the stars and the breeze and the inviting shadows over benches and under trees, the young people weren't around. No one was around. Everybody kept away from parks these nights—parks, and alleys and back streets—because of what might be lurking there.

Right now, something was lurking in the back of my mind. Call it the subconscious, the preconscious, and subliminal; the terms didn't matter. What mattered was the realization that I'd *almost* figured things out. Almost, until Kit had told me about Art Hughes.

"Do you know where you're going, Tom?"

I halted on the corner. Of course not. I didn't know where he lived. He'd told me he had a room around the corner from Swanee's.

"Over here," I said. And I guided her down the street, over, and into the juke-box jangle.

It was hard to walk in. It was hard to face the slow ripple of recognition running along the bar, accompanied by whispers and sidelong stares. The music was as loud as ever, and nobody really stopped talking when we entered. But I could sense the suppressed excitement.

I leaned over the bar and the oldest bartender came right over.

"Mr. Kendall," he said. "I'm glad to see you back! I read about it in the papers and all, but I never believed it, not even at first. Like I was telling Bernie here, you could never do a thing like that. Wasn't it awful, Mr. Kendall? I mean, the way that—"

"Let's talk about it some other time," I suggested. "Right now I'm in a hurry. Do you know where Art Hughes lives? The tall, skinny guy who was in here with me the other night?"

"Hughes?" He squinted. "Oh, sure I do. You go down to the corner, to Prentiss, and turn. It's either the second or the third house, Mrs.

Arzberger's place. Reason I know, he was telling me about how she made him turn down his phonograph—"

"Thanks."

I turned and walked out with Kit, and the eyes all followed us—the eyes of those who huddled here in the safety of noise and light, huddled with one another for protection because they didn't want to be out on the streets tonight.

"Tom, do you think he's done something? Do you think we ought to call the police first?"

I shook my head. "We'll see. I've had enough of the police for one day."

"But if anything's really wrong—"

"Then we'll get them fast. Don't worry."

We rounded the corner, and I wished I could take the advice I'd handed out. I was worrying, wondering, wavering.

Then we came to Mrs. Arzberger's place, and I knew Art Hughes was home. It wasn't the light behind the drawn blinds of the second-story window. It was the sound I recognized: the long, melancholy wail from the second movement of the *Concerto in F.*

"The saddest music in the world," Art had told me, once. "It reminds me of funerals."

Going up the stairs, running up the stairs, I remembered that. Would he have chosen that music purposely? Would he have put it on the phonograph just before he—

Kit knocked.

The music went on and on. Then the trickly, tricky piano part came in, and Art Hughes opened the door. His eyes were red marbles in a death mask.

He didn't say anything. Not "You!" or "Hello!" or "Come in!" His mouth moved slowly, but no words came.

I brushed past him and went into the room. It was small, and the phonograph stood right next to the couch. And next to the phonograph was a table. And on the table was a fifth of gin, half empty. And next to the fifth of gin was this little bottle with the bright capsules. I recognized them from the hospital. Nembutal.

He'd taken the cap off, but the pills were undisturbed as yet.

I disturbed them. I walked over, scooped up the bottle, dumped it into my pocket. The pills tumbled out but I didn't care.

Art Hughes just watched me. Then he closed the door, stumbled over to the couch, and sank down.

"She told you," he murmured.

The last portion of the second movement came on, the part I've always thought would make a terrific popular song if Ira would write the words.

"You wanted her to tell me," I said. "And you wanted me to come over, didn't you?"

He nodded. "I guess so."

I sat down next to him. "You've been wanting to tell me something for a long time, haven't you, Art? You almost told me the other night in the tavern, but you were afraid. Why?"

"I don't know. I don't know."

"Then you came around again, asking me to see a doctor, to go away. Because if I went away, you'd never have to tell me. You can't make up your mind, can you? One minute you want to talk, the next minute you don't. So you even thought of going away yourself—forever."

"I wasn't really going to take those pills, Tom. Not really."

"I know. Because you haven't got the guts to do even that. What kind of a man are you, anyway, Art?"

He didn't answer. As the music reached crescendo, he stared first at Kit, then at me. But he didn't answer until the slow wail started again.

"I'm a murderer."

Kit gripped my arm. "Shall we call now?" she whispered. I shook my head.

"Listen to me, Art. The other day you came in and hinted that I was responsible for Marie's death. That wasn't true, and you know it. You knew it then. Of course she was upset about me, about my blackouts. But she loved me, she'd stick by me, she wouldn't kill herself because of that."

"I was lying," Art said. "I just wanted you to go away, so I wouldn't have to see you, wouldn't have to think any more—"

The *finale* came in, fast. Gershwin's fierce, frenetic orchestration.

"Then you came to Kit and told her you'd killed Marie. And that's a lie, too, isn't it?"

Horns sounded, drums pounded.

"No, it's true." He looked at me now as if he really saw me for the first time tonight. "Everything I said about Marie, her brooding about you until she couldn't stand it and killed herself, is true. Only it wasn't you she was brooding about, it was me. Because of what I did while you were away, wandering around. She knew she was going to have a baby and—"

"You were the father."

He couldn't say it, I couldn't say it. Kit said it. She said it quietly, over the music.

Art Hughes tried to stand up and fell back. I clenched my fists.

And then he was sobbing, sobbing and staring up at me and shuddering out, "Go ahead, Tom! Go ahead and kill me. I deserve it, I killed her and I drove you crazy, so go ahead. Take your knife out and rip me like you ripped the others, rip me, rip me—"

I bent over him. The lull in the music came, the final lull before the climactic storm of sound.

Speaking softly, trying to reach him inside the private hell of his, I said, "I'm not a ripper, Art. I've never killed anyone and I don't want to. I'm not crazy, either, haven't had a blackout since this thing began. So you needn't be afraid any more."

He wouldn't, couldn't look at me.

"About Marie," I said. "I think I can understand. And when you understand, you don't blame. I don't blame you, or her, or myself, although all three of us were a part of it."

Kit was crying now, and there was no anger mingled in her tears.

"I don't blame you, Art, and you've got to stop blaming yourself. Maybe you should take the advice you handed out to me. Go and see a doctor, Art."

The *Concerto* ended, and Kit and I went away. We walked down the hall, out of the place, and silence followed us. There was silence all down the block until we reached the corner.

Then we heard the music. He'd gotten up and picked out a record at random, of course. More Gershwin. But why did it have to be a number called *Soon*?

SIXTEEN

KIT DIDN'T SAY ANYTHING until we were a block away, almost abreast of Swanee's again. Then, "You don't think he's the Ripper?"

"Sure of it. He's just a poor, mixed-up guy like all the rest of us." I thought of Mingo and his fantasies of punishment and pain, of the sailor whose name was Sweeney and who had to get drunk and start a fight because that's what you're supposed to do when you're Irish. "People always have their reasons for what they do, Kit. When the reasons are wrong, the actions are wrong. But you can find the reasons and even if they don't seem important or make sense to you, they do to the other fellow. Art had his reasons. Even the Ripper has reasons."

Even the Ripper.

And here we were again, right back at the beginning. They hadn't found the Ripper yet, and there were still three hundred thousand people to choose from.

"Don't talk about it any more." Kit gripped my arm very tightly. "Let's just go back to your place, shall we?"

It was beginning to seem like an excellent idea.

"I've got to tell you something," Kit said. "Remember the other night in the car? When I pulled away? Mingo had warned me then, and so had Art Hughes. And I almost believed, then, that it could be possible. Even tonight, I still had that little bit of feeling left, that doubt. But when Art told you about—about Marie—and you talked to him, then I knew. I knew I'd never be afraid of

you any more." She pulled my head down. "Let's go to your place, Tom. Now."

Why not? I asked myself. It was still a beautiful night, she was still a beautiful girl.

And there were still three hundred thousand people to choose from.

All right, so what? Let the police find the Ripper. That's what they get paid for. Lieutenant Cohen and Henley and Flint. Let them go into the alleys and the flophouses and the bars—

We passed Dick's place.

"Let's stop in for a drink, first," I said.

"But you've got a bottle at home."

"Just a fast one. I've never been in here."

It was true. I'd never been in Dick's. But Dick's was the place where Joe Calgary finished hanging one on the night Trixie died. Dick's was the place where he'd sold his knife, and perhaps he sold Mingo's stamp album here, too.

We went into Dick's.

I'd been in several taverns during the last three days, and never for pleasure. One look around and I knew I wouldn't find pleasure in Dick's, either.

The juke box was just as loud, the customers were just as noisy, the air just as thick and stale. I sometimes wonder what the vintners buy that's half as disappointing as what they sell. You go into a tavern for pleasure and you get pandemonium.

We found places at the bar and I ordered two Overholts. Then I did what I'd intended to do when I came in there.

The bartender who wore glasses didn't know, but the other one—the young one—came right over.

"Sure, I remember," he said. "Calgary sold the knife to Bruno. Bruno gave him three bucks for it."

"Where's Bruno?" I asked.

The young bartender looked around before he leaned forward and answered.

"The cops came in the next day and asked about Calgary," he said. "Bruno still had the knife, and he got scared, I guess, because he admitted it and handed it over. They asked him a lot of questions: why he bought it, and all that. Bruno said it was because he was scared Calgary might start something. Bruno scared—that's a laugh! Why he could have taken Calgary with one hand tied behind his back. You've never seen Bruno, have you? He's built like a brick—"

I interrupted hastily. "I've never seen Bruno, no. But I'd like to. Where is he?"

The young bartender raised his eyebrows and lowered his voice. "That's what we'd all like to know," he murmured. "After the cops were here, Bruno got off duty and went out. And he never came back."

"When was that? Before the second murder?"

"Four hours. I was thinking the same thing, myself." He stared at me. "You're Tom Kendall, aren't you? I thought I recognized you from your pictures in the paper. That's why I'm telling you. I wasn't going to tell the cops."

"Why not?"

"Well," and his eyes fell, "I mean I was going to, maybe tomorrow. Except that I didn't want it to get out in the papers the way it would if I told them. Because then Bruno might come looking for me."

"This Bruno—what do you know about him?"

"Well, he's a big guy, bigger than Calgary was. Awful bad temper. I don't even know why he bought the knife except that he seemed to like Calgary. They were two of a kind, you might say. Even had the same women. Bruno used to visit Trixie Fisher."

"You're sure of that?"

The young bartender shrugged. "I got no reason to lie to you, Mr. Kendall. I want to help, if you'll keep my name out of it. But that night, when we closed up at one, Bruno said something about maybe dropping around to see the little redhead. That would be Trixie."

"Did he carry a knife of his own, do you know?"

The bartender gave me a long, slow smile. "That's why I was so surprised he bought one from Calgary," he said. "Bruno went around with a stiletto about a foot long."

Kit had been poking me for over a minute. I turned around.

"Please," she said. "Tell Lieutenant Cohen or Mr. Howard. Let them handle it. You've done enough."

I looked at the bartender. "Do you know where Bruno lives?" I asked.

He shook his head. "Can't help you there. The boss would know, but he's gone until tomorrow. Comes in around noon. I know he tried calling Bruno's place, but nobody answered."

"Well, they should be able to locate him," I said. "And thanks a lot. You've been a great help."

"It's okay, Mr. Kendall. I don't like this business any more than you do. Take me, I got a wife, a kid on the way. Things aren't safe with a guy like that prowling around. I always did think Bruno was a little nuts, even before this."

I nodded. "I'll see that your information goes to the proper sources, right away."

He hesitated, leaned forward again. "Please. You won't say who told you? I'm not yellow, but if you knew this ape—"

"Sure. I'll handle it." I reached into my pocket for my wallet, then remembered I was broke. "Kit," I said. "You got any money?"

The bartender put his hand on mine. "No, Mr. Kendall. This is—this is on the house."

We walked out of there.

Going back to my place, Kit was silent.

"What's wrong, honey?" I asked.

"You know what's wrong. You promised to quit, and now you're starting out all over again. You've been too lucky, Tom—it can't last! Please, don't get mixed up in it any more."

I didn't answer her. When we got upstairs I went right to the phone and called Homicide. Cohen wasn't there, but I talked to Henley. I told him everything I'd heard. He assured me they'd get on it right away. I assured him I'd be down in the morning. We exchanged mutual good-nights. Parting is such a sweet sorrow.

Then I put down the phone. "That what you wanted me to do, Kit?"

She nodded, smiled.

"Partly."

I stood up and took her in my arms. "I've got a feeling we're going to be out of the woods soon," I said. "Just my dumb hunch, my dumb luck—stumbling onto something like this. A character like this Bruno, now, seems to be just what they're looking for. If they can find him, and find the reason—"

"Shut up about Bruno," Kit told me. "Here, help me unhook this thing."

I helped her.

I helped her, and she helped me. She helped me to forget Bruno, forget the shadows, forget the knives and the wounds they made, the wounds you can never cut out. She took me down into the dark, but it was the pleasant darkness, the good darkness where you're never alone but always together.

Then, at last, we weren't together any more. She was sleeping, and I was lying there.

And the other darkness came back. This was the darkness where the Ripper lurked, and I saw him. He didn't see me, but I saw him. For the first time everything fell into place, and what was in the subconscious came up to the conscious level, and I had my answer.

I could wait until morning, wait until daylight, but the answer wouldn't let me. It had been locked away, buried away, too long.

I got out of bed very quietly. I knew what I was going to do. I was going to do the sensible thing. I meant to pick up the phone and call Lieutenant Cohen. That's what I'd promised him, that's what I'd promised Kit, that's what I'd promised myself.

As I stood up I remembered thinking of another promise I'd made. A promise not to run any more, a promise to go through with anything I started.

Then the blackout came, and I don't remember anything for a while.

Sometimes the blackouts lasted for a day, sometimes for hours, sometimes less. This one must have been very short.

When I came to again, I was running once more. Fully dressed, and running through the park. I carried something in my hand—something I must have picked up out of the kitchen drawer as I'd finished dressing in the dark. I'd let myself out quietly, and picked this up because I knew I might need it where I was going.

It was a flashlight. I stared at it, but my feet kept on moving forward. I was out of the park now and there wasn't far to go. He'd told me himself where he lived.

I came to the place and found the side stairway. The lights were out, but I had the flashlight. The same thing in my subconscious that supplied the answer now told me what to do.

I went up the stairs very quietly. There was only one door, and I wouldn't be disturbing anyone else if I knocked.

I rapped once, twice, three times. I pounded on the door loud enough to wake the dead.

No one answered. The dead won't wake.

The blackout had been short this time. I came to, knowing who I was, where I was going, and why. There was no answer to my knock, but I couldn't stop now.

I put my hand on the doorknob and prepared to brace my shoulder against the panel. The doorknob turned. The door swung open. It hadn't been locked.

Then I stepped inside. I could have groped for the light switch, but it was easier to flick on the flashlight. The beam flooded forward, focused on the left hand corner of the small room.

I'd expected to peer and pry, to ransack and search, before I found what I was looking for. But there was no need. It hadn't been hidden. The flashlight found it for me now.

It was lying right there on the table, next to the bed. It was long and thin and shining. I recognized it right away. My poniard.

I moved toward it and the door swung shut behind me, blocking out the light from the hall. It clicked and seemed to lock. I turned to grab it, and something hit my hand.

The door closed as my flashlight fell and went out.

I stood there in the dark.

"You forget I don't need any light," said Blind Bill.

SEVENTEEN

EVERYONE'S WALK HAS A RHYTHM, and he must have been sitting there in the dark waiting ever since he heard me come and pause before the grocery store downstairs. He must have planned while he waited, planned swiftly. I knew, now, that he could plan swiftly.

"Don't move," he said softly. "I can hear you when you move. And I'm armed."

I wondered if he'd been able to come around and grab the poniard. Then I heard a scraping sound, followed by a clatter as something fell to the floor. He had another weapon. And in just a moment he'd come tap-tap-tapping toward me.

No, he wouldn't bother to tap. The realization came with chilling quickness. Here in the dark he needn't grope to find his way. He knew every inch of the room and his ears were trained to sense and search out a presence. We were both in the darkness, and now *I* was the blind man. I was blind and he was armed.

I edged back quietly, very quietly, trying to reach the door. The frame was tight, and no light shone through. But if I could only get my hand on the knob—

"I told you to stand still," Bill said. "That's better."

I gulped, searching for my voice. There wasn't much left of it when I found it, but I did the best I could.

"Don't go getting any ideas," I said. "I phoned the police before I came. They'll be here any minute now.

"Will they?" said Blind Bill. "All right, let's wait for them."

Did he believe me? His voice didn't betray anything. There was neither mockery nor fear in him.

But there was fear in me.

"While we're waiting," said Bill, "you might as well keep talking. Because I want to hear you. Then I'll know where you are."

"Sure, anything you say." Was his voice coming closer? Would he sneak up in the dark as I talked, and . . .

"Tell me something," Blind Bill said. "Tell me what gave you the idea of coming here."

Up until that time I'd thought it was all my subconscious. Now, as I spoke, I realized I'd known some things for a long time. "You made some slip-ups," I told him.

"I was in a hurry," Bill said. "What, for instance?"

"Please," I said. "The cops are coming. Turn on the light or they'll get ideas."

"That's their worry," Bill murmured. "Let them turn on the lights. Lights mean nothing to me. Where I am, it's always dark." Yes, his voice was closer. I moved back, back against the wall. I couldn't go further.

"What slip-ups?" Bill asked. "Talk fast."

"First of all, when you stole the poniard. You broke the glass on the store door, and it was a clumsy job. It was the kind of job that would either be done by a man in a hurry or a man who couldn't see."

"That proves nothing," Bill answered. "Keep talking."

"Then, in the line-up, when you told the District Attorney about my footsteps, you passed a remark about Trixie. You didn't like her. You had more to say about her, and about Joan Schuyler too, when you came to my store afterwards. I remember when Trixie and I passed you in the park that night, she said you gave her the creeps. And I wondered why. Wondered why she disliked you, why you disliked her. And I wondered about other things."

"What things?"

"Why you told me, at the store, that you'd heard Joe Calgary the night before. That was a lie, Bill. I found it out tonight. Calgary went straight to Mingo, and he must have been dead long before that second killing."

"Go on."

"Just one thing more, Bill. You told one more lie at the store. You said you had cataracts. I was in a veteran's hospital. A guy I met in there had cataracts—with that milky film over his eyes. Cataracts didn't blind you, Bill."

"You haven't said anything yet that makes sense." He was close enough now so that I could hear breathing—but where did it come from, the right or the left? "Get on with it, fast. There won't be much time." I heard another sound, a swishing sound. I edged to one side.

His voice followed me. "How do you figure it? Tell me, I want to know."

I told him. I told him, hoping he'd get excited, hoping he'd make a move so I could find him in the dark before he came for me. If I could only get my hands around his throat—

But waiting for the chance, I had to keep talking.

"I figure it this way, Bill. You killed Trixie because you were jealous of her. You tried to make her and she turned you down."

He made a sound in his throat. I went on.

"Lots of guys get turned down by girls, it wasn't quite that simple in your case. You couldn't shrug it off. You brooded about it, didn't you? You turned it over in your mind for a long time, standing on the corner night after night while you heard her go by with other men. Men like Joe Calgary.

"Maybe you had a different plan. Maybe it was only a dream, a fantasy of revenge you worked out over and over again in your head. But then, the other night, things happened. First of all, you must have met Joe Calgary when he came out of Dick's, drunk. He talked to you, told you about Trixie, made the same kind of threats he'd made to her and to me at Swanee's. And he sold you that stamp album he'd stolen—for twenty dollars.

"You bought it with a plan already in mind. Knowing Joe had threatened Trixie with a knife, you figured on killing her and planting the album on her body. Wasn't that it, Bill?"

"You're talking," Bill said. "This is all your show. So far."

"Then I came out of Swanee's with Trixie, and you recognized my walk, and that looked like a still better setup. You'd heard I had knives in my store and from somebody in the neighborhood—maybe Art Hughes— you'd picked up that story about my blackouts. I'd be an even better suspect than Joe.

"Maybe you weren't sure about going through with it, but it was worth a try. You stole the poniard and came over to Trixie's. The window was open. You waited until there were no sounds. And then you came inside."

He made that sound in his throat again. I didn't like it, tried to drown it out with my voice.

"But when you finished—what you did—you found you weren't the only one. Joe Calgary was prowling around there. My guess is he started to climb in just as you came out. He didn't see you, or he'd have hollered copper and given your name—but he must have seen a man with a weapon. So he ran, but not before you'd recognized his footsteps."

It was hot in that little room, very hot. And I felt the sweat ooze along my spine as I tried to remember how far it was to that table with the poniard on it. I turned my head, moving an inch at a time, and I kept on talking as I moved.

"Well, you left and I came to and called the cops. They picked you up, along with the other neighborhood characters, and you tried to cinch the deal by identifying me. It worked, too.

"Except that while you were in the D.A.'s office, you overhead them say they were going to question Joan Schuyler. And Joan Schuyler had been Trixie's roommate. Maybe you made a pass at her, too. More likely, it was just that you figured Trixie must have told Joan about your advances, and maybe about how you threatened her. Joan could put the finger on you, fast.

"So you waited until dark, followed her home, sneaked in, and killed her. That would take the heat off me, but you had still an out. You still had Calgary's stamp album, the one you'd planned first to use as a plant when you killed Trixie. That would work, you figured, because Calgary also was intimate with this girl. It was a clumsy device, too obvious, but it might work. And you had to move fast."

I had to move fast now, but I couldn't. My foot hit a floorboard and a creak started. I stood stockstill and once again I heard a swishing sound, quite close.

"Then you came around to me, like a good friend, and said you'd made a mistake—it was Calgary all the time. And from that point on you figured you were in the clear. The police would be looking for Calgary, and Calgary had obviously run away. It almost worked, Bill. It almost worked.

"But there was still a chance of somebody else knowing. Helen Calgary, Joe's wife. You got to thinking, didn't you? Maybe he'd run to her before he left town. Maybe he'd told her about seeing you at Trixie's—if not that, he might at least have told her that you were the one who bought the stamp album. You couldn't take the risk, could you, Bill? You were in so far already that one more wouldn't matter. And maybe, by this time, it was getting easier for you."

This time there was the sound in the throat and the swish. But I was getting nearer to the table. I had to be. Just a few more feet, a few more words—

"Certainly there was no trouble in killing Helen Calgary. You were even able to take your time, do what you'd wanted to do to Trixie and Joan. Because you didn't just murder those girls, Bill. You butchered them. You ripped them."

I felt the edge of the table against my legs. And I heard Bill's voice come close now, from behind me. He was already standing by the table. Maybe he had the poniard in *his* hand. That swish—

"Yes," he said. "I ripped them." He made a sound that was something like a laugh. I'd never heard such a sound before and never wanted to again. "Looks like your police aren't coming, after all," he said. "I don't even think you called them. So let's get it over with."

I didn't ask him what he meant. I knew.

"So you admit it," I said. "And I've got the story straight."

"Yes. You've got it down almost perfect."

"All but the most important part, Bill. The one thing I don't know. The thing that made you rip as well as kill. The reason. What was the reason, Bill?"

I heard his feet move toward me, and then they stopped. "You were right," Bill said. "It wasn't cataracts that blinded me. It was acid. Nitric acid. She burned my eyes out with the stuff, threw it in my face and burned me and took away my eyes. The dirty little bitch—"

"When was this, Bill? When did it happen?"

"In the carny, the sideshow. Years ago. I was swallowing swords. She worked in the act. Her name was Thelma. We was like man and wife for three years. And then I caught her with this razorback, this dumb bum of a boss canvasman, and I beat hell out of him. I come back to our trailer, and I guess I was kind of out of my head, because I picked up a sword and went after her. I wasn't going to kill her, honest I wasn't. But she saw me coming and she threw the acid."

His voice held a curious whine. He wasn't talking to me now, or even to himself. He was talking to the darkness. I stood there and listened to the real voice of the Ripper.

"It burned and burned. Sometimes I can still feel it burning now. That's all I got left, that and the dark. The dark never goes away, but they took everything else. They locked Thelma up. They took away my job. They took away my eyes and left me alone in the dark. And when I ask for what a man needs, when I even *beg* for it from a little floozie like Trixie or Joan, they laugh at me and tell me to go away, I give them the creeps.

"I give them the creeps, all right! I guess they know now, Thelma and all the rest of them bitches, what it feels like when the point goes in and it rips and rips—"

I moved my hand very swiftly, covering the table-top, groping for the poniard—the poniard that wasn't there. He heard me and chuckled.

"Looking for your knife, huh? I got it. But I won't use it. I never did use it, just stole it to cover up. I got my own tool. Haven't you guessed yet? It's a sword cane."

I remembered now. Bill's long black cane. I remembered the clattering sound as he'd dropped the sheath on the floor and the swishing noise. I heard the swish again, coming close.

"Don't run," he said. "I'll find you."

And he found me. The thin blade ripped out, ripped down along my shoulder. I heard the tear of cloth, felt the sharp bite in my arm.

"Cut it out!" I screamed. And my hand went into my pocket, looking for a knife that wasn't there. *When had I looked for that knife before?*

Something was happening inside me, something was coming up into my memory. But there was no time for that now. There was only time to sense the feel of the object that was in my pocket. I grabbed it, whipped it out, flicked.

My cigarette lighter flared up, flashed. I could see everything now: myself crouching in that little room, my left arm bleeding; Blind Bill standing right before me with the long thin blade poised, then plunging toward my throat.

I raised the lighter and thrust the flame against his face, into his empty eyes.

He screamed, and the sword cane slipped to the floor as he brought both hands up to claw at his seared sockets. I dropped the lighter as he staggered away, picked up the sword. He dropped to the bed, moaning.

I switched on the light, found the phone, and made my call. By the time Lieutenant Cohen arrived, the moaning had stopped.

Eighteen

EVERYTHING AFTER THAT is a blur—a long blur of riding downtown, getting my arm bandaged, making a statement, hearing Bill's confession. Somewhere in the blur was Lieutenant Cohen telling me what a good guy I was and also that I'd been a damned fool. Kit came in and made appropriate noises, and District Attorney Howard kept telling the reporters, "Not now, please. Can't you see he's almost out on his feet."

They kept me in the hospital overnight and the next day, but I didn't care about that. I slept around the clock and when I woke up I felt fine.

I felt fine because I could remember. I could think about it now, what had come to me there in the dark when the light flared up and I yelled "Cut it out!"—when I reached for a knife that wasn't there.

It was the reason for my blackouts; I knew that now. It had been blotted out by the concussion and fracture, by shock and by fear. And since that time whenever the memory came too close to consciousness, I'd black out again, just to keep the fear away. It was the traumatic incident, as Doc Greene would call it. And I could remember it clearly now. The traumatic incident back there in Korea.

Onwatong, in April, 1951. Or the place where Onwatong used to be. Now it was only a rubble of bombed-out streets, with a few steel girders rising above the smoke and the ashes in the ruins. I remembered it all.

There was no place left to hide, and the planes were coming over. No place left to hide, and Jimmy and Sam and I were together when we heard the drone. We dropped down alongside this wall and started to dig, as the drone became a roar.

We dug, and the stones vibrated, and out of the roar came a whine and then it hit.

The wall went up. Part of it came down. Part of it got me in the back of the skull, and that was the concussion. Only I wasn't out, entirely. I could still see, and I could still hear.

I could see Jimmy lying there. Part of the wall had hit him, too. The split stone had been driven halfway into his chest, and he wasn't making any sound. What I could hear was coming from Sam.

At first he only moaned, and then he began this screaming. "Cut it out," he yelled. "Cut—it—out." I looked at him. He wasn't asking anyone to stop. He meant that I should actually cut it out.

The top of the wall had fallen across his ankles, pinning him down so that he couldn't use his legs. And they'd been mashed flat. But he still couldn't pull loose. The pain was awful. He wanted to get free, and if I could only get him loose—

I reached for my pocket, for my clasp knife. It wasn't there.

That's all. As simple as that. I reached for my knife and couldn't find it. So I lay there for two hours, until the medics finally came, and listened to him scream. Me with my concussion, he with the agony in his voice as he begged me, begged someone, begged anyone, to cut it out.

I wanted a knife then, more than anything else in the world. I would have given everything to use a knife: to cut it out. But I couldn't. And when the medics came, I fainted, and they took me back to the hospital with the concussion.

That's how it started, and that's what it meant. Doc Greene would know the rest: about the suppressed guilt-feelings, the fear and the fascination connected with knives, the love and dread of the dark. Everything went back to that night in Korea: the physical shock of concussion, the psychic shock that brought the blackouts when I tried to remember what I'd done that was wrong, why I had failed, why I was guilty, and why I had to fear knives.

Now, it wasn't important any more. Finding out the reason, I realized it wasn't as bad as I'd thought. The real reason never is. It's what you do with it.

There's always a reason, I'd said, and it was true. Blind Bill had his reason, Art Hughes had his. Probably poor Anthony Mingo had a reason, too. Doctors are still trying to find it out in the sanitarium.

Art Hughes went away and I never see him any more. Blind Bill went away, too, and nobody will ever see him.

So that leaves me. Me and Kit.

I'm not complaining about that arrangement at all. The store's out of the red, and I'm out of the black. Literally. Since we've been married, I haven't had a hint of a blackout.

I had a few qualms left over, at first. I remember the day before we got married. I was back at the store, getting things in shape ready to close up so that Kit and I could leave for a week on the Gulf Coast.

She was checking off the approvals, and I climbed up on a chair and opened the knife cabinet.

"What's the big idea?"

Lieutenant Cohen came in, and I looked down to see if he was still chewing on the same old mustache. He was.

"Getting rid of these knives," I told him. "Don't want them around any more."

His face fell a bit. "Oh. Didn't know stuff like that bothered you. If I had, maybe I wouldn't have brought this."

He produced the package, then.

Kit looked at it. He handed it to her with a nod. "Brought you a wedding present," he said. "But if you don't like it—"

"Of course we like it," Kit said. "Don't we, darling?"

"Sure."

I stood there, watching her unwrap the package. And Lieutenant Cohen got redder and redder.

"Why—it's wonderful," Kit squealed. "Something we can really use, can't we, Tom?"

I looked over her shoulder.

For a moment I shuddered, then I grinned.

"Thanks, Lieutenant," I said. "Kit says, that's one gift we can really use. Something practical. Though they do say there's a trick to using it right."

"That there is," Lieutenant Cohen agreed. He chewed on his mustache thoughtfully as all three of us stood there and looked at the carving set.

FIREBUG

ZERO

MY NAME IS PHILIP DEMPSTER; I'm sleeping.

The dream is red. It's always red. Sometimes it's golden-red, like the first flash of a sulphur match. Sometimes it's blue and orange at the edges, like a glow dying away to embers, but it's still red. Red isn't always simply colors—sometimes it's a thing of emotions and the *feeling* of red. It gets to be a *knowing* what's red and what isn't. My dreams are red, always red.

My name is Philip Dempster; I'm dreaming.

In the dream I'm driving my car down a long dark road. Far ahead I see a light. It's the only light in the world, because my car has no headlamps; it's a blind car, and I'm grateful I have eyes, because if I didn't have eyes, then *I'd* be blind in this world, too. And I have to keep looking down the road toward that light...

I'm driving and my back hurts. It hurts from leaning over the wheel for so long, staring so hard at that faint trace of light far down the dark road. My eyes burn, as well, but differently. They feel as though they're turning to water, as though I haven't shut them for a long time, as though I've been intentionally keeping them open so they'll burn.

But I know this isn't so. I don't want any part of me to burn.

This must be an illusion.

The dream is real, though. So I keep driving.

The light is getting larger. It's growing much larger, much faster. I apply the brakes and the car begins to slow, but I've deceived myself. I'm no nearer the light. That's strange, for a moment there I thought the light was a flame, and I was about to say: *I'm no nearer the flame.* But it's just a light, I can assure you of that. It's not a flame. It's merely a light ... you believe me, don't you?

I step on the gas, and the car shoots forward and it isn't as far to the light as I'd supposed. It's just a little way up ahead; in fact, I can see the light is a building, really. It's a bright, glowing building, like a big glowing plastic square sitting in the middle of nowhere. I can't understand why it's out here, but since the long dark road leads back to nowhere, and up ahead, past the building of light, it's nowhere, I know I'll have to stop and ask the way.

My name is Philip Dempster; I'm lost, I think.

I pull off the road and get out of the car. I lock the door behind me. Just one door. The door on the other side is open, unlocked, and it worries me, but I start walking away from the car anyhow. I wish I had locked the other door. It's open, that door. And I know someone could—*what?* What would anyone do? There isn't anyone on the road tonight, so why should I worry? I'm still walking away from the car, and I'm bothered, but I can't turn back now. I have to walk to the building and find out where I am.

That's very important, I think.

The building is on a slight hill, a bit of an incline. I'm walking toward it, and unlike the nearness and farness of the building when I was driving, as I walk it comes much closer, much faster. It almost seems to swallow me. That's a very silly, but a very frightening thought, all at once. I stop walking, because I don't want that building to swallow me.

I stop. But my feet don't stop. They keep walking me up to the building and the building opens its mouth and I see rows and rows of lights that are very toothlike, very sharp and they're waiting waiting, just waiting to swallow me and I tell my feet to *stop Jesus for God's sake stop walking me up to that mouth will you?* But they keep right on walking me up that hill, and now I'm on a bright shining walk, going right into the mouth of the building and I can't tell if I'm large or small or what's really happening except I scream, and it doesn't take. The scream comes out as nothing ... not even a sound. I'm walking fully aware into the mouth of the bright glowing building and now I'm ...

Inside. Far inside the building, and the walls are moist and warm, like a living thing. Could this building *be* alive; could it be a pulsing, breathing thing that needs live flesh to keep it breathing? I hope not.

I'm walking very fast now, and around the bend in the white, moist pulsing breathing-walls, I can hear someone babbling. It may be talking, but it's a wet, slippery sound, like the bubbling of blood in someone's mouth. I try to hear what's being said, but the words make no sense. It's as if they were being said under water, a great depth, too far away to make any sense.

Then I round the bend and I see the cell. It's a very large cell, and the bars are glowing, translucent, as though lit from within. The bars run up to the white, glowing ceiling, and down into the white, glowing floor. And in the cell is—something—I can't make it out at first—I'm looking— I'm trying to see what it is.

Suddenly I see it clearly. It moves out from behind the bars and I see it. It's a woman. But not really a woman. My throat dries up on me and I try to force my fist into my mouth because I know I'll babble like her if I don't.

The woman is dead.

She's dead. Her limbs are charred, like blackened branches of a dead tree. But they move. She moves. *It* moves.

It's moving toward the bars now. It shuffles slowly. It's falling to pieces like burned paper, even as I watch it come toward me. My eyes feel as though they'll start from my skull and I try to back up, but I'm rooted to the spot, with the basket in my hands.

The basket? I have a basket don't I? It's filled with something.

The basket is a big basket, and the smell from it is like a hundred incinerators, a thousand furnaces where humans have been sent to die, a million grease pits with decaying flesh as their contents. I have the basket in my hands, and as the creature that was a woman bubbles and shambles imbecilically toward me, I pull something from the basket and hurl it at her.

She drops to her knees and begins tearing it with her teeth. She looks up and I see the eyes are black, moist pits of emptiness, the lips are pulled back in a stricture of pain and pleasure, and what hangs from between her teeth, is like spaghetti. But it's not spaghetti. It's a shred of flesh.

Now she beckons me to come closer. I can't help myself. I feel myself being drawn toward her, toward the face that is barely a face any longer, with a vacant pulsing hole where the nose might have been, with the lips cracked and empty of meaning. The spaces so dark and hungry where the sight of her eyes had lain. She's beckoning to me with a finger that is burned away at the second joint. A stump she crooks at me, and I go toward her.

I don't want to go near her ... she has those deformed, twisted arms extended to me. She's ... she's ... puckering her lips ...

She wants to kiss me!

I scream and my throat tightens at the thought of kissing this corpse, but her arms reach through the bars and encircle me, draw me to her, pull my face up to hers and I see myself staring down into the blackened, ruined abyss of her eye and mouth.

I can't stand it ... I'll go mad ... Help me ... please somebody help me ... save me from this thing, this dead thing ... this thing that keeps murmuring *Save me ... save me ... save me ...*

The lips reach out to me and I'm being swallowed whole by evil and filth and death and the burning of her the heat the burning the insane help the burning I'm burning burning burning I'm

My name is Philip Dempster; my dreams are horrible.

ONE

BEFORE YOU CAN HAVE an explosion, somebody must light the fuse.

I was sitting in Tracy's that evening, minding my own business, when Ed Cronin came in. He lit the fuse for me.

The big, heavy-set man took the stool next to mine, but I wasn't aware of him until he nudged my arm.

"Hello, Phil," he said. "How's it going?"

"Down," I told him, lifting my glass.

"The book, I mean."

"Which one?"

"The cult novel."

"Oh, that? So-so, I guess. I'm writing another."

"Glad to hear it," Cronin said.

"I'm not." I signaled to the bartender. "Can't seem to get it organized." The bartender looked at me and I looked at Cronin. "What'll you have?"

He ordered a beer and I took the usual.

"So that's it." Cronin nodded, more to himself than to me. "Some of the boys said you'd been hanging around here lately."

"Bully for them." I raised my glass. "Pretty bright bunch of reporters you've got, Cronin. Always on the lookout for a story. What's your head—PROMISING YOUNG NOVELIST DRINKING HIMSELF TO DEATH?"

Cronin frowned, then put a smile on top of it, "Why not? It's the truth, isn't it?"

"I drink because I like to," I said, and it was a lie. "I'm stuck on the new book, that's all," I said, and it was the truth. "But I can stop drinking whenever I want to." I didn't know whether this was true or false, and it worried me.

"Hate to see you get in the habit." Cronin shrugged. "You're a bright boy, Phil."

"And the way you figure it, bright boys don't drink," I said. "That's where you're wrong. Trying to pin down a personality with a label. In your mind you've got me pegged with that 'bright boy' tag. Therefore I'm supposed to act thus-and-so. But haven't you ever noticed that people aren't necessarily consistent? They don't run around constantly 'in character' like a bunch of actors playing roles. Sometimes I'm a bright boy, yes. Sometimes I'm a lush, too. Sometimes I can lick the world, and sometimes I'm scared of my shadow."

Cronin shook his head. "It's not your shadow," he told me. "I've been watching you. Come on, Phil, tell me. What are you afraid of?"

I smiled over at the bartender. "Look, Mac," I said. "Is it all right with you if I climb up and lay down on the bar? My friend here wants to psychoanalyze me."

"Cut it out, Phil. I'm sorry."

"That's all right. But a guy gets mad when somebody asks that kind of question, when all he wants to do is drink in peace—"

"You weren't drinking in peace," Cronin answered. "And I don't think you really want to drink at all."

"Skip it, will you?"

"All right. I didn't mean to go prying into your affairs. That's not why I came over to look for you. Phil, how'd you like to handle an assignment?"

"I'm doing a book."

"But you just said you're hung up on it. And this wouldn't interfere. Only take a few hours a day. Maybe the change of pace would help snap you out of your slump, too."

"What kind of an assignment?"

"Right up your alley. The publisher is going all out on the new Sunday supplement and he's willing to spend a little money. So I sold him the idea of a series of weekly features, say five or six. On local cult rackets."

"That's where I come in, eh?"

"Who else? You're a local boy, you wrote a book about the subject, that makes you an authority."

"Slow down a minute," I told him. "If you're going after the expos) angle, you'd better put one of the staff on it—a feature writer will do you a hatchet-job. I'm not sold on the idea that all cults are rackets. Some of them are legit. I found that out when I was on the Coast, getting material for my book."

Cronin nodded. "I know. And I don't expect you to slant your material. But we've been doing a little checking through the office. We've got a line on five or six outfits here in town that operate in a pretty suspicious manner. These are the ones I want you to work on. And I won't blue-pencil anything unless it's libel. Handle it the way you want—the boss figures it's a public service."

"And if it's lurid enough, it'll help circulation, too," I added.

Cronin shrugged. "Could be. But what do you say? Six features, about fifteen hundred or two thousand words each. We'll let staff follow up on pictures, if we need them. All you have to do is go out, take a look around, then write your story. Shouldn't take more than four-five hours a week."

"What's the price-tag say?"

"The old man was willing to go a hundred and fifty. But I told him your name was worth two hundred. With byline, of course."

Maybe it wasn't all the money in the world, but I could use twelve hundred dollars for a few hours' work a week. I could very definitely use the money, with my book-royalty check still two months away. A change of pace might snap me out of my slump. It might help me break this habit of sitting and drinking so I could sleep, sleep without dreams, without *the* dream—

"It's a deal," I said. "When do we start?"

"Week from Sunday, if you can deliver," Cronin answered. "Run an announcement in the section this coming Sunday. Today's Monday. Come in and see me tomorrow and I'll line you up with the dope we've got."

"Good enough." I thought it was good, too, because I didn't know he'd just lit the fuse. "How about another drink?"

Cronin slid off the stool. "Sorry, got to be running along. You'll be there in the morning?"

"Sure. Don't worry." I smiled at him. "I'm just staying long enough to have one for the road."

They hadn't invented a drink yet that would help you over the road I was headed for, but I didn't know that, then.

As Cronin walked out, I waved to the bartender and said, "The usual."

I had the usual, and then I left. It was a wet evening and I shivered with the chill, pulling the collar of my coat up around my neck to keep off the dampness. My car was parked half a block away and I jammed my hands in my pockets and strode away down the rain-slick walks. The streets were deserted; anybody with brains was inside with their shoes off comfortably stretched out before a nice warm television set and slugging a beer before putting the kids to bed and then turning in themselves to share bed and blankets with the better half. It was a warm, pleasant thought and I could recall a time when it was almost more than just a thought for me. But that was a long time and a lot of drinks ago.

It was nice of Cronin to think of me, I reflected, fumbling in a damp pocket for my car keys. Like offering a lush a drink. His job wouldn't help get me back to my book—if anything, it would just take me farther away. And that book would join two others gathering dust in my desk drawer.

I got in the car and old Bessie coughed to a waterlogged life. I took the usual route home, to the empty apartment with its usual litter, and tried not to look at the typewriter. As usual, it sat there waiting for me, and as usual, I avoided it, tossing my shirt over it as I undressed for bed.

I smoked the usual last cigarette before I made my usual gesture of switching off the light. Then came the usual darkness, the usual doze, and finally, the usual dream.

That's what came of not drinking enough. When I don't drink enough, I dream. When anybody else dreams they dream of flying or of being the boss while the boss has their job or maybe of making to their girlfriend or the new stenographer who started last week. Or maybe they dream of being caught on the street without their pants on. I don't dream dreams like that. Not any more. My own made-to-order dream came, the usual dream, the one I'd had ever since I got back from the Coast, whenever I went to sleep without enough in me to knock me cold.

As usual, I knew it was only a dream, but that didn't help me. I kept getting hotter and hotter, and I could feel the warmth on my face as I bent down to look at that *other* face, the usual face that was—suddenly, surprisingly, shockingly—*un*usual.

Then I saw it, saw the burned mask with the two blind bubbles oozing up, and I screamed, and my fingernails ripped the sheets to shreds.

I woke up and reached for a cigarette, but I didn't light it. I lay there trembling for a long time, wanting to smoke but not daring to. Because where there's smoke, there's fire.

And I was deathly afraid of fire.

TWO

I DROVE DOWN to the *Globe* building around ten the next morning. Even at that hour of the morning it's playing a deadly game of tag to navigate the drive along the lake shore. My gut tightened up like it used to three years before and I swore at myself for getting mixed up with something I didn't want to do, money or no. I had forgotten that Cronin could play people like violins; he'd catch you in a weak moment, say the right thing, and you'd make beautiful music for him.

All the parking spots in front of the *Globe* were taken and I drove around to the back and found a spot by the loading docks. Tony on the freight elevator practically hemorrhaged with joy when he saw me and I began to feel a touch of nostalgia. Three years ago, before I had decided to try Literature with a capital "L," I had been one of Cronin's sharpest City Hall reporters. It wasn't a bad racket, Cronin was a good boss, and I had never regretted what I learned. There were even times when I thought of going back, and Tony's delight at seeing me made me think about it again. For exactly one-and-three-quarters seconds ...

Ed Cronin was in his office, waiting for me. He reached for a notebook the moment I walked in.

"All set," he said. "Here's the list."

He handed me a sheet of names, I read it quickly.

The White Brotherhood

Church of the Golden Atom
New Kingdom Tabernacle
Wisdom Center
House of Truth
Temple of the Living Flame

"You'll find the addresses in the notebook," he told me. "And the names of the principals. We've got dope on some of them, and nothing on others. That's your job—to dig up the rest."

I nodded.

"Let me know if you need any help. I can give you a photographer if you tell me a couple hours in advance. And you'll want a press card, I suppose."

My head stopped nodding and started to shake. "These operators don't care for the press. Wouldn't it be better if I just drifted in and attended the meetings, first? Then, when I got a line on the pitch, I could go back and arrange an interview—knowing what I was talking about and what I was looking for."

"Could be."

He made a note on a pad. "I'll set up an ad to announce the series. That ought to give the *Chronicle* and the *Leader* a few headaches."

"It might give them a few ideas, too," I said. "I'd better cover as many meetings as possible before the ad tips our plans."

"Suit yourself. All I want is a good series. But be careful."

"What do you mean?"

"Well, some of these cultists are pretty far out." Cronin glanced down at his note-pad. "You carry a gun?"

"Now wait a minute!" I grinned. "This is a big town. We've got a police force, remember?"

Cronin shrugged. He still wasn't looking at me. "Just an idea," he murmured.

I leaned over the desk. "You're a newspaper man. You don't get ideas. You get facts. Why did you make that crack about a gun?"

"Well—" He shifted uneasily in his chair. "When I sent out a couple of the boys to round up preliminary data, they ran into tough sledding in a few places. The Wisdom Center gang tossed one of them out on his can when he started to ask questions. After talking to Peabody—that's the White Brotherhood outfit—another guy got a couple of anonymous phone calls, telling him to keep his nose out of it. And the Living Flame bunch wouldn't even let anyone in the place. So—"

"So you've been putting on an act all along for my benefit," I interrupted. "Is that it? Handing me a line about a press card and a photographer, knowing I'd refuse. And wanting me to, really, because you already tried to get the story with your staff, and it didn't work. That's why you picked me, isn't it, Cronin? Because an outsider might get in where your people couldn't. And because you're pretty sure the word is out already, and they're waiting for someone to come along. They're stirred up, ripe for trouble. What do you expect for your twelve hundred bucks—do you want me to go out and get killed?"

"Now wait a minute—"

"Well, if you do," I said, "I'm your man. Because I can use the money." I picked up the notebook and headed for the door. "See you in the morgue," I said.

Cronin opened his mouth to say something, but no words came out. I've seen them look that way on the rocks at the zoo, before somebody tossed them a fish.

I turned in the doorway and smiled back at him. "Forget it," I told him. "Can't you take a joke? I was only kidding."

Then I went out, still smiling to myself. Sure, I was only kidding. It was just a rib. People don't get themselves killed over a newspaper article any more, not even by cultists. Not in a big city like this one.

Or do they? Driving away, in the car, I remembered some of the things I'd heard out on the Coast. Rumors, and more than rumors. Some of these screwy outfits were big business to those who ran them—and really big, million-dollar enterprises. There was always a risk involved when anyone interfered.

I stopped smiling. Maybe I should carry a gun, at that. Only I knew I wouldn't, even if this turned out to be dangerous.

Maybe that was the real answer. I wanted it to be dangerous, I wanted to get myself knocked off. I'd taken this assignment because of a death-wish—

Crazy. But perhaps I ought to stop in and see Schwarm one of these days now, tell him about it. He'd know.

I filed that idea for future reference, and dumped all the other ideas on top of it. They've never invented a safe as reliable as the good old human skull. It can keep a lot of secrets snug and secure. Of course, lately, some of those head-shrinkers have adopted safe-cracking tactics, boring into the skull with chisels. Nothing's really inviolate any more. You can't hide anything, they always find out, and the dream keeps coming back over and over again until you see what you've tried to lock away, even from yourself. Until you see that charred face—

"Hey, whyncha look where the hell ya goin'?"

I jerked upright as the kid yelled at me, from the curb. "Sorry," I said, twisting the wheel. Had to watch myself. Watch where I was going.

Where *was* I going?

No sense thinking about *that*, either. Except in the purely superficial sense.

Right now I was going to eat lunch. Afterwards I'd read the notebook and make plans.

I slid into a parking spot, just south of the business district, and entered the Dinner Gong. I slid into a booth, slid some food into me, and started to read over the material in the notes.

The White Brotherhood was first on the list.

"Rev. Amos Peabody. Claims divinity. Predicts end of world. 1970. Check previous claim, end of world 1960. Approx. 200 followers. Gimmick—sign over all possessions. Res. in Tabernacle, 149 S. Mason. Meetings ev. Tuesday, Thursday, 8 pm."

This was Tuesday. No sense going over the rest of the notebook now. I could check on the White Brotherhood and attend their meeting tonight; maybe see Peabody himself afterwards, and get the first story out.

I looked at my watch. Not yet one o'clock. I got out of the Dinner Gong and headed the Ford toward the Court House. From there I went to the Federal Building, and from the Federal Building to the Public Library.

By the time I got around to looking at my watch again, it was almost seven. But I had my notes, plenty of them. I could almost do the article without seeing a meeting.

Peabody was a pretty standard operator, apparently. I knew now how many times he'd been married, and how many times arrested on suspicion of practicing a con game. I knew his income for last year—or what he'd reported—and where it came from. I knew how he ran his racket, and who he'd stolen his pitch from.

I'd met so many of the breed out on the Coast, and so many of the followers. That was the group which really interested me—the followers, the believers, the wonder-seekers, hungry for miracles.

Escape. Everybody wanted escape nowadays. Some found it in a television tube, others sought it in a hypodermic syringe, and it was still selling in pints and fifths.

Nobody wanted reality any more. Reality had been reduced to a simple but unpalatable recipe:

"Take one pinch of hydrogen atoms—add a dash of cobalt—and stand *way* back."

That was the little household hint they were all trying to run away from. Just as sure as death and taxes—and there was plenty of both around for good measure, today.

So, inevitably, some people sought the cults. Certain familiar types to whom spectator-sports and vicarious satisfaction or distraction was not enough. I knew whom I'd find in the ranks of the White Brotherhood.

There was the fat, frowsy housewife, elevated to the circle of the Chosen Ones. The stammering sweeper from the factory, taking his place in the Exalted Hierarchy and gloating over the Day of Doom that awaits the foreman and the bosses. The bespectacled girl with the stringy hair who becomes the Bride of Glory. The aging man whose repentance for past sins increases with his impotence, putting those sins behind him and buying his way to favor in the Coming Kingdom.

These were the people Amos Peabody commanded and commended to the Holy Spirit—all duly incorporated according to law, everything legally protected in his name; a nice, clean, tax-free little setup and growing bigger every day. Give 'em all a title, make 'em feel important, tell 'em everybody else is going to burn while the True Believers get their pie in the sky. Amos Peabody was getting *his* pie right here and now. And perhaps he wouldn't like a stranger to come around and poke a finger into it.

But I drove down to 149 S. Mason just the same, and got there about half past seven. It was just the kind of a setup I expected to find—a big three-story frame building that had once been a public meeting hall, probably. Now the first floor was a tabernacle, and the second and third given over to offices and living-quarters. Everything looked simple and unpretentious enough—but that was deliberate on Peabody's part. Never scare the suckers away with a flash front, not if you're working the "end of the world" racket and preaching the renunciation of all earthly pooses slons.

Most of the chumps probably didn't know what I'd learned in just one afternoon's work. They weren't aware that Mr. Peabody owned an eighty-acre estate out in the Heights and lived in a fourteen-room mansion. They knew he had two Cadillacs and an ermine robe, because they'd given him these gifts by subscription; a prophet is supposed to enjoy a few luxuries. But they wouldn't figure on finding all that money in real estate and in bonds—not when Peabody was spreading the glad tidings about the end of the world.

I stared at the front of the building as the lights went on. Half an hour early, but they were getting ready. Little knots of people were eddying on the walk just outside. A few older people, a surprising number of youthful ones—the good clean-cut youngsters in conservative suits and cheery smiles just a few years away from executive trainee programs and YMCA secretary-ships. Outwardly, at least, they were identical in size and shape to young Episcopalians or Methodists or Christian Scientists or Knights of Columbus. Inwardly, the mixture was probably a little different. A little guiltier, perhaps. Oddball personalities that found their sense of belonging in an oddball religious off-shoot ...

I glanced at my watch. Time for me to get ready. Half an hour to go. All at once I remembered that I hadn't eaten anything since lunch time.

Maybe I could pick up a sandwich in a hurry. I glanced down the block and realized my luck wasn't going to be very good. Once away from the yellow pool of light in front of the scrubbed white of the tabernacle, I was out of the high-rent district. Faded buildings with peeling paint, dirty, fly-specked plate-glass windows, second-hand furniture stores, a maga-zine store with a sign advertising old books and magazines in both English and Spanish, a run-down movie theater shilling for that great hit, "Los Ni9os Encantados." A candy store, still open, and a couple of kids in black leather jackets and hair to match, lounging out in front and digging the squares in front of the tabernacle.

A wind came up and old newspapers went skittering down the dusty streets; half a block away there was the sudden clatter of a garbage can and the surprised yowl of a cat. I could smell rain in the air and glanced at the sky to note the full-rigged clouds sailing slowly past the moon. Fine night, I thought. For a lot of things. All of them bad ...

The one beanery on the block was closed and I decided to try a bar. In a neighborhood like this, tavern neon always seems to burn brighter by way of contrast.

I walked across the street and down the block to the bar. *Joe's Place.* Why is it that nine out of ten taverns are identified by the first name of the proprietor? What is there about our life and times that makes us feel we must be on a first-name basis with the bartender?

Why is a raven like a writing-desk?

Lewis Carroll knew a lot about Wonderland, and I'll bet he never entered a tavern in his life. But I wasn't Lewis Carroll. I was Phil Dempster, and I didn't live in Wonderland.

I went into the tavern.

It was a Mom-and-Pop setup, with Joe behind the bar, reading the sports page. When I asked about a sandwich he said sure, and called Mom. She was in the back room, and after she took the order she returned there to slice the liver-sausage.

I had a bottle of beer while I waited. I found out I was thirsty, too, so I had another. Then the sandwich arrived, and something which Mom called coffee. The old girl had quite an imagination.

Two gulps and I put the cup down. I called for a shot, instead. At least I could believe the labels on the bottles.

I took another look at my notes. Everything seemed to be in order. Maybe I could leave the notebook here when I went over to the White Brotherhood. I wanted to make sure the stuff was safe.

Not that I really expected to run into trouble. Still, you never could tell. No sense taking chances. Taking chances on getting tossed out, or roughed up, or—

What was the matter with me? Didn't I want to go? Didn't I want to earn that money? After all, as Cronin said, this would be a public service. Exposing a charlatan, saving people from being deceived by a fast operator who wouldn't hesitate for a moment to cut your throat and—

All right. So I *didn't* want to go. I knew that, now. I'd lost my nerve. That's why I couldn't write any more, that's why I was afraid of my own shadow.

No, not my shadow. I was afraid of something else, and Cronin knew it. I knew it, too. I was afraid, and so I was drinking.

I was drinking now. Five minutes to eight, and I'd just ordered another shot. Two shots and two beers on an almost empty stomach. That ought to give me the courage to go through with it.

But I kept hoping I wouldn't have to. That something would save me, at the last minute. *Save me, save me,* the voice kept saying it over and over again in my head. I knew the voice and wanted to forget it. Another drink would help. Only there wasn't time.

I started to get up, got ready to pay up and ask Joe if he'd please hang onto my stuff for me for an hour or so.

Then the door opened.

The door opened, and this girl walked in.

She didn't belong in a Mom-and-Pop tavern. She didn't belong in this neighborhood, or even in this world. I knew where she belonged. She belonged in my dreams—the ones I used to have, a long, long time ago.

Her hair was copper, the color of a newly-minted penny; the kind you put in your pocket for good luck. And she was almost, but not quite, pocket-size. Rather short, but after a single glance you didn't notice it, because she was perfectly proportioned. Meaning that the lines of her black wool dress were molded to her body, that the white curve of her throat drew the eye irresistibly down to delight the—

I blinked and shook my head. This wasn't *like* me. I hadn't even thought about women since I came back from the Coast. Up until now, if anyone had asked, I'd have told them I didn't intend to think about them again.

But here I was, and here *she* was. Why? How had she strayed into this cheap joint, what was she doing here?

It was none of my business, but I watched her as she walked over to the bar and ordered a drink. Bourbon, on the rocks. The bartender didn't know her, that was obvious. He poured, and I stared. Stared until she became conscious of my scrutiny, and turned to face me.

I caught a glimpse of green eyes. Then she glanced away. Sure, why not? This was real life. In real life no dream girl ever walks up to you and says, "You must be Phil Dempster. I've always wanted to meet you."

I caught her staring at me again, and turned away. Time to talk to the bartender. He came down the line and I leaned over.

Then I felt the hand on my shoulder. I looked around and she was standing there. Standing there and smiling, and saying, "Pardon me. But aren't you Philip Dempster? You know, I've always wanted to meet you."

THREE

LET'S NOT FORGET OUR FUSE. It was burning now, but I didn't know it, I didn't realize how quickly a spark can travel. Even if I'd known, the chances are I wouldn't have done anything about it.

If you've ever seen a fuse burn, perhaps you can understand why. You get so that you forget about the danger and just look at the spark—the little red spark, eating its way along, moving so prettily, so swiftly, so magically. You watch the spark, and it's like something alive. Unconsciously, you *identify* yourself with it, find yourself hoping it will keep on living instead of going out. And the spark moves on, and on, faster and faster, until the explosion.

At the time, though, I was unaware. All I knew was that a dream was happening. One of the good dreams, one of the best.

And the dream said, "I thought I recognized you, but I wasn't sure. You look just like your picture on the dust jacket."

Then I understood, and it wasn't a dream any more. "So you read the book," I said.

"Certainly. We bought three copies for the library."

"Are you a librarian?"

"Not any more. I used to be. I'm working as a private secretary now." She gave me a look from under her lowered lashes. "But this isn't very polite, is it—just coming up to you this way without even introducing myself."

"Let's be honest," I said. "I love it. Doesn't happen very often—people don't remember the names of writers. You were a librarian, you ought to know that. Somebody will go on and on about a book they've read. Ask them who wrote it and they can't tell you."

"That's right, Mr. Dempster."

"What are you drinking, Miss—?"

"Bourbon."

"I see. And the name?"

"Diana Rideaux." She spelled it for me.

"French, eh?"

"My father was. Creole, rather—I was born in New Orleans."

"Wonderful city. I'm going back there some day," I told her. "Always wanted to do a definitive study of the old voodoo cults. Know anything about that?"

"No. I've lived up here most of my life."

Glancing over to the bar, I gave Joe a nod. "Two bourbons," I said. "On the rocks."

Joe brought the drinks. We made small talk. I found out that she had come down here to visit an aunt, but the aunt was out. And she'd forgotten to bring a coat, and it was chilly on the corner waiting for the bus, so she stopped in for a quick drink to warm her up. She wasn't in the habit of going into strange taverns or any taverns, alone, and she hoped I didn't have the wrong impression.

I assured her that I did not, that I had a very good impression. Which was quite true. The more I saw, the more I liked. And then she got to talking about the novel, and the more I heard, the more I liked.

Then I glanced at my watch, and it was quarter after eight. She noticed how I checked the time and said, "Am I keeping you from an engagement?"

"No, not at all. There's no place I'd rather be than right here." Which was also true. I was beginning to get a glow. Some of it came from the liquor. Some of it came from her presence; the nearness of that copper cloud, all warm and soft and scented.

It was very pleasant to sit there, drink in hand, and listen to a pretty girl talk about me. That may sound very fatuous, but I've got a hunch every man feels that way, really. Even though most of them would be ashamed to admit it.

I really should break it off, I kept telling myself. Maybe make another date for another time. I had to get over to that meeting.

But then again, suppose I missed a few minutes? Probably didn't start on time, anyway. Eight-thirty would be soon enough. We could have another drink, first.

So we did, and Miss Rideaux suggested we move into a booth, because now some of the regular customers had come in. We moved to the booth and went on talking.

By the time I checked my watch again it was quarter to nine. And we'd just ordered another drink.

There really wasn't any hurry, come to think of it. The White Brotherhood would be holding another jam-session on Thursday night. That would be soon enough; I could cover it then. Why leave now, just when everything was going so smoothly, floating along on a sea of bourbon and perfume?

I felt better than I had in months, better than I thought I'd ever feel again. This was perfect. There are some girls you like to talk to, and some girls you like to drink with; but the trouble is, one kind resents the other. Besides, it's very expensive to take two girls out at the same time, even if they *are* willing. Which they aren't.

So I was lucky, getting the combination rolled into one. A librarian who liked libations. And who stimulated the libido. Yes, indeed—almost too good to be true. That's what I'd told Margery once. "You're too good to be true. Promise that you'll be true."

"What's wrong?" she said. I realized that Miss Rideaux was staring at me. "Did I say something?"

"No. Why?" I asked.

"You're frowning."

"Sorry. I just remembered something—"

"I'll bet you did have a date tonight after all."

"Not a date," I said. "An assignment."

"Assignment? What do you mean?"

So I told her about the White Brotherhood. Somewhere along the line we had another drink, and then another. What was it—number seven or number eight? I was losing count now, but it didn't matter. Nothing mattered except that I was talking to her and she was listening and leaning forward so that I could smell her perfume and smell her hair and stare into those green eyes, those smoky emeralds, no, more like jade, copper and jade—

But I didn't tell her about that, of course. I was being very brilliant and very analytical about cults. Everything is very brilliant and very analytical after the eighth drink, or was this the tenth coming up now? Anyway, I told her all about the White Brotherhood, and she was quite interested. I explained to her why people joined such organizations, what the attraction was. I told her about some of the Coast outfits in the past—the *I Am* movement, and *Mankind United*; Arthur Bell and Riker, Kullgren, and the Man from Lemuria down in Ojai. Bell's take was better than two and a half million dollars in ten years. And the *I Am* deal grossed even more.

"Started out back in the '30s," I said. "Man name of Guy Ballard and his wife were leaders. He was a former paper-hanger. Wrote this book, *Unveiled Mysteries*, under the pseudonym of Godfrey Ray King. Ever read it?"

She shook her head. *That* was something to see. It made me want to reach out and touch her hair. Instead, I kept on talking.

"Ballard just happened to be climbing Mount Shasta one fine day when he ran into Saint Germain, the Ascended Master. Saint Germain give Ballard a drink of something called electronic essence and a tablet of the same stuff—remember, this was before the day of vitamin pills. Must have been a pretty powerful mixture, because white flames shot out fifty feet in the air on all sides of him, and he was levitated through space. Saint Germain took him on a conducted tour of Egypt, South America, India and Yellowstone National Park—showed him the location of ancient cities filled with hoards of buried treasure. Told him that there were other Ascended Masters who lived eternally in the secret places of the earth and directed its destiny. Now the time had come to reveal the truth to all, and Ballard had been selected to bring the message to the world." I paused, sipped my drink, offered her a cigarette.

"No thanks. Go on—this is interesting."

"The best is yet to come," I told her. "Ballard went home and started to write his book. Saint Germain dictated some of it to him, and he kept on through the years—but I don't think he ever got a share of the royalties. Ballard handled the money, and did pretty well.

"He set up a temple, of course, and he sold signet rings, and steel engravings of Cosmic Beings. He had a cold cream, too, and charts and books and even phonograph records of the 'music of the spheres'. There was a monthly magazine and printed lectures and study courses.

"He had classes going in his Sanctuary from seven in the morning until midnight. The pupils learned chants, and the secret of color vibrations. They bought everything, including a 'Flame in Action' machine which sold for a couple of hundred dollars."

"Fantasy," said Miss Rideaux.

"Reality," I told her. "This actually happened—it's all down in the records. You see, the pupils were learning the words and colors and prayers which would remove the layer of Evil from the earth. Saint Germain and the other Ascended Masters helped out with the Purple Ray. Once this layer was removed, everybody could attain heart's desire. You could get a 'precipitation' of anything you wanted. All you did was concentrate on the object until it appeared. If you wanted a new washing machine, 'precipitation' would give it to you.

"And there were other benefits. Didn't Ballard predict the destruction of Southern California in 1936, and then save it by pleading with Saint Germain at the last minute? Didn't he sink three submarines Hitler had sent to blow up the Panama Canal? Didn't he offer them all immortality and riches? They got their money's worth, all right."

"How did Ballard make out?" the girl asked.

"Not too badly. You see, the cult spread to other cities. At one time he had over three hundred thousand followers. If Ballard hadn't died, and if his wife hadn't been convicted of using the mails to defraud, it might have gone on to greater heights. Anyhow, when the Feds stepped in and took an audit many years ago, they estimated Ballard's take at way over three million dollars."

"Three million—!"

"Not bad for electronic essence," I said. "How about another drink?"

She nodded. The drinks didn't seem to bother her at all, but they were getting to me. When I take on a little too much alcohol my speech centers aren't affected, but my vision goes haywire.

Right now she was nothing but a copper blur. Not bright and shiny, but dim and wavering. I told myself that maybe I needed glasses. I told myself that maybe I didn't need what was *in* glasses. Not very funny. I laughed anyway.

"Mr. Dempster—is something the matter?"

"No, nothing. Just too much electronic essence, I guess. Can I drive you home?"

She stared at me and I tried to stare back. I could tell she was shaking her head.

"No. I don't think so. But if you've got a car outside, *I'll* drive *you* home."

"Sorry. I shouldn't have taken that last one. I've been drinking too much lately. Got to cut it out." I stood up.

"Think you can make it all right?" Her hand, on my arm.

"Of course I can." And I could. I walked out of there under my own power. The place was crowded now, and nobody paid any attention to us. She went first, then I followed the copper blur.

In the car I could close my eyes. I gave her my address and she drove. I guess I fell asleep for a little while, because when I came to we were parked in front of the apartment. She was opening the car door.

"Going to leave it out all night?" she asked.

"Sure. I've got a permit."

"Then I'll be on my way." She smiled, or I thought she did. "And thank you for a very entertaining evening."

Entertaining, hell. What's this modern generation coming to, I asked myself. Used to be that the woman had a few too many and the man took her home—or somewhere. And now the whole deal was reversed. *She* took *me* home. Fine thing. Phil Dempster meets his dream girl and ends up with a jag on, too woozy to even think of asking her to come upstairs—

"Hey," I said. "Where are you going?"

"Home, naturally. I live over on Fairhope. Don't worry, there's a bus stop right at the corner."

"I'm sorry," I sighed. "I'm a mess."

"Don't be sorry. I enjoyed it."

"Well, I didn't. Next time I promise—" I leaned forward. "Can I phone you?"

"Of course. I'm in the book."

"Stay home tomorrow night. I'll call."

"That'll be fine. Goodnight." She hesitated a moment. "Are you sure you can make it upstairs?"

"Sure. I'm all right, I—"

But she was gone. I heard her heels clattering away, and I leaned out the window to look, only everything was blurred. Everything was blurred, and I'd been lying. I wasn't all right. I was all wrong, *this* was wrong, this drinking and drinking and drinking every night because of a dream that wasn't real. When a reality came along I wasn't ready for it; I kept on drinking and let her go.

Why hadn't we just talked? Why hadn't I found out a few things about her, instead of doing all that ranting over a bunch of crazy cults? As it was, she must think I was just a stewbum—typical drunken writer. The kind of guy she was glad to get rid of.

As it was, she hadn't told me a thing. She was a private secretary, yes, but where? Lived on Fairhope, she said, but what address? Probably roomed with someone, and I'd never know now.

Still, she'd given me her phone number, hadn't she? No—she hadn't. Just said I could call her tomorrow night. In the book, she told me. And that was probably a stall, to get away from here fast.

Why didn't I think to ask the number, write it down in the notebook? The notebook—

I felt in my pockets. Nothing there. I groped around on the seat beside me, scrabbled at the floor under my feet. Then I remembered.

I had left the notebook back in the tavern, in the booth.

That was it. I *must* have it. And I had to get it. What if somebody from the White Brotherhood drifted into Joe's Place after the meeting and found my notes?

I had to get it. She was gone now, the bus had thundered past five minutes ago. Nobody to drive me. Late. I didn't see a taxi. Maybe I could go upstairs and call one—

No. That might take a half-hour or more, this time of night. The sooner I got my hands on the notebook the better. I could drive the car myself. I was all right.

For a while the fuse seems to burn slowly, and then at the last the spark just races along—

I slid over in the seat, groped for the keys in the ignition. The car began to purr and throb, purr and throb, crawl forward and then streak through the night like a cat pouncing on its prey. A copper cat, with green eyes. The cat-goddess of Bubastis. There was a cult idea—revive the ancient Egyptian pantheon. Didn't some associate of Aleister Crowley try that? Crowley was a devil-worshipper. The Great Beast 666, he called himself. And people believed. Everybody believed nowadays, everybody heard voices, everybody saw visions.

Even I saw them when I dreamed, and there was no sense shutting my eyes. Can't drive now with your eyes shut—

I came to, somewhere on Fuller Avenue. A voice was whispering to me, "You can't make it, Phil. You can't make it. Why don't you stop, stop, stop?"

It was my own voice, and I didn't want to listen. I didn't want to stop. I *had* to make it. Even though I couldn't see what I was doing, where I was going.

Something was wrong with me, something was terribly wrong. If Schwarm were here, he'd know. He'd tell me what to do. He'd tell me to go home, and I'd go. Or he'd tell me to park, get out and walk the rest of the way before I ran into someone.

That was it. I could get out and walk. Only a few blocks more to go. Safer to walk. Then I wouldn't kill anybody, or take a chance on killing myself.

It had started to drizzle and I was dimly aware of the dampness on my face. I didn't bother buttoning my coat or trying to keep the chill off. In once sense I hoped the rain would sober me up. But that was a faraway thought and in another larger sense, I really didn't care whether I sobered up. Then, or ever. The walks were slippery and once I almost fell and thought vaguely I should watch it or I'd hurt myself. Or bump into somebody and hurt them ...

I didn't want to hurt anyone, I didn't want to kill anyone. I didn't want to die. I didn't want to *see* anyone die. That was it. That was the most important thing. Not to *see* anyone die.

So I walked, with my eyes closed. And my mind closed. I just walked, and then I guess I must have climbed. I know, there at the last, that I ran.

I ran through a blackout, because everything was getting too clear all of a sudden—too clear, and too bright. I could see too well.

There was a time when I stood in front of a door and rattled the knob. Was it Joe's tavern, was it closed?

There was a time when I went somewhere else and walked with my eyes shut, praying for another moment of peace before I opened them and realized what my awakened senses were trying to tell me—before I had to see what I could smell now, and hear.

The fuse sputters loudly at the end—

But this wasn't a sputtering. This was a low murmur that became a roar. A roaring in my ears, and a choking in my lungs. It was behind me now, I was moving away, I was running away to the corner.

Something red stood on the corner. I opened my eyes just long enough to see it. Something red, shining in the reflection of the light that came from behind me.

I went over it it, hung onto it. My hand went out and up, finding pain and then warmth. My hand moved then, and I heard a sound.

Then the sound was drowned out in the roaring, and the roaring was drowned out in the wailing. I slumped there, wanting to pass out but not quite making it. Maybe a minute passed, maybe five, maybe ten.

And all at once somebody was shaking me, I was awake, I was sober. But how can a man be awake and sober in a nightmare?

I didn't know.

All I know is that's how they found me, standing there next to the fire-alarm on the corner, while the tabernacle of the White Brotherhood went up in flames behind me.

FOUR

IT WAS JUST BEGINNING to get light outside. I could see the first streaks of dawn through the high window in the little office.

Captain Dalton pushed a mug of coffee my way. I picked it up and took a mouthful. It had a bitter taste, like ashes. Everything tasted of ashes, smelled of smoke to me.

"All right, Mr. Dempster," he said. "We're ready for that statement."

"But I told you everything. And I told Detective Henderson on the way down here—"

"This is for the record. Official." The short, gray-haired head of the Arson Squad stabbed the stem of his pipe toward the stenographer who sat beside me, pad in hand.

I wondered what on earth could induce a man to take such a job—sit there ready for dictation at five in the morning. I wondered why the head of the Arson Squad was allowed to smoke a pipe. I wondered about a lot of things.

"Try to remember every detail, now. This is serious."

I nodded. I was serious, all right. Serious as hell. The red hell of a holocaust, walls coming down in a shower of sparks—three alarms at the last, with the streets roped off all around. They found Peabody's body in a room upstairs, and three others; members of the White Brotherhood who were sleeping there overnight. The whole building had burned up. Burned to the ground. How can something burn up to the ground? Oh, it was serious, I knew that. And I knew that they hadn't bothered to bring me down here just for the ride. I'd already talked to a detective and to the Fire Marshal, too. If they Arson Squad was in on it, that meant they suspected—

"Where should I begin?" I asked.

"Start with this evening. I want a full statement. The works."

I gave him the works. Who I was, what I was doing. I told him about Ed Cronin and my assignment. I told him about going into Joe's tavern. I told him about meeting Diana Rideaux, and what had happened. About her driving me home, and me going back for the notebook.

That is, I told him about my physical actions of the evening. I didn't mention how much I had to drink, or what the drinks had done to me. I didn't tell him how I'd walked around with my eyes shut, or where I had walked. Partly because there were long stretches I couldn't remember, and partly because there were other stretches I didn't want to remember. Certainly I wouldn't talk about those things.

It was enough to say I'd gone back to the tavern, found it locked, then noticed the flames, smelled the smoke, and turned in the alarm.

Or *was* it enough?

When I'd finished talking, Captain Dalton looked at me. "That's it?" he asked.

"That's it."

He glanced down at a sheet of paper. "Couple of other points you might be able to help us on," he said. "According to what Henderson put down here, you didn't drive all the way to the tavern. Instead, you parked over on Fuller, in the 300 block. Why?"

"I told you. I'd had a few drinks too many, thought the air might do me good."

He nodded. "So you went straight over to the tavern and found it closed."

My turn to nod.

"What did you figure on doing then? Going straight home and calling the tavern in the morning?"

I nodded again.

"I see." Captain Dalton stabbed at the notes with his pipe. "You're sure that's all you had in mind?"

"Of course. What else was there to do?"

"That's what I'm asking you." Dalton stood up. He was a short man, but at the moment he looked quite tall as he stood peering down at me. "Because if you were going right home, you'd walk back to the car, wouldn't you? And the car was in the *other* direction from the White Brotherhood tabernacle. Yet you didn't go back—you went forward. You had to go forward, because we found you on the far corner after the alarm was turned in."

"I saw the flames," I said. "I smelled smoke."

He kept staring at me. "What time was this?"

"Never thought to look. I'd been drinking, you know how it is."

"I don't know how it is. I want to find out." He turned away. "Would you say you put in the alarm immediately?"

"Of course. Wasn't that the thing to do?"

He didn't answer me directly. He talked to the wall, now. "If you turned it in at once, then somebody's cockeyed."

"What do you mean?"

"The alarm went in at exactly one-fifteen. That's on record. You say you went straight from the tavern to the alarm box, because you smelled smoke and saw flames. Is that correct?"

"Yes."

"How long would you estimate it would take to walk from the tavern door to the alarm?"

"Three minutes. Maybe less."

He was staring at me again. "Three minutes, maybe less." Now the pipe-stem was stabbing straight at my eyes. "So according to your story, you must have tried that tavern door at around ten after one. At eleven after, or twelve after, you looked down the block and saw flames. From the front window upstairs, you said."

"That's right."

Captain Dalton went over to the side door and opened it. He called into the next room. "Bring Shelby in for a minute, will you?"

A detective entered, followed by a bespectacled man wearing a cab-driver's cap and a leather jacket.

"You're Mr. Shelby?" asked the Captain.

"Yeah, I'm Vick Shelby."

"My name's Dalton. Arson Squad. I read your statement."

The cab-driver shifted his weight from his right leg to his left. "What's the matter with it? I tole you evvything I know. Look, I gotta get outta here, I gotta check in—"

"There's nothing wrong. You'll be released in just a moment. But first, I wanted you to go over it again, so I could hear for myself. You say you were coming down Mason at ten after one?"

"That's right. I turned off Claybourne at ezacally ten after. Reason I remember is this time-load come over the radio for me. One-thirty out at the airport. I called in and give the operator the word, and rules are you gotta say what time it is you get the call. So I says one-ten, see? Then I drove south on Mason, like I said."

"Let me see, now. Claybourne is about a mile north of the White Brotherhood tabernacle, isn't it?"

"Fourteen blocks, countin' the alley off the YMCA."

"And this would bring you abreast of the tabernacle at about one-twelve or one-thirteen?"

"Uh-huh."

"Did you see any flames when you passed the building?"

"No."

"Smell any smoke?"

"No." Vick Shelby shifted from his left foot to his right again. "Diden' I tell you before, if I'd seen anything I would of stopped and put in an alarm? Whaddya gettin' at—tryin' to make me say *I* set the place on fire?"

"Of course not." Captain Dalton was being very kind and very patient; he didn't point his pipe at Vick once. "Just one more thing. As you drove along, did you happen to notice anybody walking, or running, along the left-hand side of the street in the block before the tabernacle?"

"Not a soul," said the cab-driver. "Nobody was around."

"You didn't see a man in front of the alarm box on the corner, either?"

"I didn't see no one."

Dalton was pointing at me again. "You're sure you didn't see *this* man?"

"Never seen him before in my life."

"All right, Mr. Shelby. You an go now, and thanks very much. If we need you, we'll get in touch."

"Okay."

And out he went. Just opened the door and walked out, free as the air. While I sat there, and the pipe-stem pointed.

"You didn't see the cab go by, did you?"

"Of course not. I would have mentioned it if I had. I told you everything I know."

"Did you?" Dalton sat down again. He was beginning to sweat a little, I noticed, but I didn't care. Because I was wringing wet, myself.

"Did you?" Dalton repeated. "You say you were at the tavern at one-ten or a moment later. That you walked down Mason Street and crossed over immediately, seeing flames at one-twelve or one-thirteen. But the cab-driver didn't see any flames at that time. And he didn't see you, either."

"I can't help that," I said. "Maybe I was in the shadows. Maybe there was some kind of explosion and the flames broke out suddenly, in a moment or so. I wouldn't have waited a second to call after I saw them."

"Wouldn't you, Mr. Dempster?"

"Say, what is this? Do you think *I* started the fire?" My voice sounded just like the cab-driver's.

"I don't think anything." He sighed. "I haven't even said I thought anyone *started* the fire. It could have been spontaneous combustion, for all we know. But it's our business to find out. Our business, because the place wasn't covered by any insurance. If the National Board of Fire Underwriters was in on this deal, you'd really be getting some questions along about now."

"Look," I said. "I told you what I know about it. And I told you I was under the weather. A man doesn't always remember details. Maybe I got there earlier and walked around a while. But I did see flames, I did turn in the alarm. Since when is it a crime to turn in a fire-alarm at a fire?" I stood up. "Since when is it a crime to park your car down the street and take a little walk? I didn't set fire to that place. Why should I? I'd never even been there in my life. Think it over, it doesn't make sense!"

"Nothing makes sense," Dalton told me. "You start out for a meeting, but you don't go. You meet a strange girl and hang one on with her. Know her name but not where she lives. She drives you home, but you come back because you forgot your notebook. Only you don't come back all the way. You park your car down the street and walk. You claim all this happened just before the fire broke out. But why couldn't it have been earlier? Suppose you came back at twelve-thirty instead of ten after one and you—"

"Why?" I was almost shouting at him. "You tell me for a change. What's the reason, what's the motive? Every crime's got to have a motive."

Dalton tapped his pipe on the desk and shook his head. "That's the odd part of it," he murmured. His voice was soft, reflective. "Arson, yes. We get motives galore. Insurance is the biggest one, of course. Then there's revenge—discharged employee burning down the plant because he's mad at the boss. There's jealousy, too, and sometimes fire is a cover-up for murder. Lots of motives like that. Not all of them seem completely sane or rational reasons, But we can understand them. It's the other kind we're afraid of. The cases where there is no motive, no sense. The torch doesn't have a reason for setting fires—at least, not one he can understand. Voices tell him to do it, or he likes to see things burn, or he wants to watch the firemen come and maybe even run into the flames himself and be a hero. Many times a firebug doesn't even seem to realize what he's done—it's as though the whole experience was blotted out of his consciousness."

"Sounds crazy to me," I said.

"It is crazy." Dalton began to load his pipe. "There's a name for it too. They call it pyromania."

"You can't lean on me," I whispered, whispering because I was frightened. "You said yourself you don't even know if the fire *was* started by somebody. You haven't got a crime, let alone a criminal. If you want to book me, I want a chance to call a lawyer. But I've told you the truth. You can check with Ed Cronin, check with that girl—"

The door opened and the detective who'd brought the cab-driver stuck his head in.

"Girl's here," he said.

Dalton frowned at him, then rose. "Right with you," he said. And then, to me, "You stay here until I get back. Keep an eye on him, Scotty."

The stenographer nodded.

I sat there and watched the dawn come up. The beautiful, beautiful dawn. Coming up like fire—

Then I closed my eyes. *Pyromania. Sometimes you don't even realize what you've done. How long had I walked around and where had I gone? Burning. That charred mask—*

What was going on out there? What was he asking Diana Rideaux, what was she telling him?

I don't know if he was gone five minutes or five hours. The sun was shining in my eyes when he came back in. The detective was with him.

"All right, Dempster," he said. "You can run along home now. But stick around town in case we want to call you later."

I stood, nodded. "Where's Miss Rideaux?" I asked.

"She just left. But it's all right. Her story checks you out. According to her, she didn't say goodnight to you until one o'clock. Lucky for you she was around."

I had trouble standing. My feet were asleep. Captain Dalton came over to me. "All right?" he asked.

"Sure. Fine."

"Sorry I went after you that way. But you've got to be careful in this line of work. I've seen some mighty funny cases. Nothing screwier than a firebug."

"I understand." I moved away. The detective put his hand on my arm.

"Want to take the back way out?" he asked. "Reporters up front."

I nodded gratefully.

"I'll have one of the squads drive you home," he said. "This must have been rough on you." He fished in his pocket, pulled out a pack of cigarettes. "Here—have one?"

"No, thanks," I answered. "I've given up smoking."

FIVE

I WANTED TO SLEEP, now, but there was too much to do. The first job was to take a cab over to Joe's tavern. It was open, and Joe was there.

So was my notebook.

"Noticed it when I come to clear away the glasses after you left," he said. "Too late to call you. Figured you'd be back."

"Thanks," I said.

"Detective was in here asking after it. He looked at it, I guess, but he didn't take it along. Got something to do with the fire?"

"Didn't you read it?

Joe indicated the crowded bar. "Who's got time to read, business like this? Besides—it ain't my proppity."

I was willing to accept his first reason. The bar seemed to be doing a rushing morning business. So was the street, outside. Plenty of traffic, plenty of spectators, plenty of morbid curiosity-seekers come to gape at the still smoking ruins. People are always interested in fires. Why?

"No kidding," Joe said. "You have somethin' to do with the fire?"

"Sure," I told him. "I set it."

"Ah—"

"Thanks for the notebook. Look, hadn't you better be getting back to the customers?"

"Ma'll handle 'em." He leaned over the bar. "Didja see it burn, huh?"

"No. I was home."

"Boy, that was really somethin'! Flames musta been thirty feet in the air. They had five engines here—we was roped off, they wouldn't let us get any closer. Ma and me, we watched outta the window upstairs, though. You could feel the heat way over here."

I edged away from the bar, seeking escape.

"You heard about Peabody, huh? Him and three other guys got it. Jeez, that must be a awful way to die—"

This wasn't what I wanted to hear. I had to make him stop. "Did you know Peabody?" I asked.

"Him? Nah. He never come in here. Didn't even take a glass of beer. None of that gang ever showed around. Bunch a fanatics, you ask me. Give all their money to the Brotherhood. Big racket. How can people get so crazy?"

I shook my head. I didn't know how people could get so crazy. Yesterday I thought I did, but today I wasn't sure any more. Wasn't sure what being crazy meant. Did it mean you wanted to start fires, did it mean you wanted to watch fires, did it mean you were afraid of fire? If so, then everyone was crazy.

"Sorry," I said. "I've got to go. My car's parked down the street."

He opened his mouth, but I opened the door. And once again, I started walking in the wrong direction.

I *had* to see it before I went away.

The actual intersection was still roped off, and the fire department was very much in evidence; their vehicles and men were scattered all over the place.

The curbs were lined with parked cars for blocks around, and a sizeable crowd pressed against the ropes. Cops walked back and forth, ordering the spectators to stand clear, move along. But they grinned as they spoke, and the crowd grinned back.

There was an air of holiday gaiety here. I didn't sense any carefree happiness, but I could feel the excitement and the exhilaration. I shouldered my way up to the rope, and all around me people were smiling and staring.

I stared, too, but I didn't smile. The gutted core of the tabernacle still stood, although the two walls on the farther side had toppled almost from the foundation. The roof was gone, of course, but the front remained upright—empty windows like blind eyes, the open door like a burned mouth from which poured a stench of ashy decay. Shreds of burned lath and plaster hung in front of the empty window sockets like the greasy hair of a juvenile delinquent. Half the street was cluttered with debris left there when the roof had fallen in and chairs and papers and half-burned hymnals had puffed out of the burning building like dust blown out of a doorway. Something else in the street caught my eye and I almost lost my lunch. It had been an old building and harbored more than its share of the minor animal life that manages to live in symbiosis with urban humanity. Small spiders and bugs had probably gone up like bits of paper on a blast furnace. Then a small army of squealing, burning rats had made a run for it and some had gotten as far as the street outside. I started to shake. Human beings would burn just as easily. And they'd look the same way ...

Firemen poked around in the ruins, and hose-men near the corner trained a spitting serpent on the cellarway.

This was it, this was the spot where the flames had lived and men had died.

And the crowd liked it. I could see it in their faces. Could see what they felt openly, knew what they felt secretly. The crowd liked it. The Great Beast. The Great Beast who lives in a diet of violence, has lived on it through the centuries.

These were faces that lighted up in the red reflection of a burning Rome. These were the faces that kindled with glee as the torch was applied to the Christian martyrs—as the faggots fired about the feet of Torquemada's victims. In their eyes I could read the rope, see the stake, learn the love of lynching and the burning desire to burn. This was the Mob, and to the Mob all suffering was a spectacle, all destruction a delight.

Sure, they were talking about how terrible it was. They always talk that way, like old women going on at a funeral. But the old women go to funerals every day, and the Mob goes to scenes of violence and disaster. Goes and gloats. Goes and feasts upon the filth. *Supp'd full with horrors,* isn't that the way Shakespeare puts it?

Give us this day our daily dread. Blasphemy? Perhaps, but there was blasphemy all around me. I could feel the thoughts, the dark desires.

"Glad it wasn't me ... I wish I could have seen it, though ... wonder what it's like to start a fire, burn a place down ... too bad the whole neighborhood didn't go up, then there'd really be something to watch ..."

It had happened at all times, all over the world. They burned the Library at Alexandria, and they burned Rome, and Paris, and London, and Atlanta. Chicago and San Francisco had gone up in flames, too. And always, the Mob came. The Mob came to savor smoke as incense, to view the burnt offering and offer adoration to what dark gods of death? They'd stand there and watch the flames flickering orange and pink and blue and white and feel the warmth on their faces and oooh and aaah when the ceiling fell in or a wall collapsed. They'd quietly root for the flames and silently boo the firemen and stare without pity or sympathy when a volunteer staggered to the sidelines to cough the smoke out of his lungs. It didn't matter whether it was the impersonal fa'ade of the State National Bank being destroyed by the licking flames or Uncle Harry's lingerie shop. There was no pity for the owners, no pity for the victims. Only a sea of too-bright, blazing eyes, the Mob worshipping its oldest god.

I knew. I *knew.* Underneath the gay assertions—"I always look out of the window when I hear the fire-engines go by" and "I don't know what gets into Tom, the minute he hears the siren, off he goes in his car" and "There's just, oh, something about a fire that gets me"—underneath the commonplace, everyday expressions of opinion there was a need. A flaming need for a flaming deed. We're all fire-worshippers at heart. And we rejoice when we see a sacrifice.

Fine thoughts for early morning, after a sleepless night. I shivered and turned away to seek a route to the car.

It was still standing there. I had the keys in my pocket, and the cops hadn't towed it away.

I drove to the apartment, picking up some rolls and a dozen eggs on the way. I made breakfast, shaved, washed.

Then I called Cronin.

"Dempster. You heard about last night?"

"*Heard about it? My God, we're swamped down here!* And where were you, why didn't you phone in the story when it happened?"

"You know why. You must have checked with Dalton by this time."

"Yeah. I know. Fine thing. For a while there, I was afraid you'd be mixed up in this, give the paper a black eye."

"Nice of you to be so thoughtful," I said.

"Never mind the sarcasm, Dempster. I already gave you a break—a big one. We can't keep your name out of the story, because you turned in the alarm. But we're killing the part about you being questioned, and we're not mentioning what you were up to, with the notebook." He paused. "You get it back?"

"I got it. So you needn't worry about the paper's reputation."

"Go to hell." Cronin paused. When he spoke again, his voice was calm. "Sure you're all right, Phil?"

"I'm all right. Just tired, that's all."

Another pause. And then, "Phil—you sure you haven't got anything more to tell me?"

"Quite sure. I leveled with Captain Dalton, gave him everything I know on it."

"All right. What are your plans now?"

"I'm hitting the sack. Tired. But I'll keep in touch with you."

"Do that."

"Right." I hung up. And then I did hit the sack, and the sack hit me, and I slept. Slept without dreams. Slept until it was dark.

I got up, took a bath, and thought about dinner. Almost dinner-time. Almost time to call—

She must have been sitting at the phone, waiting.

"Hello."

"Oh, it's you. Are you all right?"

"Yes, thanks."

"I called you this afternoon, from the office. Nobody answered."

"I was sleeping."

"Tired?"

"Not now. Hungry. You eaten yet?"

"No."

"I'll be around in fifteen minutes."

"Well—"

"Going to be coy?"

"Make it twenty. I've got to change my dress."

I gave her half an hour before I pulled up in front of the building on Fairhope. It was a former duplex, now converted to four apartments. My girl lived in the front upper.

My girl? Well—

She looked like my girl when she greeted me at the door. Tonight the dress was green, to match the eyes and set off the hair. It set off other things, too. On her, and inside me.

"You look good," she said. "A person would never think you'd been through—" A lip-biting pause. "I'm sorry."

"That's all right."

"Care for a drink?"

I shook my head. "Not drinking at the moment. Not smoking, either. Last night seems to have cured me of all my vices."

"Did it?"

"Well, most of them. But I'm still ready to eat."

"Fine. I'll get my hat. Where are we going?"

"I was thinking about the Chateau. Would you like that?"

"You should have told me. I'm not dressed for it."

"Sure you are. You look fine. And after being hauled out of bed that way—I'm sorry they dragged you into it."

"I'm not." Diana looked at me as if she meant it. "They thought you started the fire, didn't they?"

"Looks that way. But your alibi fixed things. Sweet of you."

"You needn't thank me. I only told them the truth."

"But—" I hesitated. "You didn't really leave me at one, you know."

"I thought I did. It must have been around one when I caught the bus. Maybe five or ten minutes earlier at the most, come to remember. Should I have told them it was any earlier?"

"You definitely shouldn't," I answered. "One o'clock was just dandy. Saved my life with your story. Honey, I could hug you."

I stepped forward with every intention in the world of doing just that. Diana moved back, eyes widening.

"Phil," she whispered. "Are you saying what I think you're saying? *Did you start that fire?*"

"Of course not." I didn't like the way she moved back, but at least she was calling me "Phil," now. "As a matter of fact, there's nothing to show that anybody started it."

"Oh, but there is," she told me. "Haven't you seen the papers? The Fire

Marshal made a statement this noon. They found out how it was set. Somebody must have crawled in through the basement window and dumped a gallon of kerosene over the coal-pile and the shed down there, and on the stairs, too. That's how those men were trapped upstairs—the flames came right up the stairwell."

"How could they tell?"

"I guess they found the empty tin tossed on the coal-pile. Something like that. Anyway, it's in the paper." She handed me the *Globe*. "Read it if you want to. I'll get my hat."

I read it. Cronin had done a good job. My name was mentioned, but only as a passerby who had turned in the alarm. The cab-driver's statement wasn't included at all.

Dalton didn't get much of a play, either. The story was build around the Fire Marshal and the Chief of the Fire Department. Sure enough, they claimed arson. Various members and former members of the White Brotherhood were being held for questioning. Of course the Fire Marshal didn't actually come right out and *say* it was arson. His statement was full of "indications lead us to believe" and "apparently" and "it appears." But there was no doubt about it, now. And they were investigating.

I skipped over the second-page stories about the White Brotherhood and Amos Peabody. The whole story of the cult was there—the story I'd intended to write. Now my opportunity had gone. Gone up in smoke.

That part wasn't important. What was important was how the fire had started. It would be easy to crawl through an open cellar window and find a convenient can of kerosene lying around. Almost any basement contains something like that—if not kerosene, then oil or cleaning fluid or some old rags or wastepaper. Even wood would do. Wood and newspapers. There are a thousand ways to start a fire. And it could be done so swiftly, so very swiftly. Into the cellar, up the stairs, and out again, all in five or ten minutes. Five or ten minutes was plenty of time.

Thinking about it made me want to take a drink. But before I acted on the impulse, Diana walked back into the room. She had her hat on, carried her bag.

"Will I need my coat?" she asked.

"No. It's still quite warm. Almost like summer. I wish I had a convertible."

"This is luxury enough." She smiled. "The Chateau—I've never been there. How did you guess that's where I wanted to go?"

"Psychic," I said.

Only I wasn't. If I'd been psychic, I would have driven fifty miles in the opposite direction.

Oh, it looked fine when we came in, and the menu was fancy, the service exceptional, the food superb. But I couldn't eat anything. Not when I saw them come in with the shishkabob. The shishkabob, served to some godawful gourmets at the next table. The shishkabob, served on a flaming sword—

"What's the matter?"

I pointed. She stared at the flames, the blue and red flames. I looked away, across the room, just in time to see another waiter wheel a serving-cart on which rested *crepes suzette*.

"Does that disturb you?"

I shook my head. And I tried to believe it didn't. What was the matter with me, was I getting a persecution-complex? Maybe it was worse than that. Maybe it was a guilt-complex. Had to get hold of myself. Suppose somebody began to play *Smoke Gets in Your Eyes*. Was that any reason for me to get up and run?

"I'm all right," I said. And after a moment I was, but I still didn't feel like eating. The steak was good, very well-done, and a bit charred on one side. That's the way I liked it—charred.

Or did I?

The dinner was turning into an ordeal. And yet she was there, smiling at me, the copper curls like living flame—

Stop it!

I made myself talk, made myself ask her all the questions I wanted her to answer. And she did answer, but half the time I wasn't listening to what she said.

All I remember is that her folks lived in Ohio, she'd been born there, her mother was divorced and when she remarried Diana had come here to finish school. She worked as a secretary now for some doctor.

I pretended to pay attention, pretended to be interested. Ordinarily I would have been, but this wasn't ordinarily. This was red flames and blue flames and trying to remember where I'd been at five to, ten to, one, five after, ten after. No stains or dirt on my clothes, but why should there be? It didn't make sense, because I'm afraid of fire, afraid of fire—

Then we were having coffee and the waiter came around and started to light the candle at our table, and I stood up very quickly.

"Let's go," I said.

She looked at me, then rose. When we went out she slipped her arm through mine. "Poor Phil," she said. "So upset. Sure you couldn't use a drink?"

"Just one."

We stopped at the bar out in front, and I had just one. We were out of there in five minutes. The night was warm, but I could feel a breeze off the lake.

"Come on," I said. "Let's take a little ride."

We took a little ride and we didn't talk much. Ended up down at the lake—not near the regular beach, but farther up, in a little place I knew. We had to go down through the bushes to get there, but we made it. I carried a blanket from the car.

It was nice down there, and peaceful in the dark. I spread the blanket and we lay down. I'd told her not to be coy when I talked to her over the phone, and apparently the remark had been unnecessary. She wasn't the coy type.

She wasn't coy and she wasn't shy. I don't know what I expected when we went down there. She was probably the most attractive woman I'd ever met, but this was only the second time we'd been together, and I'm no thoroughbred wolf. I supposed maybe we could rest for a while, and talk, perhaps hold hands and kiss. That would satisfy me.

But she wasn't resting, and she wasn't talking. And it was her hand that sought mine, her lips that came to mine, not as an offering but as an onslaught. Her mouth was a moving hunger, meeting and mingling with my own. Her mouth moved, and her hands moved, and her body moved, and now I knew that this would not satisfy me. Then I was moving, and she was suddenly still, but this I did not realize until later. Much later, when I sat up and habit hurried my hand to my pocket, in search of a cigarette.

"I thought you didn't smoke any more," she whispered.

"You cured me," I said. "You cured me, Diana. Of a lot of things."

"I'm glad."

I lay beside her. "Are you? Really? I didn't hurt you or—"

"You can't hurt me, Phil. No one can hurt me, darling. Not any more."

I puffed. The red tip of the cigarette glowed like a beacon. A warning-beacon? I didn't know, but I couldn't halt my voice.

"What do you mean? Was there some man who tried to—"

She put her mouth against my chest and laughed at my heart. "Some man? Phil, I might as well be honest with you. There have been a lot of men. A lot."

"Tell me."

"Why should I?"

"You know damned well why."

"No, I don't."

"You want me to say it, do you?"

"Say what?"

"That I'm in love with you."

"Are you?"

"Can't you feel it? Did you think I'd—"

She was laughing again. "Of course I do. Any man would. You're all alike. There's only one thing you're after, and you'll say anything, do anything, to get it. And then you run away."

"I'm not running, Diana. I'm here. I want to stay here, with you." I took another puff, looking at the glowing end. "And you're being cynical when you say all men are alike. You know it's not true—admit it."

"My father was different," she murmured. "But he was the only one. And what good did it do him? My mother knew how he felt, and she didn't care. She took advantage of it, cheated on him. When I was a little girl, she used to bring the others to the house. She didn't care if I knew, didn't care if I saw her. She didn't care about him, either. And when she met the man she wanted, she got a divorce. *She* got it, and made him pay. And now she cheats on my step-father. But that's all right. He'd do it to her. He tried to get me, once, before I left home. That's why I went away."

I could feel her mouth working and twisting against my chest.

"Don't," I said. "It's all right. I'm not like that. You'll see."

"That's what they all say," she told me. "Oh don't worry, I'm not blaming you. You're a man. I can understand how you feel. But how could my mother feel that way? Like a man, I mean, really wanting to—"

The warmth of the evening suddenly seeped away and I felt cold. Diana seemed to be changing before my very eyes. She was becoming strange, and a stranger, twisting, melting—like in a movie I had once seen about a wax museum where there was a fire and the wax statues softened and the features ran together into monstrous shapes ... I caught myself slipping into the Dream and forced my mind back to reality.

"But don't you want to?"

"No. I hate it." She sat up. "If you hadn't forced me—"

"Forced you?" I took a long drag on my cigarette. "What are you talking about?"

"You know what I'm talking about, Phil."

"No I don't. All I know is that I love you, and I thought you felt the same way about me, you acted as if you did."

"That's a lie."

She was on her feet now, and I rose, tossing the cigarette away, tossing everything away because this wasn't reasonable, it didn't make sense.

"Take your filthy hands off me!"

Now my hands were filthy. Why? I hadn't done anything to her, and yet she hated me. I could see it in the way her eyes blazed. They were blazing into mine now, because I had grabbed her. I held her close.

She tried to break loose and I caught her wrists. They were like ice. Her entire body was stiff, frozen. She *was* ice.

She was ice, and suddenly *I* was fire. I was fire, my mouth matching hers, my kisses like showers of sparks kindling a flame, my hands incendiary, my body burning, consuming hers in consummation.

Fire—anger—passion—makes you see red. Copper hair against the blanket, billowing and burning and blazing. And her body a white flame, turning to a shivering scarlet. The fire was igniting the ice and that was crazy because ice doesn't burn.

But then it was all crazy, the way she turned red, the way everything turned red. It was all crazy, but it was *real*.

For I had lifted my head and I was seeing fire. Real fire, real flames. The brush was burning! The brush, where I'd tossed my cigarette—

Then I was rising and she was rising, and she stared at me and then at the blaze. Her eyes were open and her mouth was open, too, and the scream came from her eyes as well as from her throat.

The flames were like dancing devils, climbing up the slope. She turned and ran down the beach, then clambered along the bank. I stood there, trying to move, calling, "Diana! Come back—wait!"

She didn't come back and she didn't wait. I beat at the brush with the blanket, showered sand on the sparks and then stamped and trampled and crushed the burning branches with my frantic feet.

Then the fire was out. The fire was out, and she was gone.

I climbed the bluff, panting, too winded to call. It wouldn't have been any use. When I got to the top of the slope, where the car was, she had disappeared.

I gunned the engine, wheeled down the road. I thought maybe I'd catch up to her, but I didn't. She hadn't come this way. Then I found a path and turned around—went back in the other direction. It was only a few blocks to the main highway. I didn't see her anywhere along the route. She must have hitched a ride right away. Thumbed her way out of my life.

All at once I didn't care any more. Let her go. Diana Rideaux, with her twisted ideas about men and love. Just as well I'd found out when I did. You can't live with a person whose mind works like that. Full of crazy impulses, crazy notions.

But what about me, tossing that cigarette? Did I know what I was doing, subconsciously? Was I acting on a crazy impulse, a crazy notion? You can't live with a person whose mind works like that.

How was I going to live with myself?

I put the thought aside, lighted another cigarette. I didn't really want to smoke, but I forced myself to, just to prove something. To prove that it was all my imagination, to prove that it could happen to anyone. Brushfires start every day. Careless smokers, dropping matches and butts. Did they go around accusing themselves of being pyromaniacs because of an accident like that?

Driving along, I began to feel better. I felt good enough to switch on the car radio. The music was calming, soothing. At least, that's how it began. Then it began to shriek and blare and scream. And as it did so, I recognized it—recognized it, and nearly ripped the knob from the panel trying to shut it off.

Why, of all things, did they have to be playing *The Ritual Fire Dance*?

Six

HE WAS STANDING in front of the apartment when I drove up that evening, and at first I thought he was a clown—his face was so white, his eyes were so black, his lips were so red. Then, when I parked, crossed the street, and passed him under the light, I realized that the little man was no buffoon. The masks of Comedy and Tragedy are strangely alike. This man's face was unnaturally pallid, his eyes deep-set and circled with the straining stain of fatigue. His lips were red because he'd bitten them.

I stared at him as I prepared to open the hall door, and he stared back.

"Looking for someone?" I asked.

"Just waiting, Brother."

I went inside, walked up to my door. Then I finally came to—came up out of the fog of fancy and fire and fear long enough to realize what he had said. "*Brother.*" The little man was a cultist.

The key was already in the door, but I yanked it out. I turned and went down the stairs, out the door.

But the front walk was deserted now. The stranger with the bleeding lips was gone.

I looked down the street in both directions. No one was in sight. He'd vanished, God knows where or why. And what had he been waiting for?

Up the stairs, two at a time. I got the key out, opened the door, switched on the light. Then I breathed a bit easier.

Whoever he was, whatever he was, he hadn't been here. My place was undisturbed.

My place was undisturbed, but I wasn't.

There was too much I didn't understand. A fire, and then another fire. A girl who feared me, and another who feared me, too—myself.

And now, the little man with the pale face, who was just waiting outside my apartment. Of course, it could be a coincidence. Those things happen. The long arm of coincidence might have placed him there.

But the long arm of coincidence ended in a claw, and I felt it clutching at my throat. The Tabernacle had gone up in flames and the general idea seemed to be that it hadn't been that dry a summer for it to have gone up all on its own. Somebody had lit it; somebody had lent Amos Peabody a helping hand to his Final Reward—which I'm sure Amos would have willingly passed up right at this juncture. And I was something more than just an innocent bystander. One, I had been on the scene. And two, I was doing a series of articles on the cults. Maybe somebody didn't like the idea. Maybe right at that very moment somebody was mentally thinking of me as a chicken on a spit.

It wasn't very funny. When I fry bacon, the hot grease always spatters me. I used to do that trick of lighting wooden matches with my thumbnail but the burning matchhead would invariably scorch my hand. And when I smoke cigarettes, the lit tip frequently falls off and burns a hole in my pants.

I've got a grudge against life, I thought shakily. *I get burned up all too easily* ... And that thought was anything but hilarious, too.

I went to the telephone and dialed Schwarm. I needed him now, needed him at once. Sure, it was late, but Schwarm would come. I could talk to him, reason things out. He'd know. Schwarm always knew.

Dr. Milton Schwarm. They called him a psychiatrist, and he was good enough to be consultant for the police department on occasion. But I didn't think of him as a head-shrinker. For six months now he'd been my friend. He knew something about my problems, but I hadn't been able really to tell him everything. Hadn't wanted to, because he was my friend; I hated to change that for a professional relationship.

Right now, though, I was willing. More than willing. As I sat there, listening to the buzzing, I was eager.

Then the voice came.

"Hello," I said. "This is Phil Dempster. Is Doctor Schwarm there, please?"

"I'm sorry, Mr. Dempster. He's out of he city."

"Oh. When will he be back?"

"Friday evening, I believe."

"Thank you." I cradled the phone.

He'd be back Friday evening and this was only Wednesday. Two days. So much could happen before then.

But nothing was going to happen. I was just edgy, from not drinking. That's what comes when you lay off the fire-water.

Fire-water. Did I really think of it in that way?

Schwarm would know. I could tell him and he could tell me. But now now. Friday evening.

Now I had to sleep. And tomorrow there was a job to do. The Church of the Golden Atom. Professor Ricardi.

I dragged myself over to the couch, dragged out the notebook, and read about Professor Ricardi and his Golden Atoms. It was hard going, because I kept looking over my shoulder, kept jerking upright whenever I heard a noise from outside.

Eventually, though, I dozed off. Dozed off right there on the couch. When I woke up the sun was shining. Wednesday night had passed.

Curiously enough, I felt better. A shave and a shower helped still more. By the time I finished breakfast I was completely alert and ready to go to work.

I went to work.

Research is a slow business, but rewarding. I knocked off about five, after completing my rounds. My last stop was the *Globe* morgue, where I'd been digging through newspaper files on Professor Ricardi. I stopped in to see Ed Cronin, but he'd left, so I ate dinner alone.

This time I ate in a restaurant. Tonight wasn't going to be a repetition of Tuesday evening. I drove out to Grace Boulevard in plenty of time, and parked right in front of the Church of the Golden Atom.

This was no converted meeting-hall. A trim, modern brick building in a substantial residential neighborhood, with a blazing yellow neon sign projecting from one corner: CHURCH OF THE GOLDEN ATOM.

Respectable, I thought. You couldn't have told it from some of the other churches in the neighborhood. They probably had dances and Bingo on Saturday nights and a young people's club and were charter members of the neighborhood business association.

Something about the sight of the sign made me hesitate. It was so bright. I didn't want to walk under it, and then I knew why, and I told myself *the sign blazes, but the building won't burn.*

After that I could go inside.

The outer hall was already crowded. They were all here tonight—the middle-aged widows in the clutches of the climacteric, the pale young men who avoided your eyes, the man with the shaggy eyebrows who kept mumbling to himself or an invisible companion, the girl with the goiter, the old woman with the bright orange hair. I recognized the types. The comfortable middle-class, when it begins to crack up around the edges and lose its faith in the usual faiths. Salvation begins to mean more and more to them, and they don't want to wait for it after death—they want it now.

And there were others I took special pains to observe; others *with* special pains. The lame, the halt and the blind. Canes tapped, crutches clumped, wheelchairs rolled.

I passed a table bearing books and literature. THE GOLDEN KEY was the title stamped on the bright blue binding of the book. The magazine was called ATOMIC SCIENCE, and the smaller tracts were no less imposing in their headings.

A fat woman sat behind the table, breathing benevolence and Sen-Sen. At her right was a tin box, and at her left, a half-filled bottle of Coke.

"Can I help you?" she asked.

I nodded and passed on. Another table loomed ahead. This layout was presided over by an elderly gentleman who wore a hearing aid. A gaudy chart stood propped before him, and next to it was a pyramid of 5-ounce jars, each bearing a gold label reading VITAL CREAM. Marching down the side of the table were smaller glass containers. The gold label on these identified them as ATOMIC ENERGY CAPSULES.

"Yes sir?" said the elderly man.

I hesitated for a moment, then fished in my pocket. "Better give me one of each," I said. "How much?"

"That'll be six dollars for the cream and five for the capsules," he told me.

I said something under my breath which I hoped his hearing aid wouldn't pick up. But I gave him the money. It would be worthwhile to get this stuff analyzed by a pharmaceutical chemist.

Then, on second thought, I went back and bought a copy of THE GOLDEN KEY for five dollars and two issues of ATOMIC SCIENCE at fifty cents each.

Seventeen dollars for research, so far. Not a bad deal for Professor Ricardi.

No, Professor Ricardi did all right. I found that out when I went inside. His church setup was conventional enough—rows of pews on either side of a center aisle, leading down to the rostrum and the altar. The usual organ was being manned by the usual organist, who played the usual music.

Behind the altar was the banner; a huge, golden sun emitting a corona of gilt-and-rhinestone sparks. In front of the altar, a moment after I entered, was the eminent Professor Ricardi himself.

He glittered.

His robe was golden, and so was his hair, and his beard, and the rings on his long, slim fingers that rose to invoke a benediction upon the congregation.

His voice was golden, too. And it was of gold that he spoke. Not the crass, coarse gold of material riches, but the true gold of the Spirit. Nature's gold. Here was a treasure without end, lavished upon us all, by the Primal Atom which was Being.

All Life springs from the Atom. The Atom is the source of creation, the father of us all. What is the biblical "Adam" but a misreading of "Atom"?

The Earth was born from the atomic energy of the sun. The sun—the Prime Atom—is the source of all Life. Solar energy rules the Earth, and from it we can tap untold blessings if we possess the key.

Yet woe unto those wicked ones who deny the truth, who seek to harness the Atom to their own evil ends! Those who tamper with Prime Matter, who divide the Atom and release its Essence are cursed—they will bring down doom and destruction upon themselves.

They had best turn to the Church before it was too late; learn the Truth as set forth in ATOMIC SCIENCE and THE GOLDEN KEY. There all can find eternal Youth, eternal Health, eternal Life—yes, and riches and power too, for those who desire such trifles.

As for Professor Ricardi, he was above these petty needs. His years of labor as a Cosmic Scientist in the secret laboratories of Tibet had borne sufficient reward when he discovered the shining truth of what he sought.

For forty years he had journeyed through the Wilderness of Error before he found the Way. Then a few chance words let slip to jealous fellow-scientists had resulted in their discovery of the Truth, and their misuse of it to produce the Atomic Bomb.

Now, with such power in the hands of the forces of Evil, Professor Ricardi had determined to step forward and lead the world to the Truth. Time was short, and it would be a close race between Destruction and Construction. But he was ready.

Professor Ricardi had dedicated his eternal existence to delivering the message of the Golden Atom, to dispensing Nature's Own Source of Life—pure sunlight—in the form of ATOMIC CAPSULES and VITAMIN CREAM. These scientifically prepared aids to immortality were augmented by the Inner Light of Truth shining in the pages of THE GOLDEN KEY.

So said Professor Ricardi, for almost an hour. From time to time his pronouncements were punctuated and accented by the organ.

And then the light dimmed, and he offered up a prayer to the Atomic Power Who Rules All Being, and the choir rose and chanted.

The Power descended on Ricardi, haloing his golden head. And he raised his hands to draw unto himself all those who believed, who could feel the Atomic Energy flowing from him into their bodies to heal and to save. He called upon them to surrender to the Power, to let the injured atoms rearrange themselves in perfect harmony.

It was the ultimate in phoniness. The cheap pitch was as obvious as the peroxide rinse on his hair and beard. The organ came in like a soap-opera cue, and the halo was a spotlight operated by a union electrician.

But Professor Ricardi held out his hands, and they came. They came to the altar, creeping and crawling and tottering.

All eyes were on the altar, now, as Professor Ricardi prayed over the afflicted. They were filing past him one by one. He held their hands, gazed into their eyes, and prayed. The crowd watched—and I watched the crowd.

There was a fat man sitting on my left. He stared at the altar, twisting the brim of his hat as he watched. On my right, a girl began to sob convulsively. Professor Ricardi had them now, held them in the palm of his hand.

The hand went out, touching an old man's forehead. He stood there, head bowed for a moment. Then the head jerked upright and the man straightened—straightened, and let his crutches clatter to the floor.

From either side of me came gasps and moans.

Now Ricardi bent over a woman in a wheelchair. Again he pressed his fingers against her temples. Suddenly the woman shrieked and rose from the chair. She rose and walked, and the crowd made an ancient sound.

Ricardi stepped back, smiling and shaken, as the tumult rose. Then the organ came up suddenly, the lights were on, and a gray-haired acolyte was on the platform, pleading for a Free-Will Offering. Ushers ran down the aisles.

The fat man on my left reached into his pocket and came up with a ten-dollar bill. The girl on my right fished three dollars and some change from her purse. The room resounded with the clink of coins, the tonguing tumult of those who had been privileged to witness wonders.

I'd seen enough. I rose and tried to move down the aisle toward the platform, toward the man who'd tossed aside his crutches and the woman who rose from her wheelchair to walk again.

But the crowd milled and blocked my way, breathing and babbling all around me. I fought through phrases, brushed past bodies, edged excitement at every step.

And when I reached the platform, both the man and the woman were gone. Ricardi had disappeared, too. I tried to catch the eye of the gray-haired acolyte, but he was surrounded by ushers. They were emptying their collections into a tin box.

I turned to retrace my steps up the aisle. Maybe they'd slipped out a side entrance. I might still overtake them if I got out in time.

The crowd barred my path but I pushed on. Pushed on to the edge of the lobby, where yet other groups clustered around the tables, buying THE GOLDEN KEY and ATOMIC ENERGY CAPSULES. I kept searching for a sight of the three faces I sought.

I caught a glimpse of a back bobbing in the doorway ahead. Somebody was standing there, and even at a distance I knew that I was being surveyed. As I stared, the short man turned to face me fully, and I recognized him. For an instant I saw the white face, the black eyes, the red lips of the clown. Then he disappeared in the street beyond.

He'd been here tonight, watching me. *Why?*

Ricardi and the others could wait. I had to find out about this, first.

Slowly I burrowed my way through the lobby, fighting toward the freedom of the doorway beyond.

Just as I reached it, the hand came out and tugged at my shoulder.

"Phil—wait a minute!"

I turned and gazed into the smiling moon-face of Doctor Milton Schwarm.

SEVEN

WE SAT OVER COFFEE in the restaurant down the street.

"But they told me you were out of town," I said. "I never expected to run into you here—and on the same errand."

Schwarm shook his head. "It isn't the same. You're out after a newspaper feature. Mine is a clinical investigation. As I told you, one of my patients was formerly a member of the Golden Atom sect. I wanted to get a line on the organization for that reason. And on this Professor Ricardi. These so-called cures are an interesting phenomenon. If I could find a reasonable excuse, I'd like to interview the man and the woman we saw tonight. Perfectly classical examples of hysterical—"

"Wrong," I interrupted. "They were plants. Fakes, I'm sure of it. Just as sure as I know Professor Ricardi isn't a Professor."

"What makes you so certain?"

I pulled out the notebook. "I didn't walk in there cold. Did some snooping around first. You want to know what I found out?"

"If it's not confidential."

"You'll see most of it in the *Globe* a week from Sunday. Might as well get the facts now."

"Go ahead." Schwarm leaned back and picked up his coffee-cup.

I scanned my jottings. "Your friend Professor Ricardi has a very conventional history. His real name is Joseph Edward Clutt. Born in

Spokane, in 1929. Father was a plumber. Joe was an apprentice until he ran away with a medicine show.

"He came to town here in 1951, and was rejected by the draft because of narcotics addiction. In 1956 he was named corespondent in a divorce action brought against Mrs. Agatha Loodens by her husband, Frederick. Apparently he had offered her more than the usual plumbing services."

Schwarm put his cup down. "You mean he was still a plumber in 1956? What about those trips to the Orient and Tibet?"

I grinned. "The nearest Joe Clutt ever came to the Orient was an opium pad in 'Frisco."

"Go ahead," Schwarm said. "This is interesting. I've always wondered how a cult was born."

"Simple. Shortly after the divorce, Mrs. Loodens' former husband passed away. He left her a small pharmaceutical supply business. It had government contracts during the Korean war, but it was in bad shape by '58.

"Her lover, Joe Clutt, took over. It was he who continued the manufacture of what has since become ATOMIC ENERGY CAPSULES and VITAL CREAM. The idea of the cult came from there."

"You mean this plumber dreamed up the whole procedure in order to sell his product?"

"Not quite. There's a third party involved. Their business attorney, a man named Weatherbee. I'm pretty certain the basic notion came from him. He could easily have written THE GOLDEN KEY and coached Joe Clutt in his new role. Clutt had a medicine-show and carnival background, remember, and no doubt he possessed a certain amount of personal magnetism. At least the late Mr. Loodens thought so.

"But Weatherbee and Mrs. Loodens are the brains. They got him to dye his hair, change his name, taught him the catch-phrases, and invested money in printing up the books and packaging the merchandise.

"They opened headquarters, and probably used their social and business connections to spread the word and attract the early converts. And the racket caught on. They're making a fortune in daily lessons, private courses, personality-readings. The books are going out by mail-order as well as through the Church itself. The pills and the cream sell that way too. And by far the biggest percentage of profit must come from the contributions and the Free-Will Offerings. I understand they plan to open a branch in Chicago soon."

"You wouldn't believe people would be so gullible," Schwarm murmured. "A personal observation," he hastened. "Not a professional one."

I snorted. "They don't believe it because they've been convinced of anything—cultists believe because they want to believe. Five years ago I went to a pseudo-seance and I've never forgotten it. There must have been a couple of hundred cultists present in the hall. A lot of middle-aged people but a lot of young ones, too—teenagers and married couples who'd lugged their kids along. The medium was a skinny little guy about fifty who needed a clean shirt and a shave and a bath. His wife was a fat, frowzy old witch who sold tickets and booklets and did the opening spiel about how her husband would go into a trance and communicate with the Great One in the Beyond.

"On cue the little guy closed his eyes, worked up a sweat, then started spouting gibberish in a high, sing-song voice. I recognized a few words of Spanish and I suspect most of the rest of it was Chinese. His wife 'translated' on how the Great One was pleased to be called from Beyond the Veil and gave a few predictions as to what was coming in the future and then gave stereotyped answers to stereotyped questions from the audience. The act wouldn't have fooled a ten-year-old but the people there were literally on the edges of their seats. During the intermission a friend of mine made snide remarks and we were nearly mobbed. The light of truth isn't exactly what these people are looking for."

Schwarm lit a cigarette. "But how do they get away with it?" he asked. "What about the authorities? Don't they know this man isn't a professor, that he's running a phoney religious racket?"

"Please," I said. "You're supposed to be a psychiatrist. *Naivet)* doesn't become you. Clutt is Ricardi—his change of name was legalized three years ago. He is also a professor, and if he wanted to he could call himself a doctor, too. Anybody can get a degree in metaphysics if he's will to pay the dough to one of the mail-order schools. And your use of the term 'phoney religious racket' is open to question. You know all sects and cults are tolerated, providing their leaders don't indulge in fortune-telling." I shrugged. "However, my article may get a few people to thinking."

"Perhaps." Schwarm put his cigarette down. I couldn't help but watch. I was watching everything that burned these days. "But since when have you had this sudden interest in crusading? I thought you were writing another book."

"I put it aside for a few weeks. It went stale on me."

"What seemed to be the trouble?"

He asked the question casually, but I knew Schwarm well enough to realize he was serious. Here was my opportunity to tell him—tell him everything. About Diana, and the fire at the White Brotherhood tabernacle, and my drinking before that fire, and the reasons for my drinking. But there would be no backing out if I got that far. Behind the fire was the drinking and behind the drinking was the dream, and behind the dream was something I couldn't talk about.

I *wanted* to, but I *couldn't*. Because of what he might say. He was a psychiatrist, and he'd be able to tell me what was wrong, and I was afraid of hearing it.

So I just shook my head and said, "Guess I ran out of ideas. Too much introspection. This little assignment gives me a chance to get out, get away from myself for a while."

"Get away from yourself, eh?"

"Please." I smiled at him. "No bedside manner."

"Sorry. But you know, Phil, anytime you feel that you have a problem you'd like to talk over—"

"Sure," I said. "I know. And thanks." I glanced at my watch. "Got to run along now. It's late. Can I drop you off?"

"No, I've got my car." He stood up, stubbing out his cigarette in the ashtray. A few sparks still smoldered. I glanced around the restaurant. Suppose one of those sparks blew out of the ashtray and lodged against the drapes there on the wall? If the drapes caught fire they'd burn quickly, and the walls were wood, they would burn, and the whole place could go up in flames—

Schwarm walked down the aisle and I quickly extinguished the smoldering butt. It was foolish, but I couldn't help it. Suppose he saw me? What could I say, "I'm a Boy Scout and this is Fire Prevention Week"?

But he didn't see me, nobody saw me, and everything was all right. Schwarm paid for my coffee, we went outside, and said goodbye on the street.

"Call me for lunch one of these days," he said. "Let's have a visit."

"Will do."

I watched him as he climbed into his car and drove away. Then I turned and started down the block toward my own parking place.

It was dark in the middle of the block here on the side street, but not too dark to make out the figure that leaned against the side of the car. And even in the dimness I saw and recognized that white face—the clown-face.

He stood up when he saw me.

"I've been waiting, Brother," he said.

"Yes. So I see."

"I wanted to make sure you were alone." he peered up at me, teeth protruding over the bitten lips. "You *are* alone, aren't you?"

I nodded. I was alone, and didn't like it. Alone on a dark side street with a fanatic who had waited for me.

"That is good. Otherwise I would not take you. I had to be sure."

"Sure of what?" *Sure that I was alone so he could kill me?*

He was standing quite close, and suddenly his hand came out of his coat. It didn't come out alone. I caught the gleam of the knifeblade, and before I could move the point pressed in my side.

"Be very still," he murmured. "I must make doubly certain." His right hand held the knife against me. His left hand went to my coat, opened it. His cold fingers crawled across my chest, unbuttoning my shirt.

My hands went up, and the knife dug in. "Don't try that," he whispered. "I will not harm you, I seek a sign."

Crazier than hell. This was crazier than hell, he was crazier than hell, I was—

His icy fingers raised gooseflesh on my breast as he lifted my T-shirt. For a moment he peered down at my chest. His hand pressed it.

"Good," he said. "It is as I hoped. You are not one of them. There is no mark."

"What mark?"

"The mark of the Beast. The mark of the Evil One. You are not one of them after all. You are pure. So you will help me." His hand left me. I buttoned my shirt and coat.

"Help you how? Who are you, anyway?"

"I am the one chosen. Chosen for vengeance."

What do you say when you hear a thing like that? You can't come out with, "Make sense"—not when the sharp edge of a knife is still within slicing distance of your stomach. I stared down into the white clown-face and waited.

"You will help me," he repeated. "Come." He nudged me in the direction of the car. "Get in, I'll tell you how to go."

"Where are we going?" I asked—but I got in the car while I spoke, because the knife nudged.

"To issue warning."

"The police?"

"They are enemies. You know that, surely. They hate the Brotherhood."

"Brotherhood? Are you from the White Brotherhood? Is that where you're taking me?"

"The Brotherhood has ended in the Fire of Wrath. You know that. And the Fire of Wrath will consume all before it unless others are warned in time."

Little clown-face with the knife, whispering to me in the darkness. I shuddered, moving away across the front seat. His eyes and his knife followed me.

"We must go now. Hurry. It's 1902 Benson Street."

The address meant nothing to me—Benson Street was way on the other end of town, in the suburbs.

"Who's there?"

"The one we warn. Quickly, now."

I drove. I drove, hoping we'd pass a squad car so that I could be picked up for speeding. I drove, hoping for a break, a blowout, a freak accident, anything.

But there was no hope. There was only the darkness of the streets, the darkness beside me, and the little man with the big knife. I drove him, but he was driving me. Driving me into darkness and—?

"Faster," he murmured. "We may be too late. The Fire of Wrath moves swiftly to consume the world, for the Day of Doom is at hand—"

"Fire," I said. "You keep talking about fire. Did you burn down the Brotherhood tabernacle?"

The knife bit into my side, and the sweat poured out as I waited for his hand to move, waited for the car to strike a rut. I was an inch away from eternity—just a single, cold steel inch.

But the knife moved no further. "I will not kill you, Brother, because I understand. You do not know."

"Why don't you tell me, then?"

"You shall hear, in a few moments. When I tell *him*. I want you both to hear."

"Is that why you're taking me out to this place instead of going yourself?"

"Yes. If I went alone, he would not listen. He would say that I was loony. You know what 'loony' means, Brother?"

I was afraid to answer that one in any way. I drove silently, turning off Ammon Boulevard onto Benson Street.

The voice was strident in my ear, now. " 'Loony' means crazy. That's what it means, Brother. Crazy in the head. They used to say that about me when I was little. Before I joined the Brotherhood. The Reverend knew I wasn't loony, though, and he believed in the Voices. But some of the others still called me that. It makes me mad. It makes me feel like taking my knife and cutting out their tongues. Their tongues that lie and lie."

I sat there, silent and sweating, driving down Benson and watching the houses thinning out as we reached the hillside area of the suburb. Now we were climbing, and he was whispering. "But you'll know in a minute. And he'll know, too. Know that I'm not loony, that I'm telling the truth about the Fire of Wrath. He must know, because he's the next, the next on the list—"

The trees were thick on either side now, and the 1900 block was just around the next sharp turn. We made it. 1902 was the big house on the right-hand side, set back on the steep driveway.

I drove in. "Here we are," I said.

The house was dark and silent. As we climbed out of the car I fancied I could see a dim light burning on the second floor, through a rear window.

We went to the front door. "Whom do I ask for?" I muttered. "What do I say? Busting in on somebody at this hour of the night—"

"I'll do the talking," said the little man with the knife. "Just hurry."

I rang the bell. Waited. Rang again.

"You see?" I turned to him. "Nobody home. Or else they're sound asleep."

The little man pushed me aside. He began to hammer on the door with the butt of the knife.

"No use," I told him. I started to turn away. He reached for me.

"There must be," he said. "Look at the light."

I stepped back and gazed up at the window again. There was a light burning there, burning more brightly than before.

Burning *too* brightly—

I turned to him and saw that he already knew. He could see the flame, smell the smoke now.

"Down to the corner," I said. "Turn in an alarm."

"What are you going to do?"

"Got to get inside."

"Don't—it's too late—no use now. You'll be killed—"

Now it was his turn to tremble. I looked at the little clown-face and suddenly I wasn't afraid any more. Before there was time to think it over, I'd reached out and grabbed the knife.

"Where are you going with that?"

"I'll show you." No sense trying the door. I walked over to the French window off the porch facing the walk. I shattered the glass around the outside lock with the butt of the knife. The window gave.

A suffocating wave of mingled heat and smoke poured out.

"Hurry!" I yelled. "Get that alarm turned in."

Without waiting any longer, I stepped into the room. It was dark, and the smoke stung my eyes and nostrils. There was nothing I could do about my eyes, but I groped for a handkerchief to hold over my nose and mouth.

Then I moved across the room, following the wall. I almost tripped over a floor-lamp, and I bruised my knee against a sofa. But I reached the hall, felt for a light switch, then realized I wouldn't need it.

The hall was light enough, now. I could see the flickering flare from upstairs; it was like a beacon to guide me. Or to warn me.

The smoke was thick, acrid. The stench was sickening. And the fire was upstairs, I didn't want to go up there, I was afraid of fire—

But I went. I was afraid of fire, but I was more afraid of myself. I had to go. Maybe the answer was upstairs, maybe I'd learn the secret.

I took the stairs two at a time. As I rounded the curve, the stench and the smoke and the heat seemed to coalesce, forming an invisible hand; a big, hot hand that tried to push me back.

I half-turned on the stairway, choking and gasping. The hand was pushing me down, and I wanted to shrink away from it. But the blaze beckoned above. I faced the hand again, ducked, and slipped through the invisible fingers.

Then I was on the upper landing, and the smoke swirled all about me. The hall was black with it. The rug was smoldering in the hall, and there were little tongues of flame licking and nibbling and eating.

From the room at the end of the corridor came other tongues. And the smoke poured out in a choking cloud. I stumbled toward the open doorway. The heat was rising, and I could scarcely see. I stood there blinking, trying to look into the bedroom. A burst of smoke, a burst of flame, another burst of smoke—but I caught glimpses between: Glimpses of Inferno.

Somebody had set fire to the curtains. Somebody had set fire to the drapes. Somebody had torn the bedclothes off the bed and piled them in a great heap at the foot, to smolder and burn. They were cloth and gave off a suffocating odor, but they were burning more briskly now. In a moment or so the bed would catch fire—and somebody wanted that to happen.

Whoever had set the blaze and stripped the bedding had also left a single sheet for another purpose. This sheet had been torn to long shreds and used for tying the arms and legs of the man who lay on the bed—lay face down, head almost lost to view in the rising smoke.

He wasn't struggling, wasn't even moving now. I could understand why. That smoke was enough to asphyxiate anyone.

It had been planned this way. First, asphyxiation, and in a few moments now, incineration. The heat seared my hands and forehead. The wallpaper had curled and burned, and the fire ran along the floorboards.

I ran over to the bed, kicking the burning shag-rug aside. I bent down, took hold of the bound man's waist. No time to free his hands or feet. We had to get out of here, fast.

I lifted, hoisting him over my shoulder. He hung like a sack. A heavy sack, a heavy burden to carry back down through the smoke-shrouded hall, the smoldering stairway.

Coughing, wheezing, choking. Groping, staggering, almost falling. Panting, trembling, shuddering as a sudden flash of flame licked out from the window curtains halfway down the stairs and seared my temple.

I thought I could hear shouts and the sound of sirens, but there was no way of being sure—not with the crackling and murmur that followed me down the stairs.

The room was just ahead, and beyond it was the window, and beyond the window was air. That's what I needed. Fresh air, cool air, a chance to put my burden down, a chance to lay down for a moment myself; lay down where I'd be safe from the flames.

Just a few steps more, now. And now I could see beyond into the street. The engines were arriving. I tried to find the little clown-faced man, but he was gone.

It didn't matter. What mattered was that I was out at last, out in the open. I was safe. I could put him down now.

So I put him down. Put him down on his back, so I could see his face. Then I knew I wasn't safe any more, wasn't safe from the flames or what lurked behind them.

I was staring down at the face of Joseph Clutt, alias Professor Ricardi; the purple, strangulated countenance of the leader of the Golden Atom.

For a moment I stared, and then the face started to rush up toward me. No, it didn't rush up—I was going down. Going down into the fire and past the fire into darkness.

Eight

I THINK IT WAS PYTHAGORAS who put forth a theory about eternal recurrence—the idea that the same things happen over and over again.

I wonder what Pythagoras would have thought if he'd been sitting in that little room, looking out of the window and watching the sunrise.

Actually, I didn't really care what he'd think. I only wished that he, or somebody else, would be here instead of myself. Sitting here just two days after the first time, and listening to Captain Dalton say, "It looks bad. You have to admit that. It looks bad."

"I admit nothing," I answered. "I've told you all I know about it. Why don't you pick up the little white-faced guy? And Schwarm?"

"We're looking for your mysterious kook right now," Dalton replied. "And Doctor Schwarm is on his way over."

I hoped he'd get here quickly. I was tired of having that pipe point at me. Dalton managed to do it even when he glanced down and looked over his notes.

"You still insist you never had anything to do with Professor Ricardi," he said.

"I don't insist. I'm only telling you. I never saw the man until the meeting tonight."

"And this weirdo you claim you saw—"

"It's not a claim. I saw him, he was there, he stuck a knife in my ribs."

"All right." Dalton brushed his hand through his hair. "I'm going to talk to Ricardi's attorney now—this man Weatherbee. And Mrs. Loodens. Maybe they've got something to say that makes sense."

He left me sitting there wondering what they or anyone could say that would make sense. Oddly enough, though, I didn't feel too bad. Not then. Because I knew this was one fire I had nothing to do with—and I hadn't been afraid. Or had I? Even so, I'd gone in and tried to save Ricardi. I'd behaved normally, and that proved I *was* normal. Maybe.

But somebody was responsible. Somewhere there must be a firebug, a firebug; a tiger, tiger, burning bright—

What kind of creature had fastened itself on Ricardi, tied him down and left him to the flames?

I thought over possibilities. Diana Rideaux of course. But she was ice, not fire. And she'd been with me the first time, she'd been with me the second time at the beach when my cigarette kindled the brush. Then she ran away. Copper-colored moth that feared flames. Not the right sort of animal at all.

What about the clown-faced man? He could have started the first one, yes, but if so then why was he afraid of his "enemies"? Why did he want to "warn" Ricardi? Surely he couldn't have tied Ricardi up, set the fire, then come clear across town and found me, brought me back. The blaze hadn't been going that long. Besides, even for a kook, such activity was incredible.

Still, he seemed to know Ricardi was next. How could that be? And why did he connect *me* with all this?

Somewhere, somehow, there was a pattern. They'd have to find him, make him talk. He didn't actually commit arson, but he must know who did. Where there's smoke, there's—

Schwarm came in.

"Come on," he said. "Let's get out of here, Phil."

"You talked to Captain Dalton?"

"That's right. Told him you were with me. Everything's cleared up."

"The hell it is. Never saw a worse mess in my life. You know what happened?"

"Yes." He held the door open for me. "But we can talk about that later."

This time they'd brought my car downtown. I signed for it at the police garage. Schwarm waited for me.

"Can I drop you off somewhere?" I asked.

"At my office. Will you stop in for a minute?"

"I'm pretty tired."

"I know. But I thought we might talk this thing out. As a matter of fact, I promised Captain Dalton."

"You're on this case now?"

"Unofficially, yes. They call me in for consultation from time to time, as you know. Whenever something comes up which involves the suspicion of mental disorder."

"In other words, Dalton thinks I'm nuts. Is that it?"

"No. But—"

"You're a lousy psychiatrist," I said. "At least you might have figured out a way to humor me, kid me along."

Schwarm chuckled. "Maybe. Then again, perhaps I'm a pretty good man. At least, my apparently clumsy approach is working. I'm getting you to come up to my office on the strength of it, just because you resent the implication. Right?"

"You win," I said.

I drove him over to the Soames Building and parked in his parking space in the lot. It was still early morning, and his office was deserted. No receptionist; just the two of us, alone.

"Sit down and tell me all about it," Schwarm said. "Cigarette?"

"No, thanks." I had trouble speaking. My throat was dry with thirst and something else. Fear. "Is this official?" I asked.

"I'm going to make notes, yes. But I'll respect your confidences, Phil."

"Sure." I leaned back in my chair. "Where should I start?"

"At the beginning."

"You mean last night, or the other night? You heard how I turned in the alarm for the White Brotherhood fire, I suppose?"

He nodded. "Yes. If that's the beginning, start there. *You* know where to start."

I knew, but I didn't want to tell. I couldn't tell. Not about the beginning, or the dream. And if I told him about wandering around in a daze, he'd pounce on that. *Be careful,* I reminded myself. *You must be very careful.*

So I repeated what I'd given Dalton when I made my statement. The story of meeting Diana Rideaux, going home, returning to the tavern for my notes. Then I went on from there, telling him what had happened after they picked me up and let me go again. Before I could help it, I'd gotten into the part where I saw Diana again and we went to the beach.

It was too late to stop, now. I had to go through with it, even though I realized my mistake. I gave him the story of the cigarette butt and the brush fire.

I kept looking at him as I spoke, but his face told me nothing. He was taking notes, all right, and that was all. For a moment I thought of explaining how the brush fire was an accident, and then I caught myself in time. If I protested, it would just arouse his suspicion. So I went on from there, to last night. I told about the Church of the Golden Atom meeting just as if he hadn't seen me there—about the restaurant and my encounter with the little clown-faced man outside. About the drive, and the fire, and finding Ricardi's body.

"There it is," I said. "You're interviewing the wrong guy, you know that now, don't you? If we had this weirdo character here, he could tell you what you want to find out."

"Perhaps." Schwarm put down his pencil. "But we must be practical.

Your little friend isn't here, so we'll just have to work with what we've got."

"I can't tell you any more," I said. "You've had it."

"You've been very cooperative, Phil." He tapped the notes. "Your story is remarkably detailed. You have a good memory for facts."

"Got to, when you write for a living."

"But it occurs to me that you've omitted discussing one rather important angle in your story."

"What's that?"

"Nowhere in your account did you happen to mention just how you *felt* about these things. You didn't give me your reactions to all this."

"Why—" I shrugged. "I thought it was facts you were after. My feelings aren't important."

"Well, just for the sake of curiosity, then—suppose you tell me what went on in your mind during these past three days."

"I was scared," I said. "Scared as hell. Who wouldn't be? Turn in an alarm and they pick you up and accuse you of being a firebug. Then this little off-beat character started to trail me. That wasn't exactly a picnic, either. And this girl—the way she acted, you'd think I'd been trying to rape her. Right after that came the brush fire. That part really worried me."

"Why?"

I was in too deep to stop, now. "Because I wondered if it *was* an accident. I'm not entirely ignorant of your racket, you know. I've heard about the workings of the subconscious. When I tossed away that butt, I might have been acting on a concealed impulse to start a fire. In other words, seeing the first fire might have triggered me into deciding to set one myself. Maybe we're all potential pyromaniacs at heart."

"Is that what you think?"

"You're the doctor, you tell me."

Schwarm smiled. "Do you still feel that you might have had an impulse to fire the brush?"

"Not any more." I saw a way out, and I took it now. "Because of last night. I know I had nothing to do with Ricardi's death, and so do you. And when I went in to get him, I was just plain scared, again. Afraid of fire."

"But you went in."

"I had to."

"You could have waited for the fireman."

"A person doesn't think at a time like that," I answered. "The subconscious takes over."

"Then your subconscious dictated that you go into the burning building."

"Well—"

"And yet, consciously, you say you're afraid of fire."

"I—" Then I was on my feet. "No use, Doc. I can't explain it. I can't tell you any more."

"All right. I believe you. *You* can't. But perhaps this so-called subconscious of yours can. Are you willing to try?"

I had to nod. But I was beginning to sweat, now. "What are you going to do, hypnotize me? You want me to take one of those truth drugs?"

Schwarm smiled. "Let's not be melodramatic, Phil. I don't use such methods in ordinary procedure. And while we're at it, I might as well add to your education. This 'subconscious' of yours is a rather outmoded concept. In my opinion, there is no area or entity, physical or psychic, which can be identified as a 'subconscious mind.' There is only a consciousness which receives and identifies all data. Some of this data is unpleasant. It is repressed, or even suppressed. But it has been received, and it's there; available in one form or another. Sometimes as fantasy, sometimes as symbolism—yet always it remains present and available for communication even in a distorted form. The fantasy content is a clue to the reality. The mind *tries* to communicate. Do you follow me?"

"Not completely."

"You will."

He went over to the files, came back with a bulky folder.

"What's that?"

"The method I use to discover clues. You've probably heard of it. The Rorschach test. Inkblot cards. You look them over, tell me what the blots suggest. Nothing to it."

He was right. There was nothing to it. I gazed at the cards as he flashed them in turn, and he recorded my reactions. Some of the cards were red, some were red and orange, some red and orange and blue and green.

We went over them once in sequence. Then again, in a different order. Then a third time, in sequence. He asked for comments. I gave them. I didn't try to evade or avoid what came up.

Schwarm made notes. He put the cards away and sat back, reading. From time to time he came across a statement that prompted a question. I answered everything.

Finally he sat back and pushed the notes away.

"Well," I said. "What's the verdict? Am I a firebug?"

He smiled. "You answered that question yourself, a while back. Didn't you say you believed maybe we're all potential pyromaniacs at heart?"

"That was just talk, and you know it. I'm not even sure of what a real pyromaniac is."

"Neither am I. Let's discuss it for a moment. Perhaps we can find out something."

"Yes," I said. But I didn't want to discuss it, didn't want to find out—something.

I let him do the talking.

"First of all, let's think about fire. Fire is elemental, you know. The spark of life. The fire of the sun; heat, light, motion. We all recognize it, and it attracts us. That's why the color red is so important; the most primitive, the most exciting color—the first color perceived by an infant. Red is fire."

"It's also blood," I said.

"Correct. And blood is life, too, in the symbol-language we all use. So fire is blood and fire is life, and fire is something else as well. It's magic.

"You'll find the fire-magic in all the legends of all the cultures we know. The Parsees worship fire as prescribed by Zoroaster. Vesta and Agni were fire-deities. You've heard the old story of Prometheus, who stole the gift of fire from the gods—it's common in other religions as well as the Greek. Our own Bible is full of associations between fire and the supernatural. The story of Moses and the burning bush; the pillar of fire that guided the Israelites."

"Haloes," I added. "And the angels with the flaming swords."

"Right. And fire has always been used when dealing with the supernatural. Consider the altar fires, the fire kindled for sacrifice, the ritual of burning the heretic or the witch at the stake. And let's not forget the dominant concept of the fires of Hell. Even the medieval alchemists thought they could find the philosopher's stone in mercurial fire and water. Fire has always been mysterious—a source of life and creation, and a source of death and destruction. It's magic. Even a child recognizes that. When you set a fire you're creating a new world, and at the same time you're destroying an old one. Fire-setting is a simple act. I'd say that our statistics show seventy percent of all pyromaniacs have an intelligence below the accepted norm."

"Then you do know something about pyromania?"

"A little." He went over to the bookshelves, rummaged around, and returned with a volume which he opened and examined. "The American Psychiatric Association classification listing comes under Psychasthenia and Compulsive States (002-X21) with symptomatic manifestations, pyromania (902). Does that tell you anything?"

"No." I hesitated. "Except, from what you've told me, most firebugs are imbeciles or morons who have a compulsion to set fires. But why? And what about the thirty percent who have normal intelligence or above? Why would they start fires?"

"That's the question, isn't it?"

"Don't look at me," I said. "I haven't any ideas."

"Are you certain?" Schwarm opened his notebook. "What does the word 'fire' mean to you? What other words does it suggest? Let's see what you can associate with 'fire' now."

"Well—words and phrases, of course. Ball of fire. Fire-water. Hellfire. Creative fire. Spark of genius. You're fired. Playing with fire. Hot seat. You burn me up. Fight fire with fire. Better to marry than to burn. Hot number. Carrying the torch. Seeing red. Fires of love. Old flame. Hot mama. Heat of passion." I shrugged. "That enough?"

"Plenty. Now, let's examine what you've just told me. What do these phrases suggest to you?"

"Some of them refer to punishment, don't they? Hell and the hot sea. Getting angry. And most of them have a sexual meaning."

"Exactly. We all use these figures of speech in our daily vocabulary. But some people actually think in these terms, and for them the phrases have a very real connotation.

"It's not surprising to find that most firebugs begin their careers in their late adolescence. That's the period when sexual maladjustment may precipitate paranoid schizophrenia. Jealousy, rivalry, impotence or frigidity, perversion and fetishism may all play a part. Setting a fire seems to release a tension in such cases.

"Symbolically, you see, fire-setting is the sex act. It may be the substitute for incest or some other forbidden form of sexual experience. It is something feared yet desired. Some fire-setters feel they can control fires better than their own emotions. Others feel that fire is a more potent instrument than themselves. In either case, the release from tension is there—temporarily. But since it does not solve the basic situation, the act must be repeated. That's what makes your firebug."

"But if a person knows this, wouldn't he seek help?" I asked.

"That's just the point. Most pyromaniacs refuse to admit the truth, even to themselves. Some of them operate in an amnesic trance. Others hear voices that command them. They have the feeling that the fire was started by someone other than themselves. And they aren't concerned about the harm they do—they worry more over what the authorities think of them. Symbolically to destroy love, or loved ones, isn't wrong to them. Because all fire-setters are potential murderers, capable of acting on impulse when thwarted. I had one youngster in here with all of the classical symptoms: enuresis, cyclothymic traits. And the urethral sadism component. He used to bite the heads off his pet white mice."

"Charming," I said. "The part about the mice I understand. The rest sounds too complicated for me. Can't you put it into English, Doc?"

"Of course. Think of it this way. Most pyromaniacs come from a poor environment. There's a bad family situation—broken home, sexual promiscuity on the part of one or both parents. Your typical pyromaniac—although I hesitate to describe any case as 'typical'—is a compliant son who adores his mother but hates his step-father or any man she associates with, and suspects her of moral transgressions.

"He is afraid to rebel openly, however, so he runs away. Runs into alcohol, into an unfortunate early marriage. Often the situation is complicated by an unfortunate physical defect or blemish which makes a feeling of being rejected or unwanted doubly disturbing. Outwardly, of course, your firebug is a conformist.

"He never quarrels openly with authority. He appears to be gregarious, cooperative; but when a situation becomes intolerable, he runs away.

Runs away from mother, runs away from home, from the job, from the armed forces, from any adjustment with reality which seems unpleasant. And it's not his fault, he reasons. It's his father who punished him, who gave him his physical defect, who mistreated and deserted his mother, who violated her. He hates his father, but dares not openly defy him even in his own mind. So he runs away, runs away into fantasy where an evil voice—father, of course, in disguise—tells him to set the fire. Or gives him the feelings which he cannot openly satisfy, and for which he substitutes by arson."

"You head-shrinkers are always bring sex into it," I said.

Schwarm shook his head. "We don't *bring* anything. We merely try to find what is already there. And in pyromania the sexual parallel seems obvious. Tension—the urge for gratification becoming irresistible—then exaltation and release."

"Interesting," I said. "But where do I fit in? You gave me some tests, Doc. What's the verdict?"

Schwarm lighted another cigarette. "Supposing you tell me what you think."

I hesitated a moment. "I don't seem to fit the pattern very well, do I? My parents were happy together, and there was nothing disturbing in my childhood. I'm not an adolescent anymore, I have no physical handicap, I'm not too much of an outward conformist or inward rebel. And I don't get any of my kicks from lighting fires or turning in alarms; as I told you, fire frightens me. But what did the tests indicate?"

"Just what you told me. You're not a pyromaniac, though there's always a potential threat." He bent his head, then looked. "But there's a great preoccupation with fire. Almost a pyrophobia. And you've said a half-dozen times that fire frightens you. Why?"

"I don't know."

"Is there some incident, earlier, involving fire—?"

"I don't know."

"What about your dreams, Phil? Ever have any dreams about—?"

There was the sound of a door opening in the outer office. The Marines had landed. "You've got company, Doc," I said, standing up. "Maybe we can kick this around some more at another time."

"Good." He rose. "Phil, I think I could help you, if only you'd let me. And you could help yourself."

"Sure." I started for the door.

"Want to take the other way out?" He indicated a second door at the left. "I'm expecting some other people this morning. Dalton asked me to give them the same checkup."

"Good enough. Thanks for your time and trouble."

"You'll be home if—if anyone needs to get in touch with you?"

"I'm not planning to skip town, Doc," I told him. "So just tell your friend Dalton he needn't worry. I'm going to stick around for the—" I had my hand on the doorknob, and I felt like going out before saying that last word.

Schwarm said it for me. "Fireworks?"

"That's right." I grinned. "Pyromaniacs of the world—ignite!"

NINE

I GOT HOME ABOUT NINE and slept until half past three. A couple of times the dream started, but I always managed to wake up before it really got going. Then I'd doze off again. When I got up I felt better.

I was just finishing my shower when the phone rang. I dripped my way over to it.

"Hello?"

"Phil? Ed Cronin. Where the hell you been?"

"Read the papers."

"*You* read the papers! What's happening in this city, anyway? Send you out to get a couple of simple little feature yarns and you land right in the middle of the biggest local story we've hit in three years."

"*Phil Dempster, Star Reporter*," I said. "Did you call me up to tell me you want my autograph?"

"I want your copy," Cronin yelled. "Right now!"

"But the yarn's dead," I told him. "The fire killed it. Every time I go out and try to make an honest buck, somebody burns my bridges ahead of me."

"What do you mean, the yarn's dead? It's hotter than ever. You found Ricardi's body, didn't you? There's what we want. Never mind the cults. A *Globe* reporter, working on a special assignment, stumbles across—oh, you heard me. Read the paper!"

"You got a write-up?"

"Of course we have. Swiped your photo off the dust jacket of the book. Gave it a big play. Now we want a follow-up for tomorrow. Exclusive statement. How soon can you get me a thousand words? I want to put it on AP—"

"Look, Cronin, I've got to get busy and do one of those articles for you. If I can find a cult that doesn't burn up before I get to it."

"Never mind that stuff now. This is important."

"Twelve hundred bucks is more important to me."

"So we'll pay you the dough, articles or no articles. When do I get my thousand words?"

I looked at my watch. "You there until six?"

"Sure."

"I'll be down."

"Comb your hair. We'll take another picture."

"Anything you say. Want me to pose in a fire-helmet?"

"Shut up and go to work."

I shut up and went to work. I did him a thousand words on the Church of the Golden Atom. I worked in my little clown-face friend, and played him up as the key figure in the mystery. It wasn't hard to do, because I was telling the truth. *He* knew what was going on, and why. And I was just a stooge.

But why?

I couldn't answer that one, and I didn't try. I finished the yarn up, hopped in the car, and took it downtown. Cronin was waiting for me under the big clock in his office.

I threw the pages on his desk and pointed. "Fifteen minutes early," I said. "How's that for speed?

He grunted and tossed me a paper. "You read this while I read your stuff."

I did. It was quite a story. The way Cronin angled it, I—or the *Globe*, rather—was a hero. And I—meaning the *Globe* again—was going to solve the mysterious fire-deaths that were spreading terror throughout the city.

"Terror throughout the city." Big deal. But he wrote it like that, played it up big. Half of the front page was devoted to the fire. I saw my picture, Dalton's picture, Ricardi's picture. There was a big story on Ricardi, using much of the material I had in the notebook—apparently the reporter who dug up the original dope was working on the assignment.

I noted that an inquest would be held Saturday—tomorrow morning. And the police were looking for my little friend. Good. That meant Dalton had taken my report seriously after all.

In fact, everybody was taking this seriously. Perhaps Cronin hadn't exaggerated the terror angle. One of his snoops had been out rounding up comments from housewives who were buying locks at hardware stores, family men who were purchasing shotgun shells. The police were rounding up suspects, checking on every known or suspected arsonist in town. The heat—and I winced as I thought of it—was on.

"Good enough!" Cronin thwacked down the pages. "I'll just jazz this up a little and run it tomorrow. Come on upstairs now and get yourself mugged."

"You're really serious?"

"Damned right." We climbed the steps in the hall. "From now on, you stick to this yarn. Maybe you can pick up some leads tomorrow at the inquest. Maybe some of our boys will find something out. Whatever they get I'll pass along to you. The old man wants to play this story for all it's worth. And you're the logical byline for anything that breaks."

"Including my neck."

"You getting scared?"

"Not me. I already *got* scared last night. I wasn't fooling about this little loony, you know. He stuck a knife in my ribs."

"Think he set the fire?"

"Not this last one. He couldn't have. But he might have set the first. And he knows all about it. There's something going on, something connected with these cults."

"Your job is to find out about it."

"My job," I said, "is to stay alive."

Cronin stood silent as the photographer pushed me into a chair, seared me with his spots, and took three shots in rapid succession.

"That's it," he told me. I got up. Cronin put his arm around my shoulder.

"You can't let me down, Phil. Not when you're in this deep."

"Any deeper and I'll be in a grave."

"Nonsense. I'm not asking you to take any chances. Just keep your eyes open. If we can feed you a lead, follow it up. Routine stuff, really. But there may be a chance to hit the jackpot."

"I'll bet that will make Captain Dalton ever so happy," I said. "To know that one of his principal suspects has turned detective."

"Flush Captain Dalton," Cronin advised. "He's got nothing on you, Phil. Believe me, I made it my business to find out. Look, he's going to call you for the inquest tomorrow anyway. You'll have to be there. So why not earn yourself some quick money by sticking on the assignment? If nothing turns up, do us a Sunday story on this little guy. Go interview some doctors, find out about the pyromaniac bit."

I grinned. "That I've done already," I said.

"All right. Contact me right after the inquest tomorrow morning. I'll have two reps there anyway, but I want your slant."

"Will do."

I left him in the corridor and took the elevator down. It was time to eat.

The Dinner Gong was crowded, but I found a booth where I could eat alone. Only I wasn't alone. A copperhaired girl sat across from me, and next to her was a white-faced man with bleeding lips. Next to him was the golden countenance of Professor Ricardi, bit it wasn't golden any more—it was purple, mottled and inflamed. And as I stared at it, the face began to change, to melt into another charred and mutilated mask. I jerked my eyes away and now they rested on another occupant. Doctor Schwarm, I believe. Doctor Schwarm, who knew that anyone who has a morbid fear of fire may be a potential pyromaniac, who knew that sometimes a firebug doesn't remember what he's done. Alcohol sets him off, and then he wanders out in a daze, and when the flames rise he isn't sure of what happened. And if he dreams of fire, and there was an earlier time he won't talk about, then maybe—

I blinked until the thoughts went away, the faces vanished. Silly business. You couldn't get four people into the booth-seat across from me. Absolutely impossible. A lunatic, a neurotic girl, a dead cult-leader and a head-shrinker. What a combination! Why did I let it bother me? I was alone. *All alone.*

That thought didn't exactly cheer me up, either. I was all alone, but somewhere out there in the city was another. A man I'd never met, but who knew about me. He must know now, because he'd read the papers. He'd know I was dangerous to his plans, and he was clever enough to act.

Schwarm was probably right when he said that most firebugs were adolescent and subnormal. But these two crimes weren't the work of an adolescent. They weren't the work of a subnormal individual, either. Abnormal would be the proper term. Abnormal, and abnormally cunning. These fires had been set for a purpose. It wasn't arson, but murder.

Schwarm had told me that, too. "All firebugs are potential murderers."

And *this* one wasn't a potential but an *actual* killer. This man, who knew about me. Who might come after me, knowing I was all alone.

I couldn't finish my meal. I had to get out of there. When I started the car, I had to fight to keep it headed for home. Now was the time to run for it, to run away, far away.

Isn't that what Schwarm had said? Firebugs are weak, they run away from reality.

Well?

Was I or wasn't I?

The only way to find out would be to stick around. And I wanted to know. A part of me *had* to know. So I'd stick. But I'd be careful. I'd watch myself, make sure that Dalton and the cops knew my whereabouts. No more foolish chances, no more late evening prowls.

It was still twilight, and that helped. The streetlights came on with reassuring brilliance. Rows of mechanical candles to guide my way home. *Fire is dangerous, but it gives light, and light protects us from darkness. The Powers of Darkness. We fear fire but we fear the dark more. Why? Red is light, black is death.*

I turned the corner and parked, crossed the street. Then I saw it, looming before me in front of the entrance. It was a big car, and it was black. Jet black. Black as death.

Somebody was waiting for me.

Only a few hours had passed, and already, somebody was waiting. Waiting in a big black hearse.

I halted, hesitated. I tried to see into the car out of the corner of my eye, but couldn't. And I really didn't want to. Curiosity wasn't going to kill this cat. Sweat oozed across my forehead and I was suddenly acutely conscious that I knew more than anybody else did about the cults, that I had been the first man on the scene in two murders. Perhaps I had seen something I shouldn't have and had been too drunk the first time to realize what it was and too scared the second. But somebody else might not know that. Somebody else might assume I knew far more than I did, that my supposed knowledge and Captain Dalton's authority might be the perfect match ... match.

There was still time to turn around, walk back to my own car, get in, drive away. Chances are, I'd be followed. But at least I could get onto the main drag, head for the stationhouse. Dalton would protect me. It was worth a try.

I turned, took two steps.

Then the car door swung open, on the street side. And the voice reached me.

"Mr. Dempster! I want to see you."

The voice was low and musical. A woman's voice. I glanced over and saw the streetlight haloing blonde hair. "Please, Mr. Dempster. I must talk to you at once. I'm Agatha Loodens."

I turned and crossed the street again to meet Ricardi's mistress.

TEN

AGATHA LOODENS had leaned back on my sofa, holding a glass in her hand. It matched her outfit perfectly; the maize dress, the gold button earrings, the straight blonde hair gathered in a bun at the nape of her bare neck. Looking at the glass and then at her, I realized she had highball-colored hair.

"Comfortable?" I asked.

"Very." She smiled. Her teeth were very white and very regular. Everything was very about her.

"Then suppose you tell me what it is you wanted to see me about."

She laughed. Very musical laugh. "You're quite direct, Mr. Dempster. I had hope we might consider this in the nature of a social call."

"You mean a wake?" I said. "After all, Joe's dead—"

"Please." She wasn't laughing now. "I'd rather we didn't talk about that."

"I kind of thought that was what you came here to talk about."

"Not exactly." She leaned forward, setting her glass down on the coffee table which separated my chair from the sofa.

"But—you called him Joe. How did you know his real name?

"It's in the papers," I answered. "All of it."

She nodded. "Of course." Then she picked up her glass again. Before she drank she said, "Or almost all of it."

"Meaning."

"I was hoping you'd tell me."

I stood up and walked over to the dinette table where I mixed myself another drink. "This isn't a training camp," I said. "Do your sparring someplace else."

"That's rude."

"I'm a rude man. A rude man, and a tired one. I've had all the cross-examinations anybody could possibly need. Police, reporters, a psychiatrist—"

"Oh! Then you saw Dr. Schwarm too. Did he make you take that quaint little test of his?"

I nodded. "I took the quaint little test. In case you're interested, I passed with flying colors, too." I walked back, sat down, leaned forward. "Which means, Mrs. Loodens, that I'm not a firebug, if that's what you want to know."

"Why, I never even considered the possibility. You have a very suspicious mind, Mr. Dempster."

"Right. And while we're still on the subject, what about you? How did you score on the inkblots?"

She took another sip, a very delicate sip. "I didn't see any lamps or torches or burning brands, if that's what you mean. I'm afraid my reactions were purely—feminine. In fact, I think I may have shocked the doctor just a trifle." She smiled and stretched back. Her skirt crept a big higher on her leg. At another time I might have been interested. Chronologically, she could be a year or two older than I, but exceptionally well-preserved. Maybe she took ATOMIC ENERGY CAPSULES and used VITAL CREAM. Come to think of it, I was sure she did.

I forced myself back to the business at hand. "Now that we've had our medical report, what is it you wanted to ask me? Is it a deal you're after?"

"Perhaps." She leaned forward. "Did you ever meet Amos Peabody?"

"No."

"You know nothing about his outfit?"

"His religious organization?"

"I said 'outfit,' Mr. Dempster. Let's be frank—he was running a racket, the same as Joe."

"You admit it?"

"Why not?" Agatha Loodens adjusted an earring. "I wouldn't insult your intelligence by pretending otherwise. The Church of the Golden Atom was a nice little grift. In time, it might have become a nice big grift. But it's too late now, because of what happened. And that's why it interests me. What happened—and why."

I stared at her. "Suppose you ask your attorney, Mr. Weatherbee."

Her eyes narrowed. "What made you say that?"

"Seems natural he'd have a theory. After all, isn't he a partner?"

"He was, until last month." She sipped her drink. "Or do you already know that?"

"News to me."

"There was a dispute last month, about future plans. Mr. Weatherbee had some idea about combining with other outfits, with Joe as the leader. Joe couldn't see it. So Don pulled out and we went on alone."

I took her glass for a refill and talked over my shoulder. "Very interesting," I said. "Here you are, the three of you, coining money in a going, growing cult racket. And just because Weatherbee's plan is rejected, he pulls out. Gives up a nice, soft, steady source of income he's worked to build up for years. How idealistic!"

She almost yanked the glass out of my hand when I offered it to her. "Are you being sarcastic?"

"Very," I told her. "As the British are so fond of saying, I put it to you. I put it to you that your friend Joe—Professor Ricardi to his devoted followers—kicked Weatherbee out. I put it to you that he discovered Weatherbee had other ideas."

"What kind of ideas would those be?"

"The same ideas any man might get if he spent too much time around you."

"Really!" She laughed. "I've never been so complimentarily insulted in all my—"

"Never mind that. Is it true?"

Agatha Loodens sighed. "Yes. Don started to get ideas. And Joe threatened to beat him up."

I nodded. "And that was enough to scare Weatherbee away from a sure twenty or thirty thousand dollars a year? Please, Mrs. Loodens. I'm going to have to put it to you again. I think Joe had the goods on Weatherbee—something he wanted to keep hushed up—and threatened to spill it unless he got out."

She didn't answer. And that was answer enough for me. "Just what was this secret Weatherbee guarded so closely?"

"I don't know."

"Ricardi never told you, eh?" I moved closer to her, and Agatha Loodens stared at me. She had little gold flecks in the pupils of her eyes.

"I put it to you that Weatherbee's guilty secret concerned your late husband—perhaps the way he died."

She raised one hand to her mouth, and I knew I'd hit the jackpot.

"Weatherbee had something to do with your husband's death. You and Ricardi knew it. But you didn't care, because you were all profiting by it together. Until Weatherbee got ambitious and tried to move in on you. Ricardi threatened him and made him leave the setup."

I nodded to myself. "Now it makes sense. You came to me because you're wondering if Weatherbee could be behind these fires. You're wondering if he bumped off your boyfriend."

"Yes, it's true. That's the reason."

"*Did* Weatherbee murder your husband?"

"I don't know. I swear it, I don't know. Joe knew, but he wouldn't tell me. He didn't want me to get mixed up in it."

"And you never went to the police. You never wanted to because it might spoil your setup. I see."

"No you don't. The way you tell it, I sound like a criminal—suspecting a man of being involved in my husband's death, and not doing anything about it. But it wasn't that simple. Nothing's ever that simple. I loved Joe, and if I went to the police, what would they think about that? You know the answer. They'd try and make it appear as though I helped plan the killing. Weatherbee would see to that. He'll do anything to get what he wants, anything."

"He wanted you," I said. "So you think he arranged to murder Joe last night."

She nodded. "That's why I wanted to see you. To find out if there was anything more you might know about this. To see if Weatherbee had gotten to you, in case you did know, and threatened you so you'd keep silent."

"Supposing he had," I answered. "What did you plan on doing then?"

Agatha Loodens stood up. "I had my choice of two methods of persuasion," she told me. "The first was—this."

She opened her purse. Her hand dipped in delicately and emerged with a small revolver.

"Interesting method," I said. "And what about the other alternative? Would that be interesting, too?"

"You be the judge," she murmured. She took three steps forward around the coffee table, then leaned over me. I didn't have to raise my arms to pull her down. She melted into my lap, tossing her purse to the floor. Melted like molten lava. The heat poured from her body, fusing her mouth to mine.

I was to be the judge, eh? Well, court was now in session. I stared down into those gold-flecked, eyes, then stared past them to the floor.

The purse rested there where she'd dropped it—and from its open throat protruded a score of little tongues. Some red, some black, some white, some green.

I pushed her off my lap. "Excuse me," I said. "You dropped something." I stooped and picked up one of the tongues. "Book-matches, I believe." I picked up a handful and then another. "Didn't know you smoked."

"I don't smoke. I—I collect book-matches. It's a hobby. You've heard of that, haven't you?"

"I've heard of lots of hobbies."

She clung to my arm. "Please, it's the truth! You don't think I had anything to do with—"

The phone rang.

I straightened up. She was on her feet instantly. "Don't answer it!" she whispered, as if the phone itself could hear her.

I pushed her away. She watched me cross the room, pick up the telephone. She heard my voice, heard it with her ears, her eyes, her mouth, her very body intent and intense.

She watched as I put the phone down, walked back. And then her arms were around me again. "Who was it? Was it Weatherbee?"

"It was Captain Dalton."

"Anything—?"

"No. Just checking."

Her frightened breathing was replaced by a slower, more languorous inhalation. Her fingers began to trace a pattern on my shoulders. Her head came up. I stared straight into her golden eyes.

"Captain Dalton had a message for me," I murmured. "He told me to be a good little boy and go straight to bed. Because tomorrow morning I must be up bright and early. To attend your lover's inquest."

She jerked away, scooped up her purse.

"I'm glad to see you're taking his advice, too," I said. "And here's something else to remember."

Agatha Loodens opened the door so fast I didn't think she'd hear my parting words. But she did, because the door slammed shut behind her the moment I'd uttered them.

"Little girls like you," I said, "shouldn't play with matches."

Eleven

IT WASN'T UNTIL the next morning that I realized what a fool I'd been. Me and my big mouth. I should have kept that big mouth silent, left it where it belonged. It was having a pretty good time, as I remembered.

And if I'd gone on, perhaps I would have found out a lot of things. Some of them might have been very pleasant, and some of them might have been very unpleasant.

As it was, I knew nothing. Could Agatha Loodens have started those fires? Did she set the first one as a blind, to make it appear that somebody was out to destroy cults and cult leaders—so as to mislead suspicion when she killed Ricardi?

With Weatherbee out of the picture, and Ricardi dead, she was left in control of the Church of the Golden Atom. Not a razed structure, but perfectly intact. A nice setup.

But would she kill her lover?

Perhaps. She certainly hadn't behaved like one bereft last night.

Then again, with Ricardi gone, who'd front for the cult as leader?

She might plan on taking over that role herself, come to think of it. Or she could have another candidate, already chosen, in the background.

That was a possibility. Figure it as cold-blood arson, completely and ruthlessly motivated.

I thought about it while I shaved and fixed breakfast and made myself pretty for the inquest. I thought about a lot of things.

There was another angle to consider, too, where Mrs. Loodens was concerned. Those book-matches. Suppose she didn't have any particular plan, but merely a compulsion. A compulsion to start fires.

Whoever killed Ricardi had chosen a hideous method. If Agatha Loodens hated her lover, she'd certainly indicated it in the manner she used to destroy him. I wondered what kind of background and fantasies she had. What makes female firebugs burn?

Then again, according to her story, she feared this attorney, Don Weatherbee. Feared him, and suspected him of causing her husband's death. Maybe she'd told me the truth, or part of the truth. I reviewed my gallery of suspects, now. Agatha Loodens, Weatherbee, the clown-faced man or his associates in the White Brotherhood, plus that old familiar figure of song and story—person or persons unknown.

Unless Captain Dalton and his boys had been working overtime, I rather anticipated the inquest would pin the rap on the latter suspect.

And of course, I was right.

They'd arranged a rather unusual setting for the affair. Dalton sent one of his blue-uniformed chauffeurs to call for me, and I was surprised when we drew up in front of 1902 Benson Street. They were holding the inquest in Ricardi's home! The place smelled of smoke, but downstairs was intact.

Afterwards, I realized why. A man named Kleber had swung the deal—an investigator for the National Board of Fire Underwriters. Ricardi's place was covered by insurance. He seemed to have gone over the place thoroughly some time yesterday. When I came in, Dalton immediately took my arm and steered me over to Kleber. The tall, gray-haired investigator was pleasantly persistent. He asked me for a full account of the whole affair, and I told him what I knew. He'd gotten it all from Dalton, of course, but he wanted it again.

Later on he got it still a third time, when they put me up for testimony.

Quite an audience had assembled to listen to me. The fire marshal, several of his men, Dalton, a detective named Henderson, Ricardi's part-time housekeeper, and several more familiar faces.

The police and the jury sat on one side of the room. As I was examined by Finch, the coroner, I could see my friends sitting on the other side. There was Schwarm, of course, next to Doctor Oakes—he lived down the block, and he'd come over after I dragged Ricardi out and pronounced him dead. Next to Schwarm on the left was a short, squat, balding man in gray tweeds. I guessed he might be Don Weatherbee, and I guessed right—realized that when I caught him glaring at Agatha Loodens.

She was there, too, and glared right back. First at Weatherbee, and then at me.

Just one big happy family, if only the clown-faced man were here.

I wished for his presence very much, particularly when they called me and Finch asked his questions. The more I mentioned him in my story, the more worried I got—especially when I glanced over at the jury to see how they were taking it. No apparent reaction at all on those six stony faces.

For the first time I realized this occasion could be serious—these six dead-pan citizens had it within their power to indict me.

I told Finch all I knew. Schwarm smiled up at me, but all the other faces were cold, on both sides of the room. Captain Dalton and Kleber were whispering from time to time with another well-dressed man whom I vaguely recognized as the District Attorney. I didn't like that, either.

When I'd finished, I paid particular attention to the rest of the proceedings. They called Oakes, and he and the Coroner traded medical Latin for a few minutes, both gravely arriving at the conclusion that Joseph Clutt, *alias* Professor Ricardi, was legally dead and had legally died in an illegal conflagration.

The part-time housekeeper contributed her bit. She hadn't been in to clean for three days beforehand. There were questions about the disposition of rags and bedding, but nothing important.

Before I was called, several Golden Atom witnesses had established the fact that Ricardi had left the Church following the meeting the other night and driven off in his own car, alone. He had stated his intention of going straight home to bed—he thought he was catching cold. Apparently ATOMIC ENERGY CAPSULES did not contain antihistamine. But none of them had overheard or noticed anything suspicious. Ricardi got no messages, no phone calls; he wasn't agitated or upset.

So the story gradually took shape—with everything apparent but a coherent plot. Ricardi went home, I discovered his body, he was pronounced dead.

Now came the rest of the witnesses. Weatherbee, first. He had a deep, courtroom voice, out of Blackstone by Old Taylor, and a wonderfully professional way of using that voice to say absolutely nothing.

Yes, he had previously been affiliated with Professor Ricardi in a professional capacity. Their arrangement had terminated several months ago—he named the date. No disagreement; it was merely that the pressure of legal work prevented him from further fulfilling his obligations to the corporate Church. He absolutely denied having seen Professor Ricardi on the night of his death or at any time since the severance of their business relationship.

On the night of the fire he had been playing poker at the home of a friend. Captain Dalton's testimony would corroborate this.

The Coroner violated procedure and asked Dalton for confirmation. He got it.

Then Mrs. Loodens came on. She gave a good performance. This morning she appeared in black—trimmed with tears. It was all so dreadful, so very dreadful. She didn't know a thing about it. And to think she hadn't even been there at the Church on that last evening! She'd been home, with a *very* bad headache. And of course, she had witnesses. The maid, and then some friends who spoke to her over the telephone at about the time of the fire. Captain Dalton knew.

It appeared, when the Coroner turned to him again, that Captain Dalton did know.

Exit, Mrs. Loodens. I caught Weatherbee glaring at her as she took her seat again, and he noticed me. It may have been a trick of the light, but I thought for an instant that he winked.

Now Kleber was on the stand. Expert testimony, this. The fire was definitely not accidental. Whoever seized and bound Ricardi had also deliberately kindled the blaze. Whoever knocked him over the head—

I blinked. How had that escaped me? But come to think of it, that was the only possible way to account for Ricardi's being tied. Somebody had knocked him out, first.

I followed Kleber's story close now, cutting through the technicalities and listening to some of the questions he posed.

First of all, how did the murderer get in the house? All the doors and windows were locked when the firemen and police arrived—all except the French window which I claimed to have broken in my entrance. The jurors had toured the house.

If my testimony was valid—and I didn't relish the way he came down on the *if*—it meant one thing. Ricardi must have admitted his murderer himself, done so willingly. What followed is conjectural in the extreme. Was Ricardi slugged downstairs and his body carried up to the bedroom? Or did the assault occur there? No evidence one way or the other. But it might have a bearing on the matter.

More important, for the purposes of this hearing, was the indication of *haste*. Obviously the crime had been committed in a great hurry. In his opinion, the object was definitely not murder. The blow on the skull hadn't killed Ricardi. Anyone whose primary purpose was the death of Ricardi would have continued to batter in his head until he was dead.

No, the real motive was arson. The fire had been quickly improvised and deliberately so, beyond the shadow of a doubt. The house was fully covered by insurance—and the beneficiary was the corporation. Kleber would leave it to the jury regarding the matter of murder and possible suspects. But he wanted to emphasize that this was a clear-cut case of arson.

I saw what he was getting at, now. Arson meant intent to defraud—no insurance claim would be paid. Very neat. And I wasn't the only one who saw it, either. Agatha Loodens' eyes were wide. *She* was the corporation, of course, and we all knew it.

Then Schwarm took the stand. More expert testimony. I listened, wondering whether he'd say something to pin the rap on Mrs. Loodens. Or on me.

He did a beautiful job. First, the medical definition of pyromania. Then, a report of his examinations of Mrs. Loodens, Weatherbee, and myself. Plus—this was a surprise—the part-time housekeeper.

His considered opinion, as a qualified psychiatrist, was that none of us were pyromaniacal.

Kleber grinned. Clear case of arson, now. Or so he thought.

So he thought until Schwarm went on, speaking quietly and deliberately. He went over the same evidence Kleber had offered and turned it inside out.

He cited the usual motives for arson, then demolished them, one by one. If Weatherbee killed Ricardi for revenge, he certainly wouldn't have bungled the firesetting. In order to conceal the crime effectively, he had only to make use of materials at hand. There was plenty of oil in the basement, for example; he could have kindled a blaze that would spread swiftly and surely. Besides, that was his alibi.

As for Mrs. Loodens, her motive might have been to collect on the insurance. But she was wealthy in her own right, and the twenty-thousand-dollar payment to the corporation wouldn't materially increase her holdings. And even if she had acted out of jealousy or anger, she most certainly would have set a fire that was sure to blaze up. Also, she had an alibi, too.

In the matter of Philip Dempster—that was me, now—there was certainly no apparent suspicion of any motive. I didn't know Ricardi. I had nothing to profit from by his death. And the best substantiation for my statement was the fact that somebody had turned in an alarm. Since no one had showed up to admit it, the logical assumption was that my own statement was correct—the mysterious cultist had called the firemen and fled. Surely I wouldn't assault Ricardi, start a crude fire, then run out and summon the engines, run back inside, and bring Ricardi down. And Schwarm had been with me earlier in the evening, he knew I hadn't time to undertake such a mission. So I had an alibi, too.

No, this wasn't the work of an arsonist. This was a case of pyromania, in his opinion.

Everything Kleber had said pointed to it. The element of *haste* showed that the criminal had absolutely no premeditation. The fire itself was *improvised*, apparently on the spur of the moment. Nothing was planned—in all probability, the whole series of activities were spontaneous. It was Doctor Schwarm's view that the murderer was definitely a pyromaniac, and still at large.

That did it.

There was more testimony and discussion, of course, and Coroner Finch got in his nickel's worth. But the verdict was as fast as it was foregone.

Professor Ricardi had met death at the hands of a person or persons unknown.

Exit smiling. No applause, but some of us felt like it. Not Captain Dalton, of course, and not Mr. Kleber.

I nodded to the *Globe* reporters Cronin had sent down, and gave one of them a message for him—I'd have his story over this afternoon some time.

Then I jostled through the crowd looking for Schwarm. He was talking to Mrs. Loodens. As I approached, an arm reached out and clung.

"Mr. Dempster."

I turned. Weatherbee was at my side. "I wonder if I might have a word with you."

"Why—yes, I guess so."

"Let's get out of here, then. My car's right outside."

I allowed myself to be dragged away. Weatherbee and I went out together and climbed into his shiny new Lincoln. Very appropriate car for an attorney, come to think of it. Lincoln was a lawyer, too—but if he were alive today, I doubt if he'd have the kind of practice which would allow him to buy an automobile like this. It was heavy and slick. Like Weatherbee himself.

"Where to now?" I said.

"Thought we might have lunch together."

"I'm sorry. I've got to get a story out. Couldn't you drive me back to my place and talk on the way?"

"If you like." He gunned out into the street. "So you're covering this case for the *Globe*, eh? What do you think of the deal?"

"I think Schwarm's right. It's the work of a firebug."

"Does Mrs. Loodens think so too?"

"How would I know?"

"Didn't she tell you? She was up to your place last night."

I didn't answer. He grinned to himself. "Mind if I asked what she wanted?"

"I don't mind. She wanted the same thing you do—information."

"What'd she say about me?"

"She merely told about breaking up the partnership."

He chuckled again. "I'll bet she did." The car picked up speed and so did my heart. It occurred to me belatedly that Weatherbee was as much a suspect as anybody else. And I had delivered myself into his hands like a Christmas basket to a needy family. Once out in the forest preserves and I could be tomorrow morning's headlines. How did you jump out of a speeding car? Jam the door open and double up so you'd roll like a ball when you hit? Crank open the windows and holler for a cop? Or sit there, as I was doing, and drown in my sweat. Better to drown than to burn ...

"She think I killed Ricardi?"

I didn't answer.

"Good enough for me. But I didn't, boy. He had it coming to him, of course—only murder's not my business."

"What is your business, Mr. Weatherbee?" I asked. "Is it spying on Mrs. Loodens and me?"

No chuckle now. "That's kind of a harsh remark, Mr. Dempster. A fellow could resent a remark like that."

"I resent being cross-examined, too."

He sighed. "Minute ago you made a crack about what my business might be. I'll tell you, and you can make up your own mind if you want to keep it confidential or not. I'm in the cult business, Mr. Dempster."

"But I thought you and Ricardi split up?"

"That we did."

"Then—?

"Ricardi wasn't the only one running a cult in this town. There's the Wisdom outfit, and the New Kingdom gang, and the House of Truth, the White Brotherhood. Nobody knows it, but I happen to be the attorney for Dykes, of the House of Truth. And last month, after the split with Ricardi, I paid a little visit to Amos Peabody. He was quite a sharpie, that boy. I told him how I'd dragged Ricardi out of the gutter by the scruff of his neck and built the Golden Atom deal up. I told him I could do the same thing for the White Brotherhood. Take it out of the penny-ante evangelist class and really streamline his operation, put him in the big leagues. Make a long story short, I bought in on him. I owned fifty percent of the White Brotherhood Tabernacle. And somebody killed Peabody, burned the place down.

"Now do you see why I'm interested?"

I nodded. "I'm beginning to."

"Maybe you can see something else, Dempster. Two fires have been started. Two cult heads have died in them. What does that suggest?"

"Somebody wants to knock off cult leaders."

"Very brilliant observation. Maybe you can also figure out the reason why."

"Rivalry?" I suggested.

We pulled up in front of my apartment. "Go to the head of the class." His eyes narrowed. "Better still, go to the meeting tonight and see Ogundu."

"Ogundu?"

"Don't know him, eh? He's a cult leader, too. Runs the Temple of the Living Flame on the south side. Does that suggest anything to you?"

"Firebug?"

"Firebugs, in the plural. Every torch in town must hang around his setup, getting their kicks."

"Why don't you tell Captain Dalton what you think?"

"Don't be dumb. I tell Dalton, he asks me why I'm interested. I tell him that, he tells the paper. I get my name out in the open. Not good."

"But I'm working for the paper myself."

"I know that. And you're a smart operator. You'll be able to get in where the cops can't."

"It's a good lead," I said. "I'll look into it. But if I do get a story, I don't see how I can keep your name out of it."

"Well, you've got plenty of time to figure a way," Weatherbee told me. "I don't want to be tied to any cult deal. All I want is a line on Ogundu and his Temple."

"Read the papers," I said. "I'll get a story of some kind if I go there tonight. Probably run it Monday."

"Maybe. If I say so."

"What do you mean?"

"You're not doing this for the papers, Dempster. You're doing this for me. I want to get a report from you tomorrow, in person. If it's okay to write up something, I'll tell you. If not, you'll keep your trap shut."

"And suppose I don't? You aren't going to try to threaten me, are you? You said yourself that you don't go in for murder."

Don Weatherbee smiled. "No threats. You could go ahead and do as you please. You could even to go Dalton now and tell him what I said. But I don't advise it."

I got out of the car. "May I ask why not?"

"Glad you did." He started up the motor again and closed the door. "Told you I was tied up with the White Brotherhood, remember? Well, your little stranger sounds to me like one of our boys. I don't know him—wish I did, because he might have the answers—but I know a couple more like him. Nice, clean, Godfearing citizens, but a bit on the fanatical side. Open to suggestions, too, if you catch my meaning. I think some of them carry knives, same as the character you met. And if I slipped them the word that you were an enemy of the Brotherhood, that maybe you had something to do with the fire and the murder of Amos Peabody—"

He chuckled. "No threats, understand. Just something to think about. Run along, Dempster, and write a good story. I'll be seeing you about the other story tomorrow."

I went inside and opened the door of my apartment. It took quite a while, because my hand was trembling so I couldn't control the key.

TWELVE

IT ISN'T EASY to tell it this way—about how my hand trembled, about being afraid. Not after a steady diet of magazines and movies and TV, where every man is a Private Eye winking at danger.

I sat in my apartment, trying to write the inquest story for Cronin, and I kept thinking about the setup. A Private Eye wouldn't have muffed things. If a Private Eye had taken the knife from my clown-faced friend, he'd have given him a clout on the head in return—and probably snapped a couple of wrists in the bargain.

If a Private Eye had Agatha Loodens where I had her last night, he'd have hung on to her until he got everything he wanted, and that doesn't necessarily just mean information.

If a Private Eye had been threatened by Weatherbee now, he'd know what to do. Private Eyes always know what to do. They may get sapped, slugged, shot and tortured, but that doesn't seem to matter. They keep right on going, day and night, without any sleep and with only rye for nourishment. And apparently they tap some source of cosmic energy—maybe they use VITAL CREAM. Whatever it is, they're always ready for a fight with a fiend or a bout with a blonde. To top it off, they also know all the answers. The best one can apparently solve any crime in 26 minutes flat, leaving plenty of time for four full minute commercials. Good deal.

The only trouble was that my name happened to be Phil Dempster. I wasn't a Private Eye, merely a private citizen. I didn't know who set those fires, who killed Peabody or Ricardi. And I was scared.

I pecked out a few lines on the story, then called Schwarm. Right now I was ready for a nice, long talk. "You asked me if I had any personal problems, Doc," I'd say. "Well, if you can come over, maybe I can answer that one for you."

That's what I'd say, what I intended to say. But there was no answer.

I hunted up his home phone, called. All I got was the ringing in the ears. Even that was better than nothing, better than silence. I held the phone for a long time, not wanting to lose the sound of the ring.

Silence was getting on my nerves. Maybe I ought to move to a noisier place. A place where there'd be people all around me. A place where Mrs. Loodens and the clown-faced cultist and Don Weatherbee couldn't find me. A place the killer wouldn't know about.

I thought about that for a moment. Then I thought about calling Captain Dalton. That made sense. I could tell him Weatherbee had threatened me. He'd give me police protection. Nobody could touch me, then.

But how long would that last? How long would the cops furnish me with a free bodyguard—a week, ten days? Suppose they found the firebug sooner? That would end my protection. And Weatherbee would wait. He was a big man in town, he had standing, a reputation. He'd deny any threats, maybe he'd even sue me. And when something finally happened to me, who could prove anything?

Something would happen to me sooner or later. I believed that. Weatherbee warned me it would, if I went to the cops.

That made sense, too.

So there was nothing to do now except go back to the typewriter and pound out my thousand words on the inquest. I had to make four false starts before I got going, and it was after three when I finished.

But nobody interrupted me. Nobody came to shove a knife in my ribs or a gun in my back.

I put the story in my pocket, locked the place up, and drove downtown. I stopped off long enough for a quick bite, then walked in on Cronin.

"Here's the inquest yarn," I said.

"Good." He read it over. I picked up the paper and read the *Globe* account. All very straight stuff. But I noted that Dalton had issued a statement following the inquest, and so had the District Attorney. The case wasn't closed. The inquest was merely a formality, absolving previous suspects. The person or persons responsible for the crimes would be apprehended by the Department. And so on.

"This is all right." Cronin waved my story at me. "Wish you'd been here a little earlier, though. Your friend Schwarm is down at headquarters, looking over the day's haul. The boys have been out with their butterfly nets. There's a lot of cross-examining going on."

"Maybe I'll look in tonight," I said.

"You'd better. We'll want another yarn for Monday, unless they manage to snag their man."

"Think they'll get him?"

Cronin lifted his eyebrows. "Who knows? Ninety percent of these cases break only because somebody tips the police off. It's that way all over the country. If the average guy knew how many thousands of unsolved murders have been committed, how many killers are running around loose, he'd be surprised. And scared silly."

"I'm a little scared myself," I said.

His eyes narrowed. "Anybody try to pressure you?" he asked.

"No," I said slowly. But I couldn't resist fishing. "Only there's angles here I don't get. Mrs. Loodens talked to me. So did Don Weatherbee."

"Give you any information?"

I shook my head. "They were asking, not telling."

"Well, that's only natural. Everybody's antsy about this thing." He stood up. "Phil, I hope something happens soon to crack this business. It could be bad."

"How do you mean?"

"Remember last year, when they caught this kid carving up his girlfriend?"

"Miller, wasn't it?"

"That's the name. Well, within the next two weeks, there were six more cases like it. People playing sex-maniac. Something seems to set off a wave. All of the perverts and offbeats in town read about those crimes and get ideas."

"Think there'll be more fires, Ed?"

He nodded. "I know it. Matter of fact, they've started already."

"You serious?"

"Running the story tomorrow. Since Ricardi's death the Fire Department has answered twenty-six alarms in two days. The average is eight."

"Anything big?"

"No. Lucky so far. But they're all alike, and that's the point. Crank jobs. Amateur torch works. Fires in baby carriages—empty ones, thank God. Fires in alleys, in hallways, in places where there should be no fires. Kids started most of them."

"That's what Schwarm said," I told him. "Most firebugs are adolescents."

"Never mind the psychology," Cronin muttered. "Save it for the stories. But I'm worried. There's a real firebug still at large. And your little pal with the big knife."

I grinned, in spite of myself.

"What's so funny?" he asked.

"Nothing. Just glad to find out I'm not the only one who's scared about all this. But I never figured you'd feel that way."

Cronin gave me a long look. "I know," he said. "Anybody in the newspaper business knows. We get a lot of stories, and we don't run 'em all. And what we do run, we tone down. But we end up with a little different slant on people. I mentioned unsolved murders before. That's only a small part of it. This city—every town, every community—is filled with secrets. Two million abortions reported a year, and who knows how many unreported? Thirty thousand people disappear—a hundred a day, year in and year out. Just disappear, never heard of again. That's bad enough.

"Your friend with the shiv isn't exactly a news-item to us. There's probably five million just like him, and another five million who carry guns. Not professional criminals, but screwballs. The kind who need treatment, need to be put away."

He walked over to the window and leaned against the dirty glass. A big man staring thoughtfully down at his city spread out below him. You work for a paper as long as Cronin had and you wind up married to the city. You chart her progress and take her temperature now and then and when she gets sick, you worry about her. Now Cronin knew she was incubating a virulent disease and he was concerned. It was a side of the man I always suspected was there but one he seldom displayed.

"If you only knew what's going on out there," he said slowly. "If you only knew how many of the citizens are psychos. Doc Schwarm could probably make a guess—I've heard it said that one person out of three needs psychiatric treatment at some time or other in the course of a lifetime. And how many actually get it? Damned few. So we've got a city full of offbeats. People who walk around talking to themselves. People who sleep with guns under their pillows because they're afraid somebody is out to get them. People who make homemade bombs, who poison dogs, who chain their kids or their wives up in attics. Rapists. Rippers. Guys who go after women with whips and razor-blades. Homos. The stories I've heard, the things I've seen in the last ten years—nobody likes to think about them, nobody likes to believe them, but they're all true. People are naturally vicious."

"People are afraid," I said. "That's the answer. Fear makes them cruel. Sometimes they're afraid of things that aren't real. Sometimes they put their faith into things that aren't real either. That's why they join these cults."

"Cults!" Cronin spat the word. "I'd like to smash every damned one of them. I'd like to stamp out every phoney freak setup in the world—every racket that thrives on and encourages maladjustment. Only one good thing has come of this so far; the White Brotherhood and the Golden Atom setups are gone. Maybe that's what this firebug has in mind. Maybe he plans to burn out every cult in town."

I looked at Cronin. He was shaking with rage.

"You sound a little fanatical yourself," I said quietly. "Do you really mean that?"

"Of course I do. I know what goes on. For two years my wife was mixed up with some damned fake healing outfit—nobody could talk her out of it. Until her appendix ruptured and she almost died. Lost our baby on account of it. And fed a fortune to those charlatans. I hate the scum!"

"Well." I stood up. "Better run along."

Cronin sighed and wearily wiped his forehead. "Sorry I blew up that way," he said. "Pay no attention to me. Been a hard week."

"Sure."

"You'll try to find out what Schwarm did with these suspects?"

"Have a story for you Monday," I promised. "Take care of yourself."

I went out. I went out and ate and thought over the interview. Everybody was a screwball or a potential screwball, according to Cronin. And Cronin hated cults, wanted to see them burn. He'd given me this assignment to expose cults.

Where had *he* been during the fires? What kind of a potential did he have?

But that was crazy. Cronin couldn't be the firebug. He was just a normal guy—but one out of three needs psychiatric treatment sooner or later, and how many of them get it?

I ate at the Dinner Gong, and the toast was burned. *Burned*. In an hour, I was due at the Temple of the Living Flame. I didn't want to go there. I hadn't told Cronin I was going tonight. Weatherbee didn't want anyone to know.

I thought about the Temple of the Living Flame. Weatherbee had told me it was a firebug hangout, and that sounded logical. A natural, in fact. Why hadn't the police looked into this?

Come to think of it, maybe my notebook would give me a little advance information. I was supposed to see a man named Ogundu. Foreign-sounding name. Polish, or Russian, perhaps.

It was seven o'clock. I had just time enough to take a run back to the apartment, pick up the notebook, and be on my way. On my not-so-merry way.

I drove swiftly. I parked two doors down from my place, then headed for the door. Somebody honked a horn at me.

"Mr. Dempster!"

I turned, recognizing the voice. I recognized the car, too. There she was again, waiting for me.

"Hello," I said. "Still mad?"

She shook her head. The blond hair was worn in an upsweep tonight, and the earrings were pendant.

"Aren't you going to ask me up?" she inquired.

"Sorry. I've got an appointment."

"I wanted to talk to you."

"Stick around," I said. "Got to get something. Be right down."

It didn't take more than two minutes. I went up, pocketed the notebook and came out to her car. She opened the door for me. I climbed in and sat down.

Agatha Loodens seemed to be all set for a big evening. I couldn't help but take a good look at her, and there was plenty for me to see tonight. I'm not talking about jewelry or the fancy hairdo, either; just her own dainty, demure, d)collet) self. She looked like she'd been poured into her dress by somebody whose hand wasn't quite steady.

My hand wouldn't have been steady, either. I sat next to her now, staring at the cleavage.

"I had hoped to speak to you after the inquest," she told me. "But you left so quickly. With Mr. Weatherbee."

"That's right."

"What did he want?"

"Nothing. Just talked a little about the case."

"Phil—I meant what I said last night. Keep away from the man. He's dangerous." She paused. "Very."

"I'm being careful these days." I paused. "Very." Then I stopped watching the double-feature long enough to look her in the eye. "Is that what you came here to see me about?"

"Please. I'm not just snooping. When I saw you go out with Don this noon, I got worried."

"Why? Afraid he'd tell me something I shouldn't know?"

Her lips tightened. "Must you be such a—?"

"Don't say it." I grinned. "Sorry, but I guess I must. Too many people keep coming at me these days. All of them are warning me, and none of them really give a damn about me."

"Are you sure?"

She was very close, and her lips weren't tight any more. They were loose, and full, and I could see the tip of her tongue, like a little pink doormat with the word *Welcome* on it.

"I'm not sure of anything," I said.

"Must you keep that appointment?" she murmured.

"Yes."

"Is it with Weatherbee?"

"No. I'm not seeing him tonight."

"Good. I found out a few things about him today. Things you'd be interested in knowing."

"Such as?"

"He's got another cult, Phil. He's mixed up with that White Brotherhood gang."

"I already know that. He told me himself."

"But there's more to it, Phil. A lot more. Things he wouldn't tell me. I'm sure of it. If you'd only listen to me, let me help you—"

"You can." I sat up and moved away. "I'll be through with my chores by eleven. How about stopping back here then? We'll have all the time we want."

Agatha Loodens nodded. Then she leaned over and her mouth met mine. It was a cordial meeting, and I hated to break it up, but I had to. "See you at eleven," I said.

"Yes. And—take care of yourself."

"Now she tells me." I waved, and she drove away. I waited until the car rounded the corner and disappeared, then walked over to my own heap. I climbed in and opened the notebook.

Here was the stuff on the Brotherhood, the Golden Atom, Wisdom Center, House of Truth, New Kingdom Tabernacle, and—nothing.

I riffled through the pages again. I found the Temple of the Living Flame listed up front, with its address opposite the entry, and the name Ogundu beneath. But there was no inner heading, no additional notes. Apparently Cronin's people hadn't gotten around to this one.

Or had they? And had someone gotten around to them?

I shrugged. Things were getting out of hand. Now I was really letting my imagination run away with me. Figuring Cronin for a firebug, seeing a man hiding under every bed. A man with a knife and a torch.

Time to stop. And time to go. I put the car in gear and drove to 101 South Sherburne Street and the Temple of the Living Flame.

Thirteen

IT WAS MY NIGHT FOR SURPRISES.

The setting was no surprise. The Negro ghetto on the South Side. The night was hot and muggy and the odors from the cheap and dirty restaurants clung close to the pavement. Greasy ham and eggs, black-eyed peas, turnip greens—a rich mixture for a queasy nose. The no-down-payment-and-the-rest-of-your-life-to-pay furniture stores stuffed with upholstered borax in purple and orange and black, the inevitable auto agency selling long, black Lincolns, a cut-rate drugstore, the usual combination package-liquor store and bar, a former dance hall turned roller skating rink... The placid black faces that filled the walk, the rumble of the elevated overhead.

A cool wind blew off the lake and for no good reason at all I reflected that it would probably be a night like this on which I'd die. Alone and overlooked, with life buzzing quietly on about me. Just so long as I could never see myself with the flesh beginning to redden and char, the eyes start ...

I blotted it out and parked across the street from the small, two-story white frame building, sitting in the car and studying the setup for a moment. It looked like any one of half a dozen churches you can find in colored neighborhoods—a former store, converted into a mission or a tabernacle, its windows covered in heavy drapes. Over the doorway was a sign, illuminated by a large outdoor bulb. TEMPLE OF THE LIVING

FLAME—ALL WELCOME. It was the doorway which furnished the surprise.

Because now, as I watched, out of it marched a familiar figure. I recognized the pipe-in-jaw profile of Captain Dalton. He was followed by two other plain-clothes men. They went down the block to a waiting car, got in, drove off.

So they *had* got around to this place after all! Perhaps my visit was unnecessary. Even so, duty called. Duty—and Don Weatherbee.

I sat in the car a while longer. It wasn't quite eight yet. There's be time to watch the early arrivals. Might be someone worth seeing.

That's what I told myself. Actually, I knew who I was looking for. I didn't want to see him, but he might show up. My little clown-faced apparition.

They were coming to the meeting now, and so far I hadn't spotted the man I was searching for. Most of the faces weren't even white. That was another surprise. What was I getting into now—an old-fashioned Revival Meeting?

I got out and went over. People were still going into the place, and now I saw that they weren't all Negroes. There was a little man with a twisted arm who tipped his cap to me as he passed; a thin, almost rachitic girl with pale yellow hair; an elderly bum with a milk-white cast covering his left eye; several teenagers in the regulation uniform of leather jacket and blue jeans; an unshaven drunk; a well-dressed young woman in heavy makeup; three beat types, two with crewcuts and the third with a macro- or hydrocephalic bulge which needed no tonsorial garnish to attract attention.

A strange assortment. Or was it? Hadn't Schwarm told me about firebugs? Adolescents, the physically deformed, the subnormal and abnormal? If these *were* firebugs. I had Weatherbee's word for that.

Half past eight. Time to go in. I walked up the steps, opened the door.

The lobby entry was small. No comparison here with the splash of the Church of the Golden Atom. No tables offering written or bottled guarantees of eternal youth. It was just an alcove, leading directly into the Temple.

The Temple had folding chairs arranged in rows before a small platform. The walls were draped in heavy monks-cloth, but the general effect was that of a cheap auction-house.

Only the backdrop of the stage was indicative of the purpose and activities of this organization. The heavy, black drapes hung from ceiling to floor, completely covering the wall or whatever was behind them. And sewn in the center, with threads of flame, was the vivid outline of a burning bird. It was a simple symbol, but subtly compelling—and I recognized what it represented. The Phoenix, the resurrection bird that rises anew from its own ashes.

Suddenly the firebird shivered and split asunder. A man had parted the drapes in the middle and stepped forth on the platform. Ogundu—and another surprise.

I really should have expected it. He wouldn't be Polish or Russian. He was a Negro, slender and splendid, black as the night in a robe as red as living flame.

He stood there, theatrically poised, hands uplifted, and the crowd rose to its feet. There were deacons present now, I noted. One of them stood at the far wall, ready to switch out the lights, and I wondered if the Temple held its meetings in darkness. Then I noted two others, each on either side of the platform altar. They carried candles which they held over large potlike objects which stood on tripods. Now I knew their purpose. The pots were braziers.

Ogundu's hands came down. "Kindle the Living Flame!" he said.

And from all around me came the response. "Kindle the Living Flame!" It was a chant, a ritual.

The candles dipped. The lights flicked off and the fires flared up—flared from the braziers to flood Ogundu's face and send shimmering shadows across the figure of the Phoenix.

I sat there and stared. I'd admired Professor Ricardi's pitch, his smooth performance in the fancy auditorium with the organ offering accompaniment. He'd used all the trimmings to get the crowd worked up.

But he hadn't got to me. Even after the full treatment, I'd still remained an aloof, objective observer.

This was different.

I felt something crawl up into my throat.

Oh, I knew what was happening. I knew I was sitting in a dingy little converted store in a dingy little district, surrounded by a crowd of credulous cretins. I knew that Ogundu was as big a fake as Ricardi—his ebony was just as phoney as Ricardi's gold.

But he was doing something to me in spite of all I realized. This nondescript Negro in a rented theatrical costume had taken a few yards of velvet, a couple of candles, and some second-hand smudge-pots, switched off the lights, and made a Mystery.

What had Schwarm said? Something I already knew, something everybody knows. *Fire is magic.* Ogundu brought fire, and he was Prometheus and Pythagoras and Zoroaster and Mazda and Ahriman—all the gods and devils and wonder-workers incarnate.

The crowd stirred restlessly, watching the flames. I knew why they came here, now. Fire was the lure. Fire that burns, fire that destroys, fire that creates, fire that purifies, fire that is living death and death-in-life.

Ogundu was talking now. He had a deep baritone voice, the voice of the evangelist, the voice of the prophet, the voice of the sayer of sooth. There have always been such voices, there have always been men who kindled an altar-flame before which men gathered to look, to listen, and to learn. Learn the secret of Fire which is Being, which is Magic.

Some of this was my thought, some of it was Ogundu's words.

He wasn't preaching, in the usual meaning of the term. He wasn't exhorting or explaining, he wasn't promising boons or blessings, selling salve or offering unguent. He was proclaiming the true God—the Living Flame. The Flame men must willingly worship to escape destruction.

Fire is Life. Fire is Death. And Fire is also Hell. Those who do not worship will learn. Those who do not give themselves to the Flame will be given to It in Afterlife. For the World and the Universe was born of Fire, and we are all a part of it. That is the great secret—not to oppose the Truth.

He chanted the ancient, mystic words. Just so much gibberish, really. It's always gibberish when you remember it, write it down. But when you hear it in the dark, and the fire flares—real fire, that really burns—something happens.

I knew, now. Weatherbee was right, Schwarm was right, Cronin was right. The world is full of them: full of twisted bodies and twisted minds that feed on flame. I could feel them beside me in the darkness, catch glimpses of faces shining in the firelight. That's the way faces must shine in Hell. Red eyes, red teeth, red hands all about me. And the voice chanting, the breath panting, the urge rising in the room as the flames rose—the haunting wanting, the desire for fire, a burning yearning, flowing and glowing—

From out of nowhere the thought crept into my mind and it was like a voice crying *Save me, save me*. I recognized the voice, and thrust it down again; down into the dream where it belonged.

And I thrust again, burying it, and I thrust away the flame-born fancies. This was just another cheap, phoney little racket. In a minute they'd turn on the lights and pass the collection plate around. Get any group together, turn out the lights, kindle a fire and let somebody start using wizard's words in a deep voice; you're bound to get a reaction. No matter how sophisticated the group may be, the reaction will come.

Yes, but *why?* Was it because there really *is* something about darkness and fire that means magic? Is it atavistic, do we all go back to the cave-dwellers who gathered around the flame that kept back the blackness and its beasts? Do we all have some hidden heritage from the time when every temple guarded an altar of the gods, when enemies were destroyed in a holy holocaust? Was there an instinctive reaction?

Whatever it was, I felt it now. I knew why the others came here, knew why fire held a fascination.

My throat was dry, swollen. My hands were clenched, rigid at my sides, and my heart was beginning to pound in rhythm with Ogundu's baritone booming, in rhythm with the rise and fall of the flames. This was it. *This is how a firebug feels before—*

Had I ever felt this way? In the past, in the dim past, five days ago, when the White Brotherhood tabernacle burned? Did I *know* this feeling?

That was a crazy thought. Maybe all my thoughts were crazy. Maybe nobody else here felt like this. Or maybe I wasn't crazy, and they all did—and if so, that was crazier still.

I snapped my attention back to the stage. Something was happening on the platform now. The deacons were up there. They were bringing in this long box, this long, shallow trough. It came from behind the curtains, and so did the iron fire-pot. The iron fire-pot, with its long handles—it took two men to lift it and bring it forward, smoking and hissing.

Ogundu was chanting something about faith, now. The crowd responded. It was like a hymn without music, but it had a counterpoint. The hissing of hot coals, live coals.

The deacons dumped the fire-pot's contents into the long, shallow trough. It stretched halfway across the front of the platform, and sent a swirl of smoke up to veil Ogundu's face.

For a moment it seemed like a Revival Meeting once again. The shrill shrieks of Negro women, the grunting affirmations of the men rose all about me. I'd heard cries like that before, from those possessed of the Spirit.

Possession. Demoniac possession. Demon of fire.

I told myself that my name was Philip Dempster, that I was sitting in a remodeled store, watching a cult racketeer put on a show. But somehow the message didn't get through to my throat and hands and lungs and heart. The pulsing and pounding, the rigor and rictus went on.

And I watched as Ogundu ripped the enfolding flame from his body, cast off the crimson robe, and stood before us in the firelight, stripped to the waist. He stopped and flung his shoes aside.

He closed his eyes. The four deacons chanted and he responded. Somebody began to stamp on the floor with both feet. In a moment the pounding rose all around me—the rhythmic, measured stamping that's older than Stonehenge. It made the floor vibrate, made the flames quiver. I was vibrating and quivering with them.

Ogundu moved barefoot to one end of the trough. He moved swiftly, with feline grace, a black panther. His eyes were embers. One of the deacons handed him a vial, and he dipped into it and tossed something down into the long, shallow trough before him. The coals hissed and sputtered, sizzled and seared as smoke smoldered up anew.

And then Ogundu listened to the drumming, listened to it well and swell. A moment he stood there, and then he started forward.

He walked slowly, now—walked on naked feet across the bed of live coals.

Then he walked back.

I'd read about it, of course. They say it's done in Africa, by witch-doctors.

But this wasn't a case of what I read or what they said. This wasn't

Africa, and Ogundu wasn't a witch-doctor. This was 101 South Sherburne Street, right here, and I saw a man walk barefoot over fire.

Sure, the lights came on, just as I knew they would, and the deacons were only ordinary Negroes in cheap suits, coming down the aisle with the collection plates. And somebody was spreading ashes on the fire, and then pouring water—the braziers were extinguished, and people were pushing back those battered folding chairs. The show was over.

Yet I'd seen something tonight. I remembered Seabrook's old book, *The Magic Island*, and his account of Haiti. How the simple, friendly, ignorant Negro farmers gathered together, and how the beating of a drum and the summoning of the Snake transformed them momentarily into a magic multitude, votaries of Voodoo. Seabrook had sensed the summoning of a Mystery.

And I?

I wasn't sure. One thing I did know—this time there wouldn't be any slip-ups. I intended to see Ogundu, and see him right now.

Down the aisle, up onto the platform. One of the deacons barred my way.

"Where you headin' for, Mister?"

"I want to see Ogundu."

"The Father has retired."

"I'm from the *Globe*." For the first time I was glad Cronin had given me a press card. I pulled it out but he didn't bother to read it.

"Wait. I'll tell him. What's your name, Mister?"

"Philip Dempster. He'll probably know who I am."

The deacon parted the curtains. He wasn't gone long. When he emerged again, he was smiling.

"You can go right back," he told me. "First door down the hall."

I went right back.

Behind the curtains was a doorway leading into the hall corridor. I found the first door, opened it.

This was what lay behind the black curtain of Mystery—this was what lurked behind the portals guarded by the Phoenix. Just an ordinary little office, filled with second-hand furniture. At first I was disappointed. Disappointed in the appearance of the place, and disappointed in the appearance of the thin, middle-aged Negro who sat beside the desk, soaking his naked feet in a dented tin basin.

"Got to soak this gunk off," he grinned. "Stuff sticks." He picked up a cigar-butt from an ashtray on the desk. "Sit down," he invited. "How'd you like the show?"

I opened my mouth. Just then a girl stuck her head into the room—a white girl.

Ogundu turned and waved her away. "It's all right," he said. "I won't need you any more tonight."

She looked at me, nodded, and withdrew.

"My secretary," Ogundu told me. "Nice girl."

"Yeah," I nodded. "Nice girl." I stared at the doorway, trying to get a glimpse of the hall outside.

But Diana Rideaux had disappeared.

FOURTEEN

OGUNDU DRIED HIS FEET. I stared at the pink soles. There wasn't the slightest sign of a burn. I didn't see any callouses, either.

"What's the secret?" I asked. "Is it that preparation you smeared on?"

He smiled. "Partly. And part of it's the kind of coals—porous stuff, gives off heat as fast as it absorbs it. But the big thing is knowing how to talk, and not being afraid. Ever hear of the Nigerian Fire Walkers?"

"Don't tell me you're from Ghana?"

He shook his head. "Born and raised right here in town. But you don't have to go to Africa to learn a few tricks. I've got others. Fire-eating, and picking up red-hot pokers. They go for that kind of jazz in a big way around here."

"Aren't you afraid I'll quote you in my writeup?" I asked.

Ogundu chewed the end of his cigar. "Go ahead. It won't bother me any. You just got in on the last performance."

"You're quitting the Temple?"

"That's right. As of now."

"Dalton scare you?"

"Told me to lay off, if that's what you mean. Said he'd have the Fire Marshal get after me for violating ordinances. Said I couldn't mess around with torches and live coals. He leaned on me pretty hard."

"What are your plans?"

"Cutting out of here right quick. Sell this place for whatever it'll bring."

"Then you don't care what I write?"

Ogundu shrugged. "Do as you please. By the time your story's out, I'll be on my way." He started to put on his stockings and shoes. "Anything you want to know about the gimmicks I use, just go ahead and ask."

"That's nice of you to be so cooperative," I told him. "I appreciate it."

"No sense being funky, the way I figure it." He laced his shoes slowly. "When you gotta go, you gotta go. I've had all I could expect here, anyway." He sat up, smiling. "Now, Mr. Dempster, what do you want to know?"

I smiled back at him and took a deep breath. "I want to know if you have any firebugs in your congregation."

His smile melted away like butter on a hot griddle. "What's that got to do with your newspaper story?"

"Plenty. I'm not so much interested in the cult angle any more. It's the firebug I'm after."

"You working with the cops?"

"No. Not officially. I'm working for myself. Twice now I've been involved in this series of cases. I don't like incendiaries and I don't like killers. I want to find out what this is all about."

"So does your friend Captain Dalton. Did you send him here, is that it?"

"Believe me, I had nothing to do with it. But it's only natural he'd come around. Knowing what you were doing here, running the kind of racket that is bound to attract every potential pyromaniac in town."

"I told you I'm getting out."

"Yes. But you haven't answered my question."

"I can't answer it, Mr. Dempster. I don't know the answer. You think if one of my people was a firebug, he'd tell me about it?" He paused. "Or do you maybe figure I trained a couple of them to start those fires on purpose? Is that it?"

"I don't think anything. I'm waiting to hear what you think."

"Far as I know, all my people are clean. But you don't have to take my word for it. Ask Captain Dalton. When he walked out of here earlier tonight, he had a list of every name I got in the files. Does that answer your question?"

"Partly," I said. I leaned forward. "Speaking of your people, maybe you can give me some information. Does one of them happen to be a little man, about five feet three or four, who wears a brown topcoat? The one I'm thinking of is almost bald. He has a white face, deep circles under his eyes, and he's got a habit of biting his lips. Looks a little bit like a clown—"

Ogundu stood up. He walked over to the filing cabinet, opened it, took out an object and threw it on the desk. It clattered and lay still. I gazed down on the glittering length of a knife. I'd seen it before—felt its edge against my ribs.

"Does this belong to him?" Ogundu asked.

"Yes. You know him."

"I saw him last night. Worked late, and about ten o'clock I decided to go out for coffee. Just as I opened the side door, this came whizzing at me. Stuck in the door-frame just next to my right ear. I saw your little man then. He ran down the alley, but not before i got a good look. Who is he?"

"I don't know," I said. "But I want to. Did you tell the police?"

Ogundu shook his head. "Got enough troubles without that. Been like this all week, ever since that Brotherhood fire. People warning me somebody's out to get all us cult leaders. My secretary scared half to death, wanting to quit."

"Your secretary," I said. "What about her?"

"Nothing about her. Name's Rideaux. Diana Rideaux. Been with me six-seven months now. Good girl. Nice girl. You saw her."

I nodded. "Is she a—believer?"

"You mean does she go for this Living Flame line? No. She's got a head on her shoulders. How could she, when she knows all the tricks? Why do you ask?"

"Just wondering. After all, it's rather unusual to find a—I mean, a job like this—"

Ogundu smiled again. "I know what you mean. She's a white girl working for a Negro. Well, I can give you the answer to that one. It's a hundred bucks a week. That's all. But Diana's worth it, she's sensible. Or was, up until this week. Lately she's had all kinds of notions about being followed. Come to think of it, she said something about this little guy with the knife. That was on Thursday, I guess. I laughed at her."

"You aren't laughing now."

"That's right. I'm not laughing. I'm leaving."

"You're scared," I murmured.

"All right. I'm scared. I had me a sweet little setup here, no trouble. And all of a sudden things start happening. Bad things. Fires and killings and people coming on strong with knives. I don't know what it's all about and I don't want to find out. Go ahead and print it in the paper if you like—print it that I'm scared and running away. I don't care."

"You'd like that, wouldn't you?" I said. "Having people think you left town because you're frightened. Instead of having them think you left because you know too much."

"I don't know anything," Ogundu said.

"I wish you'd tell me. Maybe I could help. You don't want to see this sort of thing go on, do you? Innocent people being murdered, a whole city in danger—"

"I helped all I could," he answered. "Now's the time to cut out."

It seemed like good advice. I took it. "Good night," I said.

"Goodbye."

I walked through the deserted Temple and out to the street. The little man wasn't waiting for me there, and he wasn't waiting for me at the car. It wouldn't have startled me too greatly if he had been. This was my night for surprises.

But he wasn't surprising me. I drove home quickly, noting that it was already a few minutes past eleven.

I parked out in front and looked around for Mrs. Loodens and her car. Apparently she hadn't arrived yet. Just to make sure I went upstairs. My door was locked and she wasn't in the hall.

I came back down again and waited in the lobby. The minutes crawled past. Eleven fifteen, eleven thirty, eleven forty.

Apparently that was the last surprise of the evening. For some reason or other, she wasn't coming.

I turned to go back up the stairs when the taxi pulled up in front of the lobby door. I watched it deposit the final surprise on the curb.

Diana Rideaux came up the walk, opened the door, and stepped right into my arms.

FIFTEEN

WE LAY ON THE SOFA. Quite a bit of time had gone by, and Mrs. Loodens hadn't showed up. I didn't have a light burning for her in the window. In fact, I didn't have any light at all.

"Feel better now?" I whispered

"Um-hum."

"But why didn't you tell me?"

"What? About working for Ogundu? How could I, after what you said about cults, people who ran them? I was ashamed—" She moved away. "I'm ashamed right now."

I moved her back.

"But you came here anyway."

"I had to. When I saw you at the Temple tonight, I knew it was something I had to do. I wasn't afraid any more."

"You know I'd never hurt you," I said.

"Yes. I was a fool, letting myself think that—"

"Think what?"

The words were whispers. "I thought you were the firebug."

"Because of that business with the cigarette the other night? That was an accident."

"Yes." She sighed. "Only at the time, I wasn't sure. And then I read about Professor Ricardi in the papers."

"But you must have read my alibi, too, and what they said at the inquest."

She pressed close again. "I'm sorry. It's just that I've been so worried. And then when I was followed—"

"Who followed you?"

"Please. It's nothing. Ogundu said I was imagining things."

"Did you see who it was? Could it have been a little white-faced man?"

"I didn't actually see anyone." She clung and whispered. "Besides, it doesn't matter now. Nobody can hurt me when I'm with you, can they, Phil? You aren't angry because of what I thought, you forgive me—"

"There's nothing to forgive. You're not the only one who doubted my story. And I've been running around suspecting everybody. Including you, when you popped into the doorway of Ogundu's office." I smoothed her hair. "But it's all right now. I don't give a damn who you work for, as long as you're my girl."

"I am your girl, Phil. You know that."

"Yes."

"And I'm quitting Ogundu."

"Good idea." Apparently he hadn't told her about his plans for leaving town. And I didn't think this was the time or place to mention it. Still, I couldn't resist doing a little probing.

"Diana, when I talked to Ogundu tonight I questioned him about the fires. I wondered if some of his followers could be involved. You know the setup—what do you think?"

She sat up, suddenly thoughtful. "I never saw anything suspicious. They get pretty worked up at those meetings, but nothing's ever happened that I know about. Even at the brandings—"

"What brandings? Ogundu didn't mention that."

"Some of the deacons, the Inner Circle, they call themselves, go through a ritual. They have the brand of the Phoenix burned on their arms or chests."

"Sounds pretty barbaric."

"That's what I thought, too. But Ogundu says it's nothing; they even do it in fraternities, sometimes. Just sucker stuff, he calls it."

I squeezed her hand. "What kind of a man is Ogundu, anyway?" I kept my voice calm. "What are his habits? Does he have any special foibles or eccentricities?"

Her hand trembled, pulled away. "Phil, is *that* it? Do you think *he* might—?"

"I don't know."

"It's like a nightmare, isn't it?" she whispered. "Everywhere you turn, there's something lurking."

"Take it easy," I said. I pulled her back down beside me on the sofa. "Stop trembling. I won't hurt you."

"I know. But when I think about what's happened—please, Phil, turn on the light."

"Afraid of the dark?" I bent my head. Her mouth twisted free of mine.

"Afraid of *me?*" I had to say it, had to hear her answer. I waited for it. And it came, but not in words; only in a trembling silence that was worse than words.

I could feel her body beneath me, feel my arms holding her just as I'd held her before. Just the way I'd held Ricardi when I turned his body over and saw his face. Just the way I held the *other* body in my dreams, when I turned it over and saw its face, saw the bubbling eyes, the burned mask. I'd seen it in my dreams and I knew what it was. But I couldn't tell Dalton, I couldn't tell Schwarm, I was even afraid to tell myself.

That's why I drank, so I could sleep without the dream; but sooner or later I'd have to tell. Have to separate the dream from the reality, have to know where one left off and the other began.

But not yet. I couldn't face it now. I couldn't face the face. Drinking was better, and *this* was better. Yes, this was better. I held her now, and I could go on and forget again for a little while.

"Stop!" she whimpered.

Only I didn't stop, because if I stopped I'd remember, and that was too much to bear. *Pyrophobia*, Schwarm had guessed, and he had guessed the truth. Fear of fire. Fear of remembering a fire and a face.

I held her, and my hand went to the top of her dress, and she whimpered again but I was going on, I had to go on, and then—

She wrenched her arm free and switched on the lamp.

It flared up, the light flared up, like fire.

I held her in my arms, staring down at the charred countenance of my dreams. Then I screamed.

"*Margery!*"

An instant. Only an instant, and then it was all right. The face was gone. Diana lay in my arms, sobbing. And now I could tell her, could tell her everything. I had to tell her so that she'd understand.

"It happened while I was out on the Coast," I whispered. "About a year go. I was getting material for my book, and I met this girl. Her name was Margery Hunter. She was an artist, lived in a beach cottage south of Long Beach. We seemed to hit it off together right away. I wanted to marry her, but she made me promise to wait until the book was done and accepted.

"I finished the book and sent it off. Two months later it came back for minor revisions—but the publisher accepted it. So we held a party at her place, to celebrate. And announced our engagement.

"She had a lot of beat friends; artists, musicians, beach bums. They really believed in living it up. When we told them the reason for the party, they decided to make a night of it. One of them went out and brought back half a case of gin. Everybody got high, and I guess the party turned into a brawl.

"Margery passed out and we put her in the bedroom on the bed. The rest of us went right on drinking. Gradually most of the guests drifted off. There were only four of us left when Oscar—Oscar Ringold, the painter— suggested we go for a swim. That sounded good to everybody, so we went down to the beach and swam. The water sobered us up. When we came out we knew what we were doing. That's when Oscar called our attention to the lights in the cottage.

"You can probably figure out the rest. How the fire started, no one really knows to this day. Somebody must have dropped a cigarette. Just one of those accidents, one of those things you're always reading about.

"Only I wasn't reading about it this time. I was seeing it. There'd been a heavy wind off the ocean, and the fire had a head start. All it needed was a few minutes. By the time we got there, the flimsy little frame cottage was half gone—the whole roof caught at once, and the front door caved in.

"Margery was inside. Somebody ran up the road to hail a car. Oscar and another man held me, but I broke loose. There was no way of getting in through the door, but I found the bedroom window and crawled inside.

"And I found Margery. She'd gotten up, of course, and tried to get out, but she never made it. Nobody could have made it through that heat. She was lying face down on the floor when I reached her, and I guess I got her outside in less than a minute. Even so, my clothes were burned, and my hair and eyebrows singed off. Margery's clothes were burned, too. But that wasn't all.

"I found that out when I carried her outside. It was bright as day now, with the flames leaping all around me, and I could see everything. I turned her over, and I saw what had happened to her face—that red, grisly mass, with the oozing eyes—"

I took a deep breath. "Something happened to me when I saw that face, Diana. They said I was in shock for two days: by the time I came around, everything was gone. The cottage was gone, Margery was gone. They— they cremated her. After the inquest, of course."

"Were you accused?"

"There was no question of accusation. We were all held equally responsible—or irresponsible. Just a tragic accident, the papers called it. But I knew. It could have been my cigarette, don't you see? The way it was at the beach the other night. It could have been me. And if you'd seen her face and heard her—"

"Heard her?" Diana whispered.

"Yes. That's the worst. I didn't even remember *that* until I found Ricardi's body Thursday evening. I carried him out and turned him over. And when I looked at him it seemed for a moment as if I was back there, looking at Margery and hearing the voice coming, faint and faraway, from that burned mouth. The voice moaning, 'Save me, save me!' That's all she said. Because she died then, died in my arms."

I stood up. My shirt was soaked with sweat. "Now do you understand why I'm afraid?" I asked. "Why I drink, why I was drinking the other night? It's so I wouldn't have the dreams, so I could forget."

Margery came over to me and put her arms around me and I stared down into that ruined mask, and then it melted away and I knew I was holding Diana in my arms. Everything melted away.

"It's all right now," I murmured. And I meant it. It *was* all right. I'd talked it out.

"You're better than Schwarm," I told her.

"Not afraid any more?"

"No. Are you?"

She shook her head. "It's just that I didn't know."

I smiled at her. "Things are going to be better from now on," I said. "You'll see."

The phone rang.

I picked it up, answered, listened.

"You alone?" said the voice.

I hesitated a moment. "Yes. Why?"

"Come right down then. I just had a visitor. Your friend with the white face."

"Is he there now?"

"Took off like a bat out of hell. But not before he told me."

"Told you what?"

"What you're trying to find out, Dempster. That's why he came. Said he wanted to warn me I was next. And he knows who."

"Aren't you going to tell me?"

"When you come down. We can talk about the reward, then."

"What reward?" I asked.

"Paper said something about a thousand dollars. I could use that."

"I'll call my friend Cronin. He'll—"

"You call nobody. I don't want your friend Cronin. I don't want the cops messing around, either. I'm running like a thief. Catch me the six o'clock flight in the morning. So it's now or never."

"I'm on my way."

"Good. I'll be waiting. But no funny business. Come alone."

"Thanks."

I hung up.

Diana stood at my side. "Who was that?"

"Ogundu," I said. "I told you things would be better. He knows the identity of the firebug."

"What? But how—"

"My pal," I grinned. "My buddy. Clown-face. He came and warned him just now. I've got to get down there right away, because Ogundu's planning on leaving town."

"Aren't you going to phone the police?"

"He made me promise not to. Your boss is a pretty frightened man."

Diana put her hand on my arm. "Why should he tell you? And what makes you believe his story about the little man?"

"Seems as if he'd like that thousand-dollar reward," I answered. "That's why he's willing to talk. And that business about the little man sounds convincing. After all, he seemed to know when Ricardi's number was up."

"Yes, but—"

"Come on," I said. "I've got to hurry. I'll drop you off at your place."

"Please, Phil. Don't take the chance."

"I've got to take it." I smiled at her. "I'll leave you at your apartment and go on alone. If I'm not back in half an hour, then you can call the cops. Good enough?"

She shook her head. "I'm going with you."

"He'll be sore."

"Don't worry about him. After all, he was going to run off without telling me, wasn't he? I'd show up Monday and find him gone. I don't owe him anything."

"Is that any reason for taking a chance?"

"Then you admit it might be dangerous." Diana smiled triumphantly. "All the more reason for me to go. From now on you aren't getting into any more messes unless you take me with you."

I shrugged. "All right. But you wait outside in the car."

"We'll talk about that when we get there. Come on."

Out the door, down the stairs. It was good to feel her arm under mine, but when we reached the lobby I broke free and went on ahead.

"Phil, what's the matter?"

"Nothing. Just checking." I flattened myself against the wall and peered through the glass door, scanning the street outside.

I'd thought I'd caught a glimpse of it passing as we came down the stairs, and I was right. It stood there now, parked at the curb—the big, black shiny new Lincoln.

"Come on," I murmured. "Out the back way, quick!"

She turned and started down the hall. I took one last look to make sure.

One last look, but it was enough. I saw Weatherbee emerge from the car and start toward the door. And he saw me. One hand went to his pocket, emerged. I moved away, quickly—but not quickly enough.

He ran. I looked over my shoulder. Diana was opening the back door at the other end of the hall. I watched her disappear, then turned to face the two of them—Weatherbee and his gun.

Sixteen

"WHERE IS SHE?" Weatherbee gestured with the gun.

"Who?"

"You know who I'm talking about. What are you two trying to pull, anyway?"

"Nothing," I said. "We were just talking."

"Talking!" He moved closer. I could tell he'd been drinking, but his hand never wavered. "In the dark?"

"What's it to you? She's my girl."

"Oh, so she's *your* girl now, is she? You're a fast operator, Dempster. I got a good notion to slow you down."

"Hold on," I muttered. "You're all mixed up. You think I've been with Mrs. Loodens, is that it?"

"Think? I damned well know it."

"I did see her at seven, yes. But she drove away—hasn't come back. The girl I had upstairs just now was Diana Rideaux."

"Prove it."

"I can't. She just sneaked out the back."

"Let's go."

The gun prodded me through the exit. We stood alone in the area behind the apartment.

"She's gone," I said. "Nobody here now."

As I spoke the words, I realized the truth. There was nobody here. We were all alone in the darkness and nobody could help me. The night wind blew through the empty area-way. It would blow across the city, fanning the flames. It would blow through the hole in my skull when he pulled the trigger.

But he hadn't pulled the trigger, yet.

"I hope to God you're telling the truth," Weatherbee said. "There's nothing to gain, protecting a woman like Mrs. Loodens. I should have turned her in myself when I found out about her husband."

I blinked. "But she told me that—"

"Sure. She said I killed him. Don't be childish. Why should I do a think like that, what would I gain? *She* inherited."

"Can you prove what you're saying?" I asked.

"You mean legal proof, evidence? No. If I could, I'd go to the police. But I'm going to nail her on this arson stuff, wait and see! Why do you think I've been tailing her all week?"

"Surely you don't believe she set the fires? Why should she burn the White Brotherhood tabernacle?"

"She knew I was his new partner and that scared her. She was afraid I'd take the play away from her and Ricardi. She set the fire. Simple."

"And then killed her own boyfriend? It doesn't make sense."

Weatherbee nodded slowly, but the gun never moved an inch. "I got news for you," he said. "Ricardi was getting ready to sell out to me. I had the deal all arranged. In a couple of weeks he would have announced a merger with the White Brotherhood."

"Did she know that?"

"He must have let something slip out. So she let him have it." He nodded again. "It figures, Dempster. You heard the evidence at the inquest. Nobody broke into Ricardi's place—he let the killer in himself. Who's the most logical person to get into Ricardi's bedroom late at night?"

"But her maid said she was home with a headache—"

"For twenty bucks she could get that girl to say anything."

I stared at him. "Are you sure this isn't just a case of jealousy?"

The gun jumped up and I gulped. I could see his fat forefinger squeeze down on the trigger. It squeezed, and then it relaxed. Weatherbee sighed.

"All right. I'm jealous. You saw her—you ought to be able to understand. But I know she's in on this, and I'm waiting for her."

"Well, she's not coming back tonight, apparently. I told you the truth—I was with Diana Rideaux, Ogundu's secretary."

"Ogundu's secretary?" The gun jumped up. "Why didn't you tell me that before?"

"You didn't give me a chance." I stared at the gun. "I met her the other night, but I didn't know she was working for Ogundu. I saw her again tonight, at his Temple, when I talked to him."

"What did he say?"

"He's leaving town. Frightened of the police, I guess."

"Does the girl know anything? Where were you two headed when you came downstairs just now?"

I hesitated.

Weatherbee's mouth tightened. So did his finger on the trigger.

"All right," I murmured. "We got a call from Ogundu. He's found out who the firebug is. I was going to talk to him now, before he left."

"What about the girl?"

"I told her to wait for me at her apartment until I got back."

The gun prodded me. "Come on. Let's see Ogundu."

"But he made me promise to come alone—"

"We'll surprise him, then. March."

I marched. I marched through the area-way with the night wind in my face and the gun in my back. When we got to the car, he put the gun in his pocket, but his hand was never far away.

The Lincoln roared. It was late, there was no traffic on the street. We rode in darkness and in silence, and then we came to a place of darkness and silence. The Temple of the Living Flame stood bleak and black.

We raced each other up the steps. I couldn't see anything in the shroud of shadows. I might have lit a match, but I didn't want to light a match.

Weatherbee banged on the door. There was no response. No light showed from within, no footsteps sounded. The echoes of his pounding mingled with the whispers of the wind.

I thought of another evening, when I'd stood at Ricardi's door and vainly sought admittance. I gazed around. No French windows here.

"Maybe there's a rear entrance," Weatherbee said. "Let's find out."

We descended the steps, found a narrow walk between the Temple and the building next to it. "You go first," he told me.

I started walking and he followed, gun out now. I groped along, then rounded a corner of the narrow passageway.

There was a back door. I pushed against it, turning the knob. The door eased open.

"Come on," I whispered. "It's all right."

I blinked back into the darkness, waiting for him to come around the corner.

Then he did.

Weatherbee came around the corner very slowly. His hand clutched at the wall, and slid away as he fell.

"Weatherbee!"

I bent over the dim outlines of the figure sprawled there on the walk. I reached out and touched his face. It was cold. My fingers moved to his neck, came away wet and sticky in the darkness.

Then, as I straightened up, I caught the dull gleam in the shadows of the passageway. It was flashing toward me, toward my own throat—

I jerked back around the corner, yanking at the door, hurling myself forward.

Stumbling and gasping, I went over the threshold, then turned and slammed the door shut. I heard the lock click and catch.

This must be the basement entry to the Temple. I looked for a light-switch, then decided not to risk it. For I could hear the sound of the doorknob rattling outside. Then came a panting, the sound of furious blows against the wooden frame.

Turning, I groped along the corridor until my feet found the base of the stairway. Good. Anything was good that could take me away from that door, fast. These steps must lead up to the back hall, where Ogundu's office was located.

I rose through the darkness, reached a hall. I'd guessed right. A crack of light showed from under a door down the corridor. This was Ogundu's office and I prayed he'd be waiting for me.

I opened the door, and he was. He sat there smiling up at me calmly and quietly.

"Phil—thank God you're here!"

I whirled, shutting the door behind me. She'd been flattened against the wall, behind it. Now she came into my arms.

"Diana, what's the matter?"

She couldn't answer; she could only point.

I broke free and walked over to the smiling Negro. I moved around his chair and now I could see the back of his head—or what was left of it.

Ogundu had no reason to smile.

"What happened?" I muttered.

Diana shook her head. Her eyes avoided mine. I followed their stare to her hand; her right hand, holding the big .38.

We both looked at it for a long moment, and then she spoke. Her voice was only a whisper, but it filled the room, and its echo never died away.

"Yes, Phil. I killed him."

SEVENTEEN

I TOOK THE GUN and laid it on the desk. "His?" I murmured.

Diana nodded. "He had it ready."

"Ready for what?"

"For you." She came to me. "Don't you see? I was right—it *was* supposed to be a trap."

I lifted her chin. "What happened? From the beginning."

"I came here after I left your place. I was afraid to go to the apartment and wait. I had to know."

"You should have waited. Or phoned the police instead."

"I can't help it, it's done now. Phil, don't torment me, isn't it bad enough to realize what I've gotten into without"—she began to sob. I held her close. In a moment she was able to go on.

"I used my own key and walked in. Ogundu must have gotten an awful scare, but he didn't show it. He just asked what I was doing here. So I told him I'd come because of you—you'd been delayed. And I wanted the information he'd promised."

"Did he tell you?"

Diana shook her head. "He said he wouldn't give it to anyone but you. You were the one who deserved to know. I asked him what he meant by that, and he wouldn't answer—just told me to go away. I said I wasn't going until I found out about all this.

"Then he looked at me and he said, 'You really mean that, don't you?'

And he smiled and looked down at the floor and I saw the kerosene drum standing there."

Diana paused, and now I looked down. There *was* a kerosene drum, standing amidst a litter of papers. Something started to crawl along my spine. Diana's words only made it crawl faster.

" 'That's right,' he said. 'I was going to tell him the truth.' He pulled out the gun, then, and pointed it at me, and all the while he kept talking, telling me what he'd planned. He was waiting for you to come so he could kill you. Then he'd start the fire and phone the police—say he caught you, and killed you in self-defense. That would give the police a solution and put him in the clear. He hated you, Phil, because of your investigation. I guess he thought he could get rid of all the cults in town until you came along.

"But now, since you hadn't arrived, he was still going through with his plan. With me for a victim, instead." Diana closed her eyes. "He started to raise the gun—I made a grab for his wrist, twisted his arm around. Then the gun went off and he fell back into the chair.

"After that, I just stood there for a long time. I don't know how long. The next thing I remember is hearing footsteps outside in the hall. I got behind the door and you came in."

"That's all?" I asked.

She nodded.

"There'll be some tough sledding," I told her. "The police will ask a lot more questions."

Diana opened her eyes, wide. "You aren't going to call them?"

I nodded. "What else can I do?"

"Phil!" She stared up at me. "Phil, don't—"

"Suppose you tell me the truth, then. Suppose you tell me how you could have twisted Ogundu's wrist so the gun would shoot him through the back of the head?"

"He must have turned away—yes, I remember now, he broke loose for a second—"

She was pale and wide-eyed and the words were coming too fast. And I could feel myself slowly growing sick inside. Sick and cold. Somebody I had loved had died once. And now somebody I loved was dying again.

"Stop it, Diana! He was sitting in that chair when you killed him. He wasn't struggling. He didn't know you were coming up behind him, ready to blow his brains out—"

She came closer and put her hands on my shoulders.

"Darling—you don't know what you're talking about—"

"Yes I do. I'm beginning to know a lot of things." I caught hold of the collar of her blouse. "You came here to kill Ogundu. Because the little white-faced man had told him you started the fires."

"No! That's impossible, you know yourself, the first time I was with you—"

"You left before one, and you went back to the Brotherhood tabernacle instead of going home. When you furnished an alibi for me to Dalton, you were also furnishing an alibi for yourself. Everything worked out fine, didn't it?"

Her mouth formed words, but none came.

"But there was one thing you hadn't counted on," I said. "The little guy must have seen you. And I suppose he started following you. He saw you the next day when you made a date with Ricardi. That's how you managed to kill him, isn't it? You promised to come to his house and you did—he wouldn't keep a pretty girl out of his bedroom. And that was his mistake. You knocked him out, set fire to his room."

I didn't have to think now, the words were falling into the place. The words—the deeds—

"The little guy knew. He found out you worked here and he hung around, waiting for a chance to see Ogundu when he was alone. Tonight he did. And Ogundu called me.

"You got scared when you saw me visiting Ogundu and came over to find out if I'd learned anything. Then, when Ogundu phoned, you went into action. You killed him with his own gun and decided to carry out this crazy scheme of yours. Collected the paper, got the kerosene from the cellar—"

She froze. Frozen fire, in my arms.

"What are you going to do?"

I moved back. "What can I do? I'm going to call Dalton."

"No!"

She saw my hand go out, grabbed it. At the same time I reached for her blouse, tugged at it, jerking her to one side.

The blouse tore.

The blouse tore, down the front, and I saw what I didn't see in the darkness of the apartment, what I didn't see at the beach the time I started to open her dress and she ran away.

I saw what I'd seen on the curtain upstairs, what she'd told me about when she spoke of the Temple deacons and their ceremonies.

It was burned in her chest, burned red and deep above the breasts, burned in the whiteness of her flesh, just as it must be burned into the blackness of her brain.

I saw the brand of the Phoenix.

I stared at it, and that was my mistake. I should have been staring at her hand, the hand that grabbed the gun from the desk, raised it, and brought the butt crashing down against my skull.

I went out, cold.

EIGHTEEN

IT WASN'T COLD ANY MORE.

It was warm and wet. Not sticky, like the blood that ran down the back of my scalp. This was a creeping wetness, flowing all over me. I could feel it plainly, just as I could feel the tightness in my wrists when she tied my hands behind my back. I was still lying on the floor, but I was wet.

I opened my eyes. She was standing over me, smiling. Smiling, and pouring kerosene.

"Awake?" she said. "Good. I'm glad. I wanted you to be awake. So you could see."

"See? I don't want to see anything. Diana, let me up—"

"No. You stay there. Stay there and watch. You wanted to find out what it's like, didn't you? You wanted to know. Now I'll show you."

The fumes rose, choking me. I twisted my wrists. She'd tied them with twine from the desk; tied them very tightly.

"Don't bother," she told me. "It's no use." She walked over to the heap of papers and dumped the rest of the kerosene on the litter.

"There. That ought to be enough, don't you think?" She giggled. "I suppose you think I'm being very naughty." Something had happened to her voice. If my eyes were closed, I'd have sworn it was a little girl speaking.

But my eyes weren't closed. They were open, and I could see her—see her standing there, a full-grown woman, with her coppery hair hanging down over bare shoulders, and the livid brand blazing between her breasts.

"Mama said I was naughty. When I made the fire in the basement she caught me and gave me a spanking."

I tried to get my legs up. She came over and knelt beside me. "Mustn't move," she murmured. "Mustn't be naughty." She giggled again and hit me with the gun. The side of my head went numb.

"Lie still, now. Lie still and watch. You want to see everything, don't you? How it starts?"

"Diana," I groaned. "For God's sake—"

"Yes, for God's sake. You *do* understand, don't you? He wants me to destroy the altars of abomination, to cleanse the earth of those who bow down to graven images, and the unrighteous, those who sin against the flesh and the spirit—" She was kneeling now, kneeling beside the pile of papers. There was a match-carton in her hand.

Abruptly, her tone altered again. The child was gone, the fanatic was gone. Her voice was normal, intimately vibrant. "Oh, Phil, isn't it exciting? Wait and see. You can't imagine how lovely it is, how it makes you feel. It's like the way you must feel when you hold me. Only this is a clean feeling, it's pure and good, not like that other. No. Not the way *you* feel at all."

"Diana, stop it!"

"I'm going to stop it. I'm going to stop you. You, and all the rest of them, vessels of lust. This is what you want, isn't it? You and my mother and her men—this is all you think about!"

She crouched there, trembling. The matches fell from her fingers and her hands tore at the front of her blouse, ripping it all the way down.

"Look, then! Your hands are tied. You can't touch me. Nobody can touch me. See the brand? God told me to do that. Ogundu didn't know about the brand. God made me do it, to protect myself from evil. He sent me here to burn away all sin. To burn away all sinners."

She picked up the matches. I watched her strike a light. The paper kindled, flared.

"We won't need this now." She rose, switched off the light. The flames licked and spread, sent shadows flickering across the wall.

"You can see, can't you?" she whispered. "You can watch it spread, now. Spread, and grow. I'm going to watch, too. I always run away, but this time I'll stay and watch. I want to see it burn."

The paper was blazing. It was red and blue, and now the drapes were red and blue, too, and I could feel the heat. The fire began to race across the floor toward me.

She stood against the wall and laughed. I rolled over, trying to get back into the far corner. The fire followed, creeping and eating and creeping again.

"Yes," she said. "I want to see it burn. I want to see you burn. The way

that girl burned, the one you told me about. She was evil and so are you.
I'm going to watch God's punishment. It's in the Bible, you know. How
the wicked are cast into the flames. Don't you feel it yet, Phil? You will.
In just a minute now. Yes!"

I wedged myself into the corner, trying to curl around the base of the
desk. The fire flowed across the floor like a living lake, rising in a wave.

Diana began to gasp, but her eyes never wavered. I could see the
reflection of the flames pinpointed in her pupils.

"Burn! I want to see you burn! I want to see everything, Mama wouldn't
let me see, she said it was wicked, but Mama's dead now. God killed her,
He kills the wicked, and He told me I could see—"

It was horrible to hear the voice change, but watching her was even
worse. The features formed and altered like a waxen mask melting in the
heat of the flames; I saw Diana, I saw a child, I saw a woman in ecstasy.
This was it, this was the pyromaniac, the method and the madness that
needs no motive, the firebug—

I heard her scream

The blaze was bright and I could see everything. I jerked my head back,
staring above the sheet of flame.

Diana stood against the wall, near the door. The door was open, now,
and somebody stood on the threshold, then moved forward into the light.

I saw the face, the white face that now shone red in the reflected glare.

But he didn't see me. He stared at the girl.

"You," he said. "You burned the tabernacle. I saw you. I warned Ogundu
tonight, but then I waited because I knew you'd come."

She crouched there, edging toward the door.

"*Witch!*" he shouted.

Suddenly she turned and darted out the doorway. He moved to block
her path, then stepped aside. As she passed him, his arm rose and fell. I
heard him shout again, and for a moment the words didn't register. It
sounded like Biblical quotation—"Thou shalt not suffer a witch to live."

Then I understood why. I understood, when Diana fell forward with
the long knife driven deep between her shoulders.

The witch was dead ...

I tried to get up and almost made it. The desk toppled with a crash,
and I came down on top of it. It was like a little island in that sea of flame,
and now the flame was rising all around, and the smoke was coming up
to stifle me.

From far away I heard sounds, shouts, shots. It seemed to me that I
saw the little man fall, but then the flames came up and I was falling too.

I began to burn.

NINETEEN

IT WAS THREE DAYS before they let me sit up. Even though the burns were all first-degree, I had on too many bandages for comfort.

When Dalton came to see me, I couldn't talk at all. Schwarm visited me the fourth day, and it was a little better.

"You'll be all right," he said. "Another week here, and then a rest. You're lucky they pulled you off that desk in time. If Clark hadn't thought to wrap his coat around you and smother the flames—"

"Never mind about Clark," I said. "What about the little guy? Did you find out his name?"

"Of course. It's John Schoober. We traced his record, too. Typical paranoid—"

"Why?" I muttered. "Because he thought Diana was a witch? I think so, too. Maybe you head-shrinkers have something to learn from the oldtimers. The ones who used to explain insanity in terms of demonic possession."

Schwarm smiled.

I asked questions, then, and pieced things together. It was the little guy who'd jumped Weatherbee in the passage, of course. He hadn't lied about tipping off Ogundu and then waiting around; when he saw us he got scared and gave Weatherbee a knife-wound in the throat.

After I locked the back door on him, he broke through a cellar window and came upstairs. He waited outside the door for a long while—almost too long, as far as I was concerned—until he got up enough courage to face the witch.

Meanwhile some kid came along and happened to notice Weatherbee lying in the passageway. He called a squad car, and the squad got there just about the time the fire became visible from outside the Temple.

That's when they broke down the front door and caught the little guy making his break for it. And Sergeant Clark came in on the double and pulled me out of the blaze.

Schwarm told me all about it now. He said they'd even dug up the dope on Diana Rideaux. He asked me to tell him what had happened, and I did my best.

"Exactly," he said, when I finished. "It all fits in. The hatred of the mother. God as the father-image, idealized. Men as the actual father—feared and hated, fit only for destruction.

"The sexual pattern's there, too. Frigid but promiscuous. With fire as the symbol, fire that destroys passion and the male who can provide it; fire that at the time purifies and preserves. It makes sense."

"The hell it does," I said. "She was a witch."

I told him about the earlier part of the evening, in my apartment—and then I told him about Margery, and my dreams.

"Well, at least you have one thing to be thankful for, Phil," he said. "You won't be getting those dreams any more."

"That's right," I answered.

Schwarm told the truth. I've never dreamed about Margery since then.

But there's a new dream now, a new dream to take its place. I get it whenever I go to sleep without enough in me to knock me cold.

I know it's only a dream, but that doesn't help me. I keep getting hotter and hotter, and I can feel the warmth on my face, and then I look up and see that *other* face. I see Diana's face in the flames, see her scream.

Then I wake up and reach for a cigarette, but I don't light it. I lay there trembling for a long time, wanting to smoke but not daring to. Because where there's smoke, there's fire.

And I'm afraid of fire.

At least, I always *have* been. God knows, I've got reason enough to be afraid, and these dreams only make it worse.

But lately I've been doing a little thinking. Schwarm would say that the only way to conquer a phobia is to make yourself face it. And there's another way of putting it, too.

You've got to fight fire with fire...

Not that I'd actually do anything, understand. But I've been wondering. Suppose I could make myself get *used* to fire? So that I wouldn't be afraid of it?

I don't mean arson, incendiarism. I certainly wouldn't want to hurt anybody—not anybody who hadn't hurt me. But if I just experimented to see what it feels like, maybe down in the basement where nobody would know about it; that would be all right. I mean, I could keep water handy, put it out before anything really got started.

My idea is that I'm not actually afraid of the fire itself. Just the things that have happened to me in connection with fire.

Fire. It isn't something to be afraid of. Not if you can control it. That's the big secret, the way I see it. To *control* fire. Because when you control fire you control everything. Fire is life and it's death, too, and that's why it's so fascinating to watch it. To see it live and burn.

Maybe if I try an experiment or two, the dreams will go away. No harm in that; I'm going to be very careful. And if it helps me get rid of the dreams, that's all I want.

I suppose that's the real reason I've gone to the trouble of writing everything down this way. So that people will understand that I know what I'm doing, why I'm doing it. And there won't be any foolish talk about firebugs.

Because it makes sense, doesn't it? It's not as if I didn't know the difference between the dreams and reality. If you're logical, you can always tell the difference. You live and learn. Live and burn.

Sometimes, lately, that phrase pops into my head when I least expect it. Like a voice. But it *isn't* a voice. You see, I know that. I know the difference between dreams and reality. And I'm just going to use reality to fight the dreams.

Maybe tonight—

The Star Stalker

REEL ONE:

Once Upon a Time—

SOMEHOW the sun always seems to be directly overhead at Hollywood and Vine—even at night, when the neon creates its own illusion of high noon.

That's why the shadow always seemed conspicuous there; the walking shadow of the tall, stoop-shouldered man with the ebony cane. In his black suit and wide-brimmed hat he moved against the sunlight like an animated silhouette and always he moved in silence.

In a way he was a symbol of silence. I've heard it said that he never saw a talking picture, but that's just one of those legends. Hundreds of such legends once centered around Theodore Harker.

You've heard the name, haven't you? Even if you're only twenty, you must have heard the name. It's one of the handful that survived and will survive as long as motion pictures are made. Griffith, De Mille, Stroheim, Chaplin, Pickford, Fairbanks, Valen-tino, Garbo, and Harker. There's a street called Harker out here, and the inevitable canyon. No one has ever forgotten the name, even though the man himself became a shadow.

I don't pretend to know all he did during the last year of his life. He stalked the boulevard by day and at night he went back to the big house in the hills; they say he used to sit and stare out at the distant lights of Hollywood from a darkened room. Perhaps he did, but I don't believe he saw anything. As far as he was concerned, there was nothing left to see.

His pictures, the great pictures of the twelve fabulous years, are still shown at the Museum of Modern Art today. Perhaps that's what he was doing at night in his unlighted room—running those pictures over and over again in the secret projection booth inside his skull.

When he died the whole industry turned out for his funeral; there was almost a half-ton of flowers, and a man from the Academy made a speech. It could have been a spectacle, but it lacked the Harker touch.

Harker would have made a real production out of it. He'd make sure that Lozoff would be there, clicking his heels before the coffin and bowing from the waist. He'd want a moment spared for little Jackie Keeley, clutching his oversized cap as he scooted stiff-legged around a corner. He'd insist upon a shot of Dawn Powers' curls capturing the sunlight and Karl Druse's eyes mirroring midnight. It might have been a great show if Theodore Harker could have been there to direct it.

Maybe he's directing that show now, far beneath the synthetic surface of Forest Lawn. For the rest of the cast has joined him there through the passing years.

Wherever they are, I'm sure they're together once more, with Harker in command. Perhaps he's calling frantically for an extra spot to hit that halo over Dawn's head; maybe he's screaming for a hotter flame to flood Druse's face. But whether it be in Heaven, Hell or Hollywood, Harker remains a great director. He directed all of us, directed our destinies and our dreams.

Now that he's gone, he and the others, there's no one who can be harmed by the truth. And that means I can finally tell the story . . .

ONE

SHORTLY BEFORE nine o'clock on the morning of December 1, 1922, I got off a streetcar and moved into the scented shade of the pepper trees lining Hollywood Boulevard.

The first sightseeing bus of the day was just swinging around the intersection at Sunset and I could hear the megaphone-magnified voice of the tour guide.

"Annow folks, here onyer left, we're just passing the entrance of Coronet Studios, home of such fillum favorites as Maybelle Manners, Emerson Craig, Dude Williams, Karl Druse—"

And Tommy Post.

He didn't bother to add my name but I was there, smiling up at the busload of tourists who stared through me and past me toward the studio gates.

Someday, I thought. *Someday—*

But right now I was just a tall nonentity of nineteen; I didn't really expect to be famous for another two years yet. After all, I was still on my first job—toting scripts for Theodore Harker's production unit at $12 a week. The big thing was to be able to get past the gates, to have the guard say hello to me, and to know that I was in the movies.

In the movies. Free to wander the back lot, to move from set to set as directors uttered the Word that created Life—and, out of sputtering kleig lights, sleazy canvas, painted cardboard, brought new worlds into being.

With my own eyes I had seen the topless towers of Ilium rise against the sun, and watched the fall of the Bastille; witnessed the birth of a Gold Rush boom town and seen its death, a week later, when the set was struck. And there was more than just illusion to enchant me.

Hadn't I seen Wallace Reid, in the flesh? And Mary Miles Minter, and Larry Semon? Once I'd even eaten lunch down the street, sharing the same table with Dorothy Gish! And our regular contract players were all over the lot.

Just last week, Dude Williams called me over to his dressing room. "Tommy," he said, "I reckon I'm clean out of fixin's. How's for you takin' a run over to the drugstore and gettin' me a sack of Bull Durham? Here, keep the change."

A real cowboy star who talked like a real cowboy, and he called me by my first name! If I had to choose between Hollywood and heaven, it was no contest.

Heaven never held an angel to equal Maybelle Manners, even though *she* never called me "Tommy." I doubted if she was even aware of my existence, but it was enough that I was aware of hers. I'd edge onto the set when she was working and stare at that Mona Lisa mask framed by the dark glory of her hair; to look into her eyes was to gaze into the living depths of dreams.

But you wouldn't know about such things unless you were nineteen, and *in the movies*.

This morning I silently celebrated the end of my sixth month on the job as I headed past the main offices and across the open quadrangle to a small building at the left. The windows were lighted and that meant Arch Taylor and Miss Glint were already there.

"Hi, Tommy." Taylor smiled at me when I came in and I had no trouble smiling back. He was a junior scenarist, or as much of a scenarist as anybody could be who worked on a Harker picture. Harker usually wrote his own treatments and frequently he shot "off the cuff," improvising as he went along. But Arch Taylor got screen credit; he was a writer, and I was duly impressed. With his curved pipe, waxed mustache and snappy plus-fours he represented all the sophistication and maturity I hoped to attain when *I* reached twenty-four.

Miss Glint glanced up briefly from her desk and nodded. "Hello, Post." As far as she was concerned, that's all I was—"Post." As in wooden, or pillar-to-.

Once upon a time Miss Glint had written titles at another studio, and there was an unverified rumor that she had been responsible for the immortal "Came the dawn. . . ." If so, her contribution to the literature of the cinema went unrecognized; here at Coronet she was merely a script girl, and I was her flunky. Neither of us ever forgot it. She saw to that.

"Come on, let's get to work," she snapped, both chins jutting in double determination. "Sort these dupes out. They're shooting the arena footage."

I took off my jacket, hung it up, then walked over to the desk and began to smudge my fingers as I separated carbon copies from original pages.

Taylor walked over to the window and stared out as he lit his pipe. "Morris is here," he said. "Just walked into the front office."

Miss Glint frowned. "Maybe I better turn off the light. Him and his economy! Head of the studio and worrying about a penny's worth of electricity. But then they're all alike, aren't they?"

"Who's all alike?"

"Them. You know." She frowned again.

"I don't know." Taylor drew on his pipe. "And I've never heard Sol Morris complain about expenses. Have you, Tommy?"

I shook my head.

Miss Glint sniffed, "Take my word for it, I know what *they* are. After all, wasn't I married to one for nearly two years? All I got was complaints—the gas bill, the rent, everything. Money, that's the only thing *they* ever think about."

The chins were quivering now, and Taylor took a deep breath. "Lay off, Maggie. Come on, let's catch some coffee before the old man arrives."

Miss Glint gasped and gulped. The gasp was for the familiarity of the "Maggie" and the gulp for the sacrilegious reference to Theodore Harker. Then she turned her back on us both.

"Okay." Taylor winked at me. "How about you joining me, Tommy? Or do you have a previous engagement with Mr. Laemmle?"

"That peasant? I wouldn't sit at the same table with him," I said. "Or William Fox, either." I spread the sorted pages on the desk and straightened them out in neat piles, then reached for my jacket. "But you I like."

"Be sure you're back in fifteen minutes!" the Glint called after us.

Taylor nodded casually and we stepped out, strolling across the quadrangle to our right.

"I never knew her name was Maggie," I said. "And what was she talking about just now?"

"Sad story." Taylor pocketed his pipe as we walked. "She married a guy named Bronstein right after the war. I guess he was a bum—anyway, he just up and disappeared one day, cleaning out the savings account before he left. Ever since then she's had it in for the whole human race, with particular emphasis on a certain section."

"So that's why she's such a sourball!"

"One thing you'll learn, Tommy. There's always a reason why people act the way they do. And remember, it *is* an act. Glint got a raw deal from one man, so she tries to take it out on everybody, but she's the same as you and I underneath. She wants to be loved."

I nodded, staring across at the barn. That's right, the barn. It was still standing at the corner of the lot—the original barn, the original home of Coronet Pictures.

Sol Morris had bought it in 1913, the same year that Lasky and De Mille rented *their* barn and started making movies in Hollywood. Since that time Coronet had been spreading and sprawling its way across adjoining acreage, and Messrs. Lasky and De Mille hadn't done too badly, either.

Now the barn served as a prop warehouse, and a small portion near the door had been given over to a coffee canteen. Taylor and I stepped up to the counter and ordered. I gazed past him into the dark interior of the old structure.

"Hard to believe, isn't it?" I said. "Only eight years since Mr. Morris started here, and look where he is today. This big studio—thirty features a year, and all the two-reelers. Millions and millions of dollars, and it all began in a stable."

"So did Christ." Taylor grinned.

"Quite a cynic, aren't you?"

"Sure. It's my act." The counterman pushed the coffee mugs toward us and Taylor handed one to me. "Speaking of acts, what's yours?"

"I don't have any."

He gave me a long stare. "Maybe it's time you developed one."

"Why? I'm doing all right just being myself."

"Are you?" Taylor took a gulp of coffee, then set his mug down on the counter. "How much do you earn a week? Never mind, I know. I started the same way, in the same job, over at the old Sunrise studio just before the war. And I'd be there yet if I hadn't learned. You have to have an act if you want to get ahead out here. What's the matter, didn't your folks teach you anything?"

"You mean Uncle Andy and Aunt Minnie?"

"No, your real folks—your parents."

I stared down at the counter. "I never had any. I lived in an orphanage back East until I was out of school."

He hesitated. "Did they die, or—?"

"I wouldn't know." I talked to the coffee mug instead of looking at Taylor; that made it easier to continue. "I guess they just left me there after I was born. I didn't even think I had any relatives until Uncle Andy and Aunt Minnie showed up and took me West with them."

The coffee mug didn't comment, and neither did Taylor, so I was able to go on. "Aunt Minnie's my real aunt, my mother's sister, and she and Uncle Andy never had any kids of their own. And when my mother did, and then ran off and left me, it made Aunt Minnie feel guilty. That's what I figure—she won't even talk to me about it."

"Why didn't she take you in right away?"

"Because she and Uncle Andy were on the road all the time, in vaudeville. But when they moved out here and settled down, they came after me. Gave me a room of my own, got me this job. I owe them a lot. It's almost like having folks of you own."

"But not quite." Taylor reached for his pipe. "What you need is a father. The kind of guy you can go to when you want to talk about your troubles, or your future."

He reached out and put his hand on my shoulder. It was a big hand, long and thin, but the fingers were strong. "What about your future, Tommy? What do you want out of life, anyhow?"

I closed my eyes for a moment, trying to shut out everything except the way his hand felt; trying to imagine that it was my father's hand, my *real* father's hand, warm and friendly and waiting to guide me forward. Then, all at once, I could talk.

"I want to be like you," I said. "I want to be a movie writer and have people buy my dreams and pay money to see them. Then maybe, some day if I ever get married and have a kid of my own I'll be proud of myself and want the kid to know about it instead of sneaking off and leaving him in—"

That last sentence just slipped out because I didn't know it was coming until I said it, and I stopped and waited for Taylor to laugh.

He didn't. He just looked at me and took his hand away and said, in a very firm voice, "Well, why in hell don't you write something, then? Stuff you can show me, so that maybe I can give you a few pointers?"

"Would you?"

"Sure. You get busy and show me what you can do. Meanwhile, figure out an act."

I frowned. He waved his pipe at me.

"Look, kid. You've got to impress people. The *right* people. And who are the right people on this lot, for you? Just two. Theodore Harker—your boss. And Sol Morris—Harker's boss. Your assignment for today is to figure out a way to get them to notice you."

Taylor turned away and I followed him across the quadrangle. "I did it," he said. "Everyone does it out here. That's what's so great about the flicker business—it's all an act. Every day they're turning water into wine, celluloid into gold. Think it over, Tommy. Movies are magic. And miracles are performed by gods."

He swung off toward the gate beyond the main office. "And speaking of gods, methinks I detect the coming of the Lord. Prepare to meet your Maker!"

I didn't take his advice. I was much too interested in watching the arrival of Theodore Harker.

TWO

SOME GODS come in a fiery chariot. Theodore Harker arrived in a black
Rolls Royce. Some gods appear in shining garments. Theodore Harker
wore a midnight hue. Some gods shield their countenances from men.
Theodore Harker moved with chin outthrust, his bold features pallidly
prominent against their background of black.

Taki the chauffeur slid out from behind the wheel, padded around to
the curbside and opened the door. As Harker stepped out, the Japanese
handed him an ebony cane. For a moment Harker leaned on it, a
white-faced shadow; black fedora hat pulled down over his long black
hair, black collar rising about the choking knot of his black string tie, black
suit cloaking his bony body, black shoes planted squarely beneath him. It
was theatricalism incarnate, but who had a better right to affect the
theatrical? Even his face was the mask of an old-style Shakespearean
player—the mobile mouth, thin-lipped but pliant; the long, jutting nose
flared by pride; the sable accent of eyebrows echoing the darkness of his
garb; and finally, the eyes. The eyes that were blacker than black.

Taylor was wrong. This was no god. Magic may *come* from gods, but it
is practiced by magicians. And Theodore Harker was definitely one of
them. A black magician, carrying an ebony cane which was his wand of
power. He had but to point it and men died, empires rose and fell. Today
that wand would wave over *The Burning of Rome.*

"Good morning, Mr. Harker." Taylor spoke and I nodded, hoping he'd notice me.

But Theodore Harker wasn't responding to any greeting this morning. He swept into the studio, Taki hovering behind, and his eyes were intent on the far horizon. His own, inner horizon.

"Glad to see you back," said the guard at the inner gate, but even this allusion to his absence these past two days did not evoke a reply. Harker was down in his private darkness.

Perhaps it wasn't gloomy there, for him. But his being there brought gloom to others. For Harker now brushed past the extra-bench without a glance, and I could see the gloom sweep across each ignored face in his wake.

It was a familiar sight to me by now, but I still felt a twinge every morning that I saw it.

We had this extra-bench just inside of the front gate. It was nothing but a double row of planks set on wooden blocks, made to accommodate a dozen or so; however, it generally served to seat everybody and his brother. To say nothing of his sister, grandmother, second-cousin-by-marriage, and assorted offspring.

Casting Director Sam Lipsky called the talent offices the day before when he needed walk-ons, bits, dress extras or crowd atmosphere. It was common and accepted practice, known to all—but still these others came. Came and sat, day after day, hoping for a nod. The offchance summons, the change of schedule demanding additional help, or just a plain, ordinary miracle—the kind of miracle that was always happening out here.

They weren't supposed to hang around, of course. They probably bribed the guard to get this far. And they weren't supposed to bother Harker or any of the directors. But here they were. The little dark-haired girl who'd jumped up one morning about a week ago and kissed Harker's hand. The old man with the dyed muff. The sallow cowboy with the hangover. The blonde who *looked* like Mae Murray, but who wasn't. And that funny little foreigner with the mustache and the single white streak in his hair, who always showed up in evening dress. He'd been here five days a week for almost a month now; never missed a morning and never got a nod, let alone a call.

I watched them emote as Harker passed, watched them register eagerness, anticipation, realization, rejection, dejection. The magician did not wave his wand in their direction; the gate of heaven clanged shut behind him.

But theirs was an enduring faith and so they waited. Waited for another hour, another day, another year if necessary. That was what it would take, no doubt. Next year the little dark-haired girl could be right up there with Norma Talmadge and Leatrice Joy. Next year the sallow cowboy (sixgun in hand, all through with that bootleg hooch, pardner!) would ride the cinematic saddle behind William S. Hart. Next year the blonde would show Mae Murray some *real* dancing. Next year the funny little foreigner would—but what did *he* want?

I had no time to ponder on his problems; my own were waiting for me. *"Get an act. Make them notice you."* I had to do it, I knew that. If not, I was no better off than any of these extras on the bench.

Taylor walked ahead of me now, talking to Harker. I don't know if Harker was listening. I know *I* wasn't.

Make them notice you. But how?

"Post!"

Miss Glint recalled me to reality as she beckoned from the office doorway, brandishing a sheaf of script pages.

"Take these over to Number Three and see that they're distributed. I'll be along in a minute. Come on, get moving!"

I moved. Harker and Taylor had disappeared into the director's private bungalow, just around the corner from Number Three Stage, and I entered the set alone.

The Coliseum was a madhouse. A hundred bearded and bewigged extras swarmed across the bleachers in the background, tangling togas as they scrambled into position beneath the hot lights.

Three camera crews were setting up their positions around the edge of the arena before the bleachers and the head gaffer was busy with his men on the catwalks overhead. Carpenters banged on the flats behind Nero's throne and Nero himself was cursing one of the Penny brothers as the makeup man adjusted a laurel wreath on the imperial brow. And over it all I could hear the roaring of the lions.

The lions were penned into a double cage off at the far end of the stage. Their trainer was talking to a big, burly man in a gladiator's costume—Gus Gunther, who doubled for the star, Emerson Craig, in action sequences.

I walked around, depositing copies of scripts on the vacant seats of chairs fringing the outer edge of the arena. One for Harker, one for each of the heads of the camera crews, one for the actor playing Nero, and one for Maybelle Manners.

The lions didn't need script pages. They paced back and forth behind the bars, coughing and growling and twitching. I moved closer to the double cage and one of the lions roared.

Elmo Lincoln could play Tarzan, but I wasn't having any. I jumped about a foot, turned, moved away from the cages quickly. As I did so I saw Maybelle Manners enter, wearing the white robe of a martyr and moving with the serenity of a saint.

Becky, her maid, escorted her to the canvas chair behind one of the camera setups in a spot shielded from the glare of the kleig lights. As he caught sight of the actress, the Penny brother abandoned Nero and bounded over like a goosed gazelle, his powderpuff already poised for action.

Maybelle Manners sank into her chair, sighed deeply, and closed her eyes in patient resignation. So might an actual Early Christian have surrendered herself before entering the arena for the final sacrifice—even if there was no makeup man present to powder her shiny nose.

I took a deep breath and moved up beside the chair.

"Good morning, Miss Manners."

The eyes opened. Mona Lisa was staring at me. "Yes?"

Her husky voice did something to my spine; at nineteen, I seemed to have a spine like a xylophone. As she stared, I reddened.

"Uh—Miss Manners—"

"What is it?"

"I—I think you're sitting on your script."

She glanced down, saw the protruding edge of the pages on the seat beneath her. Then she shrugged. "Does it matter? This is the third straight day we've been supposed to shoot the death scene and *he* hasn't come near the set."

"He's here today, Miss Manners. I saw him come in a few minutes ago."

Mona Lisa frowned. "Then why are the lions over there? Don't tell me he's going to do the gladiator footage first!"

"That's right, Miss Manners." Arch Taylor moved up beside me. "The front office tried to call you this morning, but you'd already left."

"You mean I came down here again for nothing?"

"I'm sorry, Miss Manners. We've got to use the lions today because Ince has them rented the rest of the week. I'm sure we'll get to your scene tomorrow—they'll call you this afternoon—"

Maybelle Manners rose suddenly, brushing aside the Penny brother and his powderpuff. "Come on, Becky," she murmured to the maid. "Let's get out of this zoo!"

Mona Lisa made her exit.

And the magician entered, right on cue.

Theodore Harker halted at the edge of the lighted area. He waved the ebony cane. The assistant director moved out of the shadows behind him, cupped his hands.

"Quiet, everybody!"

The banging stopped. The shouting died away. The grips and gaffers scuttled to their appointed places. The camera crews stepped forward to take their posts. The extras settled down on the bleacher seats above the arena. Even the lions were silent.

Harker started over to his chair. I was there ahead of him, picking up the script pages from the seat and handing them to him. I smiled as I did so, trying to keep the pages on a level with my face. Maybe he'd associate the two. *Kid with a script. Always see him with a script. Maybe he writes them. Ought to look into that some time. What's the name of that young fellow with the script? Post, eh? Post—script. Postscript. Why, it's like a joke—*

It was a joke, because Theodore Harker didn't look at me. He didn't look at the script, either; just tossed it to the floor.

For the second time in five minutes, I blushed. Harker turned away, cupping his hands to his mouth.

"Anatole—where the devil are you?"

A fat man with a walrus mustache raced forward from the sidelines, carrying a violin. As he ran he cradled it like a little brown baby.

"A thousand pardons!" he wheezed. "I 'ave been most unavoidably detained. But I am ready to make of the music for you now."

The little mood musician bowed and scraped, then lifted his fiddle and bowed and scraped it. As I brushed past him, he whispered out of the side of his mouth. "Get that goddam stand for me, boy. I was late this morning."

I located his music stand near the door, set it up behind Harker's chair. Harker was striding out into the arena, firing orders, and I listened closely. I mustn't miss the sound of opportunity when it knocked.

"Bradshaw, the lights are *wrong*. This is an arena, the Coliseum, outdoors. That means sunshine, man. Haven't you ever been outdoors in daylight, Bradshaw? Make a note to try it sometime—but not *now*. Get your boys busy on those lights."

The ebony cane rose and stabbed accusingly at the Penny brother. "What have you done to Nero?"

"I finished him ten minutes ago, Mr. Harker."

"Finished him? You'll finish me, Penny! Look at that laurel wreath. Go ahead, just look at it."

"I am looking at it, Mr. Harker."

"And you don't notice anything wrong? Where's your tin cup, Penny? I'll drop a nickel into it and you can keep the pencil."

"Mr. Harker, if you'll only tell me—"

"I *am* telling you! The laurel wreath, Penny. You've got it set on his head like a crown."

"But Nero's the emperor—"

"Of course he's the emperor, but don't you know your Roman history? Nero was never a regal figure, and the wreath must show this to the audience. I want it worn to one side, tossed on carelessly, drunkenly—the very symbol of his character."

Penny scurried off, and then it was Gus Gunther's turn. The stunt man came up with the lion trainer. Harker fired questions, but this time he waited for answers.

Yes, the cats were safe. The trainer had a gun, but this was just for show—all four of the lions were tame and toothless. The only thing was, which did Mr. Harker want first, the whole shebang loose in the arena or Gus Gunther's special stunt work with Duke?

"We'll shoot the stunt sequence this morning and get it over with," said

Theodore Harker. He beckoned to the camera crews. "Over here, boys. I want you to follow this, because we're going to get it all on one take."

Gus Gunther was going to wrestle a lion in the arena. Long shots only, because they'd do close-ups later, with hero Emerson Craig fighting a stuffed beast. The cameras would catch the action from three angles at their prearranged positions.

The cameramen moved away and Harker glanced at Gus. "I don't want your face in any of the shots. Keep looking at Nero and the crowd. Can you do that?"

"Sure." Gus grinned. "Maybe you better tell the lion, too."

"No problem," said the trainer. "Duke's harmless, you know that. Didn't you just pet him? Come on, let's get him ready."

Gus and the trainer walked over to the double cage and opened one end. The biggest lion—the one that had roared at me—padded out on the end of a leash. The trainer led him to the center of the arena, stroking his mane. Gus stood there calmly as the lion yawned up at him, sniffed, blinked. Then Duke lay down in the sawdust.

"Oh, no!" Harker groaned. He turned to the makeup man. "Penny—get out there and brush him off!"

Penny dropped his powderpuff. Fortunately for him, the trainer was already yanking on Duke's leash. When the lion rose, he brushed the sawdust from the beast's flanks, picked flecks from the tawny mane.

"That's enough," Harker called. "Places, everyone!"

There was activity behind the cameras and lights. Arch Taylor ushered Miss Glint to her chair behind the director. The assistant director herded the extras into a tighter grouping on the benches at either side of Nero's imperial box. Nero mounted his throne and leaned forward.

Theodore Harker settled himself in his canvas chair, one finger crooked commandingly. He looked far more regal than Nero, or even the lion.

"Anatole!" he shouted. "Give me something to wake up that brute—he's dead on his feet."

The fat violinist riffled through the music on his stand, searching for proper mood music to awaken a tame lion.

Gus Gunther extended his arms, flexed them, then turned to face the audience of extras. The trainer removed Duke's harness and backed away, calling to Gus. "Okay, remember what I told you. He's trained to wrestle—just don't squeeze too hard or you'll hurt him."

Harker gazed around the set once more. Then he stood up and his eyes were everywhere. I followed his gaze across the cameras, up into the newly blossoming arc lights, out past the arena to the extras, back to the center where Gus Gunther faced the motionless lion.

Everything was silent on the set. And it *was* a set, nothing more. A crazy tangle of kleigs and tripods and flats and overhead walks and wires and men in shirtsleeves and sweating extras and a cardboard man facing a cardboard lion in a cardboard Coliseum.

Then Theodore Harker raised his magic wand and uttered the magic words. "Roll 'em!" he said.

And the dream began.

Man met beast in the bloodstained arena. An unarmed Christian braved the fangs of the jungle killer, for a mad emperor's cruel enjoyment.

Warily the gladiator advanced, arms outstretched. Sullenly the tawny terror circled him, tail lashing in a frenzy. All at once the man sprang forward—the lion rose to meet him—they stood locked in a monstrous embrace—

"Stop waltzing!" Harker yelled. "Anatole, where's the music?"

The little musician lifted his bow and sent forth the soaring strains of "Entry of the Gladiators."

"Pick up the tempo!" Harker thumped his cane on the floor in agitated rhythm. "Gus, let's look alive—you're not playing with a kitten—"

Then it happened.

Man and brute swayed together, and suddenly the lion roared. The huge paws rose, raking Gunther's back. When they came away I saw that the stunt man's shoulders were laced with red ribbons.

Gus Gunther gasped and tried to turn. The lion clawed again.

"Get him off!" Gus shouted.

"Yes, get him off!" Harker echoed. Then, to the cameras beyond, "But keep rolling until they do—we can use this!"

The trainer raced into the arena, shooting blanks from his revolver. The lion coughed, dropped to all fours, cowered as the trainer advanced, then stood silently as the harness was strapped into place. Tugging on the leash, the trainer led Duke back into his cage. An excited babble rose from the extras.

Arch Taylor was running out the doorway. "I'll call Doc Rose!" he yelled. Gus Gunther bled his way over to Anatole who gazed up at him, eyes shock-wide.

"You and your lousy fiddling!" Gus panted. "Don't you know them cats don't like music?"

Anatole lowered his eyes, and his violin. "I am sorree—ten thousand apologies—"

"Aah, to hell with it!" Gus turned away. "Get that croaker, quick. Them claws is poison, sometimes."

"Easy." Harker moved up to the injured man. "He's coming now." He caught sight of the assistant director. "Tell those extras to shut up!"

Dapper little Doc Rose hurried forward, carrying his bag. He motioned to Gus. "Over here, please." In a moment Gus was stretched out on a table generally reserved for portable props. Doc worked quickly—examining, sponging, swabbing, bandaging—

"What do you think you're doing?" Harker exclaimed. "No bandages!"

"It's necessary."

"But you'll ruin the next take! Whoever heard of a bandaged gladiator?"

"You'll have to replace him."

"In the middle of shooting? Be reasonable."

Doc shook his head, "I want this man home in bed before the lunch hour or I won't answer for the consequences. He's been badly mauled."

"It's okay, Mr. Harker," said Gus. "I'll do it again—but this time, no music."

"No. We'll think of something." Harker turned away. "Bandages!" he muttered. "The things I have to suffer—"

"I'll phone casting," Arch Taylor volunteered. "Chances are we can get somebody down here this afternoon."

"Afternoon? It's only ten-thirty now. We've got a full two hours before lunch. Don't you realize what this is costing us, with the extras and all?" Harker's voice was strident. "Besides, we *must* shoot now. It was planned this way. Can't you understand that?"

He was talking to Taylor, but all at once the words were echoing in me. And I heard a different sound; the long-awaited knocking of opportunity.

I turned and ran out.

They were still sitting on the extra-bench, all of them. I peered at the faces hastily, hopefully.

The guy with the muff wouldn't do, of course. The sallow cowhand was out—he had the shakes. What about that young man over in the corner? No good, he wore glasses. And that party down front was too fat. Then, *who?*

He stood up when he saw me staring, stood up and bowed. No one had ever bowed to me before.

"Can I be of assistance?" asked the little foreigner with the white streak in his hair. His voice was soft, with just the trace of an accent.

"I don't know." I stared even more intently. He wasn't tall enough, but—

I glanced around, then took a deep, determined breath. "Come on, let's go inside."

The guard glanced up at me as we passed the inner gate. "It's all right," I said. "Mr. Harker wants him."

I wasn't sure it was all right, and I wasn't sure Mr. Harker wanted him. But my little foreigner had no doubts. He beamed at the gatekeeper as though he were Saint Peter himself.

"What is it Mr. Harker requires?" asked the soft voice, as we moved across the quadrangle. "A dress extra, perhaps?"

"Not exactly. Scene calls for a man to fight a lion."

"I see."

Doc Rose was leading Gus through the doorway as we approached, muttering something about stitches. I nodded at Gus's retreating back. "That's the fellow you're replacing."

"Oh?"

"Think you can handle it?"

"Perhaps."

"Well, if you've got any doubts, maybe we better not go in. Mr. Harker's a little upset this morning."

"I will fight your lion."

"All right. But just let me do the talking."

He nodded. I led him onto the set, led him over to where Harker stood, still arguing with Arch Taylor.

"Pardon me, Mr. Harker."

He kept right on talking. I took another breath.

"Mr. Harker—"

He turned and looked at me. "Yes?"

"I've found your gladiator."

"You found—what?"

"I saw a man on the extra-bench. I think he can handle the scene for you."

Harker sat down. "Where is he?"

I stepped aside and nudged the little foreigner forward. Harker stared at him for a long moment. Then he stood up again, slowly. He was a tall man and he seemed to stand up in sections. Confronting the little extra player he looked even taller.

Then he turned to me and sighed. "I need a gladiator," he said. "A gladiator. Young, fearless—a big man, with an athlete's body. And you bring me a dwarf."

It was so quiet you could hear a jaw drop. But not mine. Somehow, my jaw was wagging.

"But Mr. Harker, you're only taking long shots, aren't you? He doesn't have to look like Emerson Craig, not with his back to the camera. And I got to thinking—wouldn't a small man look better in long shots? He'd make the lion seem that much bigger. Bring out the menace, the danger."

Harker didn't answer me. But suddenly he glanced at the little foreigner. "What's your name?" he asked.

"Kurt Luzovsky, sir."

"Know anything about animals?"

Luzovsky smiled. "For two years I was head keeper at the Berlin Zoo."

Harker turned away. "Penny!" he called. "Take this man down to wardrobe and get him an outfit like Gunther's. I want him dressed and back here in fifteen minutes."

I watched Theodore Harker as he walked away and I wanted to run after him. Run after him and yell, "But you can't do this—this is *my* scene—it was all *planned*."

But I didn't run and I didn't yell.

Instead, he halted. Halted and turned. "Come here," he said.

I came there.

"I want to thank you for trying to help."

"It—it wasn't anything, Mr. Harker."

He nodded. "You're probably right. I don't think this little man will do at all. But we'll give it a try. Anyway, I appreciate the effort, Mr. Post."

I stood there as Harker moved off, and all I could think of was *he knows my name, he thanked me, he knows my name*—

Arch Taylor came up beside me.

"Well, Mr. Post," he said, softly. "Welcome to Hollywood. Don't look now, but I think you've started to arrive."

THREE

KURT LUZOVSKY WAS WAITING for me outside the office door when the day's shooting ended.

"Please, you will be my guest for dinner this evening?" he asked. "I am in your debt."

"Forget it—glad you got a break."

"You will come?"

"Uh—yes. I guess so."

So I phoned Aunt Minnie I wouldn't be home for supper and we went to Luzovsky's place. He had a little flat over near Highland and we walked all the way, climbed the stairs to the landing where Madame Olga waited.

Madame Olga was a plump, raven-haired woman whose face might have passed as a bovine caricature of Maybelle Manners'. She greeted us warmly and we dined warmly, on goulash and salad. Then came the harsh Turkish cigarettes and the mellow Tokay. Luzovsky had purchased both at a little store at the corner; the cigarettes from the counter in front and the wine from under the counter in back.

"Celebration," he explained to Madame, after introducing me. "Mr. Post—the young, gentleman here—has secured me a position with Theodore Harker."

For a moment the bovine face bore a smile surpassing that of Maybelle Manners in her most Mona Lisa-like mood. And from time to time, during the meal and after, that smile returned as Luzovsky told her what had happened.

"When we finished," he said, "Mr. Harker himself ordered the close-ups. For a test, he said. And we stayed half an hour longer. Tomorrow we will see the rushes. And do you know what they paid me for today's work? Twenty-five dollars!"

Madame beamed. "Kurt—how wonderful!"

"I told you it would happen, remember? It had to happen. As Mr. Harker put it, some things are fated when a man follows his star."

"Mr. Harker believes in astrology, I guess." I smiled at Luzovsky as he refilled my wine glass. "Kind of a strange one, in a way."

"A genius," Luzovsky insisted. "A great genius. Like Wiene, and Lang, and Lubitsch."

"Who are they?"

And with that question my formal education began. I learned a lot that evening. I learned that Turkish tobacco is strong, that they made movies in France and Germany too, that Tokay brings giddiness when taken in excess, that *The Cabinet of Dr. Caligari* was a cinematic milestone.

Then we were walking in the cool California night (Tokay brings giddiness) and I learned about Luzovsky, too.

Kurt Luzovsky, once *aide-de-chief* of His Excellency, Grand Duke Nicholas. Kurt Luzovsky, who gave up his commission to marry Olga, orphaned by a pogrom in Warsaw. Kurt Luzovsky, penniless student at the Sorbonne, airplane mechanic in the Lafayette Escadrille, refugee in New York, hanger-on at the Long Island movie studios. Amateur actor, amateur director, amateur set designer and once—only once—professional production manager for a company that folded after one picture.

"They didn't even have the money to process the film," he told me. "There was nothing to pay me with except the negative. I still have it." He smiled and tapped his head, indicating the streak of white in his hair. "This is another souvenir of those days."

"Then what happened?"

A shrug. "One must live. I became a gigolo."

The word was new to me. He explained, in detail. "A paid dancing partner of foolish women. A paid bed-partner of women still more foolish. One's feet become sore—and other things—"

"What did Madame think?"

Another shrug. "We had to eat. And get money to come here."

"You'd already planned on going to Hollywood?"

"Of course. My future lies in motion pictures. Mr. Harker realized my ability at once."

I nodded. It was true. Right after the wrestling stunt with the lion—which Luzovsky had carried off without a hitch or the need for retakes—Harker had taken the little man aside and talked to him long and earnestly. Then the test was hastily improvised. Harker had seen something that interested him.

But I wondered just how long Luzovsky had been sitting on the extra-bench, at Coronet and other studios.

"Over a year," he told me.

"Without any work?"

There had been some, at first—but not enough to continue paying for the services of a two-bit talent agent over on Sunset. So he bussed dishes, and sat at the studios. He swept out stores, and sat at the studios. He peddled perfume door-to-door, and sat at the studios. "And always I studied," he said. "Night after night I studied, here and abroad. I know all there is to know about cinema."

"Didn't realize there was so much on it in the library," I confessed.

"My dear boy—one does not go to the library to study motion pictures. One goes to the movies."

That's what Luzovksy had done, night after endless night. Some evenings there wasn't money enough for food, but always a dime or a quarter for the movies. For Swanson and Arbuckle and Bushman and Chaplin and even for Pearl White. For the directorial efforts of both the De Mille brothers, and the great David Wark Griffith. Those dimes and quarters were not spent on entertainment; they were invested in the future.

"I made up my mind long ago," he said—his face was in the shadows, but I know he didn't smile—"Harker is the only man competent to direct me. He has the touch to exploit my talent."

"You talk as though it's already decided."

"Of course! I shall be a star within a year. All I needed was opportunity. This you gave me, today. And I am grateful."

We had walked a long way up Highland Avenue—past the frame porches of the Hollywood Hotel, and up the hilly slope beyond.

"Tired?" I asked.

"Not at all. It is only that the trousers are tight." He indicated the dress suit.

"You should have changed clothes."

"Changed?" He smiled. "But this is the only suit I own."

That explained a lot of things. But it didn't explain the overpowering self-assurance of the man. Certainly he seemed to know about foreign films and actors I'd never heard of—Emil Jannings, Conrad Veidt, Asta Neilsen and Pola Negri. And like millions of others, he'd been going to the picture-show for years over here. Maybe he was a good actor, too, but that proved nothing. Why was he so confident?

We climbed the hillside west of Highland and stood there at the top of the spangled night. Lights winked and wriggled across Hollywood below and the stars outshone them overhead.

I stared up at the sky. "Do you think Harker's right? Do you really believe they control the future?"

"Yes. I see my future there."

I glanced at him quickly. He was quite serious. But while I had been looking up at the stars, Luzovsky was gazing at the scene below.

"You see?" he said, softly. "From here you can't tell where the artificial lights end and the real stars begin. You can't tell the difference." He smiled. "Perhaps that's the secret—there isn't any difference."

FOUR

THE NEXT MORNING, after breakfast, I pulled out my box of Fatimas and lit a cigarette.

Aunt Minnie made a face. "Where'd you get those things?"

"Mr. Luzovsky gave them to me."

"They sure stink." Anatole came out of the bedroom. He wore pants and suspenders but no shirt.

"Hi, Uncle Andy," I said.

He sat down at the table and held out his coffee cup as Aunt Minnie filled it. "Acting mighty fancy, aren't we?"

I grinned at him. "Look who's talking. Is it any worse than pretending to be a Frenchman and pretending to play the violin?"

"Never mind about that." But he grinned back. "You know Harker goes for that phoney-accent routine. And I'm a damned good fiddle player even if I'm not a real Frog."

He scooped up the yolk of an egg and put it in his mouth, then pointed his fork at me. "Speaking of phonies, what about this joker you dragged onto the set yesterday?"

"He's no fake. You saw how he handled that lion."

Uncle Andy disposed of his egg white. "Maybe so. But you can't tell if a man's an actor just because he knows how to go into a clinch with a dumb animal. What I say is, put him up against Maybelle Manners and see what happens." He gulped the rest of his coffee and stood up, pushing back his chair.

"Must you rush so?" Aunt Minnie asked.

"Got to get into my outfit," he said. "See you later." He bowed at me. *"Au revoir, M'sieu Tommee,"* he called as he went into the bedroom, shutting the door behind him.

"Where'd he pick up that accent?" I asked Aunt Minnie.

"I don't know. He had it when I met him, playing tent shows. Comedy fiddle, in a French getup. When we got married he put me in the act."

"You never told me what you did."

She smiled. "Just stood around wearing tights. You wouldn't believe it to look at me now, but it really dressed up the routine."

"I believe you. I saw some of those pictures in the scrapbook."

Aunt Minnie stared at me over her coffee cup. "I thought that was put away."

"Uncle Andy must have been looking at it last night," I told her. "Anyhow, it was out on the table when I got home." I took a deep breath. "Aunt Minnie—do you have any pictures of my folks in there?"

She put her cup down, hard. "How many times must I tell you? I don't want you snooping around—"

"You call that snooping? All I'm trying to do is find out about my own parents!"

"Sorry." Aunt Minnie got up and came over to me. "I know how you feel—"

"Were they so terrible?" I asked. "Were they? Because if it's something like that, I wouldn't care. Even if they were—well, murderers—it wouldn't matter. Just so I *know*."

"You'll know, some day. I promise."

"Some day!"

"Please, Tommy." She put her hand on my shoulder. "I'll ask Andy before he goes—maybe he can work something out—"

"Work what out? I don't understand—"

"You will. Be patient, just a little longer. We'll talk about it tonight."

"Okay." I rose and moved to the front door. By the time I opened it I was able to smile again. "Guess I shouldn't complain, as long as I have you and Uncle Andy."

But as I went out, I knew it wasn't enough. I had to know, and I was going to find out.

Right now, though, there was a job to do.

Arch Taylor was crossing the quadrangle as I came through the studio gates. He hailed me and I fell into step beside him.

"Is Mr. Harker here yet?" I asked.

"He's not coming in today."

"But what about the rushes on Luzovsky's test?"

"I wouldn't know." Taylor quickened his pace. "Got to check with John

Frisby. He's taking over the shooting—just some pick-ups, crowd stuff."
He left me, heading for the arena set.

Frowning, I started past the canteen. One the way I saw two Arabs,
Madame Pompadour, and Buffalo Bill Cody. None of them could answer
my question. *What about that screen test?*

"Hi, sugar!"

I glanced up. Carla Sloane was sitting on a stool at the canteen counter.
She waved me over.

"How about some coffee?"

I joined her, nodding as I sneaked a peek at her legs. Carla wriggled
around on the stool and her skirt crept above her knees; according to
studio gossip, Carla's skirts were always up, whether she herself was
vertical or horizontal.

She probably knew about the gossip, because the little blonde manicurist heard everything. In her professional capacity she served (if that's
the word) the executives in the front office. Even Mr. Morris himself
seemed to require a manicure from time to time.

Because she was both inquisitive and acquisitive, many people disliked
Carla. I didn't. It isn't that I was tolerant; I just had a thing about her legs.

She sipped her coffee. "Boy, I can sure use this. Have I got a head!"

"Party?"

She nodded. "A gang of us went down to Vernon last night. Baron
Long's—you know."

I knew about Baron Long's place, and the Sunset Inn and the Ship's
Cafe in Venice. They weren't speakeasies, exactly, but few of their patrons
seemed to escape a hangover the next morning.

"Guess who we saw?" Carla was asking. "Thomas Meighan. And Milton
Sills. He's cute!" She put her cup down, leaving a kissprint on the rim. "Of
course, I always did go for older men."

"Theodore Roberts?" I suggested.

"Oh, he's older than God! Which reminds me, I just came from there."

"Where?"

"Morris's office, silly! And is *he* having a fit. When I left, he was tearing
his hair."

"This I'd like to see," I said. "With his bald head."

"He had his hands in his pockets." Carla giggled.

"What's it all about?"

"Harker had somebody deliver rushes of a test to his house. Then he
called and left word for Morris to locate some actor to go out there and
see them. Only nobody knows how to find the guy. They've called Central
Casting, Cosmopolitan, Mutual Booking—"

I stood up. "Was his name Luzovsky?"

"Something like that. Anyhow, he's not in the phone book and they
have no address. Hey—where you going?"

"To see Mr. Morris," I said.

I hurried across to the front office, nodded at Betty on the switchboard. "Ring Mr. Morris for me, please."

She stared. "*You?*"

"Tell him it's important."

Betty hesitated. "This isn't his morning for custard pies, let me tell you."

"I'm serious."

She buzzed, delivered the message, listened, then gestured to me. "You can go in. Don't worry—I'll be waiting to catch you when you sail out."

"Who's worried?" I marched forward.

But I *was* worried. Carla Sloane was right. If Harker was the great magician, then Sol Morris was indeed God.

It was hard to imagine he had ever been my age, but that's how the story ran. Once upon a time he was just a kid—little Solly Morris, who worked for a feed store in Battle Creek, Michigan, saving his pennies.

Where he got the idea nobody knows. But he took those pennies and invested them in northern timberland. He and his brothers went up there every year and cut spruce trees to haul back to the city. First in wagons, then in trucks, then in freight cars. They sold their trees at Christmas time, and even at fifty cents apiece they made money. Before long Sol Morris was on the road, setting up new markets all over the state. Somewhere he conceived the notion of the community tree in the town square, made up of a hundred or even two hundred smaller trees. By the time he was thirty, he and his brothers were wealthy men.

But Sol Morris wasn't satisfied. He kept looking for something new. When he went out for orders he'd sit in the barber shops, lie in the Turkish baths of the little towns, and relax, waiting for inspiration.

Eventually he found one, and right under his nose. ("That's a lot of territory," Arch Taylor had said, when he told me the story.) The Christmas trees went up in the town square. And invariably, inevitably, Sol Morris noticed, one side bordering each town square held a movie theater. In town after town, wherever he went, he saw a movie house.

So he told his brothers about it. "All right," they said—apparently in chorus, according to the tale—"maybe we should invest in a couple of movie houses too."

But that was not Sol Morris's idea at all. He was strictly a wholesaler at heart. A movie house made money, yes. Several movie houses would probably make more money. But who wanted the headache of running them—particularly since all movie houses, everywhere, had to buy their pictures from a studio? That's where the real money was. Why not start a studio and *make* movies for picture theaters all over America?

His brothers told him why not. Because they had a good business right here, because they didn't know anything about the flickers, because he'd lose his shirt.

Sol Morris smiled, shrugged, and gambled his shirt. He sold out his interest to the brothers and headed for Chicago. He hung around the studios there for a month, picking up information. Then he picked up personnel. Before the year was out he'd made his first trip to California, for he'd already heard of a spot where the sun was high and the price of real estate was low.

The first years were rough, but when the war came, his actors donned khaki at once and wore it for the duration. The Kaiser and his Hunnish hordes died a thousand deaths in Coronet five-reelers. The Rose of No Man's Land blossomed forth at least once a month in all its glory, the rattle of sabers turned to the ringing of cash registers, and Sol Morris was on his way.

By the summer of 1918 he was ready to risk all his resources on an epic. According to advance publicity, *The Battle Cry* would be the war picture to end all war pictures. But by fall, war pictures *were* ended. There were alarming rumors of a coming armistice—and if it came, Sol Morris and his big production would be casualties of war.

Then Theodore Harker stepped forth from the wings. He was a minor director on the lot, specializing in bogus-Bara, pseudo-Pickford and neo-Normand films, but Morris had never paid him much attention until he presented his plan for salvaging *The Battle Cry*. Yes, he could save all the war footage. Yes, he could hold down the costs. Yes, he could cut and edit. Morris listened and then, with the old familiar gesture, tossed his shirt into the pot.

And Theodore Harker raised his magic wand. He raised it and the walls of Jericho came tumbling down. He raised it and the Savior was nailed to the cross. He raised it and *The Battle Cry* became *The Prince of Peace*. Five reels grew into ten, and the story of modern warfare was given a biblical parallel praising pacifism.

Then followed a flurry of publicity, a flood of bookings, and a shower of gold. The exhibitors thought it was box office. The moviegoers said it was a swell picture. And the critics called it Art.

From that moment on, Morris never removed his shirt again, except in the presence of his wife. Harker piled success on success for Coronet, profits were high, taxes were low, and all was well in Hollywood under the reign of Good King Doug and Queen Mary.

Sol Morris was already becoming a legendary figure, and he loved it. Like Sam Goldwyn and Papa Laemmle, his pronouncements and mispronouncements were quoted everywhere. He was a member of the illiterati.

Even though I'd been on the lot for six months, I'd only seen him at a distance, but on several occasions I'd heard his voice raised in agony as I passed through the outer office. I'd seen the bookkeeper wince, watched Betty tremble, noted that even the windows shook.

Now, as I opened the door to his inner office, I heard that voice again. Apparently he'd just taken a phone call, because he was shouting into the mouthpiece now as I came in.

"No—not another dime! You know what it cost me the time you got mixed up with that little Mexican *nafkeh*? Better you should stick to studying, hurry up and matriculate or whatever they call it. No, I mean it, absolutely. So what's that got to do with a college education? Fraternity-maternity, who needs it? And stop bothering me at the office, I got business to attend—all right, we'll talk about it at home!"

Down went the receiver. Up went the hand to the head. "Troubles—what you get from kids!" He looked up and saw me. "Another kid! What kind of trouble *you* got for me?"

"No trouble, Mr. Morris. I'm Tommy Post. I work over in script for Mr. Harker."

"Pleased to meet you I'm sure get out of here."

"I understand you were looking for an actor—"

"*Nu*, so that's it. Everybody and his brother comes to me, they want to be actors. Go see Sam Lipsky, he's casting."

"I don't want a job, Mr. Morris. I'm here about this actor you're trying to locate. This Kurt Luzovsky. I know where he lives."

Morris looked at me. His fat little baby face was plumply plastic as the scowl became a smile.

"I'm sorry I hollered at you," he said. "I get excited—and on top of it, my boy Nicky has *tsurris* with his college." He gave me a sidelong glance. "This actor we're looking for—you know why we want him?"

"Mr. Harker is going to run his test out at the house."

"Smart boy. And you know where Mr. Harker lives?"

"I guess so."

"So what are you waiting for? Go get this Luzovsky fella and take him out there."

"Yes sir!" I turned and started out.

"Just a minute. What name did you say you were?"

"Post. Tommy Post."

"Good. I make a note of it." He beamed again.

I beamed, too, as I went out. It's not every day that God marks down one of your good deeds in His book.

FIVE

ARCH TAYLOR GREETED ME in the corridor outside the office. "Where the hell you been? Glint is waiting for you."

"She'll have to keep on waiting." I explained what had happened as I headed for the gate.

"But you didn't have to go through all this monkey business." Taylor shook his head. "Didn't you know Luzovsky plans to show up here at the studio around noon? He told me so yesterday."

"He told me, too," I said. "You couldn't keep him away if you called out the Marines. But Morris doesn't know that." I winked at him. "Just taking your advice. You told me to make an impression on the boss. And now I get a chance to go out to Harker's house, too."

"You work fast, don't you?"

"I've got to work faster." I waved and moved toward the street. "Want to catch Luzovsky before he leaves home. Just hold thumbs I make it in time."

I made it in time, and a taxi. Luzovsky was just coming out when I arrived, so I hailed him and explained the situation as the cab carried us off in the direction of Beverly Hills.

Luzovsky was oddly silent and I sensed his tension as he gazed out the window. There was enough to see, and I stared with him.

The building boom echoed through the canyons to the north. Estates were going up in those days, with more to come shortly—Picfair, Falcon's

Lair, the Fred Thomson-Frances Marion place, the Marion Davies beach house out in Santa Monica. Already these nearby hillsides were dotted with fine examples of Spanish Tudor, Provincial Gothic, Moorish Renaissance and Greek Elizabethan architecture. There were cathedrals with tennis courts, a Trianon with a six-car garage, a Westminster Abbey with a swimming pool. We swung past the mansions west of Sunset Strip, then angled off into one of the canyons on a side road.

Harker's hacienda sprawled over angular acres on the side of a bluff. The wall surrounding his domain was covered with rambler roses. The cab deposited us before an inner courtyard where a fountain sprayed into a pool.

Salukis swarmed out to greet us as we made our way up the tiled walk to the arched oaken door. I stared up at the silver monogram crest set in the beam beside the doorway, then ducked my head as a swarm of snow-white pigeons descended to shower greetings.

Luzovsky tugged at his collar.

"Nervous?" I asked.

He shrugged.

I smiled at him. "Nothing to be afraid of. After all, a man who was head keeper at the Berlin Zoo—"

"But I was never at the Berlin Zoo," Luzovsky sighed. "When I saw that lion yesterday I almost fainted."

It was my turn to sigh. *Actors!* I raised the silver TH of the doorknocker. Over its echo I said, "Just walk through it now like a rehearsal."

A real live butler in real live morning clothes opened the door. I eyed his real live sideburns as I stated our names and errand.

"Step inside, please," he said.

So we stepped inside—inside the Harker house, with its dining hall that seated thirty, its fireplaces in all eight of the bedrooms, the private projection room with a screen framed in 18-karat gold. I didn't see these wonders, but I'd heard about them, and now I was under the same roof, moving down a hall dominated at its far end by a huge staircase with an ornate hand-carved rail.

"Wait here."

Here was the living room and that was sufficient spectacle for me. Seventy feet long, it extended across the entire left wing of the house, and its ceiling vaulted three stories high above my humbled head. The room was big enough to hold six divans, a grand piano, a built-in pipe organ, and still leave the two of us lost in its empty immensity.

We moved to the far wall, studying the tapestry which might have come from the set of a Fairbanks film, when the butler returned and nodded at Luzovsky.

"This way, please. Mr. Harker will join you in the library."

I watched Luzovsky follow the butler into the hall, wishing I could go along. Then they disappeared and I was alone in the silence, the museum silence which seemed so oddly appropriate here. I wandered around, gazing at Louis Quatorze chairs, Spanish shawls, Ispahani prayer rugs, scimitars hanging from the walls, chandeliers dripping their crystal tears.

It was hard to imagine Harker spending an evening in this room, hard to picture him alone in this crazy clutter. But perhaps he wasn't alone; surely he must have friends, even a woman in his life.

I tried to imagine just what kind of a woman Theodore Harker would choose to share his life. She'd have to be very special, this much I knew—someone wise and warm, but with an outer restraint to match his own. And she'd have to be completely genuine. Harker was too accomplished an analyst of emotion to settle for anything less, his sense of values too demanding—

Somebody opened a door quickly down the hall, and I heard the echo of voices. To my surprise one of them was Harker's. I'd thought he was already in the library with Luzovsky, but apparently not, because it was a woman who answered him. Now I could hear them both, loud and clear.

"I've had it," she said. "Up to here!"

"Then get out. Get out and stay out this time."

"I'm going—don't you worry about that. I'm through with you and your goddam astrology!"

"You needn't shout, Mabel. There are guests in the house."

"Who the hell you think you are, giving me orders? Mister Theodore the Great Harker—why for Christ's sake, I knew you when you were peddling patent medicine!"

"And I knew you when you were peddling yourself, at two bucks a throw."

"Why you lousy sonofabitch—"

"Get out and shut up! I'll have Rogers pack your things."

"Don't bother, I'm leaving right now. Go play with your crystal balls, you phoney, stinking stargazer!"

A door slammed. Footsteps high-heeled along the hall in my direction as I edged against the wall.

I saw Mabel march past the doorway.

Mabel? It was Maybelle Manners.

"I knew you when you were peddling yourself at two bucks a throw." No, it couldn't be, the queen could do no wrong, Gioconda never fought like a fishwife, the Mona Lisa never was a whore—

Now the front door opened and slammed shut again, and I was alone, slumping back onto a sofa and trying to put the pieces of my world together again. A world where patent medicine vendors lived in palaces, where prostitutes played the role of the Virgin Queen, where baldheaded gods pleaded powerlessly to errant sons, where penniless actors fought lions to get a job.

And who the hell was I to pretend it was any different? From where I sat I could look up into a mirror. I saw the reflection of an orphan punk, a twelve-dollar-a-week flunky, bursting with delusions of grandeur because he'd just run a flunky errand for his employer. I stared deeper, trying hard to catch a glimpse of Tom Post, the successful screenwriter whose films moved millions, made millions. But he was gone, he wasn't there, he'd never *been* there because he didn't exist. All I saw in the mirror was a kid; a kid who didn't know the score, didn't even know the name of the game.

I was still sitting on the sofa when Luzovsky came back into the room. I blinked and looked at my watch, surprised to see that it was past one o'clock.

"You'd better go now," he said. "Mr. Harker has asked me to stay for lunch." I noticed he wasn't nervous any more, and for some reason he appeared to be about six inches taller.

"Did you see the rushes?" I asked. "Is everything all right?"

He nodded. "Everything's fine. We were just discussing my role in *The Burning of Rome*."

"Your *what*—?"

"I'm going to play Petronius. Mr. Harker will write the scene himself."

"But I thought they were signing Sam deGrasse—"

"Mr. Harker has selected me." He beamed. "Now, I must get back. You run along." I rose and moved with him into the hall. The butler appeared and opened the door. Luzovsky took my hand.

"Thank you," he said. "Remember what I told you last night? It's all true."

And then I was outside again, outside in the sunshine, climbing down out of the canyon. There were no cabs waiting out here in the wilderness, and I didn't want one. I didn't plan on going back to the studio, and I wasn't even interested in lunch. I wanted to walk.

"It's all true," Luzovsky had said, and he was right. The dream was coming true, for him, because he believed in himself. But I didn't believe any longer—in Harker or the stars that shone in or over Hollywood. For me the dream was dead.

I wandered past the fake fa'ades of the mansions set back on Sunset, then down into the no man's land of the Strip. In the glare of afternoon sunlight everything looked dingy and deserted. Only at night did the Strip come alive, when the stars came out to play in their own artificial little heaven of cabarets and call-houses and casinos. But even at night it was a phoney paradise. The liquor was cut with bootleg alky, the women were paid to pretend passion, and the gambler's decks were stacked, the dice loaded. Everything was cheap and commonplace, including my thoughts on the subject. Tommy Post, Boy Philosopher. Just another phoney, like all the rest.

I looked up across the street at the Chateau Marmont perched above it, then glanced ahead. I passed something called the Stumble Inn, a speakeasy masquerading as a restaurant.

That's when I saw the green Pierce-Arrow, parked in the driveway. Something about it looked familiar, and suddenly I recognized it. God knows I'd seen it often enough at the studio; I even remembered the number on its license plate. *S-2111*. It was Maybelle Manners' car.

Before I became conscious of my decision I had already turned in at the walk leading to the front door. I opened it and moved into the smoky twilight of the deserted bar. Not quite deserted, because there was a man on duty behind it, and a familiar figure seated on a stool before the counter.

She sat very quietly, hands folded, eyes downcast. The drink before her seemed untouched, but there was a bottle beside it and it was partially empty.

It was dark in there, and if she noticed me at all she gave no sign. The bartender was bored; he served me a shot without question, rang up the money, then walked over to a player piano and inserted a coin. The jangling cascade of notes resolved recognizably into a number called "Smiles."

But she wasn't smiling. Somebody had taken a knife and slashed it across the face of Mona Lisa, obliterating the smile forever. Only the eyes still burned and brooded as she lifted her glass and gulped. Then she turned and glanced in my direction. I saw her lips move but her words were inaudible above the music. I got off my barstool and moved down to where she sat.

"Tommy Post," she said.

"What?" I wasn't sure I was hearing correctly.

"Nothing. Just remembered your name, that's all." And the smile came, now. She smiled, and just for me. "You know who I am?"

"Of course, Miss Manners. Everybody knows who you are."

"Sure." The smile disappeared. And the bottle went up as she refilled her glass. "Grace Cunard. Mabel Taliaferro. Marguerite Snow."

"I'm not quite sure I— "

"I'm talking about stars. Big stars, like me. Five years ago they were. Today nobody even remembers their names. Right?" She raised her glass, then hesitated, frowning.

"What the hell are you doing here? Who sent you?"

"No one sent me, Miss Manners. I just happened to be passing by—"

"Baloney." She glanced at the player piano. "Can't hear anything with that blasting in your ears." Lifting the bottle from the bartop she moved away toward the rear. "Gonna sit in a booth. Okay?"

I followed her. As she slid in her grip on the bottle wavered and I reached out to break its fall, but she tightened her hold in time and set the bottle down on the table.

"Leave me alone, I'm all right." Her eyes narrowed. "Come on, quit playing games. They tell you to come after me?"

"They?"

"I forgot. They won't be sending anyone now." She shook her head, reached for the glass. "That's why Harker picked a fight. He knows."

"Knows what, Miss Manners?"

"About my contract. They haven't renewed." She downed her shot. "I can't get to Morris, he won't see me—it's the old routine. They're dumping me."

The glass slammed down on the table and I stared at it. "But they wouldn't do that. You're a great box-office attraction—"

"Here." Her hand gripped my shoulder, pulling me forward. "Take a good look, sonny boy. The corners of the eyes, that's where the wrinkles begin. And the sag, under the chin, when you forget to keep your head up."

"I don't see anything—"

"The camera does. And what the camera sees, the audience sees." She released me, shaking her head. "Maybe I could go to Griffith; he could shoot me under gauze. I'll find something, but the word will be out. Coronet didn't renew for three years, so let's play smart and make it a two-year contract. Or one. Or just a single-picture deal. And the pictures will get fewer and farther between. And then—ahhh, to hell with it!" She rose unsteadily. "I'm going home."

I slid out of the booth, took her arm. "Let me drive you, Miss Manners."

"Suit yourself."

The bartender gave us a bored nod as we departed. Outside the lights were already beginning to wink on; Sunset was in shadow. Nobody paid the slightest attention as I led Maybelle Manners to the car. I had a little trouble with the Pierce-Arrow's fancy gearshift, but I got it started.

Maybelle Manners slumped beside me. "Know where I live?"

I nodded. "West Adams, isn't it?"

"Good boy." She closed her eyes and I drove through the gathering dusk—past the new Chaplin studio at La Brea, past Gower Gulch, and along the clutter of cubicles lining Poverty Row. The "quickies" were made here, the films ground out on a five-day schedule by the shoestring producers. Some made a fortune on their shoestrings and others ended up using them as a suicide's noose. I wondered how long it would be before Maybelle Manners went to work for one of the shoestring operators—or went to beg for work.

We turned south on Western, heading down into the city, and now the lights blazed brilliantly. If I wished, I could have caught a clear glimpse of the face beside me, searched for the sag, the wrinkles she'd tried to show me. But I didn't want to see them. I didn't want to see her, or Harker, or myself too clearly. I'd already seen too much today, and I wanted to get away—

"Stop."

I thought she was asleep, but she stirred now, sat up, tugged at my sleeve.

"Stop here—"

She glanced off to the right and I followed her gaze as I pulled over to the curb. We were in front of a movie house.

"Come on, let's see the picture," she said.

"But Miss Manners, are you sure you're all right—?"

She didn't answer, just opened the door of the car and started to get out. I came around my side just in time to take her arm.

Then I looked up at the marquee, saw the pictured promise of the posters, the bright beckoning of the box office. Suddenly I understood. She was right, this was what to do when you were down—the thing all America did. Forget you troubles and go to the movies.

So we did.

The film was one of Harker's own—*The Love Goddess*. And it starred Maybelle Manners.

The short subjects were on as we came in. I caught a glimpse of *Topics of the Day* as she pulled me over to the stairs. "Sit in the balcony," she murmured, above the organ's drone. "Don't want anyone to see—"

We climbed up into the shadows, found seats. She was right; the balcony was deserted at this hour. As we settled down a Sennett comedy skittered across the screen. Then the curtains closed, reopened to an accompanying crescendo, and the feature began. Maybelle Manners appeared and she smiled at me.

I sat there in the warm darkness as the organ soothed, sat there and surrendered myself to her smile. Mabel was gone gone and only Maybelle existed; Maybelle the Mona Lisa, with an eternity of enchantment in her eyes.

She was up there on the screen and she was real, bigger than life and infinitely better, to me and to everyone in the audience below. They were all seeing her, just as I did, and that meant the dream was coming true again. The dream was coming true and I could believe once more—in her, in Harker, in everything.

The woman in the seat beside me, smelling of cheap alcohol and expensive perfume, was just another moviegoer. A moviegoer who stared entranced at the vision before us, clutching my arm and squeezing it impulsively as the radiant Maybelle Manners embraced the hero. I didn't recognize him.

"Who is he?" I whispered.

"Raymond Clarke." To my surprise, she laughed softly. "Queer as a three-dollar bill."

"He doesn't look it." And indeed he didn't—in the prolonged close two-shot, his face wore a look of most convincing passion.

"I fixed him good," she murmured. "Want to know how I did it?" Before I could answer her hand had left my arm and wandered into my lap. I felt her fingers fumbling, fondling, firming. "I knew it wouldn't be in the shot," she said. "Works pretty good, doesn't it?"

Rigid with response I opened my mouth, just as her warm, full lips closed over it and her tongue moved—moved in rhythm with her fingers, fingers that first freed and then captured, captured and caressed insistently, insatiably. With her other hand she pulled me toward her, grasping my hip as she slumped low in her seat.

"Easy," she whispered. "No noise—"

There was only the faint sound of her skirt rustling upwards as the fingers guided me, guided me there in the warm darkness as the organ throbbed and the lovers moved together and the love scene reached its climax up there, down here, up and down, organ rising, organ falling, and then—

Then, behind my head, the scene changed, and a brighter light flooded from the screen to fall upon the face before and below me; this time I saw her, saw her plain, and it *was* Mabel. Mabel, with the unmistakable sag at the jowls, the revealed wrinkles, the sweat-beaded forehead, the open mouth exhaling a sour stench. Framed by disheveled hair, the puffy face peered up at me.

"It's good, isn't it?" she panted. "Isn't it good, darling?" Her eyes were radiant with fulfillment.

But she wasn't looking at me.

She was staring *past* me. Staring over my shoulder, up at the screen. That's what she'd been doing all the time—staring at the image of Maybelle Manners.

Somehow I was back in my seat again and Maybelle Manners smiled down at me from afar, smiled down at a speed of eighteen frames a second as I adjusted my clothing and tried very hard to avoid looking at the woman beside me who gasped out her adoration to that flickering fantasy of light and shadow looming over us.

I tried not to look at her when we left the theater, and was mercifully spared conversation when she dozed off into sodden slumber during the drive to the West Adams Street mansion just down the block from Fatty Arbuckle's place.

After parking I roused her for a teetering trip up the walk. Becky answered the door and we must have said goodnight, but I can't remember the words. There was nothing about her that I wanted to remember, now.

I walked until I reached a streetcar stop, boarded, transferred, headed home. Hollywood was a nine o'clock town and the lights were going out all along my route. I wondered if Aunt Minnie and Uncle Andy were waiting up for me; wondered if they'd talked it over and decided to tell me about my folks. Tell me what I needed to know, now more than ever in a world where there must be something real to cling to.

The trolley rumbled and jolted but the sound lulled me and my head lolled.

Until I heard the noise. The deep roaring, and over it, the shrill wailing.

I looked up, looked through the window, saw the light blazing forth into the street.

The *blazing* light—

The trolley screeched to a halt and I swung off, running toward the searing source of light and sound. Running toward the flames, rising like burnished banners from the walls and roof of our bungalow.

I saw two fire trucks, a patrol wagon, an ambulance. A semicircle of police held the white rope of a cordon to hold back the crowd.

But nothing could hold back the flames that roared and crackled and consumed, sealing off all entry to doors and windows. Sealing off all entry, and all exit—

Fire hoses hissed and played vainly over the blaze; men in helmets and rubber coats bawled orders as inaudible as they were inadequate. As I watched, part of the roof gave way and a shower of fiery embers scorched the sky.

I grabbed the tall cop and shouted to make myself heard above bedlam. "Let me through—I live here!"

He shook his head. "Stand back."

"My aunt and uncle—are they all right?" I knew he heard me, but he was looking away. "Did you get them out?"

Still he wouldn't look at me. I shook his shoulder.

"God damn it, tell me!"

Then he looked at me and he didn't have to tell me.

SIX

SOMETIMES THE FILM SPEEDS UP and everything becomes a blur.

All I really remember about the two days is that Arch Taylor took care of me. He got me into a room at the little hotel down the street from the studio, saw to it that I ate and slept. He took on the ordeal of identifying the bodies when what was left of them could finally be removed from the charred debris of the bungalow. He selected an undertaker and chose the caskets. And he talked to reporters, the police, the people from the fire department.

They couldn't tell him very much. Apparently the blaze had started shortly before ten o'clock; a flash-fire spreading instantly. It could have been the fault of the electrical wiring, or a short in the cord of the iron. The half-melted metal legs of an ironing board were discovered in the front room, and there was a crumpled tin of cleaning fluid. Perhaps Aunt Minnie had forgotten to unplug the iron when she went to bed and if somehow the fluid had ignited

But nobody knew and accidents will happen and life goes on and did your uncle have any insurance and you've got to be brave. *Just a blur.*

Strangely enough, when the funeral actually started I was all right again.

I sat there in the little chapel on Selma Avenue, watching the studio people come in. Almost everyone who wasn't away on location showed up. Uncle Andy hadn't been the most important man on the lot, but he had friends.

Some of them came up and spoke to me before the service started.

"Sure sorry about what happened, Tommy." That was tall Dude Williams, strangely subdued as he moved past me with his tiny wife.

"My deepest condolences." Emerson Craig gripped my hand, standing before me handsome and immaculate as though he'd just stepped off the screen.

Little Jackie Keeley was harder to recognize. He looked incongruous, somehow, without his trademarkthe oversized checkered cap he always wore, even when balancing on the end of a flagpole while Mack Swain hacked at its base with an axe. But he wasn't being funny today. "Terrible tragedy," he muttered, moving past me.

The next man I couldn't identify at all. I'd seen him a dozen times, of course, but never on our lot. And never like this.

"Karl Druse," he said.

I couldn't help but stare. For Druse was just a quiet middle-aged man with graying brown hair; neither fat nor lean, tall nor short. And I didn't remember him that way, not from his films.

The Karl Druse I remembered was sometimes a giant, sometimes a dwarf. If Lon Chaney was the Man of a Thousand Faces, then Druse was the Man of a Thousand Bodies. I remembered a crook-backed King Richard, an obscenely fat rajah, a thin shadow of a vampire. Only the eyes were unchanged, the mirrors of a dark despair.

"I'm sorry," he said, and that was all. I watched him walk away with that peculiar, stiff-legged gait of his, like a man on stilts. Maybe he wore platform heels; that might explain how he created the illusion of varied height in his roles. But a horror movie star who wore a derby

There were other hands to clasp, other condolences to awkwardly acknowledge. Kurt Luzovsky and Madame Olga appeared, and I was glad to see them there, John Frisby, the director, and Sam Lipsky, even Miss Glint in a broadbrimmed black straw hat. Carla Sloane and Betty from the front office, but not Sol MorrisHe, I knew, was attending an exhibitor's convention in San Francisco. I didn't see Maybelle Manners, either, but I'd hardly expected to and I was somehow relieved that she hadn't come.

Just before I sat down, with Arch Taylor on one side and Luzovsky on the other, I noticed Theodore Harker entering; his black suit for once singularly appropriate to the occasion.

The services were mercifully brief. Neither Aunt Minnie nor Uncle Andy had been regular churchgoers and the hired reverend didn't know them. But he said the appropriate things, and when Dude Williams broke down midway through the Twenty-third Psalm and his wife led him out, it was the signal for general sniffling.

Then the organ played and we filed past the caskets, the closed caskets that somehow had nothing to do with Aunt Minnie or Uncle Andy, and it was time to go to the cemetery.

While crowd moved off I took advantage of the moment to visit the discreetly concealed front office and see Mr. Leffingwell, the head of the mortuary.

"About the bill," I began.

He nodded. "Mr. Harker took care of it."

"Harker?"

"Yesterday afternoon. He ordered that extra floral arrangement, too." Leffingwell rose. "Are you riding out in the first limousine?"

"I'd prefer to go with Mr. Taylor," I told him.

And I did. It wasn't a long drive.

"You all right?" he asked.

"I guess so. I don't know." I sighed. "Maybe I'm crazy."

"Tell me."

"Well, all during the ceremony, I kept thinking it was just a scene. Something out of a picture, with the organ playing just the way it does in the theater. I kept watching the way the lighting hit the coffins, and when the minister came on I wondered if he was somebody Lipsky would cast in the part. The crowd was just a bunch of extras—even when Dude Williams started to cry it seemed like an act"

"That was real enough," Taylor said. "He's not in good shape, I hear. Think he's worried about it; he never used to work with a double on the stunt scenes."

"Maybe he should have sent his double to the funeral," I said. Then I began to blink and my throat tightened. "What's the matter with me? Minnie and Andy gone, the only folks I've got, and I keep thinking about the whole thing as if it was a movie."

"Nothing wrong with you." His hand was firm on my shoulder, his voice was firm too. "Just shock catching up with you. You'll get over it. From now on everything is real. Right?"

I knew that what he said was true, but I wasn't entirely convinced. Although the bit at the cemetery seemed real enough. It was short and efficient; only about half of those present at the chapel had come out for the interment. The others had hurried back to the studio and their work.

It was a surprise to see Theodore Harker at the graveside. After the lowering of the caskets I left Arch Taylor with the Luzovskys and walked over to where Harker stood.

"Mr. Leffingwell told me what you did," I said. "I wanted to thank you"

"That's not necessary." He stared at the men who were arranging the wreaths and flowers over the graves. "The front office asked me to take care of it. They'll reimburse me. Andy was a good man. He'll be missed."

"Then you knew he wasn't?"

"Of course. That French accent was obviously false. But he was genuine enough. As was your aunt." Suddenly the black eyes were looking straight at me. "What are your plans now?"

"Well, I've got to find a place to live. I think there's some insurance moneyArch Taylor is checking into thatand of course I have my job."

"Twelve dollars a week."

I stared at him.

"Mr. Taylor has already spoken to me about you. He said you're interested in becoming a writer. Of course you're not ready for screenplays yet, that's out of the question."

"But"

His gesture silenced me. "You need experience. The best way to begin is to work with a production unit and learn how to structure a story. Start with titlesthey cover continuity, hold scenes together. A good title-writer can work his way up to scenarios."

Harker's eyes, and something behind them, studied me for a moment. "I talked to John Frisby this morning. He's a competent director. They're going to put him on the Jackie Keeley pictures and he's willing to give you a chance. If you're interested, report to him tomorrow morning."

I found my voice. "Tomorrow?"

Harker nodded and gestured with his cane. "Forget thisit's over and done with. Live for the present, plan for the future, don't let anyone or anything interfere. Right now you may think it's a tragedy to find yourself suddenly alone, but some day you'll realize it's better this way. You've got to travel alone. I know."

He broke off abruptly, then turned and strode away down the path, swinging his cane.

I hadn't even time to thank him.

Arch Taylor came up beside me. "Arch," I said. "Did you hear the news?"

Taylor smiled. "He told you? Good."

And it was good, very good. That night I was able to sleep soundly and dreamlessly for the first time since the fire. The next morning I went to work for John Frisby.

The next few weeks were busy ones. It turned out that Uncle Andy did have an insurance policy, and two thousand dollars was enough to buy a Ford and furnish the little apartment I found for myself over on Beechwood Drive. I had to start from scratch because nothing had been salvaged from the flames, not even the scrapbook. But the insurance money covered the essentials, and my starting salary with Frisby's unit was an incredible forty dollars a week.

I saw the New Year in with Kurt Lozoff.

Kurt Lozoff. That's the name he put on his contract, right after finishing his part in *The Burning of Rome.* And that's the name he used on the screen all during 1923, the year of *Greed, The Covered Wagon, The Hunchback of Notre Dame* and *The Ten Commandments.* Lozoff made six pictures in those twelve months and by the time another New Year's Eve rolled around, he and Madame occupied a hilltop house in the Los Feliz area; a home befitting a star.

Arch Taylor was writing his films now, with Harker directing as Lozoff strutted across the screen in his usual costumefull evening dress. There was a bit of Erich von Stroheim in his bearing, a touch of Adolphe Menjou, and a lot of Lozoff himself; the charming, cynical man of the world. Sometimes, for variety's sake, it was man of the underworld. But always he was the *rou)* with the heart of gold, ready to surrender the heroine to a younger man in the last reel.

1924 was an even bigger year for Lozoff. He moved into a larger dressing room and Arch Taylor got a private office to write in, with a modest little sign on the door which read *Stratford-on-Avon*. It was a big year for Coronet and the industry in general; the year of *The Thief of Baghdad, The Sea Hawk, The Iron Horse*. And it was the year when Miss Glint got fired.

I was present when she made her last appearance at the studio, over on Lozoff's set. Lozoff and Taylor were discussing some changes in a scene. Lozoff stood quietly as one of the Penny brothers adjusted the decorations on his coat; the ribbon of the Legion of Honor, the insignia which proclaimed him a Knight of the Garter.

"Did you read the new pages?" Taylor asked.

Lozoff shook his head. "I don't have a copy. Miss Glint must have forgotten me this morning."

A sniff signaled her arrival. "No such thing. You'll find it right on the table in your dressing room."

"Thank you," Lozoff said, as the Penny brother fussed with his lapel. "Would you be kind enough to bring it to me?"

Miss Glint frowned. "I've got to distribute the rest of these copies."

"Please, Maggie," said Arch Taylor. "That can wait."

Maybe the poor girl had difficult periods or something. But as she stalked away she was mumbling to herself, and her voice carried. "Fancy evening clothesKnight of the Garter, is he? Whoever heard of a kike knight?"

Now it so happens that Kurt Lozoff was a devout member of the Greek Orthodox Church, and it so happens that Arch Taylor was an equally devout agnostic. But someone on the set must have mentioned the incident to the front office, because the next day Miss Glint was gone.

Glint was gone, Maybelle Manners had disappeared, but I was still around and doing very well, thank you. In this fall of 1924 I'd traded in my Ford for a used Stutz and I was earning seventy-five dollars a week writing titles with the *So* method.

It was very simple, particularly when I used it to introduce characters in our comedies. For example:

A scene with Lucien Littlefield as the father:

"Papa. So tight he takes a loaf of bread down to the corner and waits for the traffic jam."

And our heroine:

"The Girl. So dumb she thinks Mah Jong is Pa Jong's wife."

Bull Montana as the villain:

"Jake the Snake. So tough he blows his nose with dynamite."

And when I exhausted the *So* method, I came up with a fresh variationthe *They Call* opening.

Jackie Keeley's first scene:

"Meet Our Hero. They call him opium, because he's such a dope."

Keeley liked it, John Frisby liked it, and the audiences ate it up. But I wanted to vomit.

Instead, I went to work. Everybody should have a hobby. Arch Taylor's was gambling at the Embassy or the Clover Club. Emerson Craig had varied tasteshe patronized Bobby Barrett's call-house on the Strip when he couldn't pick up a boy outside Kress's drugstore in Hollywood. John Frisby went to parties at the Hotel Christie or the Alexandria. Jackie Keeley spent his nights everywhere from the Ambassador to the Sunset Inn. But I stayed in my apartment and wrote.

And one morning, shortly after we'd wrapped up another Keeley epic, I paid a call on Taylor in his office, carrying a little sheaf of paper which I put down on the table before him.

"Got something I'd like you to read," I said.

He started to reach for it but I covered the stack with my hand. "Later on, at your leisure. There are carbons for Lozoff and Harker."

"What's this all about?"

"Call it a plan. I want to work on the Lozoff pictures."

"Titles?"

I shook my head. "Scenarios."

"Gunning for my job, huh?" Taylor stood up. "Maybe I made a mistake when I gave you that pep talk."

"You know better than that, Arch. I'm not working against youI want to work *with* you."

"It's not that simple. Harker rewrites everything himself."

"Yes. And it's getting stale."

Taylor shrugged. "You know what our last two pictures grossed?"

"Sure. I read the trades. But I also read the critics. And they're beginning to say that Harker's losing his touch."

"To hell with the critics."

"It's the public I'm thinking about. Another six months and the audience will start complaining too. I've been trying to analyze what's wrong and I think I know the answer. But I want you to read this and make up your own mind. If you agree, show a copy to Lozoff. Then maybe you can both go to Harker and tell him"

"What's the matter? Afraid to tell him yourself?"

Taylor said it for me. I *was* afraid. But I couldn't say so. Instead I shook my head. "I don't know him well enough. We haven't spoken to each other half a dozen times in the last two years. He'd never listen to me."

"But I *am* listening, Mr. Post."

I glanced up.

Theodore Harker stood in the doorway behind me, leaning on his cane. He scowled, head inclined like a black vulture poised to pounce.

"Please continue," he said. "You say there is something wrong with my work. You have, I assume, a solution. Might I be permitted to hear it?"

It's like a nightmare, I told myself. *A bad dream. But dreams can't harm you. Or can they?* There was only one way to find out.

I found myself talking. "It's this way, Mr. Harker. You're only making one kind of picture now, with Lozoff. Society stuff. Anybody can direct these things. It doesn't take a Harker. You're being wasted and you know it. That's why you rewrite, put in little touches like costume party scenes with Lozoff wearing a suit of armor. But you're running out of novelties and the old plot is showing through. Armor won't hide it."

"So." Theodore Harker brought his cane tip down sharply on the floor. "I still haven't heard your solution."

"Use more armor," I said.

Taylor shrugged. "You want Mr. Harker to give up society drama and go back to costume pictures?"

"No. I want him to combine the two."

They both stared at me but I kept talking. "Keep Lozoff in evening dress for a few reels, get your plot established. Then do a flashback or a dream sequence, something to point up a parallel in history. You can show the court of Louis XIV, the fall of Sodom and Gomorrah, the defeat of the Spanish Armadadon't you see the angles? Mr. Harker did just that when he came to the studio and saved that war picture turkey. That was the vehicle that made him. Why not use it now?"

Harker thumped his cane on the floor again. "You have such a story in mind, I presume?"

"Yes, I did a sample treatment. But that's not important. You can pick anything you like, modern stories from modern writers. Then turn me loose. I'll find a historical parallel for you. Just give me a chance."

"Why should I?" Harker murmured. "Let's assume your criticism makes sense. Let's assume that your suggested remedy also makes sense. Let's even assume that I've been doing some thinking about the same problem and coming up with some of the same answersI'm not altogether a fool, you know."

"I never meant" I began, but he cut in.

"You haven't answered my question, Mr. Post. Suppose I did adopt your idea. Why should I select *you* to work on scenarios for my productions?"

I stared at him, took a deep breath. And something inside my head said, *Remember the dream.*

"The dream," my voice echoed. I was talking again, only this time the prompter inside was giving me the lines. "It's the dream, Mr. Harker. I know what you're thinking, I'm just a gag writer for cheap comedies, a nobody from nowhere. But I know about dreams. And that's your secret, too, isn't it?

"That's why you've made great pictures in the past, that's why you're a great director. Because you must have come from nowhere, too, and you understand what it's like to be a nobody. You remember the dreams from those daysthe dreams ordinary people have about love and honor and the triumph of right over injustice. Sure, the highbrow critics sneer at the movies, they've always sneered. But the nobodies don't sneer. They need their dreams, and when they can't make their own any more they turn to people like youpeople who can create dreams for them." I paused. "That's what I want to do. I have to. It's like Ilike I was born to do it."

There was a moment of silence, broken only when Harker's cane struck the floor for the third time. Then he glanced at Arch Taylor.

"Call Sol Morris," he said. "Tell him I'd like to see him as soon as possible. With you, and Mr. Post. Tell him it's about my next picture."

And the voice inside my head whispered, *This is how dreams come true.*

SEVEN

SHORTLY AFTER OUR MEETING with Sol Morris I bought a new car. I drove it to all the conferences with Lozoff and Harker. I drove it to Arch Taylor's place where we sweated out weekend rewrites on our scenario. I drove it to the premiere of our first picture, *Scarlet Lady*. And afterwards John Barrymore stood with one foot up on its running board as he congratulated me on the film's success.

The day before the Fourth of July weekend in 1925, the car was parked on the lot and I was parked in my own office, waiting for my own secretary, if you please.

Arch Taylor strolled in.

"Do me a favor, Post?" (It was "Post" now—"Tommy" was dead and buried, like poor Tom Ince. Things moved fast in Hollywood.)

"What kind of favor, Arch?"

"Just want to use your office for a minute. Some people here for an audition. Forgot about the appointment and I can't take 'em out on the lot. Morris is getting ready for the party this afternoon."

"So I heard. What's he celebrating?"

"Who knows? Maybe he got an inside tip that Will Hays got caught in a vice raid with Nita Naldi. We'll find out in an hour or so."

I stood up. "Okay, go ahead and see your people. I'll take a walk."

"No, stick around, it won't take long. Some mama and her precious little darling. Another Jackie Coogan, God forbid."

"So why bother?"

"Because Sam did a test and he thinks the kid's got something. My guess would be smallpox. But he insisted I take a look. Maybe if you stick around we can cut it short."

I nodded, then sat down again and waited as he went out and returned with the three LaBuddies.

There were introductions.

Kate LaBuddie was fair, fatuous and forty. "Oh, and you're *the* Mr. Post who wrote *Scarlet Lady*?" I was ready to pick up the cue, but she stepped on my lines. "I can't *begin* to tell you how much I enjoyed it. Of course it was just a wee bit ri*scue* for the kiddies, but I insisted on taking Buddie and Mitzi with me because I *knew* they would get so much out of it. Buddie is definitely quite *mature* when it comes to histrionics and I'm sure he appreciated it, didn't you, Buddie?"

"It was thrilling," Buddie told me. "The suspense was gripping. I laughed through my tears."

That made me do a double take. Buddie LaBuddie didn't talk like an eight-year-old. But then he didn't look like an eight-year-old, either. He wore a Buster Brown outfit with long golden curls to match, but the face peering out between them was that of a middle-aged midget. Picture a child wearing eye shadow like Larry Semon and you'll get some idea of the way he looked.

"Thank you," I said. "That's quite a speech for a young man to make."

"It comes from the heart," said the child.

"Don't mind him," Kate LaBuddie trilled gaily. "He picks that up from the movies. We've gone ever since he was just a babe in arms. It's the best possible training for a car*eer*, I always say. That's where he learned to develop his talent, didn't you, darling?"

"Yes, Mummy dear."

"Won't you all sit down, please?" Arch Taylor took over. I stood up and offered my chair to the third member of the LaBuddie troupe.

"Thank you," she said softly.

It was the first time Mitzi LaBuddie had spoken. I gave her a second glance. She was slender, with wavy light brown hair and dark eyes—about seventeen or so, I guessed. Rather pretty in a quiet sort of way, in spite of the too-tight, too-short skirt and the *cloche* hat. But of course much too young to interest me.

Besides, my interest was claimed elsewhere. Mrs. LaBuddie was in full voice, her bangles and bracelets jangling as she gestured in accompaniment to her solo.

"—suppose you heard about the test. He just *couldn't* get over Buddie's performance. Of course it's only natural—my late husband was on the boards for many years, you've probably heard of him, he played *Sis Hopkins* for ages. I know Buddie has inherited his genius. Mitzi has it too, some time I'd like you to see what *she* can do, Mr. Taylor—"

"Yes, that would be fine. But right now I've been trying to decide whether or not we can use Buddie."

"Why of course you can! Buddie can do anything, simply anything! Five years in dramatic school, plus dancing lessons, plus elocution—just look at that poise and presence! Why, Kurt Lozoff himself couldn't do better."

"My impression of Kurt Lozoff." Buddie LaBuddie jumped to his feet as though someone had just wound him up. He strutted across the room to his sister, bowed from the waist, lifted her hand, kissed it—then ran his lips up her arm to the elbow with a knowing leer.

"You see?" Mrs. LaBuddie beamed at Taylor. "Now do Dude Williams, darling."

Buddie "did" Dude Williams, then Jackie Keeley. Next he crossed his eyes like Ben Turpin, and before anyone could stop him he went into the inevitable Charlie Chaplin routine. He was good, too.

"Now, Jackie Coogan," his mother purred. "Show Mr. Taylor how you would handle a Coogan part."

Buddie imitated Coogan.

To use a technical expression, he stunk.

Apparently there was a limit to this child's ability, after all. He couldn't portray a child.

Buddie must have seen the look on Arch Taylor's face because he quickly grabbed a ruler from my desk and flourished it. "And now," he panted. "I give you my interpation of the immoral Douglas Fairbanks in *Don Q, Son of Zorro!*"

He did a very "immoral" Fairbanks and was just preparing to carve a Z on Taylor's nose when the door opened and my secretary looked in.

"Sorry to disturb you," she said. "But Mr. Morris wants everybody over on Four."

We stood up. "You'll have to excuse us, Mrs. LaBuddie," Arch Taylor said. "There's a studio party this afternoon. Walpurgis Night, or Bastille Day—some such thing."

"That's quite all right. I'm sure we can arrange to have Buddie come in again for you next week. And as I was saying, about Mitzi, the dear girl is so modest and unassuming, like a bump on a log, but she's really an adorable ongenoo. The Mary Philbin type, but with more flair for—"

"Yes, of course." Taylor moved them toward the door. "I'll be in touch with you. We've got your number here."

"I could call you first thing on—"

"We'll set it up," Taylor said. "Good to see you and thanks for coming in."

I nodded at them as they left, saving my sigh until they were safely out the door. "That was gruesome," I said. "Next time you want any favors, include me out. Mama and the kid—"

"They're all alike." Taylor filled his pipe. "But that girl now, she might have something. If Mama didn't teach her how to imitate Corinne Griffith."

"Too young." I shrugged. "No personality."

"Maybe you're right." Taylor puffed on his pipe, exhaled aromatically. "Come on, let's see who they're beheading over at the Palace."

We cut across the quadrangle and entered Stage Four. It was our biggest and it was filled to capacity this afternoon. Everybody was there—props, grips, carpenters, greenery men, messengers, stenos, script girls, camera crews, the people from makeup and wardrobe, the studio cops, even Carla Sloane. Plus, of course, every contract player from Dude Williams' double up to Kurt Lozoff, and every director, writer and cutter on the lot. The entire front office was out in force, clustered together in a cloud of cigar smoke.

The two sides running the length of the building were lined with tables, some heaped with food and others piled high with glasses, bottles and bowls of cracked ice. The ice was already melting in the heat, and I knew just how it felt.

Taylor and I elbowed into the milling mob and I peered ahead at the little platform set up on the far end of the stage. The front office bookkeeper, Glazer, was up there now under a Cooper-Hewitt light, sweating his way through a speech. Over the crowd murmurs I heard him introducing "the man who has been like a father to us all, the guiding genius who made Coronet Pictures the crown of the Industry. Fellow workers, I give you Mr. Sol. J. Morris!"

Morris mounted the platform now, emerging from the throng down front. He'd been there all the time but I hadn't noticed him. I'd seen Harker standing stiffly erect like a black arrow driven into earth; Karl Druse watching at one side, his eyes inscrutable and inescapable; Lois Payne, Lozoff's current leading lady, commanding as a queen, her hair flowing like a living flame. In such a group, the bald, fat little nonentity was unnoticeable.

But now, up there on the platform, he was God again. And his voice thundered down from a clapboard Sinai.

"Fellow workers," he began. "That's what my good friend Bernie Glazer just called you. And I hope when he said it he meant it should include me, too. Because I am a fellow worker also, even if some of you think I'm not much of a fellow and I don't do any work."

He waited for the dutiful laughter, and got better than that, because there were a lot of people here in the crowd who really liked him.

"Today I'm not making a speech. First of all it's too hot, and second of all, you want to go away for a holiday. I guess you know the studio is closed until Monday."

Somebody whistled above a spattering of applause. Morris frowned.

"But what you don't know is—the studio stays closed. It don't open on Monday. Or ever."

He raised his hand before the crowd raised its groan.

"Right now we got only two units working anyways. Dude Williams goes on location in San Fernando next week. The Emerson Craig company starts shooting on the Classic lot—it's all right, I got everything arranged with Nate Fisher over there, he'll take care of you.

"And for the rest of you—goodbye and good luck. Until Labor Day, that is. Because now I'll tell you what we're gonna do. We close the studio like I said. And then we tear it down.

"But on Labor Day we're opening up again. With a brand new, bigger and better studio for Coronet Pictures!"

The applause was sudden and shattering. Somebody must have let the press in because flash powder burst now about the bald head and beaming face. Morris raised his pudgy hand once more, signaling for silence.

"That's right. I said bigger and better and I mean it. Modern, the latest thing, top to bottom. You'll read all about it in the papers and like I said, I'm not making a speech." He paused, took a cigar from his pocket, then put it back. "One thing more I got to say, though. This new studio ain't being built by me. It ain't something I decided about just so I could have my name up bigger over the entrance.

"It's being built by you. All of you who work here and helped make us a success. You get the credit.

"But I can see from the faces you ain't so worried about the credit as you are about cash. So the last thing I got to tell you is—everybody stays on the payroll, from now until we open up again after Labor Day. Goodbye and God bless you."

Then there *really* was applause. Applause, and excited babbling, and a mad rush for the side of the room where the glasses and ice and bottles waited.

I found myself wedged in beside Arch Taylor. "You know about this?" I asked.

"Not until this morning. He called in Harker, Lozoff, a few others—big surprise. Showed us the plans. Looks like we'll have the best layout in town. Better than Paramount or First National. Of course Metro and Universal have more space—"

"How about some space for me?" Carla Sloane started to struggle past us to the scotch bottles and I opened a path for her.

"Thank you, Red Grange," she said. "See you at the party?"

"What party?"

"Mine." Jackie Keeley peered over my shoulder. "We're celebrating the Fourth of July. Come on over and see the fireworks."

"But the Fourth is two days away—"

"Gives us time to catch up on our drinking."

"Lois Payne will be there," Arch said. "She's been asking about you."

I glanced across the room at Lozoff's new leading lady. It was hard for me to imagine that this regal redhead had any interest in me.

"You're kidding," I said.

"So help me, it's true—heard her myself," said Jackie Keeley. "It's gonna be a real brawl, too. All you can drink, and I ordered a whole truckload of Roman candles you can play with."

"To say nothing of Lois Payne," Arch murmured.

"Better come out." Jackie Keeley winked at me. "Maybe she'll help you shoot off your firecracker."

EIGHT

SOMEWHERE DURING THE CRUSH and course of the afternoon I lost Arch Taylor. When I tried to hunt him down I learned he'd left and taken Lois Payne with him.

"Come and ride out with us," Carla Sloane said. "I'm getting a lift from Hacky."

Hacky's real name was Hackenheimer, but nobody ever called him that. He was a big, beefy redfaced man with all the souvenirs of a former career in the prize ring—a broken nose, a cauliflower ear, and a slightly battered brain.

He'd worked for Path) and for Educational as a gag man, and that's where the battered brain came in handy. It was still doing service now, for Jackie Keeley. The addled ideas it produced were worth enough to indulge Hacky's fondness for purple shirts and orange knickers. He wasn't even a gag man any more; he was a "comedy constructionist."

At the moment he was far from sober, and he steered all over the road. But this was before the era of stoplights on Wilshire and we just thought it was funny. After the scotch we'd had, everything seemed funny, including Hacky's remarks. He habitually steered his conversation the way he steered his car.

"Think Arch Taylor's already out there?" I asked, as we weaved past the frame structure of Soldier's Home.

"Everybody's out there the way I heard it," Hacky yelled. "Everybody including Jackie Coogan and his brother."

"Didn't even know he had a brother," Carla giggled. "What's his name?"

"Coffee Coogan."

While Carla giggled, Hacky passed the flask. "Didja hear the gag about Chaney?" We sped through the sleepy, sun-baked streets of Santa Monica. "First fella says, 'See if you can use Lon Chaney in a sentence.' Second fella says, 'That's easy. Lately I been working so hard I don't have time to eat Lon Chaney more.' Get it?"

We got about a dozen others before we descended to the coast highway and began to move north in the direction of Malibu. It was a clear day, but with the contents of Hacky's flask sloshing around inside us, we didn't see Catalina.

Even so, it was impossible to miss Jackie Keeley's beach house. It was the only one that had a drawbridge and a moat before the entrance.

The drawbridge was lowered and the voices were raised in the patio beyond. We parked the car in the courtyard, between a Model T and a Mercedes, then pushed forward into the crowd congregated around the patio pool. Hacky hadn't lied—everybody seemed to be here. Everybody *except* Jackie Coogan and his brother (whose name, for the record, happened to be Robert). I didn't seek Harker or Lozoff or Karl Druse, but then I didn't expect to; they were not partygoers or partythrowers.

But Emerson Craig lurched over as we entered. The tall leading man was rapidly approaching the point where somebody would have to be leading him. "Well, look who's here! Come on and pour yourself into a drink."

"Is the liquor safe?" Hacky asked.

"Sure. Jackie ran his yacht up to Canada and picked up a good load."

"Nothing like a good load, I always say." Keeley himself wavered over and waved a welcome. "Hi, Carla—you giving me a little manicure later on?"

"Doesn't your wife look after your cuticle?"

"What wife?"

"How do I know? What wife are you on now, anyway?"

"That's a good one!" Hacky guffawed.

"I'm serious," Carla insisted. "How many is it, Jackie—four or five?"

"Five, last time I counted." Keeley slid an arm around her waist. "But she took a powder on me last week. That's why I'm celebrating. Who knows, maybe I'll meet Number Six."

Emerson Craig shook his head. "Jackie, how do you pay your alimony?"

"Seldom, that's how." Keeley urged us forward. "The bar's inside. Tell 'em I sent you."

We moved along the patio, dodging drunks, nudging neckers, elbowing past mustached men who might have been Mdivani brothers and women who might have been their sisters but probably weren't.

Inside the big living room it was louder and funnier. Louder, anyway. There was a Hawaiian with a ukulele, accompanying a blonde who did a hula wearing a fringed lampshade for a grass skirt. I saw somebody who looked like Laura LaPlante and somebody who looked like Mickey Neilan, but on second thought LaPlante wouldn't have a tattoo on that spot and Neilan wouldn't be publicly inspecting it if she had. There was a charming little brunette with a pet monkey on her shoulder; at least it *was* on her shoulder until it decided to make a hammock for itself in her d)colletage. As we moved up to the bar we almost stumbled over a barefooted old gentleman with a long white beard who might have passed as Peter the Hermit. He was sitting on the floor, staring dreamily into the eyes of a teenage girl as she lit a match and tried to set fire to his beard.

In a madhouse, you're apt to hear voices. I did.

". . . Christie Brothers, Warner Brothers, Talmadge sisters. Everywhere you go, there's nepotism . . ."

". . . sounds more like incest to me. So what's wrong with that, it's all in the family . . ."

". . . we are all worms, wriggling on the end of God's fishhook . . ."

". . . why don't you get smart and put that monkey back on bottle-feeding, darling?"

". . . million and a half it grossed and he's complaining! You should have William Fox's dough, that's all I wish on you . . ."

". . . he only uses a double in his love scenes . . ."

". . . well for chrissake, grab the monk by the tail and pull him out of there . . ."

". . . john is full, so use the pool . . ."

". . . anybody seen Billie? She said she'd drop in . . ."

". . . warned you, didn't I? Grab his tail unless you want people to think you're pregnant . . ."

". . . goddam it, I *am* pregnant . . ."

Standing at the bar, my ears eliminated voices, my eyes examined everyone, alerting myself to Lois Payne's possible presence. Suddenly I caught sight of Arch Taylor moving toward me, glass in hand. The glass was empty and he was obviously full. Somewhere along the line he'd lost his jacket, necktie and coordination.

"Sorry I lost you!" I called. "How you doing?"

"Great." He leaned against the bar for support, waving my hand aside. "Don't worry 'bout me. When I get tired I'll just crawl under the nearest blonde and sleep it off." He blinked. "Which reminds me. How about going over and cheering Lois up? She's got the blues."

"Lois Payne? Where is she?"

"Out there." Taylor gestured in the direction of an alcove off the living room. Reaching across the bar, he picked up a half-filled bottle of rye. "Here, tell her I sent a drink."

As I picked my way through the crowd I caught sight of her and moved faster, guided by the blazing beacon of her hair. The alcove, just off the hall leading to the bedrooms, was almost completely filled by a grand piano. Lois Payne sat on the bench behind it, cool and aloof, her pensive eyes downcast. I'd learned a lot since the Maybelle Manners days; enough to know that here was a true aristocrat. Perfect poise, finely chiseled features, a mouth that was almost prim despite the flaming promise of her hair. She glanced up as I approached, extending the bottle.

"Arch Taylor asked me to bring this over," I said. "I'm Tommy Post."

"Yes, I know." She smiled quietly, took the bottle from my hand, set it down beside her. "We don't really need this, do we?"

"I can get glasses—"

"No thank you." Her voice was low and I caught a hint of embarrassment. "I don't drink."

I started to move around the side of the piano. "Mind if I sit down?"

"Please do. Oh, be careful—"

She didn't have to warn me. The growl did that.

There was a dog crouching beside her, back of the piano. It had taken the bulk of a baby grand to hide the creature, because this was the biggest wolfhound I'd ever seen. Panting, it rested a massive head on Lois's lap as she stroked its jowls.

"Now you be good," she murmured. "He's our friend."

"*Your* friend," I said, eyeing the monster.

"Actually he belongs to Jackie," Lois told me. "We're just getting acquainted."

I slid onto the piano bench—on the far side of the dog. It made a rumbling noise in its throat, then subsided as Lois petted it. She stared across the alcove into the living room beyond, an enigmatic expression in her hazel eyes.

"Cigarette?" I offered.

"Sorry." She was almost blushing. "I don't smoke."

"Quite a party."

"Yes." She patted the dog's head and it licked her hand with the longest, pinkest tongue I'd ever seen. "I'm afraid I'm not much of a partygoer."

Staring off at the clamoring crowd, I could understand that. This was a girl who belonged on the cover of a candy box; hers was a face meant to be framed by the lace of an old-fashioned valentine. Her gentle grace didn't fit these raucous surroundings. As she quietly fondled the muzzle of the huge dog, he responded and so did I.

"Arch Taylor said you were feeling a little depressed," I said.

"Did he?" She gave me a shy smile. "If I am, it's his fault."

"What did he do?"

"Nothing, really." Lois sighed. "I don't want to hurt your feelings, but your friend Arch Taylor is a lousy lay."

I blinked.

She brightened. "I'll bet you're good, though. There's a bedroom just down the hall here—"

I blinked again. Lois glanced down wistfully at the wolfhound as its pink tongue lapped her fingers. "Forget it," she murmured. "All men are beasts!"

Rising, she moved into the hall. As I watched, Lois Payne went into a bedroom with the dog and closed the door behind her.

I stared after her, then turned as smoke surged from the living room. There was a sudden, shattering sound, set against a counterpoint of screams and laughter.

Hacky was standing on top of the bar, setting off Roman candles. Apparently he'd discovered his host's stock of fireworks. Rockets whizzed across the room, their flight applauded by shrieks and shouts from the crowd. One lodged on the staircase and sputtered there; another spurted sparks in the bowl of the chandelier. For a wonder, no fire started and no one was hit. Hacky balanced on the bartop and tried to light a six-inch salute with his cigar.

"Hot dog!" he shouted. "Let's start the show off with a bang!" Somebody grabbed at his leg and he fell off the bar into the crush below.

I didn't wait to see what happened. There was a side door leading from the alcove to the garden. I opened it and went out.

The garden was cool and quiet, the green of its grass and shrubbery already tinged with twilight. A breeze beckoned from the bench beyond and I sought its source on the edge of a bluff overlooking the ocean.

Dusk deepened as the moon came up over the water. I stared down as the gigantic creamy tongue of a wave lapped the beach below.

The long, pink tongue of the wolfhound . . .

What was wrong with Lois Payne? And what was wrong with me? Why did I insist on the glamor, why couldn't I take the reality for what it was worth? You couldn't have both, and if you insisted, you ended up with neither. You ended up looking down at the water, wondering what it would be like to jump.

"Hey, what gives?"

The voice came from behind me. I turned and the moonlight disclosed the haggard face of my host. Jackie Keeley had been drinking all afternoon, but he looked sober now.

He sounded sober, too. "Don't you like my party?"

"Yes, but—"

"I get it. I saw you inside there with Lois. The original Bengal Man-Trap." He grinned. "Don't worry, there's plenty more where that came from, believe me."

"I believe you. But maybe that's the trouble. Maybe I don't want any more of that kind."

"There are no other kinds," Keeley said. "I ought to know." He pulled a silver flask from his hip pocket and unscrewed the cap. "Here—have a drink."

I shook my head. "That's not the answer."

Keeley shrugged, then tilted the flask to his lips. "You come up with a better one, just let me know." He drank, then set the flask down on a ledge of rock.

"Does it really help?" I asked.

"Nothing really helps." Keeley perched on the rock ledge, glanced down wryly at his dangling legs. "Maybe I could steal a pair of Karl Druse's platform shoes or whatever it is they say he wears. But I can't wear them to bed and I wouldn't fool anybody if I did. I'd still have runt sickness."

"What?"

He shrugged. "That's the only name I can give it. Runt sickness. You get it young, when you're just a kid and shorter than the others. People start calling you 'Shorty' and 'Tiny Tim.' And they laugh. The other kids, the girls, even your own family. They think it's funny when you try to fight somebody twice your size, funny when you get licked and have to cry. But after a while you get used to it. You figure if they're gonna laugh anyway you might as well do things that make them laugh *with* you instead of just *at* you." Keeley chuckled. "So that's how I ended up in Hollywood. Star comic, but still a runt."

"You're not really so short," I said.

"No, that's the hell of it. Two, three inches less and I'd be *cute*. As it is, I'm just undersized. The kind of a guy no girl wants to dance with."

"But you've had—"

"Girls? You can say that again! And wives, too." He chuckled once more. "All of 'em married that popular star of the silver screen. And all of 'em ended up married to a runt. At least that's what they got around to telling me."

"There are plenty of women shorter than you."

"I know. I've tried all sizes, all shapes. Colors, too. But there's something about a little guy that's just plain funny." Keeley took another pull at his flask. "Most of the comics out here are small. Chaplin, Keaton, Langdon, Conklin, Bobby Vernon, Lupino Lane. Harold Lloyd's no giant, either. If we were three inches taller we'd probably all be happy bricklayers."

"Don't kid me." I shook my head. "You like being a star."

"I wouldn't mind if I was really good."

"Like Chaplin?"

"Or Buster Keaton. He's the best, but nobody seems to know it except another comic." Keeley was coming alive again; he slid off his perch and gestured. "Chaplin plays for sympathy, hoking it up with kids and dogs. But Buster doesn't cry and he doesn't mug. Don't you see what a wonderful thing it is, to be funny without mugging? Keaton's deadpan comedy—why it's like great dancing without moving your legs."

"You do all right," I said. "And you hit the answer when you talked about wanting people to laugh with you, not *at* you. That goes for me, too, and Lozoff, Arch Taylor, everybody I know out here. Maybe even Harker has a reason for—"

"Harker?" Keeley waved his flask. "Why, I knew Teddy Harker when he was still with it."

"With what?"

"A carny, that's what. Used to travel with mud shows, him and his wife. At least she said she was his wife, little redhead, Connie something-or-other. Anyway, you're right about Harker. I knew him when—and so did Karl Druse. Druse was a fire-eater and sword-swallower on the same outfit with Harker, but neither of 'em talk about it now. I don't think Karl would mind, but Harker's touchy about his past. Now, ever since he hit the Coast, he pretends he's the Great Director so nobody will laugh. Just like I pretend to be the Great Comedian. But you're right—we all have our secrets."

Keeley smiled and put his flask away. "You know something? I feel better."

"Me too," I told him.

"What say we join the party? I'm hungry."

"You go ahead and eat," I said. "I'll be along in a minute."

Jackie Keeley pattered off toward the house and I stared at his retreating figure, still wondering why comics must be sad and carny grifters play at perfection, why delicate Beauty concealed a kinship with the Beast, and why I—in spite of all my efforts to join the party—couldn't seem to settle for anything less than reality in a world where everything was founded on make-believe.

Then somebody came up behind me and put her hands over my eyes and giggled, "Guess who?"

"Carla," I said.

"Right. You win the celluloid toothpick."

"Celluloid?" I turned to face her. "Does it *have* to be celluloid? Why can't something be real for a change?"

"Such as?"

I couldn't tell her. It was much easier to take her in my arms and say, "Such as this." And kiss her, feel her lips warm and wet, her body waiting and willing.

"Come on," I murmured. "Let's go down to the beach."

We found a path and descended into the darkness. There was nothing to stop me now, nothing to hold me back, and she didn't laugh at me or at what we were doing.

And what we were doing was finding one another's flesh, finding and fusing and fulfilling. There was no pretending, no closing one's eyes and imagining—no opening one's eyes and staring up at an illusion on the screen. I knew, without words, learning from the language of her body alone, that Carla had wanted me for a long time. And I knew I needed her. Needed to hold her tight, thinking, *this is reality. You're clinging to reality now.*

I wondered how long I could hang onto it.

NINE

SEPTEMBER SUNSHINE SHIMMERED across the walk before the new Executive Building and sparkled against the walls of the Coronet stages.

"Behold!" Arch Taylor gestured with his pipe. "The pleasure dome of Kubla Khan!"

Carla Sloane frowned. "You mean Otto Kahn, don't you? And what's he got to do with it—I thought Morris put up the money for this new lot himself."

Arch Taylor winked at me, turned to the manicurist and shook his head. "You lack a classical background, honey. Haven't you heard of those immortal lovers, Balaban and Katz? Didn't you read about the Orpheum Circuit in Hades? Or Grant's surrender to Lee Shubert?"

"Banana oil," Carla said. She stared off at the avenue to our right. "I think this is just wonderful, every bit of it. And imagine getting it all built in two months!"

"A lot can happen in two months," Taylor told her. "As I hope it is never your misfortune to find out."

Carla giggled and squeezed my hand. I squeezed back until our manicures met. It had been a pleasant summer, what with getting those regular manicures and all.

"Well, we might as well see who's at the reception," Taylor said. "I understand Valentino was here this morning."

"Colleen Moore, too," Carla said. "Gee, those bangs of hers are cute. Think I'll get my hair cut that way."

"It's the new style, darling." Taylor smiled. "Look at Anna May Wong."

"Where? Oh—I thought you meant she was *here*." Carla turned as Dude Williams and his wife joined us at the edge of the walk.

"Howdy, folks," he greeted us. "Guess you all know Nina."

"Sure," I said. "Where are the kids?"

"Packed them off to school yesterday." Little Mrs. Williams smiled shyly. "My, isn't this grand?"

"Did you see the stables?" Dude asked. "They got a special corral, just for old Ranger. And his double."

"I never knew your horse had a double, said Taylor.

" 'Course he does. Gettin' along, you know. Come to think of it, I ain't no yearling myself."

Mrs. Williams bit her lip. "What are you talking about? Why, you're just a boy!"

"I'd be a mighty sad-lookin' boy if it wasn't for Max Factor's makeup," Dude murmured. "Why Karl, you old so-and-so—how's tricks?"

Karl Druse bobbed stiffly beside us. Next to Dude, the horror star seemed almost dwarfed, moving with short, jerky steps. His somber eyes were intent on the entrance to the Executive Building ahead.

"How's it strike you?" Dude asked.

"Very impressive. Almost *too* impressive." Druse frowned. "This must have cost a fortune."

"Old Morris'll git it back, don't you worry. Hey, you rate one of them new private bungalows?"

Druse nodded. "When I think back to the old days, with the dressing room in a corner of the barn, no privacy but a curtain—everybody doubling in brass and moving props—this is certainly an improvement."

"Don't remind me." Dude grimaced suddenly and his wife glanced up at him.

"What's the matter, dear?"

"Got a stitch in my side. Them baked beans." He stepped aside as we moved to the entrance. "Be all right when I take somethin'. You go ahead, I'll find you inside."

"Dude—" Nina Williams stared at his retreating back. "Ever since he had that accident on location he gets these attacks," she told us. "Doctor gave him something for pain, but lately now—"

Her voice trailed off, lost in the babble rising all about us. The lobby of the Executive Building was jammed with studio employees and invited guests.

"Look at all the flowers!" Carla was already inspecting cards attached to the floral pieces banked along the wall. "Ooh, here's one from John Gilbert. And Ronald Colman. Vilma Banky—Gloria Swanson, Jimmy Cruze, Herb Brenon—"

Bernie Glazer nodded at us as we passed; he was talking to a portly gentleman in a blue serge suit.

"Who's he?" I whispered to Taylor.

"Works for the Hays Office, I think," Arch murmured. "The vultures are gathering."

Druse nodded. "Bad enough when they censor our work," he said, "but now they're trying to control our private lives, too." He scowled. "Look what they did to poor Arbuckle, and Wally Reid."

"What about the William Desmond Taylor case?" Taylor nodded. "It's getting so a man can't sit in his car at Hollywood and Vine and rape an extra without getting a parking ticket."

Mrs. Williams sniffed. "I don't think you're a bit funny," she said. "I'm going to find Dude."

She turned away and Druse stared after her. "Something's wrong with Williams," he muttered. "He doesn't look well to me."

"Maybe he should see a veterinary." Taylor and Carla and I moved along slowly in the direction of the inner office suites.

"Wait!" Carla wailed. "Isn't that Alice Terry over there?"

"She and Rex are abroad," Taylor told her. "Come on, let's say hello to the Royal Family."

The Royal Family was holding court in Sol Morris's huge, oak-paneled audience chamber.

Theodore Harker and Lozoff were both present, and I pushed my way through the crowd to say hello. During the studio shut-down Lozoff had taken a European trip with Madame Olga. Harker had disappeared into a private retreat of his own; I'd called several times, hoping for word on the next production, but he was never in, never called back.

Now he nodded at me and shook hands. The tall director seemed unchanged at first glance—the black suit was still a little too big, the black hair still a bit too long. But something was different. I noticed it as he held out his hand to me, and then I realized the truth. Theodore Harker was actually smiling.

"Meant to get in touch with you," he said. "We must talk."

"Next assignment?"

"I've written it."

"You—?"

"This is to be something very special. I think I have what I was striving for, but of course your comments will be appreciated. Let's talk tomorrow."

"Certainly."

I turned to Lozoff. He bowed. "My dear boy, I'm so very happy to see you! Madame and I wish you to dine with us this evening—like old times, eh?"

Before answering I glanced at Carla. She nodded almost imperceptibly. "Glad to," I told Lozoff. "But I've got a date later on."

"Of course. We'll expect you at seven, then."

"Right." I moved along, greeting John Frisby and his wife, Emerson Craig, then Jackie Keeley and *his* new bride.

"Congratulations," I said.

"Thank you," said Lois Payne, coolly. She might have been meeting me for the first time.

"What a turnout!" Keeley glanced around appreciatively. "Looks like everybody in town is here."

He was almost right. The only one mission was Maybelle Manners—but of course nobody remembered her any more.

Off to our left, near the high stained-glass windows, Sol and Hilda Morris stood surrounded by the working press. They were posing for a photo, and Morris didn't have to smile for the shot. He was beaming continuously; after the picture was taken he pointed and gestured to the reporters, indicating the wonders of the dictaphone, the fans, the ventilators, the water cooler—all of which bore the Coronet trademark emblazoned in silver.

I glanced at one of the female reporters, then poked Carla in the ribs. "Hey, look who's here!"

She followed my gaze. "So?"

"Isn't that Miss Glint? How did she get in?"

"She's working for *Starland* now. Writes a monthly column—*Gossip by Glenda Glint*."

"I thought her name was Maggie."

"Well, it's Glenda now and you'd better not forget it. Columnists are important and I hear she's going to do a regular feature for the newspapers too. She knows where all the bodies are buried, and if you ask me, she's probably happy to dig them up again."

I watched Miss Glint as she joined the press of press representatives who followed Sol Morris to the corner of the room. He led them up to a pudgy young man whose jowls were pitted with smallpox scars.

Morris took the young man by the hand and stepped forward. "I got an announcement to make, everybody," he called, and the crowd quieted.

"I guess most of you already met Nicky here. If not, want you all to get introduced—Nicky Morris is the name. You're gonna hear a lot of it from now on, because he's joining the rest of us here at the studio where he belongs. You can put it down that he's our new production supervisor, with John Frisby's unit."

Young Morris clasped both hands together over his head in a gesture popularized by Jack Dempsey. "That's the story," he grinned. "From now on, Dad and I work together. I've spent the whole summer with him, just learning the ropes. And I think I can promise you some real action."

An almost inaudible groan sounded beside me. I turned to see big John Frisby's face wince its way into a smile. Arch Taylor bent to whisper. "Louis

B. Mayer has Irving Thalberg. You have Nicky Morris. How lucky can you get?"

"Yeah," Frisby murmured. "But what in hell *is* a production supervisor?"

Morris turned and moved to a small door at the far end of the room. "Let's go inside now," he said. "I think maybe it's time for the big surprise."

He opened the door, then turned as the group started forward, halting its movement with his hand. "Sorry we ain't got room for everybody. I want the boys and girls from the press, and you, and you—you—and you—"

The royal finger crooked imperiously. I was surprised and flattered when it wiggled an invitation my way.

I went inside with Theodore Harker, Lozoff, Taylor, Frisby, Nicky and a dozen others. Morris's inner sanctum was small; aside from the usual overstuffed sofa and built-in bar, there was only one other article of furniture in the room, but the reporters and trade paper representatives were already clustered around it.

What they saw was a full-size barber chair, its seat and headrest covered in ermine; a barber chair with arms and back of solid gold.

"Classy, eh?" Sol Morris strutted proudly before it; then, unable to resist the temptation, climbed up and sat down.

It was a picture I'd never forget—the king, mounting his throne. Morris leaned back and closed his eyes for a moment and the room fell silent.

Then he sat up and chuckled. "Go ahead," he said. "I ain't such a *neb* I don't know what you're thinking. Inside you're laughing; you're saying look who's sitting in gold barber chairs yet! Like some kind of high mucky-muck. I know how you'll print it in the papers.

"Well, that don't get me mad. It's good publicity, and maybe you print what I tell you now, too."

Morris smiled and his voice softened. "Some guys, they want to think, they go out in the woods, fishing. Some guys it's like they got to have a bunch of drinks to relax.

"With me, it's always barber chairs. I climb up and close my eyes and I get ideas. When I was still a salesman that's how it worked. I got the idea of going into the motion picture business sitting in a barber chair. In 1913, in Attica, Indiana.

"Barber chairs are my good luck. The first time I met Mr. Harker here, I was sitting in a barber chair down on Western Avenue. And believe me, it was a lucky day for both of us, eh, Mr. Harker?"

Harker nodded, his seldom-smiling face again alight.

"And now I kind of think we're lucky again. This great big new studio, that's one thing. Bringing my son Nicky into the business, that's good too. And the third thing—well, Mr. Harker, you want to tell them about it?"

"I'd rather show them."

The black silhouette moved to a door at the back of the room, swung it open. He waved a figure forward.

For an instant she stood on the threshold, poised and expectant. We all watched as Harker took her by the hand and drew the girl into the room.

She was a cameo come to life—all peach and rose and gold. I noted the white tulle frock, the hair piled high on her head in finespun ringlets. Her face was an oval frame for the pertly pouting mouth, the petite nose, the April-fresh blue of her eyes.

Harker released her hand and nodded at us. "I'm not going to make any predictions," he said. "I'm sure they're unnecessary. You need only to look at her to know that a new star is standing before you today, in all the glorious radiance and precious promise of youth incarnate.

"Nor shall I sully your ears, ladies and gentlemen, with sordid statistics—a full release has been prepared and will be handed to each one of you personally as you leave. If you wish, you may arrange for personal interview appointments later in the week.

"Meanwhile, I have only one announcement to make at this time. I take great pleasure in introducing the lovely and talented Miss Dawn Powers—who will play the leading role in my next production, *Daydreams*."

Yes, it was just as hammy as it sounds, but she stood there, hair haloed in the sunlight, and then she smiled—and they applauded. And before I realized it, I was applauding too, along with all the rest.

Then, as the press people converged on Harker and the girl, I drifted through the doorway. Back in the noisy outer office, Hacky grabbed my arm.

"Some layout," I commented, expecting a wisecrack.

His beefy face bore an honest bewilderment. "I'm lost," he said. "I mean it, I can't find my way around this joint. Everything's too damned big."

"Everything's new," I told him. "You'll get used to it."

"Maybe so. But I don't like it."

"Didn't they give you an office?"

Hacky nodded. "Sure. That's just the trouble, everybody's got an office now. And you know something else? I even got a private can."

"What's wrong with that?"

"What's wrong? Why it's the whole trouble in a nutshell. We're gonna be too big to be friendly now." Hacky sighed. "What the hell do I want with a private can? Man, I get *lonesome* in there!"

TEN

IT WAS ODD to watch Kurt Lozoff at ease in the privacy of his new home, wearing an old sweater as he sprawled in a morris chair and accepted a mug of black coffee from Madame.

By rights he should have been poised perfectly on the edge of his seat, spruce and stiff and starched, ready to spring up and click his heels when the butler entered the room with the silver coffee service. I wrote the scene in my mind, then discarded it as he spoke.

"Ah, it is good to get the shoes off after all that standing!" He gazed at me over the rim of his coffee mug. "What's the matter? You've been so quiet this evening. Didn't you enjoy the reception?"

"Of course. It's just, well—" And I told him about the incident with Hacky.

He smiled and slapped his knee. "But certainly! And the man is right, as far as he goes. It is only that his vision is limited." Lozoff took a gulp of coffee. "He is like a child at a puppet show, happy as long as he can see the strings in plain view. But take away the strings and he becomes afraid. He can only feel safe in this fantastic business when he's sure it's fantasy. That's why he complains about the new studio. To him it's no longer a puppet show because the strings are concealed."

Lozoff offered me a cigarette. "He probably felt safe in the old days, the cramped quarters, where he could see Karl Druse go behind a curtain and come out again with his costume on. Then he could be sure Druse was just wearing makeup. But today he might not see Druse until he's in character, and then he may mistake him for a real monster." Lozoff finished his coffee. "But you and I know better. This is only the same old puppet show on a new and bigger stage."

"Now you sound like Harker," I told him.

"Mawkish, you mean?" He laughed. "But of course; we are in a mawkish business. We deal in sentimentality, not sentiment. We create comedy and ignore humor, honor bathos above pathos. But it does not matter if we get bigger as long as we remember we're still pretending."

"You mentioned Harker—has he changed? You heard him today when he introduced that girl. Wasn't it typical?"

"Same old Harker," I admitted.

"And Mr. Morris. Certainly it will be harder to see him in his new suite of offices, surrounded by private secretaries, and the secretaries of private secretaries. But what's inside the inner office? The gold barber chair—the make-believe throne where he sits and dreams of more make-believe. No, the time to start worrying is when they take away the barber chair and Mr. Morris turns into just another businessman."

I snubbed out my cigarette. "You sound optimistic."

"Of course I do. We're going to see great things now that the screen is coming into its own. This man Murnau—have you heard of his new film, *The Last Laugh*? His cameraman, Karl Freund, has developed a technique where the camera becomes the eyes of the character, and you see what *he* is seeing. Think of what we can do with this! And the picture has only one title."

"Oh, great!" I said. "Pretty soon they'll be shooting without any script, I suppose. And then where will I be?"

"You'll move along with the developments, become a part of progress. Some day we will go beyond these silly costume epics. I will put aside my evening clothes and play mature parts in mature films. Perhaps I shall even direct them myself."

I nodded. "Have you talked to Harker about this?"

"Yes. And in time he will see it as I do."

"You mean he really isn't sold on the idea."

"Well." Lozoff's gaze dropped. "It isn't that Harker is old-fashioned. One cannot accuse him of that, not a man who has been responsible for so many innovations, who has developed the use of the visual symbol, who really created intercutting—"

"Let's be honest," I said. "Harker *is* old-fashioned. He's a complete dictator, he wants to control everything connected with his pictures. That's why we have no producers on our lot, when all the other studios use them. That's why he always rewrites what Taylor or I give him, or shoots off the cuff. That's why he insists on bringing in his own discoveries when he casts."

"He has made some fine pictures," Lozoff said, softly.

"True. But he's had his share of flops. And I wonder how his methods will work now that we've gone modern. That astrology of his—holding up shooting because the horoscope isn't favorable. He's going to have to pull his head out of the clouds and come down to earth."

"This doesn't sound like you, my boy."

"I know. Maybe I'm going modern, too. Maybe I've grown up these past few months. I'm getting a little bit impatient with all this temperament, this business of being phoney off the set as well as on."

"You've got to have the make-believe," Lozoff murmured. "Harker must play his role. The black suit and the astrology chart—he needs them both."

"Maybe you're right." I stood up, glancing at my watch. "Got to be running, now. We'll get together tomorrow, I guess, and discuss this mysterious new script he's doing."

Lozoff escorted me to the door and I paused there. "Say, I almost forgot. What do you think of this girl—this Dawn Powers?"

"Exquisite."

"Can she act?"

Lozoff shrugged. "I do not know. I've never seen her before."

"But didn't Harker run her test for you? After all, she'll be your leading woman in the picture, won't she?"

"So I learned today," Lozoff said. "Harker has never even mentioned her name to me."

"But that's incredible!"

"That's Theodore Harker."

We parted and I drove home—home to the apartment, and Carla.

She had arrived a few minutes before me and let herself in. Right now she was curled up around a big highball.

"Want one?"

"I could use it, thanks." I sat down and took off my necktie. "Big day."

"You said a mouthful!" Carla mixed my drink. "I hear you got a load of Dawn Powers. How is she?"

"Looks okay."

"Prettier'n I am?"

"Of course not."

"Oh, so's your old man! You don't have to kid me." She brought my drink and sat down on the sofa beside me. "But don't go getting any ideas about this Dawn Powers, now. She's strictly Harker's property."

"How do you know?"

Carla's smile was vague. "I get around. Confidentially—" Her smile vanished and her voice lowered. "You know how Harker is about the stars? Well, this summer he got mixed up with a new astrologer. And she introduced him to Dawn Powers."

She began opening my shirt as she spoke.

"You mean that's all there is to it?" I asked.

Carla giggled. "Act your age! The astrologer was in cahoots with somebody who wanted to get to Harker. They made a deal to sell him a bill of goods."

"But Harker's not a fool." The shirt came off and Carla started to remove my shoes.

"All men are foolish about something," she said. "Harker's a fool about the stars. And I'll bet this dame was plenty clever. Probably dug up a lot of stuff about Harker's past, told him things he didn't think anyone knew about, and said she saw it in the stars. Here, get those socks off."

I got those socks off. "Then what?"

"Then it was easy. She had his confidence, started advising him. Naturally he started talking about the future, his next picture, that sort of thing. That's where Dawn Powers came in. The astrologer probably looked into a crystal ball or whatever they use, and described the kind of a girl who'd be his next star. Predicted that she'd be a big success. And then arranged for Harker to see her. I don't know where, but my guess would be in some bedroom."

"You have a one-track mind," I told her.

"No detours in my sex drive." She stood up, unbuttoning her dress.

"So I notice." Carla let the dress fall, lowered herself beside me. "But you didn't finish. How did this astrologer get hold of Dawn Powers in the first place and figure the scheme out?"

"Somebody must have come to *her*, stupid. And made a deal—if the astrologer sold Harker on Dawn Powers, there'd be a payoff."

"Are you sure you aren't just making this all up out of your pretty head?" I touched her breasts.

Carla sat up. I'd touched her vanity, too. "Look, if you must know, I can even tell you *who* made the deal. Some dame, a widow with a couple of movie-crazy kids. She'd been trying to peddle her boy all over town and no sale. Then she started out on the girl. Maybe it was an accident, her hearing about this astrology business with Harker, but when she did she doped out a scheme. And it worked. She sold her own daughter, and that's the honest truth. The kid's name isn't Dawn Powers, you know. Something like Fritzi or Mitzi somebody—"

"Mitzi LaBuddie," I said.

"Huh? Yes, that's it."

"I thought I recognized her." I stood up. "She must have lightened her hair."

"You know her?"

"No. I only saw her once."

"Then what are you so upset about?"

"I'm not upset." I put my hand up to my eyes. "Just a little headache. Today was pretty hectic for me."

Carla sighed. "That's all right. Here, just let me get my things on."

"You don't have to go."

"Oh yes I do."

"You mad about something?"

"No. I'm not mad about anything." She smiled at me as she wriggled into her dress. "Didn't I always tell you it was that way with us—just for laughs, remember? Sooner or later it had to happen."

"Nothing's happened. You sound like you were walking out on me. Carla—"

Her hands were busy with the buttons. "I *am* walking out, before something *does* happen. You're a sweet guy, Tommy, and no hard feelings." She picked up her purse, moved toward the door. "But just remember, I warned you. There'll be trouble if you try to tangle with Theodore Harker."

"Why should I tangle with him?"

Carla turned at the door and gave me a long look. "Maybe you don't know it yet, but your headache is just starting. I saw your face when you mentioned that girl's name. You're in love with Dawn Powers."

She closed the door behind her, and left me alone.

Alone with the truth.

REEL TWO:

Came the Dawn—

ELEVEN

WHEN I WALKED into my office the next morning, my secretary was already sharpening her pencils. We must have had a hundred of them, but Miss Kress sharpened a new batch every day. What she did with them—or dreamed of doing with them—I never knew. The tall, angular spinster didn't seem to have any other vices; the moment she left work she was off to Angelus Temple quicker than you could say Aimee Semple McPherson.

I don't think Miss Kress really approved of me. I had the feeling that she would have preferred working for a more important writer—Jeanie MacPherson, Bill Counselman, or even Rupert Hughes. But she did her job efficiently and that's all I required. Never once during our association had I asked her to take off her glasses, told her she was really beautiful and swept her into my arms. If I had, perhaps she wouldn't have sharpened so many pencils.

Right now, I had other things to think about.

"Good morning, Miss Kress," I said. "Would you get Mr. Harker for me, please?"

She glanced up at me without ceasing her symbolic circumcision. "His office called just a few minutes ago. He won't be in today."

That was all I needed to know.

"Be back in a little while," I told her, heading for the door.

Miss Kress glanced up. "Is there something you want me to do in the meantime?"

"Yes. Stop sharpening and check the erasers. A writer uses them a lot more than he does pencils."

I hurried down the walk outside of the Writer's Building, looking for the brand-new cluster of bungalows behind Stage Four. Luck was with me when I found the one I wanted, and luck was with me again when I knocked on the door.

"Come in," she said.

She was sitting in front of the mirror, doing something to her hair. When she swiveled around and saw me, her mouth made an O.

"I thought you were Mr. Harker," she said.

"Sorry. I understand he's not on the lot today."

"But he told me—" She hesitated, glancing up at me. "I—I don't believe we've met."

I nodded. "Several months ago, in my office. Do you recall it now, Miss LaBuddie?"

Her eyes widened. But she wasn't looking at me now; she was staring over my shoulder at the door, assuring herself that it was closed. Then she spoke. "How did you recognize me?"

"I didn't. Not at first. You did a wonderful job with your hair and everything."

But she wasn't listening. "Mr. Harker didn't tell you," she murmured. "I know he didn't, because he said it was a secret. So how did you—"

"Aren't you even going to ask me to sit down?"

"Please," she said. "You won't tell? Promise me you won't say any-thing—"

"Don't worry, Miss LaBuddie."

"Don't call me that! My name is Dawn Powers."

"All right, Dawn. I'll keep my mouth shut. On one condition. That you have lunch with me this noon."

"But—"

"Call it blackmail." I smiled at her. "Meet you outside the front gate, twelve sharp."

Her mouth made that O again. I turned, opened the door and went out, closing it carefully behind me.

Now I was certain. However she managed to sense it, Carla had been right. I was in love with Dawn Powers.

I don't know what I did for the next two hours, and it doesn't matter. Probably my body was busily occupied in its usual daily routines, but I was somewhere else, building a dream out of vowels. I meeting the O of her mouth. Meeting with it, melting with it, merging with it.

Then it was noon and she was standing there next to the driveway exit, smiling nervously at me as I opened the door of the car. And we were riding somewhere, and then I parked, and we went inside to a table and we ordered. But all the while we were talking. Small talk, yet very important to me. Because I could see her mouth form that *O* again.

"How's your mother?"

"Please, Mr. Post. I'd be much happier if you'd consider this our first meeting. I'd rather forget what happened in your office. Mama was very foolish, and as for Buddie—"

"Has he been working?"

"Just a bit part at FBO, with Jack Hoxie, I think, or Jack Holt. Somebody named Jack. Anyway, he was terrible, of course. Mama was pretty disappointed this summer."

"Until you met Harker," I said, smoothly.

"Yes." Her answer wasn't smooth.

"That was certainly a break, you coming here as a full-fledged star in your first picture. You must have made a tremendous impression on him."

"It was—" The *O* dissolved. She began to sob. As she fumbled for her purse I got my handkerchief out.

"Use this."

I watched her dab at her eyes, wondering why women *always* dab instead of wipe.

"That's better," I said. "No sense bawling just because you're happy."

"Happy? I wish I was dead—"

More tears, more dabs. Until I reached over, took the handkerchief and did a man's job. "Blow your nose," I commanded.

"Thanks. I'm sorry."

"Nothing to be sorry about. Eat your lunch."

"I'm not very hungry."

"Scared?"

"Wouldn't you be? I'm no star. I'm not even an actress. Oh, I've had two years in one of those side-street dramatic schools and I did a little extra work, but that's all. I've never even *wanted* to act."

"Then this was your mother's idea?"

Dawn sighed, nodded. "The whole thing. Changing my hair, the makeup. Introducing me to Mr. Harker, even coaching me on what to say."

"How did that happen?"

"I—I don't know. It was at a party; she got an invitation from somewhere and made me come along. The whole thing was crazy. Mr. Harker just took one look at me and then he started to talk. All about the stars and how he guided his destiny with them and how he could make me a star—" She broke off. "I told you it was crazy."

I shook my head. "You'll be a star if Harker says so. That's the way it goes in this business."

She opened her purse, took out a lipstick and began to refashion the oval of the *O*. "You don't sound very surprised," she said, between strokes.

"I knew about the astrology."

The lipstick halted an inch from her mouth. "Who told you?"

"I can't say. But I'm sure the information will remain confidential."

The lipstick moved, then halted again. "What did they say—" Her hand started to tremble.

I reached out and grabbed her wrist. "Stop shaking. Nobody's going to harm you. Nobody's going to find out."

Her flesh was warm, smooth. My fingers wanted to tighten but I made them yield. She put her hand down, dropped the lipstick in her purse. "Thank you, Mr. Post."

"Look." I smiled at her. "If you expect me to call you Dawn Powers, you've got to call me Tom."

"All right. All right, Tommy." But she didn't return my smile. "I'm sorry to make such a fuss over nothing. It's silly for me to be frightened, only"—and her voice came out in a rush—"I can't help it, I don't know what to do, I don't want to be a star. It's just that Mama said it was the only way, we were down to our last five dollars and Buddie made a flop of it, and then she said it was up to me, I had to go through with it, our last chance—"

"Sure," I said. "I understand. I won't tell anyone and you don't have to talk about it any more."

I got the smile then, the grateful smile, and we changed the subject. At first I carried the conversation and then, gradually, I got her to talking. That's the way I wanted it; there was so much for me to observe, to learn.

I found out Mitzi had left her mother and taken a small apartment with two other girls from the dramatic school. That she had a rather wide dimple in her chin. That her mother really didn't know beans about acting, and at first wanted her to take a course with Kosloff and become a dancer. That her middle finger was longer than her forefinger. That she thought Mitzi was a stupid name for a girl but excellent for a small, properly housebroken poodle. That she had two very minute freckles on the bridge of her nose. That she had enjoyed her lunch but had to get back to the studio now just in case Mr. Harker *did* come in. That I was even more in love with her.

Driving back, I asked the inevitable question. "When can I see you again?"

"Why, you'll be seeing me every day. You're working on the picture, aren't you?"

"That's not what I mean and you know it. How about tonight?"

"I can't. I promised to see Mama."

"Tomorrow night?"

"I don't know. There's so much to do. Mr. Harker has laid out a complete schedule. There's wardrobe fittings and you know what that means. And all those interviews they've arranged for me. Tom, do you know what they're making me do? They're making me learn a *script* for interviews, and Mr. Riley from Publicity is rehearsing me on what to say."

"I still want to see you."

"Yes. I want to see you, too." She colored (or was I imagining things, just as I was imagining what it would be like to kiss that agonizing O?) and continued. "I'll need help, lots of help."

"Don't worry. I'll help in any way I can."

As we approached the studio she put her hand on my arm. "Let me off here, please. I want to stop at the drugstore."

"I'll wait."

"No, don't bother. You go ahead." She smiled. "Please."

"All right."

Then she was gone, and I drove on through the gates alone. I knew why she got out, of course; so no one would see us together. So Harker wouldn't see us together. *Met at a party,* was that the story? *The whole thing was crazy.* Yes, and I was crazy if I believed her. But she'd also said, *I had to go through with it, our last chance.* If that part was true, it made a difference.

But it didn't relieve the tightness in my throat; the tightness that came when I thought of her, when I thought of her and him together.

That tightness remained when I called Harker's house, late that afternoon. I had to call, had to know if he was there, if *she* was there—

The butler answered, of course.

"This is Mr. Post," I said. "Could I speak to Mr. Harker?"

"One moment. I'll see if he's in."

It was a long moment, for me. And then I heard the familiar voice. "Yes?"

"Tom Post. About the script—"

"Didn't my office call you this morning? I won't be in for several days, I'm afraid."

I was afraid too. "I understand, Mr. Harker. I was just anxious to get started."

"So am I." There was a pause. "Perhaps you could arrange to stop by and pick up a copy. Some time after dinner, if you're free."

"I'll be there."

And I was there, arriving so early that I forced myself to sit in the car until twilight hovered over the house on the hillside. Then I went up to the door.

Rogers opened and ushered. "Good evening, Mr. Post. This way, please. Mr. Harker is in the study."

This way was down a long hall, leading to a paneled door. I opened, entered, halted, and stared.

This was the study. A study in ebony and onyx. The wall-to-wall carpeting was black, the matching drapes hung on all sides, and I was lost in the night.

I looked up and saw the stars.

They burned down at me from the simulation of space that was the ceiling. And in their faint reflection I noted the wall hangings were not entirely black; within their folds I glimpsed the glitter of silver symbols. Here were the signs of the zodiac—Taurus and Gemini and Aries surrounded me in the eternal depths between the wheeling worlds.

Theodore Harker was sitting behind a round, velvet-covered table in the center of the room. With his sable suit drowned in darkness, he was just a disembodied face; a face and two hands that now fluttered over candles. The tapers flared up and I could see more distinctly. Harker was smiling.

"Please sit down. I've been working and meditating here all afternoon."

I took a seat across from him, noting the couch in the corner, the telltale bases of bookshelves protruding from beneath the drawn drapery.

Harker shrugged. "I seldom receive visitors here. Most of them would find my tastes too theatrical."

"It's very unusual," I said. "Quite impressive."

He nodded. "I like to work here. I find it stimulating to commune with the stars."

"Afraid I'm lost when it comes to astrology," I told him.

"Odd. I'd thought perhaps that—but no matter, another time, perhaps. You wanted to see this."

There was a drawer in the table. From it Harker took a sheaf of manuscript. "I hope you can read my handwriting. You can return it to me on Monday. I'll be back at the studio then, definitely, for our conference."

I hesitated. "Couldn't we go over it together now, perhaps?"

"Sorry. I have plans for the evening."

He extended the manuscript, carefully separating a larger sheet from the bottom and placing it on the table before him.

"Don't worry, we'll have plenty of time to talk when we meet. Taylor and Lozoff will join us too, of course." Harker rose. "Now, if you'll excuse me?"

As I stood up I glanced down at the single sheet resting on the tabletop. It was covered with designs and figures—a horoscope chart, of course.

"Good night," Harker murmured. "You'll forgive me if I don't see you to the door."

"That's all right. I know the way."

I did know the way, and I found it. But everything seemed oddly blurred. There was only one thing clear before my eyes—the name I'd seen at the top of the horoscope in Harker's study.

Dawn Powers.

TWELVE

PROMPTLY AT NINE on Monday morning I walked into Theodore Harker's office. Arch Taylor and Lozoff followed behind me.

"Good morning," I said, smiling.

Harker looked up, returning the smile and the greeting, waving us into the chairs grouped before his desk and watching us settle into them.

"Well, gentlemen," he said. "Post here tells me that you've all had a chance to read *Daydreams*."

We nodded in unison.

Harker noted the manuscript in my hand and his smile broadened. "I see you had it typed up over the weekend."

"Yes." I took a deep breath. "With a few changes."

"Changes?" The smile narrowed, disappeared. "There has been no discussion of the story yet. Unless you held a private meeting—"

"Nothing like that," I assured him. "I merely let Mr. Taylor and Mr. Lozoff read your version after I'd finished with it. On separate occasions, I might add. And it was my impression that the story line could be strengthened. Neither of them has seen my rewrite."

"Rewrite? Who asked you for a rewrite?"

"Please, Mr. Harker—I think if you'll read what I've done here—"

The smile was back on Harker's face, and now I realized that during its absence it had taken a trip to the North Pole.

"Before I do, might I be permitted to ask a few questions?" He glanced at Lozoff. "You read my script. What did you think of it?"

"I like the theme," Lozoff said. "The blind violinist and the deaf girl singer—two street musicians leading an enchanted life in their dreams. It's just that the dream sequences seemed stilted."

Harker started to open his mouth, but Lozoff hurried on. "The Napoleonic scenes with the uniforms and all—they're like an old-fashioned operetta. They are not the dreams of little people come to life."

"What's come over you?" Theodore Harker leaned forward. "I advise you to confine your theories to acting."

Lozoff ran his hand along the single silver streak in his hair. "You were an actor at one time. Now you are a director. Some day I hope to follow suit."

Harker sat back again. "Very well. But I must remind you that I am still functioning in a directorial capacity on this picture. And it will be a Harker picture—not a Lozoff production." His eyes went to Arch Taylor. "What is your opinion?"

Taylor crossed his legs casually and studied the crease in his trousers. "I'm a little worried about the girl. You've given her a lot of footage."

"She's the star," Harker said.

"I know. But she's had no experience. You can't expect her to carry a part like that alone—"

"She won't be alone." Harker brought his hand down on the desk sharply. "You seem to forget that Dawn Powers is my discovery. I created this part expressly for her. I know her potential, and you needn't worry about her ability to handle the role. Unless, of course, you no longer have confidence in me." He paused. "In that case, I presume you would rather not be associated with the production."

Taylor didn't look at the director. I was trying to catch his eye, but he wasn't looking at me, either. He kept studying that crease in his trousers. It was very sharp.

"Don't get me wrong, he said. "I can see where Post isn't too happy with the story. But I agree with you. Your direction will solve that."

Harker nodded. I glanced quickly at Lozoff, but Harker had already claimed his attention.

"And what is your final verdict, Mr. Lozoff?"

The little foreigner's eyes flickered past my face, then away. "You are the director," he answered.

"Good." Theodore Harker faced me. "And now, Mr. Post, may I see this revision you wrote?"

I handed it to him.

"Thank you." He cradled the sheaf of paper in his palm and his words came very slowly and very distinctly. "I am much obliged to you for your effort, and I'm sure you turned out a creditable piece of work. But in view of the unanimous opinion just expressed here, you will pardon me if I do not read it."

Lifting the manuscript casually, Harker tore it in two and dropped the pieces in his wastebasket.

I stood up quickly. "Now wait a minute—"

"Please, Mr. Post." His smile was quite gentle now. "No need to get upset. I can see where you might be angry, yes, because you had this all planned, didn't you? But you forget that I am capable of making plans, too. I might tell you I actually anticipated something like this. There were indications of a coming clash."

My voice shook. "What did you do, read my horoscope? I suppose you'll be shooting the picture according to astrology, holding up production again because of what you see in the stars—"

He wouldn't let me finish. "My apologies, Mr. Post. I know it is rude to destroy the creative work of another man. But I must ask you to remember that you have just made a similar, if less dramatic attempt. And failed."

The smile froze again. "As to my personal beliefs, they needn't cause you any further worry. I intend to see to it that you will not be connected with the production." He turned away. "Now, if you'll excuse us, I want to discuss my picture with Mr. Lozoff and Mr. Taylor."

Nobody looked at me as I went out.

Nobody looked at me as I crept into my own office. I sat there for a long time, all alone. Gradually self-pity faded into self-determination.

All right, I'd lost that round, but there was still a way. I could help Dawn by coaching her, suggest bits to slip into scenes that would remove some of the cloying sentimentality Harker had injected. He would probably take suggestions, coming from her. Oh, I wasn't licked yet. Not by a long shot. Or a medium shot or a close-up, either—

I looked up as the office door opened. Arch Taylor strolled in.

"You bastard!" I said. "Get out of here before I throw you out!"

He sat down calmly, puffing serenely on his pipe.

I was on my feet. "I told you what I was going to say. You promised you'd back me up, don't deny it. But when the chips were down, you chickened out."

He exhaled slowly, deliberately. I circled him.

"Lozoff I can understand. He had something at stake. But not you. You're just a two-faced, double-crossing, cheap son of a bitch—"

"Go ahead," he nodded. "Give it to me. You'll feel better."

I hesitated. "Why, Arch. *Why?*"

Taylor reached into his coat, pulled out his wallet, extracted a piece of pink paper and dropped it on my desktop.

"Here's your answer," he said. "Go ahead, take a look at it. This week's salary check. Seven hundred bucks."

He stared down at the desk, smiling. "I've been getting a check like this every week for a long time. I expect to get one for a long time to come.

And you know why I get it? Not because I'm a writer. Writers are a dime a dozen out here, anybody can tell you that. I get paid because I learned one simple lesson at the start. Always play the winning side. That's the side your bread is buttered on."

I shook my head. "Quit trying to talk your way out of this, Arch. You showed what you are—just another yes-man."

"It wouldn't have done any good to object. Harker wasn't in the mood for arguments."

"So you sold me out, just like that. Because you're yellow, because money is more important."

He grinned. "So now I'm Judas, eh? And I suppose that makes you Jesus H. Christ?"

"Get out of here," I said. "I don't want to hear any more."

"I know you don't. But you're going to listen, Tom. I've tried to help you in the past, you know that."

"I do. But I also know you're a phoney, like all the rest of them. Anything for a buck."

"Anything?" He wasn't smiling now. "Everything." His voice was hoarse, low. "I've listened to your sob story about being an orphan, but I've never told you mine." He picked up the check, twisted it between his fingers.

"I wasn't an orphan, Tom. I had parents—parents anyone could be proud of. Poor but honest. That's what my old man always used to say, poor but honest. He was still saying it when he died, coughing up his guts with cancer because he couldn't afford to quit work and see a doctor until it was too late. The county buried him and my mother took a day off from the lampshade factory—yes, that's where she worked, in a dirty upstairs loft in a stinking tenement, and my sister, too, until she wised up and took another kind of job where she didn't have to be on her feet any more." He put the check away. "Right then and there I learned the value of a buck. And I've never forgotten the lesson.

"I spent nine years getting where I am in this business. Nine years. And all I need to say is one wrong word and I'd be out on my can. Blacklisted. Washed up. Through."

I sat down again. "Where's your violin? This is America, Arch. Harker can't fire you for disagreeing with him."

"Of course he can't," Taylor nodded. "Because I don't disagree. But that's why I came here now. He's fired you."

"What?"

"You heard me. What do you think he meant when he said you wouldn't be connected with his production. You're finished."

I didn't say anything.

"Kind of changes things, doesn't it? Maybe now you can see a little more reason for my own attitude. I know what Harker's like."

"Then why didn't you warn me beforehand?"

He gestured with his pipe. "Because I know what you're like, too. When you came to me over the weekend I saw it wouldn't do any good, no matter what I said. You'd made up your mind to change that script, come hell or high water."

"Yes. That's true."

"And I think I know why. It's because of the girl, isn't it?"

I felt the flush creeping over my face.

"You needn't answer that." Taylor rose, went over to the window and talked to the trees outside.

"Maybe I am a Judas after all," he told them. "Sometimes I think Judas was just an ordinary guy who got himself in a bad spot. He didn't really want to betray anyone—he just liked to play it safe and keep everybody happy. And when he realized Christ was willing to be a martyr, he went along with it."

The trees nodded in agreement.

"In a way I envy you, Tom. You'll never be Jesus Christ, not by a long shot, but at least you'll go down trying. You had the guts to face Harker." He paused. "From now on you won't be needing my advice. I think you've outgrown it. You're ready to be your own boss."

"My own boss," I said. "That's right. I've been fired." I hesitated, but couldn't resist the final thrust. "Don't suppose you objected when Harker told you?

Taylor turned, nodded. "Of course not. You know me better than that. But like I said, Judas and me, we try to keep everybody happy. So when I got the news I slipped around to see Herb Weichmann."

"Weichmann?"

"I told him Harker didn't need you on *Daydreams* because he'd done his own script. Asked him if he was planning anything. And it turns out he is. Wants you to join his unit for the next Karl Druse picture. You'd better stop in and see him after lunch—he's expecting you."

I blinked. "But if Harker hears about it—"

"To hell with Harker." Taylor put his pipe in his pocket. "He had his big scene this morning. By the time he hears you're still on the lot, working for Weichmann, he'll calm down again. I intend to see Morris this afternoon and do a little private explaining, anyway. There won't be any trouble, believe me."

"So you stuck your neck out after all," I said. "Thanks, Arch. I'm sorry." I held out my hand and was surprised to see that it was shaking a little.

"Forget it. Just looking out for myself, that's the whole idea. Playing both ends against the middle. Who knows, you may be a big man here at Coronet some day." He shrugged. "Meanwhile, you can buy me a cup of coffee."

Thirteen

WE HAD OUR COFFEE and then I went to see Herb Weichmann. He handed me a copy of the short story on which the film was to based. I read it then and there, a yarn about a man who thought he was the Devil. Not bad, and it would make an effective vehicle for Druse. I could write this, I knew.

"Knock out a treatment," the elderly director said. "Keep the theme, but build up the young love-interest and give me a comedy character. I was thinking of Clyde Cook or Jimmy Finlayson, somebody like that. Use your own judgment. You know what goes into a Druse picture. Oh, and keep the sets simple—we try to bring these things in for around two-fifty."

That was all there was to it. I walked out of the studio with an assignment to write *The Man from Hell*, at five hundred a week and full screen credits.

Sitting in my apartment that evening, I could hardly believe it, but everything had worked out for the best. Even if Harker was my enemy now, he'd inadvertently done me a good turn. By firing me, he'd given me my chance for the big promotion—in one day I'd gone from title-writing to full-fledged authorship of my own picture, and a hefty raise in salary.

I bore no resentment against Taylor now, or Lozoff. It was easy to understand their position, and I almost pitied them, working with the Great Director. Weichmann was no genius, self-proclaimed or otherwise, but with him I could turn out a competent job without headaches, delays,

temper tantrums or delusions of grandeur to cope with. I could congratulate myself on this new association. What more could I ask for?

Dawn Powers, of course.

That was it. I suddenly realized I wouldn't be spending any time on the
Daydreams set; I'd be busy with Weichmann and Druse. How could I get
to see her?

Come to think of it, I didn't even have her address or phone number.
She'd told me she was living with two girlfriends in an apartment. But
where?

Would Carla know? Maybe I could call her and find out. Even if she
didn't know; at least I could tell her the good news. I wanted to talk to
somebody. And Carla might be happy to hear about what had happened,
just for old time's sake.

I picked up the phone and gave the operator the number, but Carla
didn't answer. Then I remembered a bit of studio gossip. Carla had been
seen at Montmartre recently with a new boyfriend—Nicky Morris, no less.
Perhaps she was with him tonight.

Carla was out with Nicky, Dawn Powers was sitting in an apartment
somewhere with two girl roommates—

Or was she?

Try as I would to prevent it, the question slipped through. Somehow
I'd have to find out, and soon. I promised myself that.

But first there was a job to do. The treatment. If I knocked out the
treatment tonight, then maybe I could get in touch with Dawn tomorrow.

So I sat down and wrote the treatment, then went to bed and waited
for tomorrow.

Tomorrow never came.

I don't know how it was with the big-name writers—women, most of
them, like Frances Marion, Anita Loos, June Mathis and Bess Meredyth.
Maybe they spent months on a script, with plenty of time to loll around
the pool at the Garden of Allah. But I know how it was with me.

Weichmann read my treatment the moment I laid it on his desk in the
morning, and then he gave it to Karl Druse.

Druse suggested a few changes, very sound ones, too—and would I
please rush through a revise so we'd have something to show to Sol Morris
by the end of the week?

I rushed through a revise.

When I brought it in, Weichmann asked me to meet with the production
staff and the set designers. And then there was wardrobe to consider and
a budget conference—

But why go on? (I asked myself that question a hundred times during
the next few weeks, but I *did* go on.) There was no end to what I did, or
what I learned. It was one thing to write titles for a script and revise them
for rushes somebody else had filmed. It was another thing—many other
things—to sit in on every phase of a picture from its inception.

I found I wasn't just writing a story; I was writing costumes and scenery and actors for Lipsky to cast and schedules for the use of certain stages and cameramen, and I was writing changes for Morris and for the Hays Office and the tastes of some nameless exhibitor in Kalamazoo.

Before I caught my breath we were well into November. I still hadn't seen the pool at the Garden of Allah, and I hadn't seen Dawn Powers.

Once in a while I'd run into Arch Taylor or Lozoff or Emerson Craig; always I asked about Dawn, and always I got the same answers. Harker was coaching her in private rehearsals, they were still readying production, Morris was screaming bloody murder but Harker wouldn't shoot until he felt the girl was ready.

"How is she?" I asked Taylor.

"All right, I guess. I haven't seen her. When I say she's getting private rehearsals, I mean just that."

"But couldn't I—"

"No, you couldn't. The set's closed. And that goes double, as far as you're concerned. He's even got a guard outside her bungalow."

"I know."

Arch Taylor shrugged. "Be patient. This won't last forever."

"Neither will I."

But I did. I lasted through the rest of November and most of December; now we were shooting the picture and I spent my days on the set and my evenings in the projection room. Then the film was wrapped up, but Weichmann wanted me to sit in while he edited; we were coming in about two reels over, and needed some cutting.

Meanwhile, *Daydreams* finally went into production, and the set *was* closed.

"Nobody gets in except cast and crew," Taylor told me. "Harker's strict orders. Even Sol Morris keeps out."

"But why? More of that damned astrology nonsense?"

Taylor shook his head. "Harker doesn't want to upset his leading lady. She's a little nervous." He shook his head. "So am I. This may be an epic, but it's no picnic."

When I cornered Emerson Craig in the commissary one noon he was more explicit.

"It's murder," he said. "I don't know what the Old Man's thinking of, using a girl like that. She's beautiful, yes, and photogenic. The boys on camera aren't having any trouble setting up their shots. They just focus on her face and shoot over the back of my head." He smiled wryly. "But that's not what I'm complaining about. The kid just can't act."

I tracked Arch Taylor down again in his office.

"Dawn," I said. "I've got to see her—"

He shook his head. "Not a chance. We're a month behind schedule right now. If Morris knew how much footage we've scrapped he'd go through the floor, barber chair and all—"

"I don't give a damn if he drops down clear to hell. It's Dawn I'm worried about. Arch—please. Help me."

Taylor took out his pipe and pointed it at me. "I am helping you. By keeping you out of this mess. You've got your own job to worry about—if your picture clicks, it means a whole new career. So don't make trouble. You can't stop what's going on, and if Harker gets riled up about you again—"

"All right," I said. "You win."

But he hasn't, I told myself. *And neither has Harker. There must be a way.*

So I went to Kurt Lozoff's party over the holidays, hoping that Dawn would be there. She wasn't, of course. But I did manage to talk to Lozoff alone.

The little man was pale, and he'd lost some weight. I didn't have to ask him how things were going. He told me, immediately.

"Tom, I made a big mistake. You were right about the picture, absolutely right. I should have backed you up."

"Don't worry, I understand. You couldn't risk your job."

"I'm risking more than my job, the way things are turning out. I'm risking the entire future." People were laughing and shouting all around us, but he kept his voice down so that even I could scarcely hear him. "This film is hopeless; it will never be completed."

"That bad, eh?"

"Harker's like a madman, I've never seen him this way before. Retake after retake, and everything wrong. I keep trying to tell him the Napoleonic flashbacks aren't in key, but he won't listen. Something's happened— you saw it coming, and I wasn't smart enough to believe you. But it's true. He's not shooting a picture. He's filming a love letter to Dawn Powers."

I could feel myself trembling. He must have noticed, but he didn't pause.

"She can't handle the role, everyone can see it. Everyone but Harker. The thing to do is build up the story line to give her a strong assist in every scene, use her for decoration. I could salvage this picture, I know it, but he won't listen. He thinks he can *make* her a great actress. And it won't work, not even for Theodore Harker."

"What's going to happen?"

Lozoff shrugged. "I wish I knew. My guess is that one day she'll just collapse. If you could see the way he drives her—day after day, rehearsal after rehearsal, take after take! One thing in the picture *will* be real—her tears—"

I gripped Lozoff's arm. "Get me in to talk to her."

"The set is closed. You know that."

"Find me a way. Some time when Harker isn't around." My grip tightened. "Remember, I got *you* past the gates."

"I haven't forgotten." Lozoff stared at me for a long moment. Then, "Will you be in your office on Monday morning?"

I nodded.

"Wait for me there. I'll try to find a way."

"That's a promise?"

"A promise." He rolled his eyes. "But God help us all if things go wrong!"

FOURTEEN

"HAPPY NEW YEAR, Mr. Post," said the guard at the gate as I swung the Stutz into the driveway that Monday morning.

And, "Happy New Year!" yelled Jackie Keeley, waving from the walk as I parked outside my office. "Don't get too close to the Crown Prince's car. I've got a bomb planted in the engine."

He gestured at the big yellow Marmon parked next to me, and I nodded. I had no intention of getting too close to Nicky Morris's car—maybe Keeley *had* planted a bomb in it. He wasn't the only one with such ideas.

For if I had been active this past fall, young Morris had been positively frenetic. He'd started out with John Frisby on a Dude Williams picture, but never finished it. Sometime around Thanksgiving, Dude Williams collapsed on the set (heart trouble, according to his wife) and was carted off to a private sanatorium under orders to rest up until spring.

So Frisby went on to a Jackie Keeley comedy, and Nicky Morris went with him. Went with him to stop the camera for idiotic suggestions, to drag sloe-eyed residents of Olvera Street before the casting director, to break up shooting with poker games when the spirit moved him, to make life miserable for the crew.

Sol Morris had left for New York over the holidays on some mysterious mission of his own, but rumor had it there'd be a showdown between Nicky and Keeley when he returned to referee.

Apparently I wasn't the only one who'd had a rough time during the closing months of the year. But this was Happy New Year, 1926, I reminded myself. And things were going to be different.

My office still looked the same, and so did Miss Kress. I glanced through the stack of mail on the desk. Cards, bills, trade papers—the usual assortment. The only thing that interested me here was the telephone. Would Lozoff call?

The phone rang and I grabbed it. "Hello—"

"Arch Taylor."

"Yes," I said, the adrenaline draining out of my voice. "What is it?"

"Haul your butt over to Projection Two. We're running final title inserts on *The Man from Hell.*"

I hesitated. "Is it absolutely necessary, Arch? I'm expecting an important call—"

"Tell your girl to switch it. Mr. Morris is here and he asked if you'd come."

"Command performance, eh? I'll be there."

And I was.

Five minutes later I sat between Morris and Taylor in the little projection room behind the Executive Offices, watching the all-too-familiar titles flicker by; each of them numbered and tagged with a few feet of the film that followed. Morris had a pad and pencil in his lap, but he wasn't using them. His cigar sent up smoke signals of silent approval.

The lights came on and Sol Morris nodded at Taylor.

"You were right," he said. "No changes." He glanced at me. "Good job. Looks like we're gonna have a nice gross with this one."

"Thank you, Mr. Morris."

He sighed. "We better. On account otherwise we're in for a little trouble."

"What's the matter?" Taylor asked.

Morris waved his cigar in a gesture of ashy deprecation. "European exhibitors. You know for the last two-three years we been booking over there and doing okay. Now, with the new studio and everything, I figured on taking out some of the profits. Only there ain't any."

He sighed again. "On account of the foreign inflation, you understand. Four million I got tied up in German banks—and Glazer tells me I can't get out with two cents on the dollar."

"What are you going to do about it?"

"I already done. Where do you think I went over the holidays? To New York. For a loan to tide us over."

"You got it?"

"Sure I got it. We'll get by. If Harker brings in a big hit and we have any kind of luck, I can pay off in a year."

Sol Morris stood up. "Only thing is, we'll have company for a while."

"What kind of company?"

Morris seemed oddly abashed. "You know how they are in New York.

They gotta stick their noses into everything. So the bank tells me, we're sending out a reprasentative. Somebody to watch how you spend the money. Maybe you can give him a title, vice-president or something."

"When's he coming?"

"He's here already. I got him staying out at the house with me. Fella name of Lester Salem."

"Vice-president?" Taylor blinked.

Morris didn't look at him. "What else? Six banks I'd been to already and always the same story; money is tight. So these guys, they'll kick in, only they want a *kibitzer*. But don't worry, he's harmless, one of those college professor fellas, he won't bother nobody. I'll fix him up with a ritzy office and when we get the loan paid off, back he goes to Wall Street."

The phone rang and I got to it first. "Yes?"

Lozoff's voice, low and urgent. "I've made arrangements," he said. "She's in her dressing room. He hasn't come in and isn't expected. There's no one on the set now. So if you could get right over—"

"Three minutes."

"Good. I'll wait for you outside. And keep your eyes open while you—"

"I'm on my way."

I hung up and glanced at Morris. "Will you excuse me? Got an errand to run."

"Sure, go ahead." He cleared his throat. "Oh, don't tell anybody about this new *schnorrer* yet. I want to make a big splash next week in the papers, a press reception and everything."

"I'll keep my mouth shut."

"Good."

I hurried out, moving down the walk on legs that had suddenly turned rubbery, propelled by a heart that was beginning to pound.

Why? I asked myself. *How can you feel this way about a girl you've only seen a few times?*

There was no answer. But my heart continued to pound.

Lozoff was waiting at the entrance.

"Get inside, quickly," he murmured. "There's a man on the door and you're supposed to sign in, but I sent him around to the canteen. I told him I'd keep watch while he was gone."

"Thanks."

"I hope this is the right thing." Lozoff was talking to himself, not to me, and I noticed he was sweating although the day wasn't warm.

"Her dressing room is on the right, over near the wall. You have ten minutes—be careful—"

I nodded, and then the rubber legs and the pounding heart moved onto the deserted set. It was a reproduction of Metternich's suite at the Congress of Vienna, with a huge, ornate table in the center, designed for diplomatic conferences. Right now four members of the crew were using it for a penny-ante poker game.

Hugging the shadows, I stepped behind a flat and walked along the wall to my right. Nobody noticed me.

Then I was at the dressing room door, tapping very softly, making a sound which seemed softer to me than the pounding of my heart.

The door opened and I saw the stranger.

The girl in the doorway had changed her name and dyed her hair and altered her features; this I knew and was prepared to recognize. But there were other differences now. Somebody had taught her how to stand, how to move her hands, how to smile at me now and ask me to please come in.

I moved past her and she shut the door behind me and I sat down on the couch against the wall. Somebody had designed a dress for this stranger, all gold and sequins, and I stared at it as she came toward me slowly. She came slowly, but realization came with a rush. *You don't know her. You don't know her at all.*

And with the realization came relief. I wanted to shout for joy, because my heart had stopped pounding; I didn't give a damn about this golden-gowned goddess.

"So you finally came," she said.

Even her voice was different than I remembered. It was softer, with a more precise inflection; the voice of an amateur actress trying to play a scene. Well, it *was* a scene, only a scene to me now. And I could take my role without a qualm or a quaver.

"I've been quite busy, writing a picture—"

"I know. Lozoff told me. He told me everything."

"Good." I smiled at her without effort as she sat down beside me. Even her nearness meant nothing now. "He told me about you, too. That's why I didn't try to visit the set. I knew you were busy, too."

She kept looking at me. "Yes. But somehow I kept thinking you'd come anyway. After doing what you did, wanting to change the script for me. That was wonderful, Tom."

Smiling came easy to me and words were easy, too. "Just doing my job, you know. I thought there should be revisions. Harker disagreed. That's all there is to it."

"I thought—" She hesitated.

"It doesn't really matter now, does it?" I said quickly. "Even if I couldn't be on hand to help, I understand you've had the most expert attention. Harker's a brilliant man, Dawn. He'll make you a real star. I know the going's pretty rough at times and you must be awfully tired, but everything's bound to work out if you obey orders. It's a marvelous opportunity."

She looked up at me, nodding.

"Yes," she murmured. "That's what they all tell me, how marvelous it is. Harker and Craig and Lozoff and Mama. I'm going to be a star and it's marvelous and I ought to be the happiest girl in the world." Her shoulders shook. "And now, you—"

Then her eyes widened, her mouth formed an O, and the stranger was gone. Dawn Powers disappeared.

I saw Mitzi LaBuddie again.

I saw Mitzi and she was crying, and then she moved and I moved and she was sobbing against me.

"It's all right," I said, wondering if she could hear my heart. "It's all right—"

"Tom, I didn't know, I thought you'd changed—"

"I thought you'd changed, too."

"I have." She tried to control her voice, but the time for that was past. "You don't know what it's like—the way he keeps after me, night and day, the things he says and does—"

Something was rising in my throat, choking me. Something I wanted to spit out.

"—and I can't do it, Tom, I hate acting. I hate the picture, I hate him and everybody except you—"

"Night and day," I said, feeling it rise in my throat, knowing it had to come out. "You hate him, but night and day he's after you, with you."

"What are you trying to say?" She drew back from me on the couch.

"Nothing. Just thinking about a story I heard once. It might make a good plot for a picture."

"Tell me."

I opened my mouth and it came out, poured out, spewed out. About the astrologer and Harker and Kate LaBuddie, everything Carla had hinted at. I didn't see anything as I talked—you close your eyes when you're vomiting.

And your heart pounds and your head throbs and your stomach churns and you say, "She sold you to him. It's true, isn't it? There's no apartment, no girlfriends. You're living with Harker in his house, you go to that room of his in the dark where the fake stars make the fake dreams and the two of you—"

Her fingers raked my face. "It's not true, it's not—"

I grabbed her wrists, twisted them away. "You mean you don't love him? I know that. You don't love him, but you're putting out for him, you're letting him paw you and play with you, you're letting him teach you all the tricks it takes to get a dirty old man excited. What do you have to do for him before he's ready, Dawn? What's it like when you're doing it—does he still direct you then, tell you how to—"

Somehow her hands were free and she came at me, gasping, clutching, her mouth moving against mine, her body straining close. "So that's why you never came to me! I've waited for so long, darling, I've wanted you for so long—"

"What about Harker?"

"Forget him. That's what I try to do, even when it's happening. Because it doesn't really happen with him, it can only happen with you, the two of us together, like this."

It was all a breathless, disjointed blur of words and phrases, but the language of her body was eloquence enough. And that's all I cared about as I clung to her on the couch, caressing her, reveling in the richness of her response.

Behind us a door opened.

We both looked up then, looked up and saw him standing there. Saw Theodore Harker in all his ebony and ice.

It was Dawn who made the first move, rising suddenly so I had no chance to restrain her. She stood before the director and she said. "All right. Now you know. So get out. You don't own me—you never have, and you never will!"

Incredibly, Harker's mouth shaped a smile. He glanced down at his hand, clenched around the head of the ebony cane. He was still smiling as he brought the cane up, swiftly—

I launched myself from the couch, grappling with him, fighting to loosen his fingers as they gripped the cane to strike. He slammed back against the wall, then thrust forward. I was holding his wrists now and it was like holding the twin, throbbing throttles of a dynamo. I could feel the pulsing of power, the same power that blazed in the black abyss behind his eyes. For a moment we struggled together, panting and swaying; both of his hands tightened around the length of the cane as I forced it down between us.

Then something snapped.

Something snapped, and our gaze unlocked. My hands fell away from his wrists and we both stared down.

The ebony cane, broken neatly in half, lay at his feet.

Harker stooped, very slowly, and picked up the pieces. I backed away as Dawn came into my arms, and we watched as he fitted the two halves of the cane together. I thought that he looked like a child working a puzzle until I saw his face in all its ashen agony.

Then, suddenly, he was erect; the cane had come together again, balanced across his palms. Once more I was staring at the magician with his magic wand. And he stared at me, stared at the girl in my arms.

"Get out!" I said.

His arm rose, lifting the cane. He hurled it past us, hurled it at the reflection in the mirror beyond. There was a splintering crash.

The echoes still resounded as he turned and stalked out.

Dawn and I stared down at the shatter of glittering fragments on the floor.

I picked up the cane and tried to put the pieces together again, but I couldn't make them fit.

"Never mind, darling," Dawn whispered. "Never mind."

Then she kissed me and I dropped the broken wand into the shining slivers of silver at our feet.

FIFTEEN

PRINCE METTERNICH WASN'T at his conference table the next morning and neither were the cardplayers. There were no diplomats and no poker faces in the group that gathered on the closed set.

When they called my office I hurried over and found them all waiting—Sol Morris, Nicky, bookkeeper Bernie Glazer, Lozoff, Arch Taylor, and the surprise.

I had a feeling they'd been discussing me before I arrived, but I could hardly blame them for that. The axe had been hanging over my head for the past twenty-four hours, and when Sol Morris rose and approached me, I almost expected to see him holding it in his hand.

Instead he smiled and steered me over to the surprise. "Just in time," he said. "I'd like you to meet our new vice-president, Lester Salem."

As we shook hands, I took special care to observe the newcomer. Since then I've seen him hundreds of times. I've glanced at his picture in the papers, the magazines, the publicity releases. But I still have trouble remembering what he looked like.

That, of course, was Lester Salem's secret. He didn't look like anybody one would remember. He was just a presence.

This morning he wore a suit that wasn't gray, wasn't brown; a pepper-and-salt tweed combination blending with the background. His shirt was white and therefore nonexistent, his tie a blurred blue. He had gray hair, gray eyes, and a pale complexion; even his thin lips seemed unaccented by color. His gestures were unobtrusive, his handclasp offered only a shadow of sensation. His voice, as he acknowledged our introduction, was flat.

Sol Morris waved me to a vacant chair before the table. "We got started already," he said, as I sat down. "I been telling them the sad news so you might as well hear it, too. Harker is out."

They were all staring at me now, ready for a reaction. I shifted in my chair, saying nothing, waiting for the axe to fall.

Morris nodded. "That's right. Out of the picture, out of the studio. I got a call from his lawyer last night. He's selling his stock, everything. After all these years together—through, just like that!"

Still they stared at me. I sensed their anticipation; the crowd gathered before the guillotine, eyes fixed on the victim just before the blade descends. Well, at least I could die bravely.

"I'm sorry, Mr. Morris," I said. "I suppose you know the story."

"We all know it."

"It's my fault," I continued. "I had no business interfering. Miss Powers isn't responsible in any way for what happened. I was the one who—"

Morris shook his head. "Never mind that. I told you we know the story. Now it all comes out. From Taylor and Lozoff, how you wanted to change the script and Harker wouldn't listen. From Emerson Craig about what kind of shenanigans went on with the shooting."

He pursed his lips. "If anybody's to blame, it's me. I shouldn't have let him close the set, take his word for it that things were going smooth."

"Then you understand what—"

"Sure. I already told you that. It happened, and it can't be helped. So we don't waste any more time. Harker wants out and he *is* out."

Lester Salem made a brief sound in his throat. "What about our legal department? Couldn't we take steps to make him fulfill his contract?"

Morris shrugged. "Who's talking contract? God knows I ain't a genius, but I got sense enough to know you can't stick a policeman behind a guy and make him turn out a masterpiece. Anyway, I wouldn't try. He wants to quit, that's his business. Our business is, what are we gonna do about the picture?"

He glanced across the table at Bernie Glazer. "You got the breakdown on costs? Okay, let's hear the figures."

We heard the figures. Boiled down to essentials, the film at its halfway mark had run expenses of a little over three hundred thousand dollars. Estimated cost of completion, including sets and costumes already contracted for, totaled another hundred and fifty thousand.

Morris sighed. "We got too much tied up already to junk it. If we do, we lose all the money and get a bad name with the exhibitors besides. We promised *Daydreams* for spring release, we been selling a lot of dogs against it, so we got to deliver. Also, everybody's going to be watching to see what we do after he walks out. If we quit, they'll say we can't get along without him. Right?"

Lester Salem leaned forward. "Might I make a suggestion?"

"Go ahead. That's what we're here for."

"Actually, it's not my idea, I don't presume to know anything about this business yet, although I assure you I intend to learn." Salem paused, nodding at Nicky down at the end of the table. "However, I did take the liberty of discussing this problem with your son. He offered what I think is a practical solution, and he was kind enough to permit me to speak for him."

Nicky wagged his gum-filled jaws in agreement as Salem continued.

"As I understand it, this studio is rather unique in that it does not employ the services of producers. Instead, once you and Mr. Glazer have approved a script and worked out a budget, you delegate authority solely to the directors."

"That's right," Morris told him. "We don't need that kind of fancy business here, executives all over the place." He pointed his cigar at Salem. "You know we even get along without supervisors. Nicky is the only one we got, sort of an experiment. But I like to keep things simple, keep the expenses down. I told the bank—"

"I'm aware of that," Salem murmured. "And at the time you explained, I was inclined to agree with you. But now I'm not so sure. If there had been a producer assigned to *Daydreams*, this unfortunate situation would never had arisen. He would have held the reins on Harker, kept costs down and production rolling.

"Now what I propose is this. You son tells me he is supervising the Jackie Keeley unit. He is the only one on the lot with this particular background of experience. I therefore suggest you appoint him as producer on *Daydreams*. At the same time, we can take Herb Weichmann off his schedule and let him finish the direction of the film. Then we'll control the situation."

Morris puffed on his cigar. "I dunno. Weichmann's a good man, but this isn't his kind of picture."

"Then we can get somebody else, somebody from outside. The director isn't that important, as I see it. The main problem is coordination—keeping an operation running smoothly and efficiently, without waste motion. Don't you agree?"

"Makes sense to me." Bernie Glazer spoke up. "Probably save us some money if we handled it that way."

"Of course." Salem smiled at him, then faced Morris once more. "Everyone has his function. We have scenarists to do the writing, actors to perform, technicians to handle staging and designing, and a director to put them through the paces. But we need an executive to keep them all in line." He turned to Nicky. "Your son knows this, Mr. Morris. He realizes what I told them at the bank before I came out here—in spite of all the phoney glamour, if you'll pardon my frankness in saying so, the movies are a business like any other business. And sensible business methods will get results—"

"I don't agree."

Salem's head swiveled. He stared, we all stared, as Kurt Lozoff rose to his feet.

"I don't agree," he repeated. "We're not in a business. We're in an *endeavor*. Sometimes we succeed, sometimes we fail, depending on just how well we translate imagination into visual terms on film.

"This picture we're talking about happens to be called *Daydreams*. But that's a good title for all of them, because that's what motion pictures are. Daydreams, individually conceived. Not uniform products stamped out on an assembly line."

"Please, Mr. Lozoff. We're not talking theory here. We have a specific problem for which I'm proposing a specific solution."

Lozoff shook his head. "I know that. And I'm offering another solution." He glanced at Sol Morris. "We're in the middle of shooting now. If we set up another system it will take weeks before we can resume. If we go out and find another director, he can't just step in and take over—he'll have to familiarize himself with the production, study the footage already filmed. Meanwhile, costs will mount. So what I propose is this." He took a deep breath. "Let's start work again tomorrow morning. And let me finish directing the picture."

"You?" Morris put down the cigar.

"Why not? I know the story. I've worked for Harker ever since I came here and I know his techniques. I have studied production methods for years. I directed a film in the east before coming to Hollywood, and I have a few innovations I would like to use in *Daydreams*. I assure you, I will not fail."

Morris shook his head. "You got a point there, about getting started tomorrow and all, but it's a big project, we got a lot of money tied up—"

"You'll be saving a lot," Lozoff said. "You'll save by starting immediately. And you'll save your director's fee. What would you have to pay a good outsider to come in—fifty, seventy-five thousand dollars?"

"I suppose so."

"Very well." Lozoff's voice was firm. "I shall do it for nothing."

Morris blinked.

"That is correct—nothing. I will even forego my salary as an actor. If the film nets a half million or over in profit, you can give me a bonus. I'll leave that up to you. Fair enough?"

Morris started to pick up his cigar, then changed his mind. "You really think you can do it?"

"You have my word."

Sol Morris sighed. Then his hand went out again. "Shake," he said. "You got yourself a deal."

Salem cleared his throat. "In that case, I'd like to assure Mr. Lozoff of my complete cooperation. I know what a tremendous responsibility he has assumed, and I'm placing myself at his disposal, to help in any way I can."

Lozoff bowed from the waist. "Thank you. But it won't be necessary. All that remains is for Mr. Post here to assist me on the scenario. There are a few changes in order, I believe."

I shot a quick glance at the ceiling. There was no axe suspended there now. I could smile at Lozoff as I answered. "Anything you say—if Mr. Morris doesn't object."

Lozoff nodded. "I have already told him about your ideas for revision. And I believe we'll have no further problems with Miss Powers' role once those necessary changes are made."

"Go ahead," Sol Morris said. "It's your baby."

"Then if you will excuse us?" Lozoff bowed again. Morris gestured, the others stared. Only I fancied I could detect a subtle change in the rhythmic motion of young Nicky's jaws; a new, set intensity in Salem's waxen smile.

But there was no time to think about that, now. I was following Lozoff off the set.

Once outside, he turned to me. "You have a carbon of your treatment? Good—get it at once. We have much to do."

"You're using my story? But that means reshooting—"

"Don't ask questions. Get the carbon and meet me in Projection Four in fifteen minutes."

That's how it started.

And that's how it continued, through the next six weeks. The Congress of Vienna was disbanded, and we went to work on my version of the script—with a few surprises in the form of Lozoff's suggestions.

Lozoff had surprises for everybody. He surprised Emerson Craig with his directorial ability. He surprised Dawn by treating her with gentle patience, leading her through their scenes together and watching carefully over the rest of her work. There was no more hysteria on the set, and he surprised everybody by removing the ban on admittance.

Lozoff surprised Glazer rather unpleasantly, though, by running the costs up well over the budget estimate. The changed sets were expensive, the shooting and reshooting even more so. We had to redo many of Harker's scenes to conform with the new treatment.

But Glazer never said anything, and if Salem complained to Morris we were not told. Everyone was waiting to see what the outcome would be.

The picture was wrapped up by the first of March; on the twenty-first the editing was completed, my titles were in, and we sat there in Projection Two and watched a miracle unreel into reality.

I'd seen it in the making, but couldn't comprehend it at the time. Now I witnessed what my script and Lozoff's imagination had done to the utterly lovely, utterly untrained automaton that was Dawn Powers.

I came prepared to suffer the vapid smile, the faltering gestures, the awkward mannerisms I'd seen when we ran Harker's rushes. And I sweated through the opening moments until she made her first appearance.

On the screen, the vapid smile became an ethereal invitation to enchantment. The flat, faltering gestures evoked a suggestion of delicate hesitancy. The subdued expression of emotion took on a subtle semblance of reality. In an era when broad grimaces and exaggerated pantomime were still the rule, her underplaying seemed to bring a new dramatic dimension into being.

Whether it was my script, or Lozoff's handling, or Harker's touch on certain retained scenes, or just the fact that Dawn wasn't afraid any more—we had a winner.

I hugged Dawn there in the dark as the film faded out, and I was still hugging her when the lights came up. I didn't care; nobody cared, because they were all talking and laughing at once and you could feel the excitement in the air that comes when you know you've won.

Then everybody was gathering around Lozoff and congratulating him, and Ryan was talking to Morris about exploitation and building a campaign for Dawn, and even young Nicky was slapping the little foreigner on the back.

"This is it," I told Lozoff. "You'll see."

And, of course, he did see. It wasn't until six months later that the returns were in, but they told the story. *Daydreams* scored with the critics, with the exhibitors, with the public. It made Coronet almost a million in net profits and it put Kurt Lozoff in the ranks of the ten best directors of the year.

But right now he nodded at me as though all this was a foregone conclusion.

"Come to my office for a minute," he murmured. "Just you and Dawn and I—please? A little celebration."

So we managed, finally, to break away. And in Lozoff's office we sat quietly while the little man poured brandy in tiny glasses and handed them to us with studied ceremony.

"To our success," he toasted.

I looked at Dawn and smiled. She smiled back. Then we both looked at Lozoff and suddenly I wasn't smiling.

"That's right," I said. "This all started with the three of us, didn't it?"

He nodded, Dawn's eyes clouded and I knew she was remembering what I remembered now—that day in the dressing room when Harker burst in. Harker, who wasn't supposed to be coming to the studio, according to Lozoff.

I put my glass down. "I've been meaning to ask you something," I said. "About the way it all started."

Lozoff beamed.

"You remember the morning I went to Dawn's dressing room—when you promised to stand guard for us? How did Harker manage to sneak past you before you could warn us?"

Lozoff beamed.

"He didn't get past you, did he? You knew he was coming. You set the whole thing up so that he *would* discover us together."

Lozoff beamed.

"Damn it, you had it all planned! But if it hadn't worked, we would have been finished—"

"It *did* work." Lozoff began to laugh. "That's all that matters."

I scowled, but Dawn began to giggle. Lozoff's chuckle rose and all at once I was laughing, too. I raised my glass again.

"That's right," I said. "Nothing succeeds like success."

The brandy had never tasted sweeter.

SIXTEEN

IN THE SPRING OF '26 I was in love, but I was also in the movies. And the movies were in their heyday.

That was the year they made 750 features and showed them in over 20,000 theaters across the country, at $2,000,000 a day. Nice round numbers, nice round dollars, made in America.

That was the year of the foreign invasion—Jannings and Veidt, Asher and Murnau, Lya de Putti and Camilla Horn. The Hanson brothers came from Sweden and so did Maurice Stiller and a towheaded young nobody named Greta Garber, or Garbo—some such name.

That was the year when Hollywood went crazy over horses. Every morning Hobart Bosworth rode the bridle path along Santa Monica Boulevard, and on Sunday afternoons Will Rogers and the gang played polo. The Vine Street Brown Derby put up a hitching post for Tom Mix's horse, Tony. Just a gag, of course, but wasn't everything?

Everything, that is, except what was happening between Dawn and myself. We laughed a lot, but we were serious about it.

There was never enough room for her clothes in my closet, but outside of that we had no problems, as long as we were together. And we were together now, except for one memorable occasion.

That was the night Dawn left to spend the weekend with her mother. "I've got to," she told me, struggling with the reticence she showed whenever Kate LaBuddie's name was mentioned. "She's been having such a terrible time with Buddie, she can't seem to get him a job." Dawn smiled at me. "Don't be such a sourpuss, darling. I'll be back Sunday night."

"This is only Friday."

"Get some rest. It won't hurt you to go to bed early for a change."

"I *have* been going to bed early."

She stuck her tongue out at me, then came into my arms. "Only two days," she murmured. "Be patient."

"No man is an island," I said. "And damned few are even continent."

"Huh?"

"Just my improvement on John Donne."

"Who's he?"

"Writer. Does screenplays for Rin-Tin-Tin."

And then she was gone and I was alone and somehow it didn't feel good. *So why don't you marry the girl?* I asked myself.

For a while I sat there, playing with the idea. It wasn't the first time the thought had occurred to me. No man is an island and no two people are an island, either. Sooner or later Dawn and I would have to think about a future in relationship to other people.

The wheels were beginning to spin and the picture started to unreel. It was time to think about this in terms of a picture. My next picture, and Dawn's.

Daydreams was in release, and we were on our way. Dawn could be a star, a big star. But a lot depended on her next vehicle, and that part would be up to me.

I'd work out a story line for Lozoff's approval, then get the go-ahead from Morris. And after that I'd spring it on Dawn—tell her about the picture, tell her about the wedding, tell her about the honeymoon after we finished shooting—

I could see it all and it looked good. One of those good dreams I could believe in, the kind that can come true.

Then the doorbell rang and the dream dissolved.

I opened the door and nightmare walked in—stumbled in, rather, and sank down sobbing on the sofa.

"Carla! What's the matter?"

It had been months since I'd seen her, and never like this. She'd never cried before.

Hardly a pretty spectacle; Carla Sloane with her eyes bloodshot and her nose red. And yet there was something poignant in the sight, perhaps because she had always seemed so self-assured, so controlled.

Whatever the reason, I reacted. I sat beside her, patting her shoulder and making vague male sounds of propitiation.

"Please—tell me what's wrong."

Her eyes were wide, wild. "You oughtta know. I'm knocked up."

"But—"

"Oh, it isn't you, couldn't be. I wish it was. No I don't—I wish I'd never been born!"

"Who, then?"

"What's the use of saying? It won't do any good, nothing'll do any good now. I don't know why I came here except there's nowhere else to go—"

She started sobbing again, and only a few phrases came through. But one emerged quite clearly.

"—that goddam yellow Marmon—"

Then I knew.

I let her cry while I mixed a drink. By the time I put it in her hand she'd calmed down a bit.

"Take it easy now. Maybe we can get this thing straightened out. Did you tell Nicky?"

"Of course."

"And—?"

"He gave me some guy's name. A doctor."

"Well, let's think about that. He certainly won't marry you. *Is* the doctor any good?"

"They're all good, until something goes wrong. Then you're on your own, they won't let you come back for treatment even if you get septic-whatever-they-call-it, anyway it's blood-poison." She shuddered. "I know. It happened to a girlfriend of mine."

"But couldn't Nicky find someone who'll keep you there for a few days, just to be sure?"

Carla shook her head. "He gave me the name of one of *them*, too. Only what he doesn't know is, the croaker's gonna be raided next week."

I stared at her. "How do *you* know that?"

Her eyes left mine. "Glenda told me."

"Glenda Glint?" I blinked. "Since when did you get so chummy with her?"

"Oh, you might as well know. I've been working for Glenda on the side now for almost a year. At first, when she just had her magazine column, she used to slip me a fin every time I gave her an inside tip about the studio. Then she got this daily column with the paper—syndicated, all over the country—"

I nodded. "That's all you hear about lately. Glenda Glint says, Glenda Glint predicts, Glenda Glint has an exclusive."

"Well, I'm on her regular payroll. I suppose she has somebody at most of the other studios, too. She wants to get the scoop ahead of Lolly Parson."

"She picks some funny methods," I said. "This latest notion of hers, this 'Clean Up Hollywood' campaign—dragging out all the old skeletons again. I imagine that's the kind of snooping that helped her find out about your doctor friend being raided."

Carla put her drink down on the end table. "She's been getting dope on a lot of this stuff. Took it to the D.A. and asked for a showdown."

"Since when did she get so righteous?"

"Since she figured out that if she did, the D.A. would give her first crack at the story when he made his move. Besides, you know something? This dame really hates the movies."

"But you played along with her."

"Like a damned fool. At first I just thought it was an easy way to pick up a little extra dough. I never gave her any real inside info, you ought to know that. And I didn't realize the way she felt until lately. Until I told her I was in trouble—"

I stood up. "You told *her*?"

Carla sniffled. "Go ahead, tell me I was crazy; I know it but I'd just found out and I was upset. I had to talk to someone; some woman. Only she isn't a woman, she's pure bitch, and now she's going to break the story—"

I pulled Carla to her feet, shook her. "She wouldn't dare run it!"

"Of course she'll run it, it's just what she wants for her campaign. What do you think I meant when I said I was in trouble?"

"Does Nicky know that, too?"

"No. Not yet."

I went over to the phone.

"Tommy, what are you doing?"

"Calling Sol Morris, of course."

"Oh, please—if he finds out he'll kill me!"

"It'll kill all of us if he doesn't." I paused before picking up the receiver. "Now listen to me. I'm going to try and help you get out of this mess. Only you've got to promise to cooperate."

"All right. I trust you."

I picked up the phone and called Morris at his private number—the one we all had "for emergencies" and never used. Well, there comes a time, and no man is an island.

"Mr. Morris? This is Post. Yes, I know what time it is. But somebody else doesn't. That's why I had to call you. Now please, listen carefully."

He listened all right.

Then it was my turn to listen. "Yes. Yes. Half an hour. We'll be there." I hung up.

"What did he say?"

"We're going over to the Studio."

"Now? Why it's almost ten!"

"I know. But we have to work fast."

We did. And apparently Sol Morris had not been idle, either. In exactly thirty-two minutes we were sitting in the big executive office, around the conference table. There were five of us—Carla, myself, Sol Morris, Nicky and Lester Salem.

The harsh overhead light accentuated the already heightened pallor of every face. Carla, staring down at the glass-topped surface of the table. Nicky, seemingly shrunken in his chair. Lester Salem, a waxen window dummy (*what was he doing here?* I wondered). Sol Morris, perhaps the most self-possessed of all; he didn't look stricken, haggard, or afraid—just tired. And myself, shifting nervously in my seat.

For a moment it was pantomime and then Morris broke silence. "Well, folks," he said. "There ain't much for me to do, is there? What I got to tell Nicky here I already said, believe me." He glanced at the beefy young man, who cringed as though shielding off an actual blow; I could imagine what had gone on during the ride down to the Studio.

Morris glanced at Carla now. "As for you, young lady, I got only two things. One is, I could beat your brains out for making such troubles for us. And the other is—I'm sorry. I apologize to you for my son."

The watery blue eyes (*water, or tears?*) sought mine. "Post, you I must thank." He paused. "Mr. Salem I am ashamed in front of. That he should be in my house, a guest, when he hears this thing."

That explained Salem's presence, all right.

But Morris went on. "Not but I wouldn't have told him, anyhow. Because he is one of the family now and he ought to know. He came along on account of maybe he can help. Isn't that right, Mr. Salem?"

The window dummy nodded gravely.

"So let's not waste time. I was going to get Riley down here, on account of the publicity angle, until I figured that's just what we don't want—publicity. So far nobody knows about this except the five of us and one more."

"Who?" I asked.

"Glenda Glint, who else? I called her right away when you told me. She's coming over. So like I said, we got only a couple of minutes for suggestions, so—"

The phone rang and Morris picked it up. "Sure, Fritz. Pass her in."

Morris put the phone down again and shrugged. "She's here already."

And then we heard the footsteps in the hallway, and Carla squeezed my hand, hard, and she *was* here.

Glenda Glint. Not *Miss* Glint, but *Glenda*. Glenda in the all-too-solid flesh. Prosperity agreed with her. It enveloped her in twenty pounds of additional weight; clung to her neck in the form of a mink fur-piece, glittered from her fingers, shone from her hennaed hair. Only the sniff was the same—the sniff and the petulant voice.

"Well, this is certainly a fine time to call a press conference, I must say."

"No, Glenda, you know I wouldn't ask you to come over unless it was important. Here, sit down." Sol Morris led her to a chair, and it was curious to see God playing usher to Miss Glint. "How about a drink?"

"I haven't time." She glanced at her watch. "I'm supposed to be at the Montmartre right now. Doris and Milton are having a *very* special party."

"This'll only take a minute," Morris placated.

"Would you mind tell me what it's all about?"

Morris shrugged. "I think you know."

She wheeled on Carla. "You told him?"

"She told *me*," I said. "I gave the facts to Mr. Morris."

Glenda Glint produced an especially spiteful sniff for my benefit. "Then there's nothing more to be said. I'm using the story in my Sunday feature. And if you called me in here with some idea you could talk me out of it, you're sadly mistaken."

Sol Morris stood up and went around behind her chair. He put a pudgy hand on her shoulder. "I wouldn't fool you, Glenda—that story's gonna hurt us. It's gonna hurt us bad. Not only the Studio, but it's a black eye for the whole Industry."

"It's news," Glenda Glint said. "Good or bad, it's news."

"News?" Sol Morris bowed his head. "Who's talking news? I'm talking people. Carla, my boy Nicky here. What's it gonna do to them?"

"That's their lookout. They should have thought about it before—"

"Who thinks about such things? You know how it is."

I'll be she doesn't, I told myself. But Morris continued.

"So I'm not even talking any more, Glenda. I'm begging. Like a father, and because you belonged to the family, once."

She stared up at him. "I've never been a member of your family. Don't you remember, you fired me yourself, because I spoke up and told the truth. How could I belong to your family? I'm no kike."

"Kike." Morris sighed. "That's a word, Glenda. Like sheeny, yid, a lot of other words. I heard them all in my life, many times. They don't bother me none. They just mean Jew. Is that what you're trying to say?"

"You know what I'm trying to say. Jews! This whole business is run by them."

"That's not true, Glenda. Look around. Nicky here, my son, he's Jewish. Though God forbid you'd never know it, and I'm not proud of it. But Mr. Salem, he's not a Jew. Or Carla, or Tommy Post. Frisby and Jackie Keeley, they're a couple Irishmen. Be honest, Glenda. Is De Mille a Jew, or Pickford, or Gish, or Mickey Neilan or Mack Sennett or—"

The sniff cut him short. "I have no time to waste discussing religion with you. Anyway it doesn't matter. I'm printing that story."

"Supposing we deny it?"

"Then I imagine the papers will be happy to print your denial, probably right on the front page. Nothing would please me better."

Morris straightened up. His voice was suddenly sharp. "All right, how much do you want?"

"Money?" She flipped her fur-piece. "I'm not interested. I *have* money."

Nicky rose. "Look, Pop, let me talk to her. You don't know it, but I got a couple friends in this town. Maybe she won't be so snotty after I send them around to pay her a little visit—"

Sniff. "Are you by any chance trying to threaten me?" She faced him.

"Let me tell you this, young man. I don't like you and I don't like your father. And after my story hits the papers on Sunday morning—*including a full report of this incident here tonight*—you might just as well close your doors before the Hays Office does it for you. I'm going to tell the American public the truth about Coronet Pictures!"

"One moment, please." The window dummy came to life. "Miss Glint, before you leave, might I clarify a point?"

"Make it snappy."

"Very well. Did I understand you to say that your interest lies in presenting news?"

"That's right. I'm a reporter, and proud of it."

"And an account of this—unfortunate affair—has a certain news value to your readers?"

"Naturally."

"Well, a thought occurred to me while you were speaking. Miss Sloane here, Carla, is not a well-known personality. Am I correct?"

"So?"

"And Nicolas Morris—his only claim to fame is his connection with this Studio."

"What are you driving at?"

"Simply this. I wondered if it might be possible to make a straight business deal with you. To exchange this story for a better one. A more newsworthy item, let us say."

"Such as?"

"A story that really ties in with your crusade to expose the seamy side of Hollywood. Something involving a prominent motion picture personality known to all you readers. I am prepared to furnish documentary proof, affidavits if necessary, for your exclusive use. In return you must promise to forget this minor, unsubstantiated affair—which, in any case, I warn you, it would be our duty and obligation to deny completely."

"Well, I'd have to know what the story is, first."

"Precisely. But let me emphasize my last point. You realize it would be very easy for us to arrange for Miss Sloane to disappear. Her—condition—could be corrected without anyone being the wiser. And young Mr. Morris, I'm sure, would be happy to issue a complete denial. You might find yourself in a very unpleasant legal suit for defamation of character."

"Quit trying to frighten me," said Glenda Glint. "You know damned well what a lawsuit would do to your Studio, with all that publicity. Give me a better story and I'll drop this item. But it has to be good."

There was a moment of silence. Sol Morris peered at Salem with anxious curiosity. "What story you got?" he asked.

Salem made a steeple of his fingers. "You may remember that when I arrived at your home you were out, paying a call on a certain party. You son told me who the party was and what his—difficulty—is. I admit it shocked me when I heard it. I think it will shock Miss Glint's readers. But, in view of the circumstances—"

Morris snapped at Nicky. "You *told* him?"

"Why not? Like you said, Pop, he's one of the family. He'd find out anyway; sooner or later everybody's gonna find out. You can't keep stuff like that a secret." His voice became a defiant whine. "Mr. Salem knows what he's talking about. Come on, let's tell her, make a deal."

Morris shook his head. "But it's ruin the poor *schnook*, you can't do that to him when he's down!"

"He's washed up anyway," Nicky answered. "And you know it."

Lester Salem nodded. "It's no longer a personal affair, I'm afraid," he said. "This involves the welfare and prosperity of the Studio as a whole. It's business, Mr. Morris. And the company I represent happens to be financially interested."

Morris shook his head again. "Never mind, Glenda," he said. "Go ahead, print the story, do whatever you like. I ain't throwing an old friend to the vultures, after all the years he's been with us—"

"*Been* with you." Salem cocked his head at Miss Glint. "Please remember that. This party is no longer connected in any way with Coronet Pictures. His resignation, retroactive as of January first, was accepted immediately upon the discovery of his condition."

"No, please—" Morris whispered.

But the window dummy went on talking, his voice as expressionless as his face. "It's Dude Williams," he said. "At the time, you may remember, Mr. Williams collapsed on the set and was sent to the Star of Hope Sanatorium, supposedly suffering from a heart ailment. Actually, to the horror and shame of his employers—who immediately asked for and accepted his resignation in the name of common decency and the welfare of the motion picture Industry—it was found that Dude Williams was, and had been for more than a year, an habitual narcotics addict. Heroin, wasn't it, Mr. Morris?"

Nicky nodded eagerly. His father faced the wall in silence.

"Well, no matter. I'll have the medical statement ready for you in the morning, together with a signed copy of the resignation. I'm going out to the sanatorium right now."

"You got no right to—" Morris began.

"In my capacity as vice-president of the organization," Salem added, calmly.

"I'll go with you," Glenda Glint declared. "Maybe he'll give me an exclusive on an interview. He's going to need every friend he's got now."

"Then it's agreed?"

"Certainly. Do you think I'm crazy? I know a real story when I see one." She paused at the door. "Well, goodnight, all."

Nobody answered her. She and Salem left together.

I rose slowly. Morris turned around.

'Tommy, you're not walking out on me?"

"No, I'm just tired. Besides, I thought you and Carla and Nicky might have—other things to settle now."

He followed me into the hall, keeping his voice low.

"Tommy, this you got to believe. I'm ashamed for myself. Ashamed because of Nicky, ashamed because I let Salem tell. But what could I do, what could I *do*, I ask you? Nicky's still my son. A man's son, he's got to protect him."

"I understand," I said.

"You heard Salem threaten," Morris continued. "He wasn't fooling—he could wreck the Studio just by calling the loan right now, I'm in that deep."

"Sure," I nodded.

"And he was telling the truth about Williams. I been going out there every week. The poor guy isn't getting better—the doctor says he's all shot, he'd never be able to work again, anyway. I'm gonna make it up to him, Tommy. I'm gonna give him a pension, see that Nina and the kids get everything they need. You know that, Tommy."

"Of course I do." I smiled at him. "You did what had to be done."

"I'm glad you see it. Because it hurts me like you'll never know. A man's son—" His voice died away, then returned. "You did me a favor tonight, Tommy. Like you did years ago. I don't forget."

His hand came out. "Have a cigar?"

I hesitated. Then, "No, thanks," I said. "I smoke cigarettes."

SEVENTEEN

I DIDN'T HAVE TO TELL Dawn what happened when she came in on Sunday evening. She had read about it in the papers. Everybody read it in the papers, watched Dude Williams make his exit *via* the front page while Carla Sloane slipped out the back door. I'd learned she was going to Mexico, but she hadn't come around to tell me goodbye.

"The poor kid," Dawn said. "It must have been awful for her."

"That's right," I said, and nothing more. Dawn knew about me and Carla, of course, but that isn't why I steered clear of the subject now.

I wanted to think. I'd been thinking for the past two days, trying to figure out why all my big plans for the future suddenly seemed remote and unreal again.

I kept trying to find the source. Was it when I'd refused Sol Morris's cigar? Or was it something he'd said? *"A man's son, he's got to protect him."*

Maybe that was it. Envy. *Nobody had ever protected me. Even a guy like Nicky has a father. But me—*

I felt rejected, so I'd rejected Morris. And what did that mean?

Dawn raced around the apartment, unpacking, taking off her shoes and stockings, chattering away about Kate LaBuddie and the brat. It seemed he had a break after all, he was going into one of those imitations of the *Our Gang* series that was always springing up. Dawn explained it all gaily, then paused.

"What's the matter?" she asked. "You look sick."

I didn't answer. I couldn't answer. I couldn't explain gaily that I'd just discovered the persistence of an old, old pattern I'd thought was long outgrown. But it was coming clear to me now.

How could I tell Dawn? How could I tell her that I was still a goddam kid after all, would probably always be one? Running around looking for surrogate fathers, trying to invest my faith in any authority that came along? *Even Harker,* I thought. *Yes, even Harker. If he'd only been different. Something happened to me when the magic wand broke.*

Who would be there to wave the magic wand in the future, over all the big, brave plans I'd made for Dawn and myself? Maybe they weren't plans—just dreams. That's why I needed a father with a magic wand.

Dawn sat down next to me. "Tell me," she said. "Is it because of Carla? Do you still feel that way about her? I—I won't be angry, darling, I can understand."

I turned blindly to the quivering *O,* turned away from the whole morbid, maudlin mess I'd made of myself. "No," I said. "It's not Carla. She doesn't mean anything. I was just—alone. I'm always alone, when you're not here. Dawn, stay with me, promise you'll stay with me."

She promised. She promised with her mouth, her eyes, her hands, her eager flesh. And this was real, I could cling to it, it was better than the father-dream.

First the room became the world, then the bed, then our bodies, and after that there was nothing but sensation blending imperceptibly into satiation. It was always the same.

And it would always be the same.

"Always," I told her. "Always like this."

"Always."

Now I could talk. Now I could go on again. "I've got plans for us, darling. You'll see. You're going to be a real star."

"I don't care about that—"

"I'll make you the biggest star this town has ever seen, bigger than any of them—"

Her eyelids fell. "Please. Go to sleep, darling."

So I went to sleep, and I dreamed it; and I knew it could come true, even without a father. The answer was there, in the dream. If I couldn't find a father, couldn't make one, the answer was still there. *I could be my own father.*

That was it. The real answer, the only real answer.

The next morning I went down to the Studio, to see Lozoff.

"I'm thinking of the same team," I told him. "You, Dawn and Emerson Craig again, in an original story. With you directing."

"Excellent." Lozoff smiled. "Have you anything definite to show me?"

"It's not down on paper yet," I answered. "I've got an idea about *Carmen.*"

"But that's been done so often—"

"Not the way I see it. I'm thinking the story in terms of motivation, with the *Daydreams* technique. We'll see what impels our soldier, our toreador. We'll look into the mind of our little gypsy factory-worker—what a part for Dawn!"

Lozoff looked up. "But *Carmen* calls for the exotic type, the brunette. "Maybe we could get somebody like Maybelle Manners—"

"That old bat?" I shook my head.

"Well, we have Lucille Hilton under contract. Or perhaps we could work out a deal with Estelle Taylor; she has the looks for the role."

I shook my head again. "Don't you see, the whole point of the idea is to bring the same cast together again?" I paused. "What's the matter, are you trying to tell me Dawn isn't strong enough for the role?"

"No, not exactly. It's just—"

I slammed my fist on the desk. "You know what you can do for her! After the performance you got out of her on *Daydreams* how can you possibly doubt it? Let's not worry about her looks. The Penny brothers have plenty of wigs over in Makeup. This can be a big thing, believe me. I've got some ideas for a quality picture, but I'm not forgetting the box office, either. And I know Dawn, I can write for her. Wait until you see the treatment."

"All right." Lozoff stood up. "I have faith in you. I'm going to notify Morris of our tentative plans. How soon can you show me something?"

"Ten days," I said.

"Good enough."

And it was good enough, or bad enough, depending on how you looked at it.

I didn't have time to look at it. During the next ten days I scarcely had time to look at Dawn.

She was there, of course, and she must have realized that I was working on the next production. But she also realized the wisdom of not asking questions, not bothering me as I curled up in the creative coma, retreated into the womb I wrought for myself with words.

That's the way it was all day, every day: I ignored her physical presence and concentrated on the artificial Dawn, the one I was fashioning afresh. *Dawn-Carmen* or *Dawn-Carmen-Post*.

But at night, when I'd finish, she'd come to me and the reality would begin again. She dragged me out of the apartment, insisting that I needed a change after a hard day's work.

So every night there was a change, and yet it was always the same. Always the same when our bodies, hands, lips, or even our eyes met— funny, just looking at her across the room could bring the same sensation. Let them argue all they please about the Fourth Dimension. I know what it is, it's love. Being in love, and the giving and the taking and the sharing.

Sharing the sunsets and the sunrise and the songs and the syncopation and the symphonies. That's part of it, and so is learning about yourself.

Feeling a sudden surge of anger when you see her talking and smiling up at another man and saying "Why, that's *jealousy*—I never knew I was jealous before." And looking at her while she sleeps and wondering if you ought to wake her up the way you *want* to wake her—then letting her sleep because it's enough just to watch her breathe, watch the rhythmic rise and fall of the blossoming breasts.

And above all, there are certain moments. Moments when a voice whispers, "I'll always love you, never forget that." And the eyes assenting, and the body offering confirmation. *"Always—never forget."*

No matter what happens, you keep *that*. They can't tear it out of your brain with knives, they can't etch it away in the slowly dripping acid of the passing years.

Nothing can take it away from you, that moment which is more than a memory. Not even *she* can destroy it.

I found that out.

Eighteen

"DARLING, I've been reading this over and I just don't know."

"You mean you don't like it?"

"Oh, of course not. It's wonderful."

I grinned at Dawn. "Glad to hear you say that. You're in good company. Lozoff and Craig are crazy about it, and Morris says we can go all out on the budget. This is going to be the big production for our fall schedule."

"But you've given me so many scenes—"

"Of course I have. Aren't you the star? And haven't you learned the ropes out here in Hollywood, being nice to the writer and everything?" I squeezed her.

"Don't muss me," she said. I mussed her and then she looked up. "I'm serious, darling. I don't think I'm good enough for the part."

"Good enough? Why, you'll be perfect! You can dance, can't you? That cafe number will knock 'em dead."

"I'm not worried about the dancing. You know what I mean."

"I don't." I took her hands. "Look, there's going to be plenty of time to learn. Lozoff himself suggested that we do the crowd stuff and the bits first. We'll shoot around you and give you a chance to rehearse, get everything down pat. He'll coach you, darling. And I'm going to help. You'll see."

"Tommy, I wish you'd get somebody else for this."

"Somebody else? But it's *your* picture. Dawn." I paused. "More than that, it's *our* picture. The one I wrote for us. The one that's going to make you big."

"I wish I had your confidence," she said.

"I've got enough for both of us. I've given this story everything. Even Lozoff can't find any flaws. And you know what a stickler he is."

"Yes." Dawn sighed. "I know. I can't fool him."

"Quit talking about trying to fool anyone! You'll be fine." I glanced at her. "What are you doing?"

"Changing my blouse. Don't you remember, we're going over to Jackie Keeley's tonight?"

I shook my head. "Nope. Forget to tell you. I called it off."

"Why?"

"I thought it might be just as well to cut out parties and that sort of thing until this picture is over. If you don't mind."

"No, I don't mind."

"I remember what a strain you were under when you did *Daydreams*. This time we won't let you get upset about anything." I smiled at her. "Come on, let's you and I just run through this script again, shall we? I want to point out a few things about some of your scenes with Don Jose."

So it began.

I'd told Dawn the truth. Lozoff and the others were excited when they saw what I turned in. And Morris was enthusiastic. Their confidence was contagious, and oddly enough I found that I really didn't need it any more. I had my own, and it kept growing.

Somehow, the decision had been made. No more conscious or unconscious leaning on others. From now on I'd be the father, the strong man.

Dawn could lean on me if she liked. I'd support her—I was determined to give her all the help she could possibly need on this picture.

And even though Lozoff was directing, I had the feeling that his position was purely nominal. Actually it was my creation, mine to control.

For the first time I began to realize the way Theodore Harker must have felt about his films—the films he conceived, wrote, produced, directed. I began to realize how he must have felt about actors and actresses, too.

As a matter of fact, I got into the habit, whenever I ran into a problem requiring a decision, of asking myself, "What would Harker do?"

And there were many such problems, now. I sat in on the preparations every day, stood at Lozoff's elbow as he approved or rejected costume designs, watched the sets go up on the back lot; and always I was able to come up with a suggestion or a solution. So much so that Lozoff finally commented, "It looks as though we'll have to give you two credits on *Carmen*, Tommy—one for writing and one for directing."

"Quit kidding," I said. "You're the director. I'm only putting in my two cents' worth."

"We're going to be ready for Dawn in another three weeks," he told me. "How is she coming along?"

"Just great. You're due for a big surprise."

I meant that part about the surprise, but to myself I admitted Dawn wasn't just great. Not yet.

We'd rehearse at home every night, with me taking the other parts and Dawn going over her scenes patiently, persistently. But patience and persistence weren't enough. She couldn't seem to capture the spirit of the role.

"Look, darling," I explained. "This isn't an opera. It's a movie. You don't have to strike a pose every time you open your mouth. That's the secret of *motion* pictures, you know—keep them moving. Just glide through this scene, the way you do when you dance."

And I'd go through it again with her; once, twice, three times. Until it was late and she made coffee and I'd sit there and check over the notes I'd made about her work of the evening—then read them back to her for study tomorrow while I was at the Studio.

It was a tough schedule for her, I admit, but she was due to start in three weeks.

Then the filming actually began, and I was busier than ever. I worked with Lozoff on the mob scenes, the little bit-player episodes which would lift *Carmen* out of its stilted operatic-triangle groove and project it against the background of a living Spain.

And at night, I did my best for Dawn. My very best, in all the sweltering heat of summer, hour after hour. No matter how hard a session I'd put in at the Studio, I still found strength to carry on with her, for her.

I tried to explain that.

"There's no need to look that way," I'd tell her. "You know there's nothing personal in it if I shout at you. It's just nerves. The grind gets me down, I guess."

"Then why don't you forget about these rehearsals and relax?" she asked. "Leave my part to Lozoff. He can help, you told me so yourself. You said there's nothing to worry about. So why go through all this?"

"You know why," I told her. "Of course Lozoff can help you do a good job. But a good job isn't enough. You want to be perfect this time, darling. Perfect." I wiped my forehead. "Before I forget, I meant to tell you something. I had them run off *Daydreams* again for me this afternoon, just so I could check your scenes. And I noticed a few things I want you to watch out for when you work with Emerson Craig—"

For three weeks it went like that.

And then it was time to begin, time for Lozoff to don his uniform and time for Dawn to put on the black wig.

Somewhere outside it was July now, and the big sails bellied on the yachts at Balboa, and the kids went up to Arrowhead, and the tourists sniffed around Harold Lloyd's estate.

But we were inside, on the set, under the lights, and July was far away. This was Spain, this was sweat, this was torture—the endless torture of take after take. A bit, and then "Cut!" Another bit, and then "Cut!" Isn't there a Chinese torture called "The Death of a Thousand Cuts"? Well, we improved upon it.

Or *I* did. Something had happened to Lozoff; he didn't seem to care. Oh, he was patient enough with Dawn, and considerate. Perhaps that was the trouble—he was *too* patient, too apt to consider a scene satisfactory. He let her spend too much time in the dressing room, gave too many breaks for coffee and cigarettes.

"What's the matter?" I finally demanded. "Are you slipping?"

He smiled at me. "You know me better than that. It's not myself I'm thinking of. Dawn is under great tension. You are perhaps too close to her to realize. You think of her only as a woman. I think of her as an actress, and I know there are limits to the amount of effort one can demand."

I couldn't smile back. "It doesn't matter what you and I think," I said. "What's important is the way she thinks. And I want her to think of herself as a *star*. If she believed she was a star we wouldn't have this trouble— tears, and tiredness, and all the rest."

Lozoff put his hand on my arm. "She's not a star, Tommy," he murmured. "She'll never be a star. A fair actress, perhaps, in time. Adequate. Maybe even adequate for this part, if we humor her and carry her the way we carried her in *Daydreams*. But face the truth. You're asking too much, expecting too much. This is no Garbo, no Negri, not even a Renee Ador). So why don't you accept the fact and try to make things easier for her?"

"But the picture, what'll happen to the picture?" I asked.

"Don't worry. It's going to be a success. You have the story here. I know what to do." He hesitated. "Actually, your part of the job is over. Why don't you take a vacation for a few weeks, come back when we're finished?"

"And leave Dawn to go through this alone? I couldn't."

"Suit yourself. But please, remember what I said. And don't drive her, or yourself, this way."

It was no good talking to Lozoff, I could see that. To him, this was just another movie. Sure, he'd do a good routine job—my story had the commercial ingredients, it would make money for the Studio, and Lozoff's position would remain secure.

He could afford to feel that way because he was already established. But Dawn needed a great picture. I needed a great picture. Something to justify that adjective they were always using out here. Something colossal.

I wasn't going to sit back, not now. Would Harker be content with a routine production under such circumstances? Of course not!

And Harker hadn't been content, I remembered; even on *Daydreams*. He'd driven Dawn, no doubt about it. But she had hated him and wouldn't respond. I didn't have that problem. She'd respond to me because she loved me.

So we went on, on into August. And I tried not to drive. Instead I soothed and sympathized, begged and pleaded. But I kept after her, outlining and explaining and interpreting every scene as we came to it.

Until one day, in her dressing room, she broke.

It happened suddenly, as though something snapped.

(*The cane had snapped here once,* I thought, *but I have no cane.*) One moment we were sitting there, going over a simple little scene we'd tried to shoot in vain all morning long. I was very patient about it, too, talking calmly and quietly.

Then she began to sob. Not cry, but sob. Her shoulders, her breasts, her whole body shook.

"No—no, Tommy! I can't! I just can't! It's too much—I know what you want, I've tried, God knows I've tried— But it isn't there. Don't you see? It isn't there!"

I comforted her, thinking, *You expected this all along, really. And you know what to do, now.*

I did know what to do. I'd planned it in advance, it was all part of the pattern.

So I waited until she was quiet again. And waiting for me to speak. Waiting, no doubt, for me to begin about the scene once more.

Only I didn't. When I spoke, I didn't even mention the scene. I knew just what to say.

"Dawn, in four weeks it will be Labor Day. The picture should be finished by then. We'll have a holiday. A very special one."

She looked at me, waiting.

"I was thinking perhaps we might go to Mexico. Not for the weekend— maybe a month or so. And then to the east. New York. For the premiere, in December. Would you like that?"

"But a two-month vacation—and traveling together like that—how could we?"

"We could," I said. "On our honeymoon."

She didn't say anything, but I watched her mouth, watched the small *o* grow into a capital *O*.

"Why do you think I want this to be a good picture, a great picture? Because of the future we have tied up in it. Our future. I want you to marry a great writer. I want to marry a great star. Now you understand?"

"Tommy, Tommy—"

She was close to me again, we were together; I'd won, just as I'd known I'd win.

"Let's get this job done, once and for all. The minute we wind up this thing I'm going to Morris and tell him. We'll tell everybody, have a real Hollywood wedding, with all the trimmings. Wait until Riley gets hold of this idea, he'll go wild over it—tying in with the picture and everything! How'd you like to see your name on the front page, darling? Dawn Powers, star of Coronet Picture's super-production, *Carmen*, to wed—"

There was a discreet rap on the door and then Emerson Craig thrust his brilliantined head through the opening.

"Everything all right?" he asked. "Lozoff's ready for another take."

I glanced at Dawn. "Everything's fine," I said. "We're on our way."

And it was, from that moment.

We had our troubles, of course. Naturally, the glow didn't last. Dawn would fluff or miscue or fail to register in a scene, and the heat of August didn't cool my temper. But there was something to look forward to now, something to anticipate. And anticipation carried us through.

By the end of the month, we had our rough cut ready. And we ran it.

It was a repetition of the *Daydreams* screening all over again. Frankly, I was perhaps the least enthusiastic of anyone in the projection room that day. I could see too many places where Dawn hadn't fully realized the potentialities of a scene, too many places where Lozoff would have to cut and edit. But Morris and young Morris and Glazer and Salem were satisfied, and Arch Taylor winked at me and said, "Got to hand it to you, Post. This is it."

So I was feeling pretty good that night as we dressed for Lozoff's party. He'd opened his home to the cast and crew, rather than hold the usual little farewell ceremony on the set. Lozoff was like that; he knew when to make a grand gesture.

And I thought, why not? I'd made a grand gesture, too.

I told Dawn about it.

"Just got a wonderful idea," I said. "This party tonight—everybody's going to be there. Morris and all the rest. Even Karl Druse is coming, and you know how he is about parties. But this is a big celebration. And I was thinking—we couldn't find a better chance to announce our engagement. What do you say?"

She sat down. "Well—"

"Then it's all settled," I said. "Of course I haven't picked out the ring yet, but we can do that Monday. And start making plans for the wedding. I'll talk to Riley if Morris himself doesn't suggest it."

"Darling, wait a minute."

"Yes?"

"This idea of yours, about the big wedding. Does it have to be that way? I mean, couldn't we just go off and get married?"

"And miss all those wonderful opportunities for a tie-in with the picture? Think of the publicity! Why, we couldn't buy such coverage. Front-page stories all over the country, and every story will carry a mention of *Carmen*. Don't you see, that's the whole idea!"

She nodded. "Yes, I see. That's the whole idea. The picture."

"Now wait a minute. You sound as if—"

"*I* sound?" Dawn stood up again. "You haven't heard a peep out of me in months. You're the one who's been doing all the sounding off around here. Telling me about our plans for the future. Not *asking* me. Telling me. Tommy, you've changed."

I smiled.

"I'm glad you noticed it," I said. "I think the others are beginning to realize it, too. You see, I made up my mind about a few things recently. It's about time I grew up, started to take on responsibilities, direct my own life."

"Fine," she said. "But there's one think I'd like to say about the future. You can direct your own life if you want to, but not mine."

"What do you mean?"

"Just what I said. You've been playing director for months now, Tommy. At first I thought it was just the picture. That was bad enough, but I tried to endure it, for your sake. Even though it was just like Harker, worse than Harker—"

"You don't know what you're saying."

"Oh yes I do! You haven't been Tom Post since the day you came to me with the script in your hand. You've been Theodore Harker. Talking like him, thinking like him, plotting like him; draining me and dragging me and driving me. You think I haven't heard it all from him before? About making me a star, a great star? Only he was old, he was trying to make a dream come true, trying to get something he could never hope to possess. And you have it, only you don't want it, you prefer the dream."

"Dawn, I never knew you felt this way."

"Of course you didn't, you don't know how anybody else feels, you don't care!"

"Shut up," I said. And held her. "Shut up and listen. Maybe you're right. I don't know and I don't think you really know, either. But one thing you've got to remember. I love you, we're going to be married. I don't give a damn whether we have our wedding in the La Brea Tar Pits or the May Company's window." I stepped back. "Come on, let's get dressed."

"But remember," she said. "No announcement."

"Whatever you say," I told her. And meant it.

The party was very gay. Everyone was gay but me. I kept thinking of what Dawn had said. She was right, of course. I'd consciously modeled my behavior on Harker's. What I hadn't realized is that I'd begun to think like Harker, too.

Then came the moment when Glenda Glint sailed over and began to coo at Dawn. It would have made a great opening for our announcement, I was thinking, but I remembered my promise and kept silent. I let Dawn do all the talking.

"And now that you're a star," the Glint was saying, "perhaps you can give me just a wee hint about your plans for your next picture."

Dawn hesitated and I saw that I'd have to fill the breach.

"As a matter of fact," I murmured, "I was just discussing that with Mr. Morris. I haven't told Miss Powers yet, but we intend to hang on to our winning team. She and Mr. Lozoff and Mr. Craig will be together again in her next picture."

Dawn smiled at me. "There won't be a next picture," she said. "Not for me."

That stopped me cold. And it stopped the Glint, too. But Dawn went on.

"I'm retiring," she said. "Since I have no long-term contract, I'm free to leave when I choose."

"But—"

"I'd appreciate it if we didn't discuss the matter further right now," Dawn told her. "I seem to have something of a headache. Would you take me home, please, darling."

I took her home. I took her home, and *I* had the headache. All the way I kept saying over and over again, "But why? Why?"

"Because I'm not a star. I'm not an actress. I don't want to be one. I've always told you that and you'd never listen. Now you know I mean it."

"But why did you have to tell Glint? She'll print it and we'll have to issue a retraction—"

"Retraction? I wasn't fooling. I *am* quitting."

"All right. But don't you see, if the announcement comes now, it'll kill the picture?"

"Picture! I don't care about the picture, or any pictures."

We got home at last, and I went right over to the cupboard and mixed a drink.

"All right," I said. "You win. You were going to show me, weren't you? Well, you have. You don't care about pictures, so that's okay with me. I'll handle the pictures in this family. You can play housewife, since you're so fond of the role."

"You mean it?" She gave me a long look. "You really mean it?"

I nodded. "Drink your drink," I said. "And let's pour another. A toast—to us."

We poured and drank. And then the tension seemed to slip away, the mood changed, and she was beside me on the sofa. I kissed her hand.

"Don't do that," she said.

"Why not?" I grinned. "That's the way Lozoff does it. And you know something? You look like Garbo. Lozoff and Garbo, our greatest performances—"

"Stop it!" she said.

"Now wait a minute," I murmured. "Garbo wouldn't say a thing like that. She's sophisticated. Maybe Bessie Love would, but you're not the Bessie Love type, are you, love?"

She sat up and pulled away. "I've had enough."

"Enough of what? Don't you like my Lozoff technique? Maybe you prefer a touch of Richard Arlen, something a bit more boyish—"

I blinked. "Hey, where do you think you're going?"

"Out."

I sobered up in a hurry, stood up even faster. "Sorry," I said. "I didn't know I was really bothering you. Is something the matter?"

"No, nothing's the matter. Everything's fine. God's in His heaven and this must be the place. Only not for me. I'm leaving."

"Leaving?"

"This. And Hollywood. The whole damned business."

"Make sense."

"I *am* making sense. That's what I want to do—make sense. And you, all you want to do is make movies!"

"But—"

"You've changed, Tom. Everything's an act with you now. Everybody plays a part—like Garbo, like Lozoff, like Gilda Gray. You don't see people as people any more. A cross-eyed man is Ben Turpin, a girl in pigtails is Louise Fazenda. If you saw Christ ride a bicycle, you'd think He was on His way to an appointment with Cecil De Mille."

"That's pretty good," I said.

"It isn't good. It's awful! I'm sick of listening to movie talk, seeing movie people. First it was Mother—for years I got filled up to here with Hollywood. Then Harker. And then I had to go and fall in love with you."

"But you *do* love me," I murmured. "And you're going to marry me. Remember?"

"I've made up my mind about that, too. You really don't love me. You're in love with a whore named Hollywood."

I went to her then, grabbed her, shook her until she clung to me as I knew she would. Tears, then, wetting my shoulder. And my hands moving over her back (*damn it, she was right, I kept thinking of it in terms of a scene, wondering which angle they'd shoot it from to catch both our faces*) and my voice saying, "You're just tired, it isn't that bad really, it won't be like that when we're married—you'll see. Being a wife is good casting."

"*Casting!*"

"Sorry," I said.

"So am I." She stepped back. "But that's just what I mean when I say I have to go. *You're* not quitting pictures, not even for me—are you? Don't give me a fast answer. You wouldn't quit if I asked you. You know it."

"I guess you're right. What else is there for me to do?"

"Nothing. And you should stay, I want you to stay. I'm *proud* of you. But I can't live the kind of life you want, even as a housewife. With you gone nights, off for weeks at a time on location; always worrying about the next day's shooting, the next story, the next picture, the next contract. None of it means anything to me."

"But I love you."

"I know, I know! I wish just loving was enough. But *living* is important, too."

"What are you going to do?"

"There's Mother. And I'll find something. Something in the real world you don't know about, or want to know about. They say there's a hundred and twenty million people living in this country. And believe it or not, they don't spend *all* their time at the movies."

"Dawn, I don't know. I don't know what to say."

"Then be quiet." She smiled at me. "I'm going to walk out of that door without hearing another word about the movies."

Her mouth made an *O* and all I could say was, "Mitzi!"

Then the smile came back. Not the smile I'd gotten used to all these months, but the *real* smile. "Of course, if you can keep your mouth shut meanwhile, I could wait until tomorrow morning."

I didn't say a word. Not "darling" or "sweetheart" or anything you'd see in a caption.

Neither of us talked until a long time later. Until I whispered, "I can't believe it. I can't believe this is really the end."

"It's the beginning. You'll see."

"But I don't want to be alone."

"You must. Darling, some day you'll realize that being alone is part of you. Until then you'll compromise. Try to imitate other people, try to impress other people, use your work to fool them instead of telling the truth. The way you did with *Carmen*, writing everything so as to make them think I was an actress. I—I'm not saying this very well, Tommy. But I know you. And if you could only understand how important it is to accept being alone—"

"You're what's important."

"I'm a dream. Tommy. Tomorrow you'll wake up and I'll be gone."

"Is this a dream?"

"Don't talk."

So I didn't. And in the never-ending darkness, all she said was, "I'll always love you, never forget that."

I never have, either.

And she was right; right about everything. This wasn't the end. It was only the beginning.

REEL THREE:

The Plot Thickens

NINETEEN

IT TOOK SIX WEEKS for the Studio to recover from the sudden shock of Dawn's departure. Morris pleaded, Riley reshuffled his publicity releases, Lozoff cast about for a new vehicle. Then *Carmen* came out, made a fair success, and Dawn was gradually forgotten by everyone except myself.

My own personal recovery took six months. I tried to call her at her mother's, tried to see her again, tried to get through the days and nights following what I somewhat mawkishly told myself was a cardiac amputation. And even when my convalescent period was over, I still got occasional unexpected twinges—like the amputee who feels pain in his nonexistent limb.

But there comes a day when the amputee is up and about once more, ready to face the world again.

I did another assignment for Weichmann on a Karl Druse film. I jumped in at the last minute—the regular scripters had fumbled it, and he was practically shooting off the cuff. If I remember rightly, it was *Black Bargain*.

We managed to bring it in under the budget and ahead of schedule, so on the last night Weichmann closed the set and Druse held a little party for the production unit. Nothing out of the ordinary; just a buffet supper and drinks for the cast and crew.

After we ate, somebody got out the dice. Arch Taylor, Weichmann and a couple of cameramen were the players. The rest of us gathered around the table and watched, or congregated near the improvised bar where Druse held forth with Lucille Hilton, his leading lady.

Weichmann had the dice in his hand when somebody stepped up quietly and tapped him on the shoulder.

"Hey," he said. "What's the big idea?"

Then he looked up and saw Lester Salem standing there.

We all saw him at once, apparently. I doubt if anyone noticed his arrival, but there he was—Mr. Nobody from Nowhere.

"I'm afraid I'll have to ask you to break up this affair," he said.

"Affair?" Weichmann was genuinely puzzled. "What affair?"

Salem surveyed the set with an expression of controlled distaste. "This—gambling. And those people over there, with the liquor. You know how the Hays Office frowns on such things. The Eighteenth Amendment—"

"Oh, a ribber, eh? Prohibition agent in the crowd!" The elderly director began to laugh; he could always take a joke.

"Please," said Lester Salem, quietly. "I see no reason to permit the use of studio facilities for a private party."

Weichmann stopped laughing. "Now hold it—"

All at once Karl Druse stood between the two men.

"What's the trouble?" he asked.

"No trouble at all. I was merely suggesting to Mr. Weichmann that his studio is no place for a private party. Particularly when it involves violation of the law. If a story ever leaked out—"

"Why should it leak out?"

"Those things happen."

"You mean, like Dude Williams?"

Salem shrugged. "Perhaps."

"I've always wondered what kind of a skunk pulled that one," Druse continued, slowly. "I'm sure, whoever he is, he wasn't invited here."

He stared at Lester Salem, who licked his lips nervously. "Nevertheless," he said, "in my capacity as Vice-President in—"

Druse shook his head. "Never mind your capacity. This happens to be my picture. This is my party. You're welcome to stay, now that you're here. Help yourself to a drink if you want. But don't try and tell me what to do."

He turned his back on Salem and said, "Come on, boys. Drink up."

Salem left without a word.

"Better look out for that bastard," Weichmann said. "He'll be sharpening his knife for you."

Druse scowled. "He'd better do a fast job, then. Because I'm going to see Papa Morris tomorrow morning. It's time for a showdown."

"No, you're not." Arch Taylor was emphatic. "I know you, Karl. You'd go storming in there, yelling at the top of your voice, and Morris would yell back. That isn't the way."

"What do you suggest then?"

"Leave it to me." Taylor smiled. "Post, you remember a promise that was made last year in your presence? Something about paying off a loan and then showing somebody the gate?"

I nodded.

"Good. Then let's you and I breeze in on Morris tomorrow. I think it's about time we reminded him of a few things."

And that's just what we did.

But when we got into the private office, Morris didn't wait to hear our story. He beckoned us over to the big table and pointed to an imposing sheaf of blueprints.

"Just in time!" he said. "Boys, this is it."

"This is what?" Taylor asked.

"The plans. Lohmiller, biggest architect in New York, he figured them out. Six to start with, all alike—we buy everything in quantity and save. Gonna cost a fortune even that way, but we'll get it back. Wait and see."

"I still don't know what you're talking about."

Morris thumped the blueprints. "Theaters. That's what. I just got back from New York. We took another big step for the Industry. Coronet's building a chain."

"Our own theaters?"

"It's the smart thing to do," Morris said. "It's in the air. Now we're really gonna go places."

I looked at Taylor and he looked at me. There was no comment.

For this was, definitely, *the* thing to do. All over the nation the palaces were rising—Roxy's fabulous showplace in New York, the Balaban & Katz cathedrals in Chicago (where Paul Ash ruled the Oriental with an iron baton) and the myriad Avalons, Uptowns, Granadas and Tivolis where honest owners of Model T's could spend an evening admiring the fish-filled fountains, the maroon carpeting in the lounge, the gold leaf on the ceiling. Even the sticks could now boast of a brand new photoplayground, complete with ushers wearing military uniforms which had apparently been designed by Roy D'Arcy.

"You said this would cost a fortune," I ventured. "Have our profits really been that heavy this year?"

Morris shook his head. "No, not exactly. Tell the truth, I went for another loan. A pretty big one. Of course, the bank could see the point right away; with our own showhouses we'll always have outlets for our productions. We can't lose. So we really didn't have to do much arguing."

"We?" Taylor murmured.

"Me and Salem." Morris beamed. "I got to hand it to that fella. Maybe he is sort of a cold fish, but he's not so bad when you really get to know him. Look at the way he's getting along with my Nicky—the two of them are regular pals, and just between us, he's straightened the boy out.

Besides, he's got some real ideas. All those months hanging around with his notebook, they're gonna pay off."

"Salem got you this loan?"

Sol Morris hesitated. "More or less. Sure, what the hell, I can trust you boys. He got me the loan. On account of figuring a sure-fire way of paying off."

"Which is?"

"We're gonna enlarge production. Salem and Nicky, together, they're gonna open a whole new series of units. Produce 'em together."

"But I thought you didn't want producers?" I said.

"Not on our high-class stuff, no. Only this is different. Low-budget, that's what they'll be making. Fast shooting, fast profits. Everybody does it now."

"Quickies," Taylor muttered.

"All right, so it's quickies. Plenty people out here make quickies. Nobody's got to be ashamed for the kind of money they gross."

Taylor didn't say anything more. He just looked at Sol Morris until the old man's eyes fell.

"I know what you're thinking," he said. "But you're wrong. There won't be no trouble. This is something special, it doesn't interfere. We've got a big loan to pay off now, and it's the only way to do it. And let me tell you, if it wasn't for Salem, I don't know where we'd be at."

"Then he stays," I said.

"What's that?"

"Nothing."

Morris turned and looked up at Arch Taylor. "You said you had something on your mind. Do you want to talk about it before you look at the plans?"

"No, that's all right." Taylor put his pipe away. "Come on, Post. Let's look at the plans."

So we looked at the plans and we didn't say anything. Not then, or ever.

"Better keep your eyes open," Taylor advised me, when we got outside again. "Looks like a lot of things have been going on behind our backs."

I nodded. "Guess you're right. It's time I woke up."

"Sure. It was a tough deal for you, Post, but I think you're over it now." That was the first time he'd ever referred to Dawn Powers since she'd left. "Time to wake up and join the party. This is 1927."

It was 1927, and the party was on.

I took Taylor's advice and began to look around. First of all, I looked at the movies.

There were new faces on the screen. Gary Cooper, Evelyn Brent and W. C. Fields at Paramount. William Haines, MGM's flaming youth. Ray Griffiths and his bright, satirical comedies. I caught up on *The Big Parade* and several of the oldies I'd missed—here it was, the summer of 1927 already; had Valentino really been dead a year?

For a long time I went to the movies every night, and that's how I saw *The King of Kings* and Lozoff's new vehicle, *The Lady Accepts*.

That's how I saw the newsreel shot of Theodore Harker returning from abroad in a black Bond Street suit, ready to begin production of his independent film, *Mankind*.

I looked at all the new teams, too. Gilbert and Garbo, Gaynor and Farrell in the romance department. Plus Wallace Beery and Raymond Hatton, Karl Dane and George K. Arthur in comedies.

And that finally focused my attention on the brand new team operating right on our own lot. They weren't romantic and they weren't intentionally funny—but they were functioning.

Nicky Morris was a figurehead, of course. You didn't have to be around him for more than half an hour to realize he was incapable of making a move, let alone a movie. Salem pulled the strings, and he had found the formula.

It worked like this. Instead of buying an original scenario, Salem went to some place like the Stone Film Library, specializing in "stock shots." He bought newsreel-type footage of fires, accidents, train wrecks, blizzards, disasters at sea. And the stories were constructed around the stock scenes.

A thousand feet of forest fire? Good. Then let some hack bat out a treatment involving a heroic Mountie, a French-Canadian girl and her villainous step-father (as long as we're hyphenating, let's make the villain a half-breed) who flees the Mountie and sets fire to the Great North Woods in order to trap the lovers.

And by all means, let's keep the treatment simple, so that anybody can understand it.

Here's where Nicky demonstrated his worth—if *he* could follow the story line, anyone could. I remember one day when Arch Taylor was unhappily involved in presenting a story idea to the Morris heir. Gertrude Ederle was still in the headlines, so this had something to do with a Channel swimmer. There were also spies and a submarine, so help me—and so help Taylor, who sweated it out.

He finally managed to boil his treatment down to a single typewritten page, double-spaced.

"So I take it in," Taylor told me. "And I lay it on the desk. And Little Jesus looks at it and says, 'What's this?' So I say, 'It's the treatment you asked for. I'd like to know what you think of it.' And he says, 'I can tell you right now what's wrong. It's too long.' And he tosses it back to me."

"What did you do about it?" I asked.

"Guess." Taylor winked. "I waited three days. Then I typed the same thing over again, word for word. Only this time I did it single-spaced, so that it only took half a page. I walked in, threw it on his desk, and he said, 'Well—*this* is more like it.' End of story."

Only it wasn't the end, by a long shot. By fall, Nicky and Salem were in the quickie business up to their ears, turning out cheap six-reelers by the gross.

They were doing documentaries, too; Patriotic Movies with a Message. They supplied the latter while our armed forces supplied backgrounds and footage at no cost. Our units began turning up at Annapolis, West Point, and all points west.

To the inspired duo belongs full credit for removing those shots of bobbing battleships from the newsreels and placing them in full-length features. Nicky could probably tell you all about it. I recall him telling me, one noon, in the commissary.

"Here's the pitch, see? These two guys are in the Navy, on this battleship. One of 'em is an oldtimer—sort of a Victor McLaglen type, like *What Price Glory*, only the switch is, he's in the Navy and not the Army. And the other guy, he's a young fella, more of a smart aleck, you might say. Edmund Lowe, always wisecracking you know.

"Anyways, we got an old Commodore or Admiral running the ship— George Barbier or Claude Gillingwater, *that* kind. Tough as nails, but he loves his daughter. Even brings her along on this cruise for manoovers, get it?

"Maybe she's got a pet dog or monkey or something for comic relief. Say, don't the Navy have a billygoat for a mascot? I'll check on it this aft. Anyway, the pet gets washed overboard and the hero, this young guy, is suppose to rescue it. Only he won't. He's yellow. Turns out he's afraid of water!"

A pause, for emphasis.

"Of course the girl sees him and she won't have nothing more to do with him. Somebody else rescues the pet. And he catches hell from the Sarge or the Coxswain, or whatever this old buddy of his is called. Then they get ready to test this newfangled submarine and of course the old Admiral and his daughter, they want to go down in it the first thing. And the Coxswain is supposed to run the test.

"Only they take this pet along—maybe we better keep it a monkey, a monk would be more *believable*—it gets loose and fiddles with a valve or something, and there they are. Trapped under the sea!"

Another pause.

"Well, I guess you can figure the rest. The only guy who knows what to do—turns out he really designed the new gadget or something—is the hero. And he's a weakling, remember? So we have a scene here with the chaplin—that's what they call a preacher in the Navy, a chaplin—and he shows the hero a picture of the girl. This guy, Alec B. Francis or O. P. Heggie, he gives the hero a big pep talk about Navy spirit and all that crap, and down he goes. In a diving helmet, with sharks and this here octopus. Big fight scene—I got a whole reel from someplace, we can fake the close-ups in a tank with a rubber one. Like the whale in *Moby Dick*, only cheaper.

"Anyhow, he wins out. The girl and the old guy are watching him through the porthole, and he fixes the gadget just in time to save them.

"Then we're gonna use all these Fleet Review shots in the last scene, where the young guy is standing up on the poopdeck or wherever, getting married to the girl by her own father—you know they got the authority to do that at sea. Maybe we fix the McLaglen type up with Hedda Hopper, somebody like that.

"Anyways, the hero gets a medal, too, and salutes. And we fade out on that goddam monkey, see, wearing a little sailor suit and saluting like crazy. How about that, now?"

I never told him how about that, now, or any time. He went right ahead and made it—and then he made the one about the Marine and his comic Jack Oakie-type buddy, and the one about the West Point Cadet who took the blame for the heroine's cheating brother in the final exam, and the one about the World War rookie who didn't believe in fighting until he saw Gustav von Seyyfertitz-type Germans trying to rape his girl.

You name it, he made it.

And always Salem was in the background, working with his writers, his slick-haired juveniles and bee-lipped jazz babies who would do these assignments for peanuts or even shells; badgering Riley in the newly-created Publicity Administration Department to step up the budget on advertising.

All at once, late that fall, he wasn't in the background any more. No one could mark the exact moment when the change took place—but suddenly he was right out in front, under a great white light. Acclaimed by the press as the new Boy Genius. That seemed to be the typecasting triumph of the year, Lester Salem, Boy Genius at forty-three.

Before the year was out, the Nicky Morris units were asking for, and getting, A-picture budgets and treatment. And Salem's name kept turning up in the trade papers and in the public press. Glenda Glint's column, to be specific.

I noticed Glint was printing a lot of inside gossip about our operations. That would be Salem's method of paying her back for favors received. They were working together, now—for Salem and against his enemies.

There was the matter of Lozoff's new picture, which I hadn't written. Morris gave him the director's job and he called in an outside team to work on the story. Glint dutifully reported, "Story trouble with a certain temperamental foreign director whose sudden rise to eminence seems to be affecting his hat size these days."

Druse was getting it, too.

When he turned down an offer for an outside film with PDC, or some such outfit, Glenda Glint wrote, "What rival of Lon Chaney, the Man with the Thousand Faces, is currently rejecting work on the grounds of ill health? According to our sources, the real reason is pure laziness, which promotes us to nominate the character actor as the Man with the Thousand Excuses."

Catty stuff like that, nothing specific—yet. Just enough to show which way the wind was blowing. At the moment no storm warnings had come my way. But I kept watching Salem and Nicky.

Then, late that fall, I took on another Druse assignment. This time I did an original story, *Spider Man*. It was beginning to feel good to work again, and what I turned out wasn't half bad. Druse himself was very enthusiastic.

"This is what I want," he said. "Now that Chaney is going in for stuff like *The Unknown,* we need a strong story line. You and Weichmann are a good team for me. As long as they keep young Morris and Salem off our necks, we'll be all right."

"You still angry about that night on the set?" I asked him.

"No. I'm not angry. But Salem is. You've read some of the cracks Glint printed. It isn't hard to guess where they come from. Salem's out to get me."

"Maybe you're just imagining things."

"No. I never imagine things." Druse was grave. "I tell you, he won't rest until he drives me out of pictures entirely."

"Come on, now, it can't be that bad."

"Wait and see."

I thought he was kidding me. Until—

Until the week before we were scheduled to start rehearsals on *Spider Man*.

That's when the front office sent through a memo that the Druse unit had been shifted. No change in cast or assignments, but the production would be under the supervision of Nicholas Morris.

I went around to talk to Druse about this, but he wasn't at the Studio.

He didn't show up on starting date for rehearsals, either. We called his home, but there was no answer.

The next morning Weichmann was almost frantic. We rang the house, and I was just about ready to suggest stronger measures when I got a summons to stop in at Nicky Morris's office.

I went over to the Executive Building and gave my name to his receptionist—a new one, of course; he switched regularly every month.

"Oh yes, Mr. Post. You're to go right in."

I entered the boudoir (to this day I can't conceive of that upholstered, overstuffed, purple-plush suite as a business office) and was surprised to discover Lester Salem seated behind the bleached mahogany desk-bar.

"Where's Mr. Morris?" I asked.

"He left yesterday for the East," Salem told me. "The Trianon opening in Philadelphia, you know. But I asked you in here on another matter. Where is Karl Druse?"

"I don't know. Have you called his home?"

"Of course we've called his home. So have you. Betty, at the switch-board, told me."

So now he had spies in the office too. I bit my lip. But he wasn't waiting to observe my reaction.

"Are you sure you don't know his whereabouts?"

"Of course not. He seemed satisfied with the script when I gave it to him last week. Of course, Druse isn't very talkative—"

"Oh, he can talk when he wants to. And usually, out of turn." Salem stared at the wall.

"Perhaps you ought to send someone out to the house," I suggested, breaking the silence.

"That is just what I had in mind. Post, I'm delegating that little duty to you. I don't want to send an ordinary messenger, because I have a rather private communication to deliver.

"I want you to find Druse and tell him that if he isn't on the set promptly at nine tomorrow morning, he'll be liable for breach of contract. Is that clear?"

"Yes."

"Then make certain it is equally clear to Mr. Druse. I'll be waiting here for a report from you. Good day."

If it was, I hadn't noticed it.

I went out into the sunshine and started searching for a shadow.

TWENTY

I DIDN'T KNOW Karl Druse very well, but I had a great deal of affection for him. That's because he came in handy whenever I encountered the Argument.

The Argument was a common occurrence in those days. It arose whenever I, as a member of the "movie colony," was introduced to an outsider. Immediately, Hollywood was attacked by the Hollywoodn't.

The approach was as invariable as it was inevitable. Why were "you motion picture people" so *crazy*? Oh, *you* know what I mean—all those loud clothes and costume parties and comic-opera castles.

To which I'd reply by reminding them of a few hallowed names in the Sacred East, near Mecca itself. Jim Fisk, the Vanderbilts; the party where the naked chorus girls came out of the pie to entertain the Social Registrants. I'd mention Diamond Jim Brady's rather conspicuous manner of dress, and the architectural monstrosities created by and for the *)lite* in times when business magnates were magnatizing just as our *nouveau* rich did now.

Stalemate, but only for a moment. Then it was, "What about the scandals, the divorces?" Followed by the usual names.

My answer always took the form of more names—the scores of cinematic celebrities who were happily married and stayed that way, whose social activities never made the headlines because they were neither scandalous nor even exciting. I'd give them Bebe Daniels, and H.

B. Warner, Ernest Torrence, the Costello girls, the Lloyds, Lozoff and his wife.

But they'd come right back at me. How about Mabel Normand, taking that whole gang to Europe the time they came down to see her off at the boat? Tom Mix, earning $19,000 a week and driving a $35,000 car? What about Theodore Harker?

Wasn't it true, they asked me, that movie people got delusions of grandeur, that they tried to "live" their screen roles?

No, it wasn't true, I said. Look at Karl Druse and his horror films. Karl Druse, the horror star—a quiet middle-aged man who wore a battered derby and smoked a pipe. Why, he came to work in a little Chevy, with no chauffeur. And he probably lived in a duplex.

That usually stopped them cold. And it helped to reassure me, as well, because there were times when I wasn't any too certain I believed my own arguments. Then the memory of Karl Druse came to my rescue.

Of course, I stretched my story a bit. I didn't know whether Druse lived in a duplex or not. I'd never been invited to his house.

As a matter of fact, right now, after leaving Lester Salem's office, I had to stop and look up Druse's address before driving out to his place.

I found him listed in a side street off Benedict Canyon, and as I went Stutzing along I wondered just what sort of house he occupied.

In order to gratify my curiosity I had to make three sharp turns, climb a small hill, and then climb a larger hill in back of the first one. Druse certainly liked his privacy.

The place itself was reassuringly unpretentious. It was a two-story white affair, hidden by trees; the grounds bordered by hardy native shrubbery. There was no swimming pool, and the garage was small.

I walked up to the big open porch, picturing Druse as he must sit here in the evening, puffing on his corncob and staring out at the sunset. Here, in a setting of almost rural seclusion, a man could enjoy peace. Walden Pond is where you find it.

There was a bell to ring. I rang it. There was a door to open. Somebody opened it.

"I beg your pardon. I'm Mr. Post, from the Studio. Is Mr. Druse at home?"

"Come in."

I dived into Walden Pond and came up with a mermaid. Or something equally exotic.

The girl who had answered the door wore cloth-of-gold pajamas, Chinese-fashion. This was not inappropriate, because she was obviously Chinese. From silver sandals to carved ivory cigarette holder, the oriental *motif* held true. And the lotus-look, the almond eyes, were exotically authentic.

There was only a single discrepancy. The Chinese girl's hair, worn in a pageboy bob, flowed to her shoulders. And it was platinum blonde.

I tried not to stare as I followed her into the living room. Once inside it was easier, because I found other things to stare at.

Here were Tutankhamen's tomb, and Angkor-Wat: here were Cathay and Cambodia and Ceylon. Reared against scarlet walls was the black and baleful bulk of a brooding Bubastis, a somber Set, a trumpeting Ganesha, and the Thunder-God of Tibet. Incense rose form a tripod and swirled over the divans, the prayer seats, the tear vases, the ceramic-inlaid coffee tables from Turkestan.

I thought of Harker's self-consciously lavish layout for comparison, but no—his romantic *rococo* was recognizable. This was different, disturbingly so. Idols and altars, incense and amber, ivory and jade and a carved replica of the Peacock Throne—but no chairs.

And the Chinese girl with the platinum hair—

"I know who you are," she said. "You're the one who's been writing *Spider Man*. Karl has spoken of you often."

"That's right. I came to find out where Mr. Druse has been. The Studio's a little worried because he hasn't reported in for rehearsals."

She nodded. "He hasn't been feeling well for several days and he went away for a rest."

"What's the matter with him? If he's ill, he should have notified us. There's an expensive production involved."

She shrugged, then stiffened. I stiffened, too, because we both heard it. The voice, from upstairs.

"Sin! Where are you?"

I stared at her. "Isn't that Druse?"

"I heard nothing."

"Sin, is somebody here?" The voice again, unmistakable.

She moved to block my way, but I was faster. I went up the stairs two at a time, noting its unusual double railing. At the landing I paused, wondering momentarily which turn to take.

A sound decided me.

I heard a rustling, a slithering in the hall. Then a head came around the corner of a doorway. It bobbed forward and I saw arms inch out, a body emerge. Something writhed toward me, crawling.

Crawling.

He didn't see me because his head was down. But I saw him. Saw the outstretched arms, the widespread legs—and *the place where the feet should be.*

I stared down at the Man of a Thousand Bodies. The man was always too short or too tall, the man who walked stiffly, the man whose legs ended above the ankles.

Then he glanced up and his eyes met mine.

"Sin!" he shouted. "Why didn't you stop him?"

The girl came up the steps behind me. Her eyes were impassive, but her mouth worked. "I tried, but he was too quick—here, let me help you."

She stepped forward, stopped, but he waved her aside. Slowly, painfully, he crawled into the doorway at my right. I followed him and found myself in a small sitting room. He moved to a low divan, lifted himself by the arms, leaned back with a sigh.

Flame, framed by the fireplace, reflected redly against his gaunt face. He looked like something out of one of his own movies.

"Sorry to disturb you," I said. "I didn't know—"

"Damned right you didn't!" He barked a laugh. Then, "Sin, how about a drink?"

She moved out of the room.

"Dumb as they come," Druse murmured. "Sometimes I wonder why I ever married her. Then, again—" He glanced down at his legs.

"Welcome to the freak show," he said. "Stop gawking and sit down!"

I found another divan across the room on the other side of the fireplace. There were no chairs, of course; he wouldn't want chairs. "Please." I shook my head. "I came here on Salem's orders. We're ready to start rehearsals."

Druse nodded. "Sorry. You'll have to excuse me. I've been doing some drinking these past few days. And I intend to do more. Ah, here we are—"

Sin entered with the tray and the glasses. She poured scotch, all around, then stood for a moment with her glass held at her side.

Druse scowled up at her. "Don't worry, it's all right! Another one won't hurt me. Take the car and drive into town for a while—I want to talk with Post."

She left the room without a word, then almost instantly reappeared. In her hands she bore a strange assortment of straps and silver that gleamed in the firelight as she placed them on the floor beside Druse.

"I'm going now," she said. "But you'll need these if you're alone. Please, try to be careful."

"All right. See you later."

She bent to kiss him, rose and nodded to me. "Goodbye, Mr. Post."

"Goodbye."

Her footsteps in the hall—on the stairs—the slight sound of a door opening and closing—then silence. Karl Druse reached down and picked up the straps and the silver.

"Ever see anything like these before?" he asked. "Finest job in the country. I've got six pair. Cost me three thousand apiece to have them made up. Worked on the design myself. Those orthopedists don't know how to do it."

He began to adjust the straps at the knees, the calves of his legs. "Talk about feet of clay," he chuckled. "Me, I've got feet of silver. With a little steel and aluminum here at the joints. See how they bend and flex? But I can use the muscles of my legs for support and balance. Watch."

Druse stood up, stiffly but swiftly. "Of course it's even easier when I'm wearing shoes," he said. "This is one of the long pairs. The short ones are more comfortable. Hardly notice them under the pants-legs, do you?"

I nodded. He reached out, downed his drink, then refilled his glass from the bottle next to the divan. "How about you?" he asked.

"No, thanks. I still have some here. Besides, it's not noon yet."

"Of course, I'd forgotten."

"Did you forget about the rehearsals, too?"

"Hell, no! Why do you think I'm drinking?" He eyed me for a moment. "Look, Post—you're not going to go back and tell them about *this* are you?"

He pointed at the artificial feet, and I shook my head. "You know I won't," I said.

"I thought I could trust you. You're all right, Post." He sat down again. "So I might as well let you in on the rest of the secret. I've been stalling on purpose. I don't want Salem and that gum-chewing ape on my picture. I don't want them on any picture. They're going to ruin it."

"But they won't really interfere," I said. "It's probably just one of the Old Man's gestures."

"Well, I don't like his gestures. I know where they lead to. You've seen those turkeys the two of them are turning out. Before long the whole Studio'll be run that way—we'll be making Poverty Row serials next, wait and see."

"Morris wouldn't let that happen."

"Oh, wouldn't he? He needs money, and Salem is calling the tune. I know what I'm talking about—the day is coming when they'll take the movies away from the moviemakers and turn everything over to the bookkeepers. To the moneymen who don't believe in making anything except dollars. What are you shaking your head about?"

"I don't know," I said. "Sometimes I think the big trouble with all of us is that we're too self-conscious about what we're doing. Always trying to analyze the movies and ourselves. I'll bet the Industry will outgrow this sort of thing, twenty years from now."

"Sure it will," Druse answered. "But it won't grow up as a result. It'll grow down. Twenty years from now there'll be damned little analysis left except cost analysis. Hollywood will be filled with pale-faced fish like your Lester Salem. There won't be room for a Stroheim or a Chaplin or a Griffith or a Harker. And when that day comes—" He finished his drink instead of his sentence. "But I'm not going to see it happen without a fight. I want to do *your* version of *Spider Man*, not that watered-down abortion Salem sent me last week."

I took a deep breath. "Salem sent you another version? I never knew that."

"Of course you didn't. I doubt if he planned to tell you—just intended to let you find out when rehearsals started. You're on his list, boy, same as I am, ever since that night I told him off." Druse smiled with his mouth, but the dark eyes never smiled. They couldn't smile; they were crippled, like the legs—the smile had been cut away.

"I won't even show you the thing he sent over," Druse continued. "Take my word for it, it's terrible. One of those fakes where everything turns out to be a dream at the end. That's Salem's thinking for you. He wants to tell people it's all a dream, wake up and hear the birdies. What he forgets is that people pay their money because they *want* a dream, and they want to believe it's real. What he forgets is that we've got to live and suffer to make it real for them. He'd just as soon get rid of me—he thinks you can *buy* a horror star in the open market, just take any old character actor and slap a lot of makeup on his face. I know better. I know you have to pay another kind of price. I gave my feet."

He leaned forward. "Tell this to your Mr. Salem. Tell him how I learned about horror. Once there was a little boy, nine years old. His father was crazy, but the kid didn't know it. Until one day his father grabbed him and held him down on the kitchen table. He tied the kid up tight, see? And then he took a hatchet and cut the boy's feet off above the ankles. All the time he was doing it he kept laughing, laughing—"

Druse reached for the bottle. "That's how I found out about monsters. By becoming one, myself. And it was real, I tell you. I try to make it real for others, now. I try to show them what it means—without Salem's phoney endings."

I was silent for a moment, watching him pour his drink. "Does the Old Man know Salem has another story?" I asked.

"I don't think so."

"Well, let's do it our way, then." I rose. "I'm going back and tell Weichmann. We'll talk to Morris at once."

"Salem's going to have his knife out for you, if you do," Druse warned me.

"I'll take that chance."

"Why stick your neck out?" Druse groped for words and his bottle simultaneously. "You don't owe me any favors, you of all people—" He shook his head and then his mouth smiled again as the somber eyes stared. "Sorry for me, aren't you?"

"That's not the reason."

"Don't be," said the mouth, while the eyes mirrored an agony of their own. "I've got everything I want. You may not approve of Sin, or the way I've fixed the house up here, but it suits me. Maybe my old man wasn't the only crazy one in the family."

The mouth chuckled and the dark eyes glanced toward the fireplace. "This is what I've always wanted, every since the carny days. Harker knows—"

"Jackie Keeley said you two started out together."

The eyes met mine quickly, and then Druse nodded. "True. And as long as you're interested in my little secrets, here's another one. I get a kick out of wearing a derby and smoking that goddam pipe, looking like a rube. And knowing, all the time, that I'm really a monster.

"You understand that, Post? I'm a monster, just the way it is up there on the screen. I'm *real*, and nobody's going to change me. Not a fool like Salem. Sometimes when I get to thinking about him, I could—"

Shaking his head, he barked a laugh. "I'm talking too much. And not drinking enough." Druse extended the bottle. "One for the road?"

"All right." I poured for both of us, lifted my glass to the firelight. "You come in tomorrow," I told him. "Everything will be straightened out by then. That's a promise."

"Thanks. I'll drink to that."

He drank to that, and I drank my own toast. A toast to a monster, to the man with the silver feet.

TWENTY-ONE

I NEVER REPORTED BACK to Salem at all. Instead I went straight to Sol Morris. I told him all about it, without making any complaints—just gave him the straight story.

He made a clicking sound with his tongue, then ground his cigar out in the big gold ashtray.

"Weichmann said you wrote a good one," he murmured. "That's enough for me. So start the rehearsals tomorrow. Never mind about Salem. I'll talk to him."

"I don't want any hard feelings," I said.

"Of course you don't. Leave that to me. Somebody's getting too big in the britches."

Just what kind of a custom-tailoring job was done on Salem's britches, I'll never know. But neither he nor Nicky bothered us during the filming of *Spider Man*; they never showed up on the set. The next time I saw Salem he was his usual nonsmiling self, and he made no mention of the incident.

Druse came back, turned in an excellent job, and the picture—when it was finally shown—did all right.

We released it early in 1928, with plenty of exploitation. That was Salem's innovation. He sold all his turkeys with "showmanship," and the lobbies of the growing Coronet Chain were now filled with college pendants, palm trees, circus banners, burglar tools, machine guns, model airplanes, boxing gloves—depending on the type of bird he had in the oven at the moment.

He sponsored Black Bottom Contests and Treasure Hunts and Talent Searches. He had Beauty Parades and Flower Matinees and Personal Appearances and Ukulele Amateur Nights.

People were talking about his stunts. And people were talking, now, about Joan Crawford and a new cartoon character named Mickey Mouse. We began to hear about the big New York gross on *The Jazz Singer*— Warner Brothers were pushing another one of those novelties called Vitaphone, with music and voices. It caught on, just the way color did when Doug made *The Black Pirate*, a few years before. And like color, it was a very interesting experiment but way too expensive, of course.

In mid-year we finally got a chance to see something really important. Theodore Harker brought out his new picture. *That* was big news.

For a week before the premiere I heard about it on the lot. From Hacky, for example:

"Going to see *Mankind*?"

"Of course I am."

"Where's the premiere?"

"Grauman's Chinese."

"He doesn't look it! Haha!"

I showed up on the big night, with Lozoff and Madame Olga. It was a fullscale production—searchlights, the red carpet, the radio announcer, the special cordon of police, and the rope to keep back the crowds. We stood in the lobby, watching Theodore Harker make his entrance.

"That's Stella Ballard with him, his new discovery," Lozoff told me. "And George Conway."

I nodded, my eyes on Harker as he paused before the microphone and said "a few words" as requested by the master of ceremonies. He had a new cane, and that gave him the old look—no, Harker hadn't changed. He was still the master magician, and when I saw him everything came back in a rush. The cane moved, the wand waved, and there were Carla and Dude and Maybelle and Dawn. *Dawn. Why, it was a year and a half now, almost two—I'd thought I'd forgotten. But I hadn't. You never forget.*

In the mob just beyond the doorway, people stared and pointed, and a voice recalled me to reality. A girl, asking her boyfriend, "Who's he?"

She pointed at Harker. I smiled at the time, but during the course of the picture I recalled the question and I didn't smile, then.

After it was over, the Lozoffs and I went to a little place on Sunset for a bite to eat.

"Well," I said. "What do you think?"

"Ballard's a fair actress. But this Conway—he has something. I'd like to use him soon."

"That's not what I mean," I told him. "What do you think of the picture?"

Lozoff selected a cigarette. "If you'd asked me that question in 1922, you know what my answer would have been. But now, in '28, I don't know."

"The audience seemed to enjoy it."

"You know premiere audiences. And right now there's a big party at Harker's place, with everybody gathering around and telling him this is the best thing he's ever done. But it's dated."

Madame Olga nodded. "I think I understand what Kurt means," she said. "The love scenes, the orange blossoms, the doves—too old-fashioned."

"Well, we don't have to make everything into a Clara Bow opus, do we? Must it all be hey-hey stuff, redhot mamma and palpitating papa?"

Lozoff smiled. "Of course not. That's false, too. And it won't last. What *will* last is the mature approach, the honest approach. Telling your story, no matter whether the setting is ancient Greece or modern America, in realistic terms. The technique you find in *The Crowd* and *The Wind*."

He leaned forward. "The time has come, I think, to take the big step. I am going to see Morris next week and tell him my plans for the coming year. I want you to work with me. I'll see about getting this George Conway; if not, I have someone else in mind. I want Lucille Hilton for Sonia and Druse for Porfiry. As for you, you'd better get started reading the book."

"What book?" I asked. "What are we making?"

"*Crime and Punishment,*" said Lozoff.

"All right." I stood up. "But better not tell Nicky. He doesn't like gangster pictures.

Madame Olga laughed. "It is good to see you happy again," she said. "Making the jokes. For a while there, Kurt and I were troubled because of you. After that girl—"

Lozoff gave her a look and she subsided. But I smiled. "It's all right," I answered. "That was a long time ago."

"I'm glad." Madame Olga smiled. "I thought that maybe when you heard about her getting married, you'd be—"

"Married?"

"Yes, it was in the papers tonight. Didn't you read—"

"Married? Who's she marrying? What's his name?"

"I don't remember. Please, Tommy, sit down, don't get excited. I thought—"

I didn't wait to hear what she thought. I was out of there, running down the street to the newsstand. I was buying a paper, ripping through the pages, cursing because it was an early morning edition and not from the previous evening.

Then I was in the drugstore, looking for a phone. I was calling Kate LaBuddie's number. I was trembling and my hands were shaking, and now my voice was shaking, too.

"Hello-this is Tom Post. Where is she?"

"She?"

"Dawn. Mitzi. I must talk to her!"

"She's not here. Mr. Post, do you realize it's almost midnight?"

"I'm not asking you what time it is. Where is she?"

"She's not here. Really, Mr. Post—"

"Are you going to tell me the truth or must I come out there?"

"Well—"

I slammed the receiver down. Then I was back on the street.

"Taxi!"

I opened the door before it had come to a stop, hurled the Vine Street address at the driver and myself into a seat. Then I sat there, shaking and shaking as we knifed through the night. My stomach was churning and my head was churning, too. I kept wanting to throw up and all I could regurgitate was memories.

Then I was getting out in front of the apartment house, going into the lobby, pressing the buzzer. I rang and I rang and I rang. I began to curse as I held my finger down and listened to the drone.

"Answer, damn you!" I yelled. "Answer!"

Finally the lock clicked on the inner door. I yanked the handle and careened down the hall. Apartment 2-B. *2-B or not 2-B. It is good to see you happy again. Making the jokes.*

I stopped in front of the door, raised my fist to pound. The door opened. Kate LaBuddie peered out at me.

"Are you crazy?" she whispered.

"Let me in."

"All right, but no noise."

"Let me in."

She slid the chain off the lock and I entered.

"I must say this is most irr—irrigelur." I took a good look at her, then a good sniff. Kate LaBuddie, I suddenly realized, was drunk. I could smell the reek of juniper essence in the untidy front room, and now I couldsee the bottle and the tumbler on the table.

Kate LaBuddie peered up at me, trying to push her hair back from her forehead. "What do you *mean*, breaking in here at this hour?" she began, in a curious mimicry of her usual affected manner. Then, abruptly, the hair slid down across her forehead and the mask came awry, too. "What the hell's the big idea?" she demanded.

I wasn't wearing a mask, either, now. "That's what I want to know," I said, and shook her. "Where's Dawn?"

"Take your hands off me," gasped Kate LaBuddie. Then she sat down and began to sob.

"I'm sorry," I said. And I was, suddenly and intensely, as I looked at the drunken, middle-aged woman huddling there on the sofa. Somehow, at this moment, she bore a mocking resemblance to Dawn. Perhaps it was the way her mouth made a wavering *O* as she sobbed.

"Please," I said, sitting down beside her. "I'm not here to cause trouble."

"Trouble? You're the one who started all the trouble in the first place. You and your ideas." The sobs ceased and she began to talk with renewed animation. "If it hadn't been for you, she'd never have quit the movies. She'd never have left Harker. She'd be a great star today, instead of—"

I saw the tears coming again, so I did the sensible thing. I stood up and walked over to the table, poured a stiff slug of gin into the tumbler, and carried it back to her. She accepted it without a word and gulped greedily.

"Feel better now?" I asked.

"Better? Why should I feel better? I'm a mother, Mr. Post. A poor woman, alone in the world with two innocent children to protect." She was going into her act again, but I was willing to watch, and to wait.

"I worked my fingers to the *bone* to provide them with every oppor— oppratunity. And just when things began to go the right way, *you* came along and spoiled it all.

"Look!" she cried, waving the tumbler and sloshing some of the contents on the rug with the force of her gesture. "Is this the home for the mother of a star? Why, we'd be living in a palace today if it wasn't for *you*. You took her away from Harker, you took her away from me, you took her away from the movies. And now here I sit, all alone, with Buddie out God-knows-where and Mitzi off with that mis'rable little wholesale grocer. All those years of planning, and she ends up with a wholesale grocer. It's funny—"

I didn't give her time to laugh. "Off? You mean she ran away?"

"Last night. They drove to Nevada, to get married. Didn't even ask me along—her own mother, and she didn't even—"

"You're sure they're married? What's his name?"

"Shotwell. Kenneth Shotwell. From Pasadena. He's fat, he smokes cigars, he *looks* like a wholesale grocer. And it's all your fault, all your fault. I tried so hard." Her mouth began to quiver again, but I no longer felt pity.

What I did feel must have shown on my face because she looked up at me and said, "Better help yourself to a drink."

I nodded. I found a glass in the kitchen and returned.

I poured myself half a water glass full of the stuff. I hated raw gin, but it didn't matter, because I hated everything.

The liquor burned as it went down, and I poured again.

"Go ahead," she said. "See, there's another bottle. I better open it."

She opened it and poured for both of us.

"You really loved her, didn't you?" she wheezed, between gulps.

I nodded.

"Then why'd you let her go? Why'd you let her quit? She could have been rich—even without Harker. There'd been enough for all of us—"

"Shut up!" I said.

She stared at me for a moment as if she hadn't heard. Then she put down her glass. "Who the hell are you to tell me to shut up, you little bastard?"

"What's that?"

Kate LaBuddie laughed. "Guess you thought I didn't know, eh? Thought it was a secret, huh? But I found out. How'd you think we got to Harker in the first place? I was the one who worked, I was the one who did the planning. I told her what to say—"

"What are you talking about? The astrologer?

"Of course I am. So you *do* know that part of it. Did Mitzi tell you?"

"No. Someone else. About how you and some astrologer got Harker's confidence by telling him a lot of things about himself, about his past, and—"

All at once I was dizzy. It was the hatred again, it was the gin, and it was something else. Something that came up in a great wave of sound, of voices that shouted *bastard, bastard, bastard*, over and over again.

I heard Aunt Minnie's voice. "*We got you from the Orphanage just because it was our chance to—*"

And Jackie Keeley, saying, "*Why, I knew Teddy Harker when he was still with it . . . used to travel with mud shows, him and his wife. At least she said she was his wife, little redhead, Connie, something-or-other—*"

Everything fitted, now. Everything fitted into the pattern, and the pattern made a single word. *Bastard*. That's who I was, what I was. Theodore Harker's bastard.

I stood up. The room was spinning now, but I didn't care. Let the room spin, let the world spin, let Kate LaBuddie drool into drunkenness and Dawn Powers honeymoon with her wholesale grocer from Pasadena. That was funny, everything was funny, and the funniest thing of all was the spectacle of a dumb bastard, a goddam kid who'd always wanted to find his father.

I lurched over to the door.

"Where are you going?" asked Kate LaBuddie.

I didn't bother to tell her. But I knew.

TWENTY-TWO

IT WAS TWO O'CLOCK in the morning, but the lights still glowed and glared through the windows of Theodore Harker's house.

I left the taxi and stared up at them, blinking. Lights in the window. *A light in the window for your wandering boy—*

Then I remembered what Lozoff had told me and I understood. Harker planned a party after the premiere. It must have just ended, for I heard no sound from within.

The steps seemed to slant in the moonlight, to curl like pale lips. *You're full of gin,* I told myself. *That's not the effect of moonlight, just moonshine. Go ahead, you bastard, knock on the door. It's time for a reunion.*

I swayed there for a moment, and I couldn't help myself. The whole family reunion script swam into my head; written, produced, directed by and starring Thomas Post. Thomas Post, the well-known, unknown bastard.

Cutting and editing automatically, I unreeled the finished film, reeling. Post, making his dramatic entrance. Harker stepping forward in front of the assembled guests, the curdled cream of the motion picture colony.

"What are you doing here?"

"Is that any kind of welcome for your beloved son?"

No, that wasn't the way. That would be melodrama. I'd have to revise the script, start over again.

"What are you doing here?"

I clung to the door. I must be drunker than I thought, because now I was actually hearing a voice. Harker's voice.

Then I turned, and I could see him. He stood beside me in the moonlight. He was real. This wasn't a script any more, and I didn't have any cues.

"I—I thought you were giving a party."

"It's all over with. Taki and Rogers are cleaning up. I stepped out for some fresh air." He inhaled deliberately. "You've been drinking, haven't you?"

I nodded. Nodded and stared up into the proud, pallid face, wondering what to say next, where to begin.

"Did you hear about Dawn?" I murmured.

"Oh, so that's it." He took my arm and led me down the stairs, across the lawn toward the first of the two swimming pools. "Yes, I read something in the paper. She's getting married."

"She is married," I said.

Theodore Harker said nothing. He gazed down at the moonlit mirror of the pool and his reflection smiled. "You're young," said the reflection. "You'll get over it."

"Great!" said my reflection. "That's why I came out here—for a helping of two-bit philosophy."

Now I could speak, speak freely, as long as I kept watching our reflections. For our reflections removed reality; it was like gazing into a vast silver screen and seeing a movie.

"Why *did* you come out here?"

My reflection faced his, mouth opening. But Harker's image was still speaking.

"Surely you can't blame me for her marriage? What happened between the three of us is all in the past. I'd forgotten about it long ago, and hoped you were wise enough to do the same. One can't afford to look backward, you know."

"I didn't know." I wasn't looking backward, I was looking down at our reflections. "And that's why I came. Because I saw something tonight for the first time. Something that concerns both of us."

"I told you, Dawn isn't important to me any more."

"I'm not talking about Dawn. This is something I learned from Kate LaBuddie."

I waited for a reaction, but his reflection was immobile. And I thought, *what if he doesn't know, doesn't realize?* But my voice went on, the voice of my image in the pool. Narcissus spoke.

"She told me how she went to that astrologer and supplied her with information about your past—got the woman to gain your confidence so that you'd believe her predictions of the future, about Dawn. She told me how you were taken in."

He didn't answer; the reflection never wavered. And I shouted, "What's the matter, don't you believe me? It's true, you know—the great Theodore Harker, duped by a couple of stupid, conniving women!"

Harker's image rippled the water with a shrug. "Why get so excited? Some of this I already know, the rest I suspected. And it doesn't matter. It's all past."

"The past is dead, eh?"

"Of course. I tried to convey that lesson to you years ago, at the funeral. One lives for the present, plans for the future. The past is unimportant. One travels forward, alone."

"I remember now," I said, and I did. "The funeral. The one you paid for. You said the Studio would foot the bill, but that was a lie, wasn't it? You paid for the funeral out of your own pocket."

"What if I did?"

"Nothing. Except that it proves you don't live up to your own philosophy. You can't shut out your conscience—"

"Please, Post! I'm trying to be patient, but—"

"Get your hands off me!" My reflection retreated a step, treading water. "You'll listen just the way I had to listen tonight, when I found out."

He turned away, and his back made a black stain across the water. I spoke to the shadow, to the reflection of a shadow.

"Yes, I found out. Now I know how it must have been, in that past you don't like to remember. When you were in the carnival, with the little redhead."

The shadow stiffened.

"You ran away, didn't you? And when I was born, I went into the orphanage. You were beginning to make progress, traveling forward alone, as you say. Alone! I wonder how many bodies you trampled on in your climb from the carny to Hollywood? You were never alone—there was always a woman, always women when you wanted them. Don't tell me about loneliness. *I* was the one who knew what it was to be really alone. For fourteen years in that vacuous vacuum.

"I'm not sure what happened next. I'd like to believe that once you came out here, even your calloused conscience gave you a few qualms; enough so that you asked your old friend Minnie and her husband to take me out and adopt me. Actually, I suppose it was just the other way around—Minnie must have come to you and hinted that she knew the facts. So you let her take me to shut her up, and you gave Uncle Andy a studio job. You even let me have one. And that, to your way of thinking, closed the matter. But it isn't closed, after all."

I could see his face again, in the water. Turning and moving its lips. "I don't know what you're talking about."

"You know, all right. And how it must have hurt you to see me take Dawn away from you—losing a woman to your own son!"

Harker's mouth opened and his features shivered in the pool as though someone had hit the surface of the water with a stone.

Now I could look at him, look at his actual face in the moonlight. And now that I'd said it, I wanted to look at him. There was no hatred left in me any more.

"I'm—sorry," I said. "You don't know how it was for me, but I think I'm beginning to understand how it must have been for you. All these years, hiding the secret. Trying to pretend, even when you saw me every day. Trying to live up to your own code, shutting out the past. I used to think nothing could be worse than this ache of mine, this need to find a father. But there's something far more terrible to bear—fear. That's what you had, every day."

I moved closer, watching the wavering lines of his mouth.

"Don't worry," I murmured. "I won't tell. And I didn't come here because I wanted anything from you. I don't need your money or your fame or even your name. It's just that I must know there's truth between us. Because you're my father—"

Suddenly the wavering lines dissolved on Theodore Harker's face. They exploded, exploded in a peal of laughter.

"You're crazy!" Harker said. "Father? I'm not your father. I have no son." He chuckled again. "Go back to that idiotic woman and tell her it's no good. No more blackmail. Just a pack of lies."

Theodore Harker stood there, proud in the moonlight, his head thrown back. He laughed and he laughed, and I made a noise in my throat and then I turned and I was running, running back into the darkness and the silence, running until the sound of his laughter was only an empty echo inside the hollow of my skull.

TWENTY-THREE

TWO WEEKS PASSED before I went into Sol Morris's office, to confer about *Crime and Punishment*.

Not a long time, two weeks, but a lot can happen in such a period. You can go on a honeymoon, or example. Or a blind, tearing drunk. Or you can reason things out for yourself, and then sit down and decide to write a script.

Somewhere along the line I got excited. I'd suddenly learned that it was possible for me to do a job for its own sake. That doesn't sound like such a startling discovery, but it was, for me. To find myself writing fluently—not for Dawn's sake, or the approval of a father, real or imaginary—was something new. And I enjoyed it.

Lozoff looked at what I'd done and approved. He'd never asked me what had happened the night I rushed off and left him, and I never told him. But he read my treatment and he said, "This is what I was hoping for. You are writing the way I wanted you to write—as if what we are going to do is something fine, something important."

So we went to the Executive Offices.

"I don't know," Sol Morris said. "I had Salem get the dope on it for me. Arrow-Pathe made it back in 1917, and nobody got excited. Somebody did it in Germany in '23."

"I saw it." Lozoff nodded. "Wiene made it, under the title of *Raskolnikov*."

"All those foreign names." Morris frowned through the cigar smoke. "And Russian, on top of it. We ain't so friendly with Russia. What about that?"

"This won't be a Russian picture. The theme is universal. That's why Dostoevski's novel is a classic. I want to put it on the screen as a classic, too. With all respect to Mr. Salem, this Studio hasn't been producing enough prestige pictures lately. We need a contender for the Academy Awards."

"That nonsense! Those arty guys with their newfangled Academy—it don't mean a thing. And what about this fella Dostoevski? Is he working out here?"

"He's dead," Lozoff said. "Look, Mr. Morris. You saw my budget estimate. It isn't out of line."

"That's right."

"We've got our principals right here under contract. Hilton and Druse. I was thinking of the actor Harker used in *Mankind*—young Conway. He'd be excellent for the student role and he isn't expensive. Post is working with me on the treatment. You can have it in a few days."

"Well, let's wait and see. We can talk about it then."

So we sent him the treatment and came back the following week. And Morris said:

"It's a good story. Gloomy, sort of, but you can feel it. That business where the girl Sonia decides she's gonna go with him to Siberia at the end—I see what you mean, all right."

"Then we can go ahead?"

"I don't know." He paused. "I been talking to Nicky. He sort of wants to use Lucille Hilton in that new thing of his—the dirigible picture. Salem has a lot of stuff on a zeppelin crash, and he tells me it's a natural. Besides, Hilton can't act."

"Yes she can," Lozoff said. "I want her."

Morris shrugged. "All right. But Druse is out."

"Out?"

"We're not renewing his contract. Ever since *Spider Man* there's been trouble. Salem tells me he shows up drunk half the time—"

"Mr. Salem doesn't want me to make this picture. That's the truth, isn't it?"

"You put it that way, the answer's yes. He says there isn't enough action, enough punch."

I broke in. "Action? It starts with a double murder. The whole plot is built on suspense—the inspector versus the student. Didn't you say you liked the treatment?"

"I do, my boy." Morris faced me. "But sometimes you got to think of other things. Like keeping peace in the family, here. Salem's doing a good job for us—don't worry, I know Nicky has nothing to do with it—and he's entitled to his opinion."

"His opinion, yes," Lozoff said. "But you are still the head of this Studio."

Morris was silent. Lozoff stood up. "I have been with you a good many years. I have acted, I have directed. My pictures made money. I think you can rely on the soundness of my judgment. Now I am asking you to let me make this picture. What do you say?"

"All right. Go ahead. I'll tell Salem." Morris hesitated. "But on one condition. Druse is out. Fair enough?"

Lozoff bit his lip.

"I know what you're thinking," Morris said. "It won't be your fault. I told you we're letting him go anyway. So if you compromise, Salem will. Right?"

"I suppose so. Only that means we need another name to strengthen the cast—"

"I've got a name for you," I said. "A strong one. Just the man to play the inspector. It's going to be a change of pace for him, but I know he can do it."

"Who do you have in mind?"

"Kurt Lozoff."

Lozoff raised his eyebrows. Then he smiled. "Why not? Von Stroheim acts and directs in his films."

"Please, no Stroheim," Morris sighed. "Just a nice, simple masterpiece, without too many retakes."

"You'll get it," I told him. "This is going to be one picture we can all be proud of."

And I meant it.

During the next six weeks, while Lozoff signed Conway and handled the problem of tests, casting, wardrobe, art, sets and advance publicity, I worked on the scenario.

By the time we were ready to turn the crank, it was mid-November, and our delivery date was February 1.

But we had our story, and it was a good one. I knew it without being told, although I *was* told.

"This is what I talked about a long time ago," Lozoff exulted. "An honest picture. Realism *and* imagination. Now we get to work."

So we set up our shooting schedule, checked the sets and arranged their sequence of construction, arranged rehearsals, then chopped the scenes up into a new order for actual filming.

About this time Lucille Hilton came down with a case of grippe, which meant we'd have to shoot around her if we wanted to start without delay. So we rearranged the shooting schedule accordingly. This meant Lozoff had to get up on his part at once. His costumes weren't ready. The wardrobe people went into overtime.

Research now came up with a few problems concerning our police station set. Changes were made. Lucille Hilton came sniffling back to the

Studio. And when she returned, Arch Taylor, who was working on titles, sprained his ankle playing golf. I took over for him.

Total so far: five thousand man-hours, six thousand cups of black coffee, seven thousand cigarettes.

And then the shooting started.

Lozoff worked from the middle to the end. Then he jumped to the beginning, skipped a few scenes (we wanted to kill off the old pawnbroker and her sister first, in order to take them off salary) and then we went to the end again.

We looked at rushes, and Lozoff insisted on editing as he went along—he wanted fades, dissolves and inserts to work with.

Arch Taylor came back to help me with the titles.

George Conway got a rash that covered his entire left cheek and jaw. We shot around him and did the street scenes, with a double in the long shots.

It was the end of December, now, and the parties began. We shut down for a week over Christmas holidays. Lucille Hilton went to Agua Caliente with Emerson Craig. Lozoff and I spent the time rewriting the sequences between the student and Sonia.

Somebody from the front office suddenly discovered that Sonia was a prostitute. Glazer came back and wanted to know what the hell? We showed him the scenes. He was afraid of the Hays people. We told him he had the soul of an accountant and rewrote the sequences again.

Then it was January, and we rolled once more. Lozoff began to look funny in the rushes. He weighed himself and discovered why—he'd lost twelve pounds so far.

A heavy rainstorm leaked in on the tenement set and the roof cracked. We held up shooting for two days while the damage was repaired. Lucille Hilton fainted on the set after the twenty-fourth retake of her big scene.

So much for the glamorous side of the motion picture business.

But Lozoff was merciless. If Harker had been a tyrant, and I had been a pseudo-Harker, Lozoff was autocracy incarnate. He got something out of Hilton I'd never suspected she had—but it was something I'd tried to put into the script.

He did the same for Conway and for the character actress who played the role of Sonia's mother. And then he went to work on himself. He knew what he wanted to do with the inspector, and he did it. No more evening dress, no more bowing from the waist, no more urbanity. He was Porfiry—but not until retake after retake.

They brought in the machines that made fog, and shot the scenes at the river, where Sonia and the student decide to go to the police. Thirty-three times, and the scene was short.

But Jackie Keeley happened to wander onto the set during the final take, and when he saw it, he cried.

There were times, during the cat-and-mouse sequences between

Porfiry and Raskolnikov, when I found myself clenching my hands until the nails pierced the flesh. And when I saw the opening reel—the entire footage leading up to the murder, where Raskolnikov's face is never shown; only his back or hands, or shadow—it made something tighten all along my spine.

Then I knew it was worth it. We were making a great picture, the one I'd always dreamed about.

And finally, one day in the third week of January, I saw it all.

The air in the projection room was blue with smoke. I could smell Morris's cigar, the distinctive odor of Lozoff's cigarette, Arch Taylor's pipe. Over the dull whirring of the projector I caught the rhythmic snick and smack of Nicky's mastication as he chomped his way through the twelve rough-cut reels of *Crime and Punishment*. From time to time I heard a scraping sound as Salem or Lucille Hilton shifted in their seats. Once George Conway cracked his knuckles, and Treedom, the cameraman, had a coughing spell. But I kept my eyes on the screen.

Then, abruptly, the screen went blank and somebody snapped on the lights. Lozoff put away his pen and closed his notebook. Morris found a fresh cigar. There was silence.

Somebody had to say it. I think Taylor opened his mouth first. "Well?"

"You were right." Treedom turned to Lozoff. "It has to go just the way it is. Twelve reels."

Bernie Glazer nodded at the director. "A masterpiece. I wouldn't change a foot of it."

Lozoff smiled. It was hot in the little room, and he was perspiring. He stared at Sol Morris, waiting. Morris examined the end of his cigar. I could see that he was sweating, too—and then I realized something else. *He* was waiting.

Salem stood up and walked to the front of the room. His shadow moved across the blank screen. He smiled at Morris.

"I'd like to say a few words," he murmured. "With your permission."

"Go right ahead, Lester." It was *Lester*, now.

"Thank you." The smile broadened now to include all of us.

"First of all, I feel I owe somebody an apology. When Mr. Lozoff came to us with the intention of making his picture, I was opposed to it. Although I have a feeling of reverence for the classics and I respect Mr. Lozoff's ability, I thought this film would be a mistake. But you people who know me and work with me realize one thing—I'm man enough to admit it when I'm wrong. And I was wrong about *Crime and Punishment*. You did a magnificent job, Lozoff, a magnificent job! Acting *and* directing."

"Thank you."

"That goes for everyone connected with the production. Miss Hilton, your work is terrific. Mr. Conway—I congratulate you on a performance that's going to make motion picture history. Mr. Treedom, you and Mr.

Besserer and the rest of the crew have come through with a great piece
of photography. Don't you agree, Mr. Morris? Nicky?"

"He said it would be a winner." Sol Morris put the cigar back in his
mouth and smiled happily.

"Got to hand it to you, pal," nodded Nicky.

"There is just one thing I take exception to," Salem continued. "Mr.
Treedom. You made the remark that you wouldn't change a foot of the
film."

Treedom tugged at his mustache. "Well, that was just a way of putting
it, you might say. We've got a lot of extra footage—if you or Mr. Lozoff
wants to go another reel or so, if you want to make a couple of substitu-
tions—"

"That's not what I mean," Salem told him. "I'm sure the editing has
been excellent. And I like what Mr. Taylor and Mr. Post did with their
titles." He smiled at me. "Unfortunately, it's largely a case of love's labor
lost."

"You want to run it without titles, like *The Last Laugh*?" I asked. "But—"

"No. I want to run it without titles, but *with* sound."

"Sound?" Lozoff sat up straight.

Lester Salem nodded. "Perhaps the matter has escaped your attention,"
he said. "You creative people sometimes bury yourselves entirely in the
work of the moment, I know. But speaking as a businessman, I can tell
you I've been keeping my eyes open throughout the past year—and my
ears, too. And I'm convinced the sound picture, the talking picture, is
really here to stay.

"I've got a few figures here on the grosses from Warner's and Fox and
the independents. They're really quite surprising. And that's not just my
opinion. MGM and United Artists and the others are getting into this
thing. Paramount, too. They tell me Westinghouse can't keep up with the
orders—theaters are converting to sound all over the country. We can't
afford to miss the boat."

"Isn't it a rather expensive gamble?" Arch Taylor asked.

"Expensive, yes. A gamble—no. The past months prove you can't lose
with a talkie. The public wants voices and we've got to give them what
they ask for."

He leaned over the back of the front row, talking earnestly. "This isn't
just an offhand opinion. It's something I've already talked over with Mr.
Morris at great length. It's something my people are prepared to back up
with cold cash. As a matter of fact, we *have* backed it up. With Mr. Morris's
permission—right, Mr. Morris?—I think I can tell you a loan has already
been negotiated. We're ready to invest three million dollars in preparing
this Studio for talking picture production. Plus another two million to
convert our own theaters and publicize the fact. Next week we'll shut
down for the entire month of February and let the technicians go to work.

During that time we can get ready to resume shooting on *Crime and Punishment* and our other scheduled releases as talkies.

"Mr. Lozoff, you'll have all the cooperation I can give you. You'll have the aid of trained engineers, sound experts. We'll be using new equipment, microphones. It's going to be a big job, but I know you can do it. The picture will be a sensation."

Lozoff gripped the arms of his seat. "I disagree," he said, softly. "First of all, I must correct you on one point. I am not unaware of these new developments in the sound film. I know what has happened here in Hollywood during the past year or more. I have seen Mr. Jolson and Miss McAvoy, and heard them. I attended *The Lights of New York*, and *Abie's Irish Rose*, *Mother Knows Best*, *The Terror*, the rest of the releases. There is only one fault to be found with them. One and all, they stink."

Lester Salem opened his mouth, but Lozoff wasn't finished. "Inevitably, talkies will replace the silent films. There will be some wonderful advances. But all this is several years in the future. We won't be ready in a month, or in six months."

Salem shrugged impatiently. "We can't let the others get the jump on us."

Lozoff nodded. "I'm all in favor of starting now, converting the Studio to sound. Turn out the photographed stage plays, the films with singing and dancing. Experiment a little with part-talkies. That's good business. But don't try to change *Crime and Punishment*."

"I understand how you feel." Salem was smiling again. "But what I propose can't possibly harm the picture, only improve it. We'll merely reshoot some of the sequences with dialogue, add a sound-effects track, give the public something to really rave about."

"*Merely*." Lozoff sighed. "I wish it were that simple! For example, in those scenes you saw between the inspector and the student—"

"Exactly what I was talking about!" Salem broke in. "Think of what dialogue would do there, to bring everything out."

Lozoff shook his head. "Those scenes were created in terms of pantomime. With your recording apparatus in its present stage of development, pantomime is virtually impossible. The microphone is stationary—performers must remain motionless in order to have their voices picked up properly. This means the camera is immobile, too. Every change in shooting, from close-up to long shot, requires a complete change of electrical setup. And that's only the beginning.

"The microphone magnifies and distorts the slightest rustle of cloth, the squeak of shoes, offstage noises. That's something we can learn to control. Directors and actors must work in silence. Actors must memorize lines, and there'll be more exacting rehearsals. Scripts will be different. These things we can and must learn. Once a picture is *written* the new way—so that sound and dialogue play their proper parts to bring out dramatic values-we'll overcome the mechanical obstacles.

"But what you propose now is out of the question. Here's one basic difficulty. These sound cameras photograph at a speed of ninety feet a minute. Our present cameras shoot at sixty. Actors are conditioned to this speed; their entire technique must change or else they'll appear slow. Scenes will drag until they learn to make the transition—and you can't expect them to do so overnight. Another thing, we have no way of predicting how the voices of our cast will record."

Salem turned away. "We're set up to handle those problems," he said. "We'll have voice coaches, stage directors, playwrights from the East. The engineers will know how to mix the sound. Don't worry."

"But I am worried." Lozoff walked over to Sol Morris. "You see what I mean, don't you? This picture was conceived in terms of silent techniques. It tells its story through pictorial values, pantomime. And it's perfect. Don't you agree?"

Morris nodded slowly. "We never made a better one," he said.

"Then why change it? Why rip it up, break the mood. I came to you and begged for a chance to make this picture. I promised you a fine job, and I haven't failed. Now I ask you to let it stand."

He turned to face us all. "And as for business—this film will make money. There's still a market for a good silent picture, will be for at least another year."

Lozoff's glance included Salem now. "Look, Mr. Salem. From now on, I'll go along with you. I'll work with sound. It's something I want to do, it's a challenge to me. I don't promise my unit will turn film out as fast or as soon as the others, because I want time to study and experiment. I want to do nothing but the best.

"But I can promise you just that. And in return, I ask only one thing. Let *Crime and Punishment* stand. Release it. I know it will find an audience. It will bring you a profit, it will bring you praise and prestige. This picture means something to me. It represents everything I know, everything I believe in. And I say to you, honestly and sincerely, you are wrong. Sound cannot improve it, only spoil it. It is a *silent* picture."

Lester Salem shook his head.

Lozoff's forehead was wet. "Mr. Morris—"

Sol Morris lowered his face. "I'm sorry," he said. "That's up to Mr. Salem."

"I see."

We all saw, then. *Three million to prepare the Studio. Two million to convert the theaters.* Salem had paid the piper and he was calling the tune.

"Getting late, gentlemen," he said, glancing at his watch. "I suggest we postpone further discussion until tomorrow. We'll be fresh, then, and perhaps Mr. Lozoff will feel better if he sleeps on this idea. After all, the important thing to remember is, we have to keep up with the times." He smiled, walking over to the door. "One thing has already changed. As I said just the other day at the Association Luncheon, that old motto—*Silence is Golden*—has been erased from the copybooks."

We filed out, moving slowly.

Arch Taylor's pipe bobbed beside me as he bent his head and murmured in my ear. "Yeah, that's right. We've got a new motto, now. *Money talks.*"

TWENTY-FOUR

IN FEBRUARY the Studio closed down for the changeover. This gave me a breathing-spell and a chance to look around. But I didn't breathe easier, and what I saw wasn't pleasant.

The panic was on, the handwriting was over Hollywood, the lid was off the Brown Derby. Sound was here, with a vengeance.

Goodbye Jannings, Nissen, Langdon, Pringle, Billie Dove! Some of them would hang around, hang on for a couple of years yet—but the curtain was coming down. Goodbye, then, to John Gilbert and D. W. Griffith and the Sennett Bathing Beauties. Farewell to the little Wampas girls and to the big girls like Pola and Vilma and Baclanova.

And hello John Boles, Warner Baxter, Lawrence Gray! Welcome Tibbett and roll out the red soundtrack for Ruth Chatterton! A nice fat raise for Marie Dressler and Conrad Nagel, a big boost for the Barrymore brothers, and congratulations to Norma Shearer and the rest whose voices came through clearly.

Watch those musicals, they're going to be BIG! Listen to that *Broadway Melody*, everybody. Maybe we can get Wynn and Cantor and George M. Cohan out here—they didn't set the world on fire in silents, but we can use 'em now. Look at the way Jolson is cleaning up. Understand Mayer is signing an m.c. named Jack Benny. Who are these Four Marx Brothers you hear about? They say Chaplin won't talk, but Doug and Mary and Gloria are going along with it.

Did you hear what happened to Gloria and Erich on *Queen Kelly*? What's the word over at Universal, will Uncle Carl be ready? Fox is out to corner the market—Gaynor and Farrell are set for a musical. Anybody know anything about El Brendel, Roscoe Ates, Benny Rubin? Here they come, get set, everybody!

Get set for the Chief and the Twentieth Century, get those extra porters out to carry bags for the dialogue directors and the dramatic coaches and the diction specialists. Reserve those tables at the Troc for the New York play doctors, the booking agents who can find the talent, yank the acts off Orpheum Time. And don't forget a box of cigars for the engineers. Without the engineers, we're licked! Thank God we can always get another loan from the banks—this is costing real money, but wait until we hit Main Street with our new, jazzed-up version of *Way Down East—All Talking, All Singing, All Dancing*!

I looked around and I saw what was happening, heard what was happening. There was a new threat called RKO, and the voice of Vitaphone thundered in the land. Fox had gone Movietone, Hollywood had gone—

Hollywood had gone.

I looked in vain for the once familiar figures; the cameramen with their caps turned backwards; the directors in puttees, the mood musicians, the beard-wearing bums on the extra-bench. They were suddenly dated and departed, like the Keystone Cops. In a few years they'd be cameos or caricatures of a dim and distant past.

Where was Harker; where was Karl Druse?

Druse hadn't signed anywhere for another picture. Maybe he was ill, as the rumors said.

As for Harker, I'd scarcely given him a thought. *Mankind* hadn't done too well at the box office, and he hadn't announced a new production. But that wasn't the real reason I didn't think about him.

I didn't think about him because I didn't *need* him any more. The dream of Dawn had vanished, and the dream of a father was discarded, too. I'd learned, at last, that his advice was best. Forget the past.

Maybe I wasn't his son, after all. I could have gone back to Kate LaBuddie, searched out the astrologer, checked and verified. But it didn't matter any more. It was part of the past.

That's why Harker laughed at me; he could see the absurdity of my attempt to resurrect a dead reality. And I was no longer angry with him for laughing, because I understood.

Suppose he was my father, what then? Suppose Teddy Harker had married little Connie back there in the carny days? Suppose he'd settled down with a wife and a kid, given up his delusions of grandeur and tried to make a living?

Chances are, he'd have stuck with the carnival—had to stick with it. Selling patent medicine, doubling in brass as a spieler. Maybe he'd have taken a winter job somewhere, as a filling station attendant or a grocery clerk (takes money to feed three over the layoff season, and what kind of skilled work can a carny get?).

I could see him as he might have been, and I could see myself. That was the clincher—I could see myself. There wouldn't have been any Hollywood for Harker if he'd stuck, and there wouldn't have been any Hollywood for me.

No, it was all for the best. All for the best that Theodore Harker had followed his flamboyant fancies into the future, believed in stars and destiny and dreams.

I couldn't complain. If it came to a choice, I'd rather be Tom Post than Tom Harker any day—because Tom Post was sharing the big dream. Hadn't I written myself into that last picture, just as I'd always promised I would?

That was the important thing, the only important thing. No sense searching for phantom fathers, worrying about people in the past. They were phantoms, too. You couldn't believe in them. You could only believe in yourself, in what you were doing. The way I believed in *Crime and Punishment*.

I made up my mind, and then Lozoff and I went to work again. We had plenty of time.

It was the middle of March before they actually got the Studio open again, and the first week in April before they'd done tests of Lozoff, Conway and Hilton. Lozoff's voice was surprisingly good, with just a touch of accent. Conway sounded effeminate, and Hilton might just as well had gone over to Disney and dubbed-in for Mickey Mouse.

"That's it!" Lester Salem said, when he heard the soundtracks. "We'll dub for Conway and Hilton. Get a couple of good people out here from New York. Right?"

I didn't say anything. I'd spent a little time chumming around with a few of my friends, men who were already doing dialogue and talkie scripts. I thought I could handle the technique all right, but I wasn't up on dub-ins.

"Come on over to my office," Salem suggested. "Nicky's there. The four of us can get our plans set."

"What about Mr. Morris?" Lozoff asked.

"He's asked me to handle this." Salem's voice was bland.

I glanced at Lozoff but said nothing. There was nothing to say. We followed Lester Salem down the corridor.

"Don't worry about a thing," he said. "Just go right ahead and show me what you can turn out."

"It's all done," I answered. "I handed it in two days ago. Didn't know what sequences you planned on doing in sound, so I just went straight through from beginning to end—wrote dialogue for the entire thing. All you have to do is select what you want. Lozoff and I have been running that print for weeks, studying it."

Lozoff nodded in agreement. "Maybe it can be done," he murmured. "With dub-in, we won't have to reshoot any scenes. Just add the soundtrack. I have in mind a composer, a friend of mine—he has done some very fine things. He could write a musical score."

Salem waved us into his office. Nicky sat there, glancing up in greeting as we entered.

"Sit down," Salem said. Then, to me. "I'm afraid you don't understand. I've read your dialogue, yes. It's good, but it won't fit."

"What's wrong—too talky?"

"No." He hesitated. "I was meaning to tell you this before, but there's been so much to do that it slipped my mind. Anyway, I've gone over the whole proposition here with Nicky, and we've decided on a few changes. We'll dub in the voices all the way, but we'll shoot some additional scenes."

It was very quiet there in his office, and the sound of Nicky's cud was all too audible.

Lozoff looked at him, then at me, then at Lester Salem. "What did you have in mind?" he asked, softly.

"Well, I don't pretend to be an expert, you understand, just a business-man. Nicky and I have made pictures together for several years now, but we certainly can't claim to be in *your* class. Nevertheless, our modest little efforts have made money for the Studio. Because we have learned something about audience appeal. And with all due respect to you, Mr. Lozoff, there's one thing your picture lacks. Nicky put his finger right on it."

"What is missing?"

Nicky stopped chewing and slapped his hand on the desk. "Comedy relief, that's what! Whole damned thing's like a funeral or something. I'm kinda surprised at you, Lozoff—an oldtimer in the game and everything. You ought to know you can't feed the public a tearjerker like this without a comic in there someplace!"

Salem smiled. "Tell them what we planned, Nicky."

"Sure. We got to thinking, and it's a natural. I never read the book or nothing, but it seems to me like we could give this here Raskinikoff or whatever his name is—that's another thing I wanted to mention, we're gonna change his name to something people can pronounce—but any-ways, we can give him a few scenes with his buddy. You know, one of these wise guys, maybe an Eddie Quillan type. Only with an accent, to show he's Russian, see?"

Nicky glanced at me. "You can work out some kind of a running gag, can't you, Post? Maybe this guy is always hungry, moaning for *borscht*. Or he's a vodka-hound, a real character. And—hey, here's a twist—maybe he's got a lot of stuff hocked with this old babe, this pawnbroker, and he thinks the cops are looking for *him* instead of the other guy. So whenever the inspector comes around, he quick beats it and hides under the bed. Some gimmick like that, give the folks a chance to laugh once in a while, get me?"

"I get you," I said.

"And another thing, while we're on the subject," Salem interposed. "Introducing dialogue brings out a new element. We might have shown the Russian background without comment in a silent film. But in a talkie, it's not safe. I don't want to see us open to criticism here. So when we write the lines, we'll have to inject a subtle note. To show the barbarity of the Bolsheviks, the fallacy of the Communist doctrine."

"But this picture is not laid in present-day Russia," Lozoff said. "There were no Communists at that time."

"Which reminds me." Salem paced the floor. "One more point. We're using sound. That's modern. The whole trend today is to the present, to new things. Suppose we set this picture up in a frame —tell a story within a story, you might say. We can open with a modern sequence; perhaps an old man, an immigrant maybe, telling his grandchildren about the way it used to be in the old country." He paused and raised a finger. "I've got it! Why not show Raskolnikov himself, thirty years after? He's served his time in Siberia, married Sonia, come to America—to start a new life in a new world. And he has these children, or grandchildren. And he tells them the whole story, in a flashback. Then we close with a modern sequence again, where he tells them crime doesn't pay and the American Way of Life is superior to anything the Czar or the Commies can ever offer. In other words, a happy ending."

"Swell!" Nicky grinned up at him. "That takes care of everything, wraps it all up. You hit it that time!"

Salem squared his shoulders. He put his hand to his chest. "As I said, gentlemen, I don't pretend to be in the same class with your creative geniuses. But experience has shown me one thing. When I feel it here"— the hand pressed the heart, then suddenly extended—"the box office feels it out there!"

"So that's the way we're gonna do it," Nicky said. "Yes sir!"

Lozoff stood up. He seemed very short, standing next to Lester Salem. "I don't suppose you'd be interested in hearing my objections?" he asked.

"Of course I would." Salem put his hand on Lozoff's shoulder. "Only right now, we must take time into consideration. We haven't a moment to spare, we're months behind on everything. I'd like to see a new script ready within a week. We'll want to shoot the new scenes as quickly as possible."

"In other words, you're going ahead with it just the way you told us? With the comedian and the modern sequences?"

Salem nodded. "I think it's best."

Lozoff took a deep breath, and it was queer to see a corpse breathing.

"Then I wish you luck," he said, tonelessly. "But I advise you to find another director, and another New York actor to dub in my voice. I am afraid I must bow out."

"See?" Nicky slapped the desk again. "I told you he'd get his bowels in an uproar!"

Salem ignored young Morris. "I'm sorry you feel this way," he told Lozoff. "But I quite understand. And if you don't think you can go along with us 100%, then perhaps it's for the best."

"Thank you." Lozoff started for the door. Salem turned to me immediately. "Now, about the script changes and the dialogue we want from you—"

I stood up. I didn't feel like a corpse. I felt very much alive.

"You know what you can do with your picture," I said.

Salem stared. "Look, Post, you're a young man. You can't afford to take this attitude. Mr. Lozoff here, with all due respect, has had his day. Maybe he can go back to Europe, take a job directing there. That's his business. But your business is to play ball with us, for the sake of your future."

"I'm sorry," I said. "But my answer stands. I don't care to think of my future as some sort of ballgame."

Lester Salem frowned. "You don't like me, do you, Post?"

"That has nothing to do with it. The important thing, first last and always, is the picture. That's all I know about, all I've ever learned."

"Well, it's time you so-called artists learned something else," Salem declared. "Movies are an industry, and we on the executive end must remember that. Try to think of it from my angle, Post. I'm not in business for my health."

I nodded. "Why is it that your kind always makes that statement, says it as if it were something clever? Why *aren't* you in business for your health, and everybody's health? Must it always be profit—over health, self-respect, sanity?"

Salem had stopped smiling, and for a moment his lips drew back. I noted that Lester Salem had very bad teeth. "Now see here, Post, you're on salary—"

"I was." I moved over to join Lozoff at the door. "But I imagine you'll correct that, after the first of the month."

I made a little bow. It was nowhere as good as one of Lozoff's: a poor effort, but my own.

"Good afternoon, gentlemen."

Lozoff and I walked out into the slanting sunshine. The lot was swarming with people—no actors, but plenty of stagehands carting equipment; no extras, but a multiplicity of electricians. Everything looked strange.

Arch Taylor waved his hand at us from the doorway of one of the new soundstages, and ambled over.

"Well," he began, "how'd it go? Everything straightened out all right? You come to an understanding?"

"We did." Kurt Lozoff smiled. "We understand one another perfectly now, Mr. Salem and I."

"He's walking out," I said.

"Quitting?"

"Or being fired." I smiled. "Me too."

"Fight?"

"No fight. Only Kurt won't make the changes. And I won't write a part for Skeets Gallagher or Ned Sparks into the script."

"But you can't!" Taylor wasn't smiling now. "Look, I don't know how it is with Kurt, here. Maybe he's saved his dough. But you haven't got enough to quit on."

"I'll get by. I've got some property out in Encino—"

"Don't kid yourself. I understand how you feel. Hell, when I see some of the stinkers they've got lined up for me to work on I could almost cry, if it wasn't so funny. But I want to stay in this business—even if sound has turned into a racket. And Kurt was right when he said things won't always be like this. They'll learn. They'll change."

"Not Salem," I answered. "He'll never change. Maybe some other studio—"

"You won't have a prayer at another studio," Taylor told me. "You and Lozoff both. Salem will spread the word."

"Sorry," I said. "That's the way it's got to be, then. Come on, Kurt."

"Wait!" Taylor called after us. "Where are you going?"

I didn't answer him.

I didn't answer him, because I didn't know.

TWENTY-FIVE

CRIME AND PUNISHMENT was released on the third week of July. Lozoff's name stayed on it as director, but I didn't get writing credit. I was just as glad, for the picture—with sound—was a resounding flop.

Lozoff and I didn't go to the premiere. As a matter of fact, we weren't even invited. We caught it later, downtown, in a regular showing that August. The big house had been "wired for sound" and we sat there, uncomfortably aware of the dubbed-in voices. Salem had been at work, cutting down on Lozoff's scenes, building up his "modern" introduction and closing sequences. A brash young comic named Flip Kelly was ever so funny as Raskolnikov's (I beg your pardon, Ivan's) pal, and it was he who discovered the murdered pawnbroker and her sister and did a comedy pratfall down three flights of stairs. But the crowning touch, to me, lay in the prelude and epilogue, as the aged hero told his story to his grandchildren. The part of the oldest grandson was played by Buddie LaBuddie.

Afterwards, Lozoff and I took a walk. We ended up on a bench in Pershing Square.

"Pretty bad, wasn't it?"

Lozoff said nothing.

"Guess this is where we end up. On a park bench, with the rest of the bums."

Lozoff didn't answer.

"They sure cut the hell out of it. Wouldn't know it was the same picture."

Lozoff was silent.

"Why, they could still run your original print as an entirely new production."

Lozoff kept still.

"Oh, what's the use? We did our best and it wasn't enough. Taylor was right—all we got was the gate. I've been trying to get in all over, and nobody wants me. Might as well face it. We're through."

"No we're not." Lozoff raised his head and his jaw tightened. "What you said about the original print makes sense, Tommy. It gives me an idea."

He faced me, suddenly alert. "Why can't I go to Morris and tell him what to do? He can release our original film for showing in all the theaters that aren't equipped for sound yet. He can play it abroad, in the European market. Salem can't object to that—as he would say, it's good business."

"You think Morris will listen to you?"

"We're still good friends, I trust, even though I'm no longer with the Studio. Why not? It's worth trying. I have faith in what we've done, Tommy. And once this picture is shown, you'll see."

"I hope you're right."

"I'll make an appointment with him tomorrow."

So I went back to my apartment and waited. Three days passed before Lozoff phoned.

"Well?" I asked. "How'd you make out?"

"I didn't. At first he said it was a good idea. But he would have to think it over."

"That means he had to talk to Salem, first. And Salem queered it."

"Evidently."

"What did Morris say when you saw him again?"

Lozoff paused. Then, "I never got to see him again. He was too busy, they said. But Betty had a message for me, out in front. Mr. Morris was sorry, but he had decided against releasing the film as I suggested. That was all."

"Why, that dirty—"

"Please, do not upset yourself on my account. I'll be all right. It's you I am thinking about. We'll have to get together some day soon and see what we can plan."

"Fine," I said. "Let's do that. But don't worry. I'm in good shape."

I hung up. Then I got to wondering just what kind of shape I really was in. Time to take inventory. New car, good for at least three or four years. Good wardrobe. Some furniture—nothing fancy, but adequate. An excellent library and a good Victrola. The addresses of a reliable bootlegger and a reputable call-house. A couple of lots out in Encino. Plus—let's see now—$17,000 in the bank.

I began to think about my next move. The world was full of jobs, but I wasn't qualified for anything outside of movie work. Even if I was, I needed contacts. And I had no contacts, except for motion pictures. The only acquaintances I'd made were movie people.

Now I remembered what Dawn had told me. About the real world, the world of a hundred and twenty million people. The world I'd never bothered to find out about, because it wasn't important to me. She saw it, she had broken away and found a place in that world. She had been right, was right, all the time.

I couldn't go to her now, but what she said came to me. She was helping me now, telling me that I'd be a fool to dramatize myself, indulge in self-pity. I had those lots, and the money. I'd find something to do. And I could start immediately.

There was the stock market. Wall Street was going great, in August, 1929. Plenty of easy money to be made for the asking. Seventeen grand, buying on margin, would go a long way—

No. Not for me. Wall Street was too far off. I needed something I could watch, something close at hand. Like those lots in Encino.

Well, real estate, then. I could buy on mortgage. Worth looking into, at any rate, and I had nothing else to do.

I started nosing around. In the end, it wasn't a question of mortgages. I put $10,000 into six more lots. Corner properties, intersections, improved.

I still had enough capital left to build, if I wanted to. That was another idea to toy with—how about putting up a house, maybe a small building of some kind on one of the double lots? Perhaps I could go into business.

Six months ago I would have told myself it was crazy. Now, in September, I was sitting up nights reading the Business For Sale columns, running down leads, actually working at it. And (I told myself) I loved it. Hadn't felt better in two years. The addresses of the reliable bootlegger and the reputable call-house rested untouched in the drawer. And I hadn't heard from anyone in the movie colony for almost a month.

I was out most of the time, anyway, running down leads. One day in mid-September I drove over to Pasadena to look at a filling station that was up for sale in a residential section. I had a little trouble finding it, and I wasn't exactly eager to go into the gas business, but I worked on the theory that it paid to look around. Never know what you might run into.

I parked across the street from it and examined the corner before getting out, checking traffic flow. Then I glanced down the block. I eyed the neat array of white bungalows and green lawns—prosaic pearls in an emerald setting. A few houses down, a woman was hanging up the wash in the side yard. I watched the breeze whip the clothing high, saw the woman pause and run her hand across her forehead, just the way that—

You never know what you might run into.

I got out of the car, crossed the street, walked into the yard.

"Thursday," I said. "Don't you know Monday is supposed to be the day for washing?"

She looked up.

"Tom!"

"Hello, Dawn."

"What in the world—"

"Just passing by," I said. "Looking at Nelson's filling station, down the block. You know him?"

She nodded. "Ken does."

"Ken?"

"My husband."

"Oh." I smiled. "Hard for me to think of you as an old married lady."

"Do I look different?"

"Well, not really. Put on a few pounds, I'd say, but it went to the right places. Of course, I've never seen you in a housedress before."

"You're not likely to see me in anything else, these days. But come on inside, sit down."

"What about the wash?"

"I'm finished, can't you see? You're not the domestic type at all."

I didn't answer her. We walked up the back steps, into the kitchen.

"Don't mind the mess. It's always like this. I hate to do the dishes on washday. Let's go into the parlor."

The parlor was small. Brown rug, a three-piece suite, some floor lamps, a table with a radio and loudspeaker. There was a gas log in the fireplace, and over the mantel was one of those Spanish galleons.

"Ken made this," she told me, noticing my stare. "It's a hobby of his—building model ships."

I said nothing.

"Aren't you going to sit down?"

"I've got to be running along in a minute," I said. "Just wanted to say hello."

"Couldn't you stay for dinner? I know Ken would love to meet you."

"No, thanks."

"Tom, is everything all right? I hear you're not with the Studio any more."

"Everything's fine." I hesitated. "I've got something else on the fire now."

"Pictures?"

"I can't talk about it yet. But don't worry. I'm doing okay."

"I'm glad to hear that. Things are fine with me, too."

"Are they?" I shook my head.

"What's the matter?"

"That's what I want to know," I said. "I don't understand this. You, in a housedress, hanging up underwear. Dishes in the sink. Sitting here listening to the radio night after night, while he's futzing around with a tweezers, making model ships."

Dawn giggled. Then, all at once, she wasn't giggling any more.

"I wish you *could*," she said. "I wish you could understand. This is it. This is what I want."

"Oh no it's not," I murmured.

She nodded. "It's something real. Can't you see that?"

"Real? What the hell's the difference between building ship models and creating a motion picture? Who's going to get excited about it when he finishes one of these jobs—the neighbors who come in for a bridge game once a week?"

I stood up and put my hands on her shoulders. "This isn't right for you, Dawn," I said. My hands tightened, I could feel the flesh, the familiar flesh beneath the dress. "My God, you don't know what it's been like for me, two years now, and every moment of it—"

Suddenly my hands were empty. She stepped back, only a foot, but she was a million miles away.

"I know about that part, too. But the answer is still the same, for me. There's nothing wrong. I made a choice, and I'm not sorry. Ken's okay. You'd like him—no, don't scowl that way, I mean it. And I've always wanted kids." She smiled. "That's right. I'm pregnant. Just a little bit pregnant, now, but it'll be April."

"Congratulations," I said.

"You'll have to come and see us," she told me. "When you have time."

"Yeah, of course. I'll do that."

We were outside again. The sun made me blink. She was blinking a little, too.

"Got to get back," I said. "There's a deal cooking."

"What's all this about a filling station?" she asked.

"Oh, that. Just a sideline. Picking up a few pieces of property here and there. But you know me—the movies are the main thing. And this time I'll surprise everyone. Wait and see."

"I will. Good luck, Tom."

"Good luck." I smiled. "Say, I never kissed the bride."

Then she was in my arms, and the clothes were shipping at my face, one of Ken's sleeves slapping against my cheek. But I didn't care, because it was still true, it was still the same, it would always be the same for me. *I'll always love you, never forget that . . .*

I walked away. She waved, and the sleeves were waving, too.

Then I climbed into the car and drove away. I didn't stop to look at the filling station. *Damn it,* I thought, *why try to fool yourself? You still want the movies, don't you? And you've got to get back in, Poverty Row, anywhere. You've got to show them all, show her—*

When I got back to the apartment, the phone was ringing. I opened the door and picked up the receiver.

"Post speaking."

"Good afternoon. This is Theodore Harker."

He didn't have to tell me. I'd never forget *that* voice.

". . . may be a bit awkward under the circumstances, but I'd appreciate it if you could join me this evening for a little discussion which might be of mutual interest. If you are not otherwise engaged, of course."

"Certainly. I'd be glad to."

"Excellent. Eight o'clock then, at my home. You know how to get here."

TWENTY-SIX

I KNEW HOW to get there. The way hadn't changed, and when I entered the canyon I realized nothing else had changed, either. The hacienda loomed ahead, the rambler roses ran riot along the wall, the two pools glittered in the moonlight.

The real live butler was still there, his real live sideburns untouched by the graying fingers of Time. The fireplaces blazed, the Salukis prowled the halls, the living room still displayed its divans and tapestry.

But the butler led me straight down the hall to the dining room, with its mahogany table and its thirty chairs. Not all of the chairs were occupied, but enough to again remind me that nothing had changed. Because we were together once more.

I stared at the familiar faces, saluting and securing answering smiles. Here was Kurt Lozoff, the white streak a trifle wider across his scalp, but trim and erect as ever. Here was Karl Druse, somber eyes sunken into his skull, yet still clinging to the ridiculous incongruity of his corncob. Here, surprisingly, was Jackie Keeley, with that incredibly childish face and that incredibly ancient smile. Here—another surprise!—was Emerson Craig, and the paunchy actor who had played Nero in those far-off days when Rome had fallen. The only stranger was the tall woman with the touch of gray in her hair, the tall woman with the ageless eyes. Suddenly I recognized Maybelle Manners.

Then I saw the man sitting in the armchair at the head of the table, and everything was assured. The white-faced shadow was the same. Long black hair, black brows, the dark dominance of the eyes. The flowing collar, the tie, the black suit— Time had not dimmed, nor custom staled, their infinite monotony.

Monotony? Infinite excitement, as Theodore Harker rose and held out his hand in greeting.

"A pleasure to see you. Won't you find a chair? Rogers, bring Mr. Post something to drink. No? Then we shall proceed. I was waiting for you."

I tried to read something into the words, into the eyes. It wasn't there. This wasn't the man who'd laughed at me. This was Theodore Harker, the famous director. Nothing had changed.

As I seated myself next to Karl Druse, Harker remained standing. The thin lips parted, the long fingers splayed across the tabletop.

"I have taken a great liberty in calling you here tonight," he began. "And I shall take an even greater liberty now, by speaking frankly."

The Shakespearean pause, and a slow, searching scrutiny of the silent faces. Then:

"This meeting would have created a sensation just three short years ago. The press and photographers would have been present. Yet tonight we sit alone, surrounded by silence. Or shall we say, we sit alone, surrounded by sound?

"That is why we are here, my friends. Why try to deny it? Sound has come to Hollywood—and we have departed. The truth is that none of us has departed willingly. We have been cast out; some of us eased, some of us rudely ejected."

Harker pushed back his chair, standing tall and towering.

"They say we're finished. They say times have changed—there's no longer a place for a great director, a great character actor, a great comedian, a distinguished leading lady, a talented writer, a famous leading man. It's not that we're too old, it's merely that we're inarticulate. And when we would speak, they tell us to be silent, say that we belong to silence and therefore to the past.

"But we can, we will be heard. The time has come for us to speak up!"

So that's what it's all about, I thought. *A signed protest to the trade papers.*

"Less than ten years ago, Hollywood history was made when the Big Four—Pickford, Fairbanks, Chaplin and Griffith—formed the United Artists Corporation. Theirs was a great dream; to assemble the top talent of the screen in the finest productions.

"I call upon that dream once again—tonight—and I tell you we have the power to bring it into reality!"

Harker stood silent for a moment, hands folded. His voice was brisk, matter-of-fact. "What I propose is this. We, all of us, will incorporate as an independent motion picture production company. We will produce, release and distribute our own films through regular outlets in the United States and abroad.

"We'll start with sound—not talking pictures, but films with a musical background and sound effects. As we develop our technique, learn the new dimension of dialogue, we will produce talking pictures; perhaps within a year. I have spent much time analyzing the problem and I feel this is the correct solution, to make a graceful transition.

"Other have plunged in blindly, produced trash. We will not make their mistakes. We will make pictures meanwhile, instead. Great pictures. Great pictures with great names. We still have a public, a world-wide audience. We are not alone."

Jackie Keeley opened his mouth. Harker glanced at him and nodded. "I know what you're going to say. This costs money.

"I've done more than study this proposition. I have taken it before the proper people in New York. And I waited to call you until tonight—because I can now assure you of financial support. Unlimited financial support. We have our backing, guaranteed in writing. I lack nothing now but your cooperation and consent. What do you say—are you with me?"

What did we say? Were we with him? No cheerleader could have asked for a better response. Suddenly there was a babble of voices, a milling $m+l)e$ of handclasps, backslapping, smiles, gestures.

Everybody wanted a drink, now. Harker wandered from group to group; answering questions, resolving problems, anticipating arguments, stating solutions.

The moneyman's name was Breck. Reginald Breck. One of the biggest brokerage houses in the country. *Distribution*? Of course the big companies would fight us, but we could book through at least two chains already, and if necessary we'd set up our own. *Studio*? Build our plant, of course, as soon as we found a suitable location. We could break ground in November, get into limited production after the first of the year. *Executive staff*? That was important, there would be future conferences on just that point. *Publicity*? Of course, it was no secret—but for the present, not a word. Best to tie in the announcement with the location, once we found it. Besides, we could buy the land at a lower price if the purpose wasn't revealed. *Technical men*? That would be the next step—

I wandered through it all, sensing the overtones of elation, the summoning of hope, the parting with the past, the fixation upon the future.

". . . hardly believe it. I wouldn't want this to get around, but when he called I was just talking to the bank. I'm down to my last three hundred dollars. It's a miracle." So said Mona Lisa, Milady with the graying hair.

- ". . . got to hand it to the old boy. They can't write him off so easily. Wait until Parsons and Glint and the rest of them hear about *this* deal!" Thus Jackie Keeley.

". . . like old times again. Wouldn't it be wonderful if Griffith came in on this, and Chaplin? I had been thinking of Europe as a last resort. But this is perfect." According to Lozoff.

". . . given up hope. They didn't have anything for me anywhere. You know why. This man Salem and his vicious rumors, they're all whispering about me behind my back, don't think I haven't realized. He thought he could put me out of pictures. But he'll see. He and Morris. There'll be a day of reckoning now. It's coming, soon. We're going to be back where we belong when Salem is burning in hell. Just remember that." Karl Druse speaking, his voice subdued, his eyes unleashed.

". . . thought I was all through with this business, but now I can see it's only the beginning. This is what I want to do, this is where I belong." Myself talking, and meaning it.

And Harker, the walking silhouette, the silent shadow, smiling and moving about the room; truly the Great Director now, with an All-Star Cast assembled, ready to embark on his biggest production . . .

The night sped past, and the days sped by.

There was so much to do.

I went out to the San Fernando Valley with Druse and Lozoff and looked over the site Harker purchased for the studio. A hundred acres, plus an option on fifty more—twenty-five adjoining on either side.

"A little off the beaten track," Lozoff commented, "but I have confidence in Harker's judgment. He seems to think some of the big companies will be moving out this way as they expand. We'll have room to grow, here."

"Do you think we'll be able to start in January?" Druse asked.

"Well, you know how it always goes," I told him. "Bound to be some delays. Harker's out East now—he'll bring Mr. Breck back with him before the first of the month. But I think we're safer if we plan on the first of February as our tentative target date."

"I hope so." Druse gave me a wry smile. "Why it's over a year since I made my last picture." The smile disappeared. "Last picture! That's what Salem and Morris thought it would be, too. I can't wait to see the look on their faces when they find out."

Lozoff nodded. "I know how you feel, Karl. But this is a constructive move, not an act of revenge."

"Speak for yourself. I'm not turning the other cheek. Not after what they did to me, saying that I'm a drunkard, whispering about me as if I were some kind of freak. Do you want to know something? I haven't taken a drink since that night at Harker's house. And I won't take one until my first picture is released—until I see the look on their smug, stupid faces! You're the last person who should talk that way, after what they did to your reputation."

Lozoff sighed. "Well, I can't blame Morris for it. He had no choice. Since the last loan, Salem is running the Studio."

"They're all alike," Druse spat. "Morris knew what he was doing—he and that son of his. They sold out to save their own skins. And they let Salem throw us all to the wolves. It's a conspiracy, I tell you! Well, they'll see. They thought they could run us out of the movies. But we *are* the movies. I'm not afraid of them and their threats. I'm not afraid. We'll pull the whole rotten setup down around their ears."

Druse entered his car, pulled away.

Lozoff shook his head. "I'm worried about Karl," he said. "Something is very wrong."

"Persecution complex," I said. "He'll snap out of it when we get started, though."

"I hope so." Lozoff smiled at me. "Tommy, this may be the opportunity we've always dreamed of."

"That's what we thought about *Crime and Punishment*," I said.

"I know. I still regret what happened there. I keep thinking about the original, the master print, just gathering dust in the files." We climbed into my car and I started the motor.

"You know something, Tommy? That film—I know just where it is. Exactly. The top shelf of the laboratory, down the corridor from the Executive office wing. Before this happened, I even had some idea of getting in there and . . ." His voice trailed off. "But that was crazy, of course. That's the way Druse would think. I'm glad now I don't have to think that way."

We left the Valley, headed back. "Big things ahead," Lozoff mused. "We'll make the change, and perhaps it's for the best. I'm no fanatic. The silent film wasn't the final answer. It was only the first step, and a faltering one."

"Glad to hear you say that," I told him. "You know, Harker and some of the others aren't really sold yet. They cling to the silents, no matter what they say. Why, twenty years from now, I'll bet you'll still find diehards who'll claim the silents were the only thing. I can see a sort of cult springing up, the way it already has with Chaplin. His stuff will endure, of course, and I'm willing to bet that Fairbanks and Griffith and Keaton and Stroheim will stand inspection in the future. But there was a lot of bad stuff, let's not fool ourselves. It isn't just that the styles and the hairdos will seem funny in years to come. The hokum, the hamming and mugging, will be obvious. That's going out now, thank goodness, Jannings and Veidt and Chaney will survive. Things like *Crime and Punishment*, in our version."

I dropped Lozoff off at his house.

"See you in a few days," I said. "Harker is due back on the 27th."

Lozoff nodded, and we parted.

But Harker did not return from New York on the 27th. He did not return to Hollywood until November 8th.

That was ten days after the Crash.

TWENTY-SEVEN

WE CAME OUT to Harker's place, most of us, early in the afternoon.

Maybelle Manners wasn't there, and Druse was missing, but it didn't matter. They already knew. Just as we knew, before we gathered in the dining room. And what could anyone do, what could anyone say?

"There is nothing to say," Harker told us. "You have the story. The panic—you can scarcely believe some of the things I heard, saw with my own eyes. It's incredible. But it's true. Breck is wiped out. He has nothing left, nothing."

"What about us?" Jackie Keeley stood up. "I thought I was a smart one. I pulled out of the market when this deal came up. Made a killing, too. And I sunk every dime into the corporation here. Now what?"

"Yes." Emerson Craig paced the floor. "Where do we go from here? Couldn't you find somebody else—?"

"I tried. But the way things are, nobody will make a move." Harker shook his head. "We still have the land, though. It's bought and paid for. We're not beaten yet; we'll make the rounds. Things are bound to straighten out. With what we have to offer, we'll find backing."

"Who? Somebody like Salem, who wants to make epics about the Horse Marines?" Craig looked down at the table. "Meanwhile, what are we supposed to do? What about Lozoff, here, who went into hock up to his neck on this proposition? How do we eat?"

"Give me time," Harker said. "I'll manage. You have my word, all of you."

They started to file out. I waited for Lozoff, who sat there staring out the window. I followed his gaze. He was looking at nothing. There was nothing to see except the swimming pool. Now, in November, it was utterly empty, except for a few dead leaves swirling on the bottom.

Harker came up beside me.

We watched the leaves blow across the bottom of the pool.

"I'm sorry," he said. I don't know if he was talking to me or to Lozoff.

"It was a dream, wasn't it?" I murmured. "A great dream, but only a dream."

"No." Harker shook his head. "We'll still do it. If I can only convince them, make them see it as I see it."

"It's useless. All for nothing." Lozoff stood up, slowly. "Oh, I don't mind about the money. It's something more I have at stake. My name. Tommy knows what I'm talking about. If they'd only listened to me at the Studio, released *Crime and Punishment* for the silent houses, for Europe—"

"Wait a minute," I said. "You're convinced there's a profit in it. The original version is just sitting there. Maybe Salem wouldn't release it himself, but he might be willing to sell it. If we could buy it ourselves and distribute it—"

"What's all this?" Harker asked.

I told him.

I told him about the picture we had made, the picture I had written. I told him what it meant to us, what it meant to me. I told him why it was important—and not until the words came tumbling out did I realize just how important it was. It was *my* dream.

"Why not?" I said. "Suppose we could get it for fifty, even seventy-five thousand? Working through the regular exchanges we could still clear a profit of two or three hundred thousand, perhaps more. It wouldn't be a loan, it would be an investment. We'd have money to get started with. And it's a great picture. A world-wide showing would give us something to offer. It would give Lozoff back his reputation. Then we could go and ask for backing—can you see it?"

"Of course." Harker looked at me. "I can see many things. What this picture means to you."

I stared into his eyes. "Yes," I said. "When I wrote it, when we made it, I felt the way you do."

"I understand."

Lozoff coughed. "Tommy said something about a loan. If you have your own private funds, Mr. Harker, couldn't you—"

"Of course." Harker smiled. "Come on."

"Where?"

The director glanced out the window, peering at the gray prelude to twilight. "It's not too late. We can probably catch Morris if he's still at the Studio."

He strode to the door. "Rogers! Phone Coronet Pictures, Mr. Morris. I want an appointment now—tell them it's urgent."

We waited a moment. The phone rang in the alcove off the dining room. Harker hesitated, then picked it up. "Hello, Mr. Morris? Oh, I'm sorry, I expected another call. Yes, this is Harker speaking. No. No, he didn't. Yes, if he comes I'll have him call you immediately. That's right. Goodbye."

He replaced the receiver. "Karl Druse's wife."

"Looking for him?" I asked.

"Yes. She knew about the meeting and wondered if he was here. She's very upset about him, ever since he heard the bad news."

"I can imagine." Lozoff needed. "He knew what you were going to tell us. I spoke to him yesterday myself. He sounded bad—I think he'd been drinking. He has the odd idea that the Studio is somehow responsible for our not getting the money."

"There are some queer portents," Harker said. "I meant to recheck my findings."

Lozoff nodded again. "Still interested in astrology? Strange the stars didn't foretell all this."

"Perhaps they did." Harker sighed. "It's just that sometimes you don't want to believe, even when you see the truth plainly forecast. There are times when a man must rebel against the stars—"

Rogers entered. "Mr. Morris will see you whenever you arrive, sir."

"Good. Then let's be on our way."

We drove in twilight. Taki slid skillfully through the traffic. We stared out at the violet sky. The stars were beginning to break through. I watched them and wondered. Lozoff watched Harker and Harker, for some strange reason, kept watching me.

Lozoff began to tell the director about his wild plans for stealing the print of *Crime and Punishment*. He spoke of how the negative was stored in the laboratory, and Harker nodded. But he watched me.

It wasn't until we approached the Studio that he spoke. And then he said, "I'm glad I called you. At first, I didn't know—I thought you might have been angry. But you were entitled to a place with us. You *belonged*. Even though it didn't work out the way I wanted it to. You understand what I mean?"

"I understand," I said. "I've forgotten the—the other. That's all in the past."

"What are you two talking about?" Lozoff demanded.

"Nothing. Just a private matter," I told him. "It isn't important any more."

"But the picture is important, isn't it?" Theodore Harker murmured. "To you?"

"Yes," I answered.

"Then you'll have it. This much at least I owe to you."

For a moment we stared at the stars together.

It was dark now, as we arrived. The gates were closed and Taki had to slide out from under the wheel and go over to the guard's office.

Then we rolled onto the lot, noting the changes, sensing the difference, each of us equally oppressed and uncomfortably aware of the passage of time.

The extra-bench was gone, and so was the casual litter of the outer office. We entered the Executive Building after a backward glance at the new soundstages to our right, halted at the outer desk while a trim young thing buzzed Mr. Morris.

She smiled brightly. "He'll see you know, Mr. Hecker."

Hecker. Yes, times *had* changed.

But we went in, and there was Morris, big as life, standing up and holding out his hand. *He* hadn't changed, not good old baldheaded Sol—

Oh yes, he had! Good old baldheaded Sol was wearing a neat little brown toupee now. Just a partial hairpiece, nothing extreme, *but after all, a fella has to keep up with the times, no sense letting people think you're an old hasbeen.*

I didn't like the toupee, somehow. It bothered me. All during the hearty exchange of greetings, all during the "How are you?" and "Great to see you!" and "Sit right down" preliminaries, I kept watching, wondering, worrying.

Then we were all seated, and it was time to begin. In a moment Harker would get down to business, start the ball rolling. All I had to do now was sit back and wait.

Instead, I opened my mouth.

"Say, that must be a new brand of cigar you're smoking, Mr. Morris."

He smiled. "No, Tommy. The same like always. You remember."

"Well, it smells different to me."

"Must be something wrong with you nose." Morris chuckled, then leaned forward. "Hey, wait a minute now. I *do* smell something."

"So do I." Lozoff sniffed.

"Smoke." Theodore Harker rose. "Something is burning."

"Wait, I'll take a look." Morris got up and opened the door of his private office. The barber chair was revealed in all its golden splendor. "No, nothing in here." He stared. "Look—under the door! That's where it's coming from, the hall."

We trooped after him, crossing the room to the door leading to the corridor beyond. He yanked the knob. "Here, let me get my key—"

The door swung back, the smoke billowed forward.

"Fire!" Morris yelled. "There's a fire down there—quick, somebody call—

Lozoff turned away, heading back to the outer office.

Morris coughed, tears running from his eyes. "Maybe it's the lab," he said. "All them chemicals and stuff—"

Suddenly a siren sounded from outside. I stared through the window of the corridor. There was a red glare rising off to the right.

"The new stages, they're burning!" Morris brushed past me. "I got to see—"

"You can't go through that hall," I said. "You'll suffocate. Close the door and wait for help to come. There's nothing you can do, anyway."

"That's right. There's nothing you can do. It's too late. Too late!"

The voice came croaking out of the corridor, and then the figure came crawling out of the smoke. The face was blackened, but I recognized the eyes. They stared up at us now, and we stared down in turn—at the body hunching on hands and knees, at the lolling legs, the silver feet. *The silver feet—*

"Druse!"

"Yes, I'm here." He peered up at us, laughing. "I've been here all the time, Mr. Morris. All day. You didn't know that, did you? I wasn't invited, I'm not welcome here any more, but I came. In makeup, if you please—as an extra. You see, I wanted to do another job for you. Just one last job. And I did it."

"Why you—"

"Keep back!" We saw the gun then.

"Karl—stop it!" I said.

Druse shook his head and leveled the gun at me. "Stand still and you won't get hurt. Mr. Morris and Mr. Salem, they're going to hurt now." He grinned with his mouth but his eyes were mirthless, merciless. "It'll hurt bad to see everything go up in flames, won't it, Mr. Morris? All those nice new soundstages you built for others to use, because we weren't good enough any more. What did Salem say about me, eh? Did he say I wasn't convincing as a monster? Maybe he's changed his mind now."

Harker started to gesture, but the gun brushed him back.

"No use. It's going good. In three places. The lab was the last. Wait until all that film catches—then you'll really see something!" Druse started to laugh, but the gun wavered.

"Karl, you're sick—"

"No. Drunk, maybe, but I'm not sick. This is the first time I felt good since I heard the news. About the money. I know why we didn't get the money. Salem and Morris queered it, they wanted to stop us. But I stopped them."

He stared at Harker and the grin came back, crawling over his face. "I'm good at setting fires. You ought to know that, Harker. Didn't I do a job for you, years ago—?"

"Shut up!"

Now *I* stared at Theodore Harker, and I knew. *Years ago. The fire that killed Andy and Minnie wasn't an accident.*

I moved toward Harker, my throat throbbing, my fists clenched. "So that's it! You were afraid they'd tell me the truth, the only two people who knew, so you sent Druse to get rid of them—"

His face went white. "No—"

"You son of a bitch, you're the *real* monster!"

"Stop!"

But I didn't stop. I went for him, my hands opening and reaching for his throat. And then Karl Druse fired.

The shot went wild, but it stopped me; stopped me long enough to turn and lunge. The hands intended for Harker's throat grasped Druse's wrist instead. I twisted it and the gun clattered to the floor.

"Get some help!" I yelled. I had to yell because of the sirens making all that noise outside—and because of a series of muffled reports from down the hall.

"Chemicals!" Sol Morris turned away, holding a handkerchief to his nose. "We got to get out of here before the film catches."

"Film—" Harker murmured. He wasn't looking at Morris or Druse or me; he stared off into the swirling smoke of the hall beyond the doorway.

Druse struggled, trying to break my grip, and I felt the surging strength in his arms. I shouted at Harker.

"Come on, help me hold him—we've got to take him outside."

Harker turned for a moment, shaking his head. "Your film. It's in there." He started to move toward the hall doorway.

"No—you can't! Come back!"

I released my hold on Druse's wrist and started across the room, but Harker was already in the corridor. For an instant I saw his face before the smoke shrouded it. His lips moved and I caught the words very faintly.

"I'm going, son."

He said "son." I heard him, *I heard him.*

Then he disappeared in the blinding billow of the hall beyond. The muffled blasts echoed, and Sol Morris grabbed my arm.

"Quick, let's go! You can't stop him anyway. He's crazy, like Druse."

"No." I shook free, pushing Morris against the wall. His hairpiece slid off and I stared down into his frightened face. "You know why he went in there? To get the print of *Crime and Punishment.*"

"He'll fry—look at the flames now!" Morris clawed at my arm again.

"The firemen are here," I yelled. "Tell them to run a hose in, quick. I'll get Harker out of there."

"No you don't!"

I turned. Druse was on his knees. He'd picked up the gun from the floor and he trained it on us once more as he edged back slowly, moving to the hall doorway.

"You stay here. I'll go back for him. I have to go back anyway." He laughed. "I forgot my shoes. Must find my shoes, put them on. Don't want anyone to see me without my shoes." He moved back along the corridor, still facing us. A surge of smoke surrounded him. His clothes were beginning to smolder.

"I'm not a freak, you know," he said. He laughed again as his hair started to burn, as he moved into the fire and the smoke billowed up, blotting out his face.

"Don't!" I yelled. "Come back! *Father!*"

But nobody heard me. There was nothing but the crash of a falling beam, the roar of the fire, the shouts of the men who came up behind me then and held my arms.

They had the hose, and they tried to get in. I remember how they played a stream of water along the hall, and I think they finally managed to get as far as the lab door—or the place where the door had been. Now there was nothing but thunder and flame, thunder and flame and then a blazing burst that ended in utter darkness as I slumped forward and passed out.

When I came to I was at the hospital, and it was all over. Morris was there with me, and Lozoff. They told me the rest.

The lab and half the Executive Building were gone. Two stages up in smoke, completely demolished. One watchman and one gaffer dead, three injured. Two firemen out—suffocation. Damage roughly estimated at four hundred thousand.

"But what about—?"

Morris gulped. "I already told the papers. How Harker was back there looking at some film when the fire started and Druse went in after, to save him. That's how the story's gonna be, we had to tell them something—"

Lozoff pushed the little man aside. "They never came out," he said. "Druse was pinned under a beam when they found him. Harker almost made it. He got as far as the door, anyway, carrying all those reels in his arms. He was still holding them when the wall caved in. He wanted to save our picture."

"Sure," I said. "I guess we all did."

Morris shook his head. "Terrible," he muttered. "Believe me, I don't care about the Studio. We got insurance, anyway. But to see a fine actor like Druse go to pieces that way—terrible! And Theodore Harker. He was a fool to try and get those reels out. What kind of business is that, to kill yourself for a movie? But he was a great director."

Kurt Lozoff sighed. "No, he wasn't. He was a great man."

I turned my face to the wall and they left.

TWENTY-EIGHT

I WON'T TAKE YOU with me to the funeral. It was one of those big affairs, with too many people, too many flowers, too many reporters and photographers and bit players and curiosity seekers who stood outside the chapel and asked for autographs. The sermon by an eminent local divine was a glowing tribute to the heroic sacrifice of two men whose contribution to the art of the screen would never be forgotten. Two men whom, incidentally, the eminent local divine had never seen.

But it was a great spectacle. And almost all the stuff about the unforgettable contribution was printed in the evening papers which were used to wrap the garbage in, the following morning.

And that was that.

I'd seen them all at the cemetery, of course, Lozoff, Madame Olga, Jackie Keeley, Hilton, Craig, Maybelle, Arch Taylor, and the people from the Studio—all the studios. Glenda Glint had a wonderful time just listing the names and describing the floral offerings.

Nicky and Hilda Morris were there, with Sol, in a new hairpiece—it was black for the occasion, and attracted favorable comment.

Morris came up to me, as I was leaving, and shook my hand. "You come and see me one of these days," he said. "Don't forget, now."

I nodded and said yes, but I never did. I never went back.

He probably would have been much too busy to see me anyway. Because a lot of things happened during the months that followed.

They bought Harker's land in the San Fernando Valley from his estate and rebuilt out there. He would have laughed about that, I think—Salem and Morris erecting their new Studio on his chosen site. It was, somehow, the final touch.

From time to time I heard rumors about the others, but I gradually lost track of them during 1930. Lozoff and Madame Olga went to Europe. Lucille Hilton and Emerson Craig both announced their formal retirement. Maybelle Manners just disappeared.

In the fall of '30 Coronet Pictures opened their new plant, with Lester Salem cutting the pink ribbon, and shaking hands with Sol Morris—the Grand Old Man of the Industry, as Salem now called him. Nicky got himself some kind of title with the new setup, but the Grand Old Man gradually drifted out of the news reports and the publicity blurbs, and I guess the gold barber chair went with him when he sold out the following year.

As for me, I went back to Encino. I still had the lots, and a little cash. I had enough to put up a small building and take a stab at going into business. Used cars, of all things. Turned out pretty well, too—plenty of people wanted used cars at the beginning of 1931.

That was the year Chaplin made *City Lights*. The rest was talk, punctuated by the chanting of chorines and the spattering of machine guns on the soundtracks.

That was the year, though, when I found out what had happened to Jackie Keeley.

As a matter of fact, he drove in to see me early one Friday evening when the lot was still open. It developed he had a Rolls to sell. Rolls wasn't exactly a hot item in 1931, but I made him a deal. He looked as though he could use the money.

"Things aren't so good right now," he admitted, as we sat in the office, afterwards. "You probably heard. Oh, I did a couple of supporting jobs here and there, but I'm on the way out. And we can't all produce our own, like Charlie."

I got out a bottle and let him sample the latest production of the reliable bootlegger. He seemed to approve of it.

"Funny how fast things change," he said. "Most of my bunch is gone, already. All the Sennett people, the oldtimers. Langdon is through. Lloyd and Keaton, too, but they don't know it yet. They will, in a few more years. But they won't give up—they're just like the characters in the comedies. Brave little guys who never quit."

I poured him another drink.

"Thanks, Tommy. You know, you were lucky in a way. Still young yet, so you can start over again like this and make a go of it. But me, I'm still *in* pictures, even if I'm out."

"What do you mean by that?" I asked.

"I can't explain. This new bunch, the New York crowd and the young people growing up with the talkies, they're in business. Producing, directing, acting—that's just a job to them. It was different with us. We *lived* our work. Old D. W. Griffith, with those brass-hooked shoes and the loops in back for pulling them on, remember? He was a Great Director twenty-four hours a day. Harker, too. Valentino was the Great Lover, on screen or off. Just like Karl Druse was a monster, and I was a funny little runt. We lived our work, so that's why we died, when the silent movies died. Some of us actually passed on, and the rest of us are only partially alive." He helped himself to another drink. "Yes, you're lucky. You got out, got back to reality, just in time."

I nodded. "Here, wait a minute until I close up this place." I switched off the lights on the lot outside. Keeley sat there, watching me. God knows what he was thinking. I had my own thoughts at the moment.

Curiously enough, I wasn't thinking about myself or what he'd just told me. I was thinking about Dawn—out there in Pasadena, hanging up the wash every week, watching the model shipbuilder, looking after the kid. Must be about two years old now. Funny to think of Dawn with a kid. Funnier still to think *I'll always love you—never forget that.* But it was all true, it was all real, and it wasn't so funny that I couldn't take a drink on it.

I did. I took several, and Jackie Keeley joined me. We sat there in the dark for a while, until we'd killed the pint. It was after nine, so I drove him home in my car.

It turned out he lived way up near the Reservoir, and somehow I found myself taking a route up Mulholland Drive. Mulholland Drive, with the lights glittering below and the new convertibles parked in the darkness (*Dawn, where are you now, do you remember, do you still share it?*) and the night air was cool across my burning cheeks.

"Let's stop for a minute," I said. "Take a look down there."

"Sure." We climbed out, walked along the rim overlooking Wonderland. At first glance, nothing seemed to have changed. Then I noted the new neon, the increased brilliance, the enlarged arc of the sweeping spread stretching before us.

"Growing fast," I murmured.

"That's right." Jackie Keeley teetered on the edge. I joined him, my arm unobtrusive on his shoulder.

"Don't worry." He chuckled. "I'm not going to fall. Just faking—you know."

"Of course. It's a reflex, isn't it? I've been thinking over what you said, Jackie, about the old days. And I can't agree with you. We were all faking, weren't we? Fooling ourselves, because none of it was true."

"Oh yes it was." The small face was earnest. "Don't ever let them tell you differently. It was true, every bit of it. That's the way it happened."

"But it doesn't *seem* true any more. Even after a few years—"

"Of course it doesn't. There's been so many jokes about illiterate producers, we're beginning to forget they actually existed. So many wisecracks about the great director with his megaphone that it's just a stock gag—but did they ever see De Mille?"

Keeley nodded up at me. "Yes—God help us—it was all true. But none of it was *real*. That's your secret. True, but not real."

He was quite sober now. "What the hell," he said. "It doesn't matter one way or the other. In a couple of years, we and everything we did will be museum pieces. Radio's the big thing nowadays and then we'll be having this other stuff they talk about, where you see pictures right in your home—television, isn't it?" He grinned. "No sense making a fuss over it. Only it's hard to admit that your whole life, everything you ever did and believed in doing, isn't important any more."

I smiled back at him. "Don't you ever think that," I told him. "It *was* important, and it *will* be, again. Some day men will look back. Some day men will go to the old films to recreate a culture, read the history of an era from its movies. There are newspapers and books and written records, but they're cold and dead. The movies live on. It's all there, if only they look; all that you can ever hope to know—a mirror of the manners, the modes, the mores of a people. The foolish ones won't see it, of course. They'll laugh and pass by, and think themselves sophisticated because they have eyes only for tomorrow."

Keeley shook his head. "I wish I could believe you."

"I mean it. The silent movies *were* America, for that dazzling decade from 1919 to 1929. They're as much a part of our way of life as the cowboys and the pioneers. Some day there'll be legends about them, and folk heroes. Fairbanks and Tom Mix, Chaplin and The Great Profile and America's Sweetheart. And even twenty years from now, when the flapper is forgotten, women will remember Clara Bow and men will speak of Garbo as a goddess glimpsed in youth. And as the years roll on, the stories will grow. About the Great Goldwyn, and the unconquerable Erich von Stroheim; the heroes and heroines of the good old days. First will come scoffing, then reminiscence, then the myth. Silence *is* golden, and the movies were our golden age."

"I wish you could have said that at Harker's funeral," Keeley murmured.

"I didn't have to. He knew. And it didn't really matter that he died, or any of the others. Because they all left something behind. The things men create from their imagination.

"Yes, we'll die, too, Jackie. But we're the lucky ones. We've preserved something after all, preserved it on film, for generations to come. What we lost won't matter then. It's what we saved that really counts. And we saved our dreams."

We took a long look, a last look at all the lights, then climbed back into the car and started down the dark road ahead.